4|16   HMT

Books should be returned or renewed by the last
date above. Renew by phone **03000 41 31 31** or
online *www.kent.gov.uk/libs*

THE SECRET OF
the Journal

REALM OF
DARKNESS

C. F. Dunn

LION FICTION

Published by Lion Fiction
an imprint of
Lion Hudson plc
Wilkinson House, Jordan Hill Road
Oxford OX2 8DR, England
www.lionhudson.com/fiction

ISBN 978 1 78264 196 4
e-ISBN 978 1 78264 197 1

First edition 2016

A catalogue record for this book is available from the British Library

Printed and bound in the UK, February 2016, LH26

Contents

For my friends, past and present.

Acknowledgments

This is my opportunity to thank all those involved in helping breathe life into Emma and Matthew by bringing *Realm of Darkness* out of my imagination and onto the shelves. So, to start with, I owe grateful thanks to the Lion Fiction team, who always responded cheerfully to my author queries: editor Jessica Tinker; Jess Scott, who saw it through to production; Jonathan Roberts (design), and Kylie Ord (production). A special thank you to copy editor, Julie Frederick, who kept *Realm* on the straight and narrow, and to Sarah Krueger of Kregel Publishing in the USA.

Much appreciation and thanks goes to peerless authors, Liz Fenwick (*The Cornish House*) and Fiona Veitch Smith (*The Jazz Files*) who sacrificed their precious writing time to generously offer endorsements for *Realm Of Darkness*.

No acknowledgments would be complete without thanking my former publisher and editor in the UK, Tony Collins, who looked beyond my novice blunders and saw the potential in my debut novel, *Mortal Fire*.

I am indebted to the many people who, in their professional capacity, have generously given their time and advice, especially Consultant Psychiatrist Dr Kiki O'Neill-Byrne MB, BCH, BAO, Dip Clin Psych, MRCPsych, for her insight into psychological conditions.

Thanks also to author Sue Russell, and friends and colleagues Dee Prewer and Lisa Lewin for their feedback and support, to North Kent Writers' Group for putting up with me, and to Michelle Jimerson Morris, of Seamlyne Reproductions, and Norm Forgey of Maine Day Trip, who once again provided regional information.

My everlasting gratitude to my husband and daughters, my mother and father, my brother and his family, whose love and tireless encouragement keep me going, step by step, along the road. Finally, to Stig, who although now treads an eternal path, kept me company on many a long walk as I untangled plots and conjured new ones.

Characters

ACADEMIC & RESEARCH STAFF AT HOWARD'S LAKE COLLEGE, MAINE

Emma D'Eresby, Department of History (Medieval & Early Modern)

Elena Smalova, Department of History (Post-Revolutionary Soviet Society)

Matias Lidström, Faculty of Bio-medicine (Genetics)

Matthew Lynes, surgeon, Faculty of Bio-medicine (Mutagenesis)

Sam Wiesner, Department of Mathematics (Metamathematics)

Madge Makepeace, Faculty of Social Sciences (Anthropology)

Siggie Gerhard, Faculty of Social Sciences (Psychology)

Saul Abrahms, Faculty of Social Sciences (Psychology of Functional Governance)

Colin Eckhart, Department of History (Renaissance & Reformation Art)

Kort Staahl, Department of English (Early Modern Literature)

Megan, research assistant, Bio-medicine

Sung, research assistant, Bio-medicine

The Dean, Stephen Shotter

MA STUDENTS

Holly Stanhope; Josh Feitel; Hannah Graham; Aydin Yilmaz; Leo Hamell

IN CAMBRIDGE

Guy Hilliard, Emma's former tutor
Tom Falconer, Emma's friend

EMMA'S FAMILY

Hugh D'Eresby, her father
Penny D'Eresby, her mother
Beth Marshall, her sister
Rob Marshall, her brother-in-law
Alex & Flora, her twin nephew and niece
Archie, her baby nephew
Nanna, her grandmother

Mike Taylor, friend of the family
Joan Seaton, friend of the family

MATTHEW'S FAMILY

Henry Lynes, his son
Patricia Lynes (Pat), Henry's wife
Margaret Lynes (Maggie), his granddaughter
Daniel Lynes (Dan), his grandson
Jeanette (Jeannie) Rathbone, Dan's wife, and their children:
Ellie Lynes
Joel Lynes
Harry Lynes

Dei sum leonis

THE LYNES FAMILY TREE

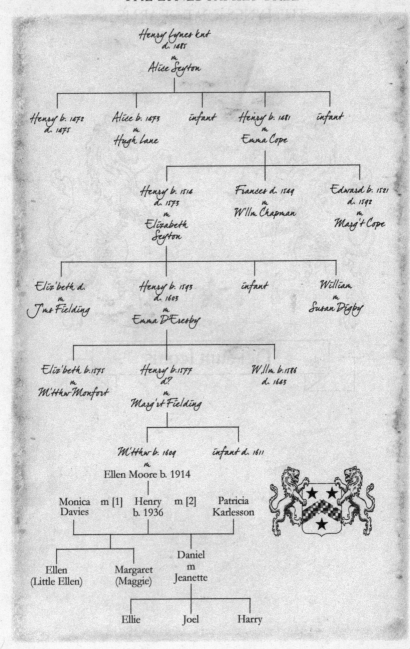

Henry Lynes knt
d. 1485
m
Alice Seyton

Henry b. 1472
d. 1475

Alice b. 1473
m
Hugh Lane

infant

Henry b. 1481
m
Emma Cope

infant

Henry b. 1514
d. 1573
m
Elizabeth
Seyton

Frances d. 1549
m
W'llm Chapman

Edward b. 1521
d. 1592
m
Marg't Cope

Eliz'beth d.
m
Jms Fielding

Henry b. 1593
d. 1603
m
Emma D'Eresby

infant

William
m
Susan Digby

Eliz'beth b. 1575
m
M'tthw Monfort

Henry b. 1577
d. ?
m
Marg'rt Fielding

W'llm b. 1586
d. 1643

M'tthw b. 1609
m
Ellen Moore b. 1914

infant d. 1611

Monica
Davies

m [1]

Henry
b. 1936

m [2]

Patricia
Karlesson

Ellen
(Little Ellen)

Margaret
(Maggie)

Daniel
m
Jeanette

Ellie

Joel

Harry

The Story So Far

Independent and self-contained British historian Emma D'Eresby has taken up a year-long research post in an exclusive American university in Maine, fulfilling her ambition (and that of her grandfather) to study the Richardson Journal – the diary of a seventeenth-century Englishman – housed in the library there.

Single-minded and determined, Emma is wary of relationships, but she quickly attracts the unwelcome attention of seductive colleague Sam Wiesner, and the disturbing Professor of English, Kort Staahl. Despite her best intentions to remain focused on her work, and encouraged by her vivacious Russian friend, Elena Smalova, Emma becomes increasingly attracted to medical research scientist and surgeon Matthew Lynes, whose old fashioned courtesy she finds both disarming and curious.

Widowed and living quietly with his family, Matthew is reluctant to let her into his life, despite his clear interest in her, and Emma suspects there is more to his past than the little he tells her. His English-sounding name and the distinctive colour of his hair intrigues her, and Emma believes there is a link between Matthew and the very journal she came to the United States to study. Against her nature, she smuggles the historic document from the library to investigate further.

Events take a sinister turn as a series of savage assaults on women sends ripples of fear through the campus. Emma is convinced she is being followed, and during the prestigious All Saints' dinner at Halloween, is viciously attacked by psychotic Professor Staahl, leaving her on the edge of death. Only Matthew's timely intervention saves her and, as he cares for her

13

in his college rooms, their relationship deepens and Emma finds herself battling between her growing love and her need to learn more about him.

A near-fatal encounter with a bear raises questions about Matthew she can no longer ignore.

Frustrated by the mystery surrounding his past and his refusal to tell her who he really is, Emma reluctantly flees Maine to her claustrophobic family home in England. Hidden from sight, but not her conscience, she has also taken the journal.

Years of acrimony with her family and a bruising affair a decade before with her tutor, Guy Hilliard – a married man – have left their scars. Now broken both physically and emotionally, and facing an emotional crisis, Emma drifts, until a chance meeting refocuses her attention on the unanswered questions she had left behind. Using her historical training to trace Matthew's family to an almost extinct hamlet in the tiny county of Rutland, she makes a startling discovery. Her instinct had been right: Matthew is a relic of the past.

Born in the early years of the seventeenth century, Matthew had been betrayed during the English Civil War, when a clash with his uncle left him fighting for his life. He not only lived, but *persisted*, growing steadily in strength and surviving events that would have killed any other man. Diary entries by the family steward in the same journal now in Emma's possession reveal that in the overheated atmosphere of seventeenth-century England – where rumours were rife and accusations of witchcraft frequent – Matthew faced persecution because of his differences, and he fled to the American colonies.

Coming to terms with Matthew's past, Emma is all too aware that she possesses knowledge that could destroy his future and, when she learns he has disappeared from the college, sinks further into desolation. But as winter descends on the old stone walls of her family home, Matthew, unable to remain separated from her, comes to find Emma and takes her back to America.

Looking forward to the future, Emma believes she has all the answers, but Matthew has one more revelation that could end their relationship once and for all. In a fraught confrontation in a remote snowbound cabin high in the mountains, Matthew tells her that he is still married. Over a harrowing few days, with their relationship hanging in the balance, Matthew recounts his story, and Emma learns that his wife, Ellen, is a ninety-six-year-old paraplegic, and the man she thought was his father is, in fact, his son. Emma is faced with a stark choice: cut all ties with Matthew as she once did with Guy or face an uncertain future with the only man she has ever really loved. Emma believes that her life is inextricably linked with Matthew's and makes the decision to stay with him with all the complications it will entail.

As she prepares to meet Matthew's family at Christmas, the last thing on Emma's mind is college professor Sam Wiesner, but it becomes apparent that she has been very much on his. After a brief, but unpleasant, encounter in which Sam acquires a broken jaw, Emma is forced to warn Sam off. But, despite her best efforts to protect Matthew's identity, wheels have been set in motion that one day could expose him to the world.

In the third book of *The Secret of the Journal* series – *Rope of Sand* – Emma meets Matthew's family for the first time when she goes to stay with him for Christmas. Here she is introduced to his son, Henry, and learns how unique the family really is. As Christmas approaches, it is clear that Emma is not welcomed by all members of the Lynes family: what does Matthew's great-granddaughter Ellie have against her, and what might his sinister clinical psychiatrist granddaughter Maggie be prepared to do to prevent Matthew and Emma being together?

When one evening, out of spite, Ellie gives Emma coffee instead of her usual tea, Emma suffers an extreme reaction and her heart stops for a few seconds. In those moments Emma discovers that coffee heightens all her senses, and she can detect the emotions of others around her in colour, revealing their deepest feelings – a form of synesthesia.

As questions of mortality and faith interweave, the bond between Emma and Matthew grows even stronger, but they accept that they must wait until his wife dies before they can have a life together.

After Christmas, and very reluctantly, Emma goes to meet Matthew's wife, Ellen – a frail and disabled elderly woman with a core of steel – and learns how a lifetime spent with Matthew will be one that demands the sacrifice of normality, and be full of obfuscation, concealment, and lies.

Blaming Emma for coming between Matthew and his wife, and destabilized by her presence over Christmas, Maggie reveals – in a threatening and vitriolic confrontation – that she has been in charge of assessing Kort Staahl's mental state since his vicious attack in October, and is determined to get rid of Emma. It is only a matter of time before ticking resentment explodes.

Just as Emma settles down to the new term's teaching at Howard's Lake College, and looking forward to the history conference in the summer, she receives, without warning, a writ of prosecution issued on behalf of Kort Staahl. Emma is accused of defamation *per se* – a serious offence – and goes to trial worried that the spotlight will fall on Matthew as a key witness, and is shocked to find that Maggie is involved as a witness for the prosecution. But there is more to the trial than it seems. Partway through, Matthew's wife dies, and, as he buries her a few days later, Henry's first wife, Monica, appears at the graveside, revealing that she instigated the trial in revenge against Matthew.

Her sudden appearance after an absence of forty years drives her daughter, Maggie, ever closer to the borders of madness.

The following day the trial resumes, with Maggie teetering on the edge of sanity while under fierce cross-examination on the witness stand. Emma fears she will reveal who Matthew is and, in one last desperate effort to protect his secret, she doses herself with coffee in an attempt to connect with Maggie emotionally using her newly discovered ability. She succeeds but suffers a near-fatal heart attack. The trial is cancelled and, as winter turns a corner and Emma recovers in hospital, Matthew puts aside his past. Together he and Emma look forward to the future with renewed hope.

Little Blood

Before the present there is always the past.

There was never any doubt in my mind the career I would follow and I defended my position with all the tenacity of a zealot. The more my father battled to change my mind, the more resolute I became, until – had there been another choice – I wouldn't have given it a second thought, so determined had I become to thwart him.

My father approached boiling point, his face beetroot, his eyebrows knotted in an angry "V" as I confronted him.

"I won't change my mind."

"History is not a proper career, Emma. You can't expect to make a decent living as a historian."

"Grandpa didn't do too badly."

"Don't be infantile. Your grandfather was a Cambridge professor; you couldn't possibly emulate his success in this day and age. No, your mother and I think you need a profession you can rely on – law, medicine…"

"I'm not interested in anything else."

"… the Armed Forces, dentistry, accountancy…"

"Dad, dentists scare me and I can hardly add up. I want to study history; it's the only thing I want to do." We faced each other across the length of his study, he as pugnacious as ever, I staunch and unyielding. We were father and daughter bound by blood and so far removed from each other that we could have been inhabiting parallel worlds.

"We only have your welfare in mind; you can do much better than being an academic. Now, I've spoken to your headmaster, and in his opinion…"

* * *

Blah, blah, blah, on and on for what seemed like a decade but proved to be less than half that by the time I won. I took my A levels early to escape, driven by the twin desires of achieving my goal and proving him wrong. I'd just had my seventeenth birthday when I went to Cambridge – only seventeen when I left home. It was more than I expected, everything I hoped for, and I fell into the life of an undergraduate as if born to it.

I was seventeen when I left home, eighteen when I met Guy Hilliard, and nineteen when I slept with him for the first time.

I knew about him long before I met him. He epitomized everything I wanted to be, and I devoured his books with an appetite I never showed food. His insight, his attention to detail, his wit – as caustic and apposite as slaked lime – had me hunger for more, driving me on in search of greater understanding. So, when I met him for the first time, it was a trap already baited and waiting to be sprung.

"Ladies and gentlemen," he said as we waited outside his study for our initial supervision of the second year, "I have you in thrall."

I should have known better, but I was young and naïve.

Over the previous year I relished every moment spent at lectures and supervisions, absorbing each new experience like a sponge. I worked hard, gave my essays in on time, stayed up too late talking or watching films. We went punting on the slack waters of the Cam, avoiding missiles flung from the bridges and the ducks as they swam between boats. I had friends, even a boyfriend of sorts – Tom – who made me laugh and understood if I'd rather stay in and read than go out to the pub. I felt no longer alone or lonely; life was good and it could only get better.

As a renowned lecturer, Guy maintained the highest academic standards, and students fought to get on his course. He would take five where other supervisors took three, because he could guarantee to have whittled them down by the end of the first term. His style was indomitable, formidable. When anyone spoke, he listened intently, often with a frown deeply embedded, and when he answered he spoke assertively and without pretence to flatter. Without a doubt his manner and intellect were intimidating; he did not suffer fools and he told them as much. If he displayed any kindness at all, it was in his single-minded pursuit of what he believed to be in his students' best interests. Lean, spare – broad enough in the shoulders not to look scrawny and nearing six feet tall – his dark brown hair and faintly olive skin betrayed his Anglo-French parentage. He seemed more English than anything else, and I say *English* rather than *British* because he identified with an era that predated the Act of Union, and he had Royalist leanings. He appeared attractive, but not handsome, and, although many of his female students claimed they did not like him because of his manner, they blushed when he praised them and, after tutorials, twittered endlessly like sparrows in a dust bath.

Partway through the Michaelmas term I waited with nerves of jelly as Guy returned our first essays. Constantly watching, summing up, assessing – restless energy directed his eyes and one foot that tapped with impatience. Smoke from a late summer bonfire drew a fragrant haze across his study. He rose, shut the window, and sat down. He moved with purpose – short, precise movements designed to get him where he wanted to go but no more.

We waited expectantly. He smiled. He didn't smile often, but when he did it meant one of two things: either he felt genuinely pleased – which was rare – or someone could expect a rocketing.

"Right, let's get started. Mr Vine, dross, raise your game or you're off the course. Don't expect an easy ride on the back of your school scholarship – that means nothing here, you've got to earn it." He all but threw the essay at the pink-faced boy. "Mr Horton – a passing attempt. One or two acceptable points, but don't rely on your A-level notes. Blake was good in his day, but he's way off-beam now."

Greg surveyed his returned essay glumly, the furious red slashes and comments visible from where I sat. I raised an eyebrow in sympathy and he grimaced, still hungover from the rave the night before.

"Miss Cam-er-ron," he drew out Steph's name. "Well, what can I say? If you continue to produce work like this you're looking at graduating by Christmas and collecting your doctorate in a couple of years. Quite remarkable." Steph beamed, but she missed the sarcastic undertones. Tom glanced at me and we both looked at her hoping she would read the signs, but she was a lamb to slaughter. Dr Hilliard cast his eyes over the lengthy essay. "What's the going rate for this on the internet now? And don't bother denying it; I had a student sent down last year for plagiarism. If you're going to pay good money for this offal, give me credit and find something original – better still, write it yourself. Now, who's next..."

Tom dropped his pen and fumbled picking it up. I smiled encouragement.

"Mr Falconer, ah yes, not at all bad. A collaborative attempt, was it?" Guy shot me a look. "Well, make sure you use spellcheck next time; there's no excuse and I have a hang-up about bad spelling. Last, but by no means least, Miss D'Eresby... now there's a name to conjure with, ladies and gentlemen – good, solid gentry stock – the backbone of England." He tapped my essay against the side of his leg as I writhed under his gaze. "Who helped you with this?"

Taken aback, I probably came across more defensive than I meant to be. "No one."

"Whose work is it based on – whose research?"

"No one's; it's my own."

He said nothing more and I don't know whether he believed me or not, but his stare became speculative. I didn't know then what I know now – that he knew who I was, that he had been waiting for me and, until that moment, I believe he thought me overrated. And that is when it all began.

I think he tested me at first; it certainly felt like it. He fired questions like bullets – *thud, thud, thud* – until I felt bruised from the onslaught.

"'*Grave sins and shameless vices…*' Heinrich Bullinger, Zurich, 1540. So, Emma…" he would begin before I had time to sit down, "… if the common rural practice of sexual intercourse before marriage was approved, why did virginity become a valuable commodity in the economy of Upper Bavaria during the second half of the seventeenth century?"

"Um…" I would say, blushing, as mice scurried around my brain looking for answers and my fellow students cowered in case he asked them.

"Come on, Miss D'Eresby, this is well within your capabilities."

"Er… the new Reformation Ordinance of 1637 stated that all non-marital sexuality between men and women was forbidden, so what had been considered to be minor infringements became crimes in the Morality Courts, leading to severe punishment as a result of the Morality Decree of 1635. This was largely due to Counter Reformation – principally Jesuit – interpretation of morality laws. I think."

He clapped slowly. "Bravo, Miss D'Eresby, and quite rightly so.

The Morality Laws – '*Hurerei*' – or fornication '... *that have grown rampant among so many...*' What grave sins have grown rampant among us, ladies and gentlemen? What indeed." He skewered me with a look and I hurriedly dropped my eyes from his.

I found it embarrassing. I worked out once that three-quarters of questions asked during any one session were directed at me. If I answered correctly he praised me fulsomely until I squirmed. If not, his comments were scathing. Either way I flushed lobster, and when I did, his eyes became almost hooded and he watched me carefully. I dreaded his supervisions at first, but gradually – as he saw that my interest in my subject equalled his own – his questions became less barbed and more intended to guide and teach, and my dread turned into anticipation, and then from pleasure to want.

I experienced a frisson of excitement every time I entered his room, aware that he saw everything about me: the way I walked, how I wore my hair, whether I had worked all night or slept in that day. I began to dress for him, to leave a strand of hair loose so that it curled in the fenland mist. His self-assurance seemed almost arrogant, yet I found his confidence reassuring because I thought I knew where I stood with him. Like high stone walls there would be no room for manoeuvre, no space for reservation. He knew what he wanted and he wanted *me*. This man I so admired, whose work I emulated, whose passion for his subject matched mine, wanted me. Tom saw it, the others felt it, until Guy drove a wedge between us and they drifted away. But I sought his approval more than I feared their distance. I longed for his recognition of my work above all else because he withheld it, dangling it in front of me, feeding me tit-bits of praise – feeding my ambition, fuelling my desire. Stupid, stupid... but I was young and I was naïve.

I should have known better.

He indulged my obsession with the past. We spent increasing amounts of time in each other's company but, despite his relentless pursuit, not once did he allow the standard of my work to drop. He demanded more from me than any other student. His criticism stung if I did not live up to expectations. He shredded my research if not as meticulous as his own. He set tasks I could not hope to fulfil; except that, because he thought I could, I did. Now, in retrospect, I understand he intended grooming me in more ways than one, but then I saw only the interest of an older man who gave me what I wanted: his undivided attention, his absolute acceptance that what I pursued was mine by right, a validation in itself – no other justification needed, none sought, none offered. For the first time since the death of my grandfather I felt my interest in my subject vindicated.

I missed the warning signs. Either I did not look for them or my lack of worldliness made me unaware. I was not deceitful, nor did I look for deceit in others, but I couldn't deny the excitement I felt when I realized that his interest went beyond the professional. When Guy suggested a research project outside the demands of my coursework, I accepted without a second thought. When it involved long hours spent alone with him in his study, I did not demur. I might have been naïve, but I was not a fool.

I did not flaunt his attention. I did not seek it when among others. When he first tried to touch me one evening, I surprised us both by the vehemence of my rejection. I upheld my moral integrity, and my natural reserve and self-preservation did the rest. He once said that I led him on and I grew hot and angry, denying it until he looked almost sorry he said anything, and he never accused me of flirting again.

To give him his due, he didn't rush things. He didn't paw me like some scabby boy or try to touch me up like a dirty old man. He took his time, like a game of chess played over the following two terms, so I deluded myself into thinking I must be mistaken and his interest was purely academic.

He arranged for his group of students to travel to London to see a Jacobean play. The first daffodils dotted the banks of the river as I made my way to our agreed rendezvous point. Roads became bloated with traffic as rush hour beckoned and fumes hung in the air, a choking sweetness clinging to my throat. Guy drew up to the kerb, hazard lights flashing, window down.

"Get in, Emma."

I checked over my shoulder at the park beyond. "But the others…" A car honked behind him. He released the door lock and pushed it open from the inside.

"They can't make it. Get in, you're holding up the traffic." Keen to avoid his impatience, I did as bidden, and it was only later that I discovered he had bought just two tickets for that night.

He drove us to London and he put on a Rolling Stones CD. I heard him laugh for the first time when he asked me what I thought about the music and I told him they were my mother's favourite group. He made a comment about our age difference and I said that seventeen years to a historian was irrelevant in the grand scheme of things. When he went quiet, I realized he hadn't been referring to our generational taste in music.

We watched *'Tis Pity She's a Whore*, and over dinner spent the rest of the evening debating Ford's portrayal of Giovanni as a virtuous and noble man overcome by passion and condemned by a moralistic society. Guy made me feel like an adult; when he asked my opinion he listened with genuine interest to my answers. I no longer felt the need to impress and began to drop my guard.

There followed a series of theatre dates, concerts, a foreign film – always on the same day each week and followed by dinner beyond the immediate vicinity of Cambridge. Each time he took one small step towards intimacy and each time I let him. But I wasn't a fool even if I behaved like one. I knew what he wanted from the way he slipped compliments into sentences like lovers between sheets, and I let him flatter me, lifting a strand of hair to the sun to admire the fire in it.

For those first two terms after Michaelmas, as he nurtured my intellect I resisted his attempts to seduce me. Old-fashioned as it may seem, I believed in holding out for the man I wanted to marry, and without that level of commitment I could only foresee heartbreak and misery. I must have harboured hope, but more than my desire for his love, I ached for recognition as a serious academic contender.

It was all academic. Teetering on the verge of love and with my resistance wafer thin, I went home one weekend for my birthday. It was hot. Indolent air, heavy with suppressed heat, pressed against skin already tacky with sweat. Mum and Nanna knew immediately, of course, as they read the light in my eyes, and I begged them not to say anything to my father. None of us wanted an argument. We needn't have bothered. After a long career in the Army working to other people's demands, Dad had yet to lose his abrasive attributes against which I frequently rubbed, and proved quite capable of initiating a confrontation without any help from me.

He snapped open his starched napkin from its precise quarters and placed it on his lap. Friction sparked the moment he opened his mouth. "Have you given any thought to what you will be doing when you graduate, Emma?"

Nanna and Mum exchanged looks. "Hugh, darling, not now; can't this wait for another day?"

"No time like the present," he barked. "Well, Emma, have you made any enquiries yet? Most decent jobs will require a conversion course I expect, but with a good degree behind you – even if it is in history – you should stand a chance with the big boys." Light faded from the tall breakfast room windows as a storm approached, and the first of the heavy drops began to fall onto the wide stone flags of the courtyard – dark splashes – like tears. The distinctive scent of summer rain on damp stone rose on warm currents of air. "Emma, I asked you a question…"

I reluctantly faced him. "Yes, Dad, I have given it some thought." The same thought as always; nothing changed – neither his questions nor my answers. "I'll be applying for a place to study for a doctorate and, when I've completed that, I'll look for a position at any university that'll take me."

Nanna gave a little sigh, stretched out her arm, and lightly clasped my hand in hers. I smiled back at her.

"Utterly ridiculous!" Dad growled, his fists on the table. "You know my thoughts on this matter…"

"Yes, and you know mine," I countered. "Look, please, can't this wait until later? Mum and Nanna have gone to so much trouble to get this meal ready and there's nothing we have to say to each other that won't keep. Please."

He twitched his neck to free it of his stiff, starched collar in that annoying way he had when he knew he was in the wrong. "Of course – for your mother – but I expect a sensible response from you, young lady, no more of this… nonsense."

Mum shot him a cautionary "Hugh…"

He tweaked his collar again and allowed a tight smile. "This looks splendid, Penny. What a feast."

I made an effort but I barely touched my food. I drank a glass of wine and instantly regretted it as a headache set in. All so familiar, this face-off across the dining room table, this simmering rancour that boiled over into bitter recrimination.

Most of the time when at home I avoided my father, studying in my room at the top of the house, coming downstairs when I knew him to be out, or asleep, or in his potting shed, but my family upheld the traditions of mealtimes around the table, when neither of us could avoid one another.

Mum put her arms around me when we were alone in the steamy kitchen. "I know, darling. I spoke to him before you came home but he won't listen. I don't think he can. He's so worried about your future he can't see what you've already achieved."

I rested my head against her shoulder, breathing in her comforting smell of freshly laundered cotton and the scent Dad always bought her for Christmas.

"I'm doing fine, Mum – better than fine. Guy thinks I'm heading for a First. I already have an idea for my doctoral research, and Guy thinks..."

Mum raised an eyebrow. "*Guy* seems to think quite a lot of you, it seems."

I reddened and smiled self-consciously. "Dr Hilliard then – he's helping me put together a proposal. He thinks it stands a good chance of being accepted."

"Is that all he's helping you with, darling?"

"Mum, honestly! I'm the teenager – I'm the one who should be doing the innuendo, not you. Oh, but really, Guy has been wonderful. Without him I don't think I would be doing as well as I am. I owe him big time."

Deep lines between her eyes puckered as she placed her hands either side of my face, the little calluses where she gripped her tennis racquet tickling my skin. "Darling, he sounds wonderful and you're old enough not to need me to tell you to be careful, but... be careful, Emma, you know what I'm talking about. His motives might not be as clear-cut as you are making them sound... Emma?"

My eyes slipped from hers. "Yes, I know, Mum. I am careful – I'm always careful – don't worry."

She pressed her cheek to mine. "I'm so glad you're doing well; wouldn't Grandpa be pleased?"

The door opened behind us, letting in a draft of air as Nanna carried some glasses rattling on a metal tray. "What would Douglas be pleased about, Penny?"

Mum took the tray from her and I started to wash the glasses. "That Emma is doing so well, Mum. Her supervisor – Guy, didn't you say his name was?" I pulled a face at her because she knew perfectly well, "… seems to think she'll get a First. Isn't that marvellous?"

Nanna's eyes twinkled at me from behind her old-fashioned glasses. "Grandpa would be so proud of you, poppet; we all are."

"Except Dad," I couldn't help grousing, remembering I still had to face him.

"Even your father. He just has a blind spot – he'll grow out of it." We all laughed at the family joke. She paused suddenly. "*Guy*, did you say? Guy… Guy – the name rings a bell. Oh, this old brain of mine needs a good spring clean. It's a shame it's too late and will have to wait for another year. No, I can't place it. Never mind, it probably wasn't important anyway. You never know, poppet, perhaps one day you'll have Grandpa's old position at Cambridge. Does the post still exist?" I nodded, grinning – Guy held it, but I didn't think he would want to relinquish it to some upstart like me anytime soon. "Well, I look forward to your graduation ceremony – and if I'm not around for it, my darling, I'll make sure I come as a ghost and bring Grandpa with me. Dead or alive, I'll be there." She laughed her clear, girlish laugh that lit up the whole room with her jollity.

I handed her a dripping glass. "It's a deal," I said, although the thought of her not being around in person to help celebrate the culmination of Grandpa's ambition for me was unbearable. She wasn't the sort to be maudlin, so I couldn't be. The door opened again.

"Ah, Emma, there you are." My father's gruff voice filled the small space and I bristled. Where else would I be? "Ready for that little chat?"

Reluctantly, I followed him upstairs to his study. The rain had stopped temporarily, and from between engorged clouds the sun slanted through the sash windows. I sat on one of the deep window seats feeling small again and not on the verge of womanhood as Guy made me feel. Even in summer, Dad wore his tweed jacket and tie. He looked all stuffed up, permanently fuming like a volcanic vent. I imagined steam rising from the fissures of his eyes and mouth. It helped a little.

"Emma, it won't do." *Here we go.* "We tolerated you taking a degree in history" – *Hah! I hadn't given him much choice in the matter* – "but there can be no question of you continuing with this foolhardy plan. You're only nineteen; you have plenty of time to change your mind."

I slid off the window seat, fingernails digging into my palms as I focused my rising temper. "Well, that's OK then, Dad, because I'm not going to change my mind and there's no point trying to bully me out of it. I don't need your permission, I don't need your say-so. You can cut me out of your will or never speak to me again – whatever – but that is just about the limit of what you can do to me."

"Perfectly absurd, girl!" he boomed across my rant, using his height to try to dominate me.

That did it. I'd had enough. "Yes, you are, you're ridiculous – you're being ridiculous. You have no right to tell me what to do. I'm an adult and I can make my own decisions…"

"Then behave like one and not like a spoilt child. Your grandfather indulged you with this history farce. I should never have let it continue for as long as it did. He *ruined* you."

I gasped, choked, staring in horror at the antipathy behind his words. Turning, I fled the room.

Guy answered his mobile after a couple of rings. "Hold on," he said, and I could hear sounds of movement, of doors opening and shutting. "What's the matter?" His voice sounded louder. I managed a few garbled words before I finally broke down and begged him to come and get me. He didn't answer for a moment.

"Please, Guy, I need you."

"All right, but it'll take me an hour to Stamford; think you can hang on until then?"

I stifled a sob. "I'll be outside."

It started to rain again, heavier than before. My thin top clung to my back and drops escaped down loose strands of hair. Mum hurried across the cobbles to where I huddled beside the wall of St Mary's Church, conspicuously alone.

"Darling, come in and wait, you're soaked. You haven't had your presents yet and Beth is on her way over with Rob – I think they have something they want to tell us. Your father is so sorry he upset you, he didn't mean to."

I wanted to believe her. I wanted to go back inside and find that it had all been a big mistake and sit down with my family and have tea and presents and convivial chitchat about nothing much at all. I wanted to have a father who would engulf me with warmth and love and accept me for who I was and not what he wanted me to be. But I didn't, and he couldn't, so I stood there in the pouring rain instead.

"I can't, Mum, I'm sorry. I'm sorry to have ruined everything. Tell Beth, tell Nanna..." And I began to cry again because it was all so wretchedly hopeless.

"I know, I know, my darling, we understand, but come in out of the rain. You can wait inside, can't you?"

I might have done, but at that moment I happened to glance up and see my father's face scouring at the first floor window like a malignant troll. I shook my head and she sighed at my stubborn resignation. We were both saved from her persistence and my denial by the sound of a car bumping across the uneven surface towards us.

"I have to go, Mum. Thanks for trying, for everything."

Inside the car it felt warm and quiet except for the rain on the windscreen and the steady swipe of the blades across the glass.

"You're drenched – here..." Guy reached behind the seat, keeping one hand on the steering wheel, and pulled out a travel rug. A shiny sweet wrapper fell from its folds, lodging between the seat and the handbrake, and he grunted and stuffed it in his pocket.

"Thanks," I said.

"What was all that about?"

I couldn't answer.

"You didn't tell me you were going home for the weekend."

I pulled the rug around my shoulders and stared miserably out of the window. "It's my birthday."

"You didn't say. Happy birthday."

"Yeah..." Slow tears began to seep down my wet cheeks, mingling fresh and salt when they reached the corners of my mouth. He frowned and concentrated on the road. Guy didn't do tears. He gave short shrift to any student who tried them as a tactic when he returned a failed assignment. But mine were genuine and I asked for nothing more than to be taken back to college.

The A1 was unusually quiet for an early summer evening. Rush-hour had come and gone and only the occasional lorry spewed spray from its tyres as we passed.

"What did your father say to upset you?"

I rubbed the back of my hand across my face, tasting my tears as I tried to stem them. "He thinks history is a waste of time."

Guy laughed shortly. "That's apt given what we deal in. What does he want you to do instead?"

I pouted. "A profession – law, accountancy, medicine – you know, something *respectable*, something that earns real *money*."

A lorry flashed its lights at us as we overtook it. Guy skewed his mouth in displeasure. "He doesn't know you very well," he remarked.

I glowered at the flat, sodden landscape. "No, he doesn't."

We travelled on in silence. Despite the heat in the car, I felt cold. "Emma, have you eaten?"

I shrugged. The wipers thrashed across the windscreen but made little difference to the onslaught of rain. "I can't see the bloody road. Look, we're going to have to pull over, I can't drive in this."

He slowed right down, but through the sheer volume of water only the smudged outlines of buildings and trees distinguished their surroundings. He drew into the first promising car park and assessed the illuminated sign through the rain-smeared window. "This will have to do. Wait here."

He ducked through the rain and disappeared from view. He came back minutes later, opening the door, holding out his hand. "I've got us a room; come on."

I baulked. "A room?"

"Yes, a room, there's nothing else. Come on, I'm getting soaked."

"But a *room*, Guy?"

"For Pete's sake, Emma, you don't want to sit in the foyer looking like *that*, do you?" I caught a glimpse of myself in the mirror. I looked a sight – my hair plastered to my face, my eyes puffy and still bleary with unspent tears. My pale shirt was too thin and the rain made it almost transparent, showing my bra. I wrapped my arms across my chest and climbed out of the car.

It looked a modern box, all featureless corporate colours and side lighting to take off some of the starkness, but the room was warm and dry and offered privacy while the rain beat down outside. I perched on a chair as Guy went to fill the kettle from the basin in the tiny bathroom. I felt more conscious of being alone with him now than I ever did at uni. He came back in and switched on the kettle. He stood surveying me with his hands on his hips. I shivered.

"You're a mess." He swung around and opened the door of the wardrobe, the thin hangers rattling emptily. "There's nothing here to change into, but there are towels in the bathroom. I'll go and see what I can find to eat. I won't be long." The door shut behind him. I went into the bathroom and fingered the white towels. My shirt would dry quickly enough if I hung it on the heated towel rail; the skirt might take longer. I locked the door and stripped down to basics, draping my top and skirt to dry. My skin roughened with goose-pimples and it was all I could do to stop shaking.

My clothes were still damp, but dry enough, and I felt better for my shower when I emerged a little time later. Guy lay stretched out on the bed with his hands behind his head, watching the evening news on the feeble television, his burgundy shirt – taut across his chest and shoulders – already dry. His mobile lay beside him on the bedside locker, the face still glowing – he must have made a call – and next to it an ice-bucket and a long-necked bottle. My heart skipped a beat, but it wasn't the pleasant sensation of anticipation, rather that of uncertainty.

He patted the bed next to him. "Come and sit down. There's been another car-bomb in the Middle East, killed dozens, poor sods; what a benighted region."

I sat on the furthest corner of the bed from him and watched the unsteady camera work of the media team under fire against a background of pockmarked concrete and bloodied faces and torn limbs.

"Unbelievable." He waved a hand in the direction of the television, inviting comment. I said nothing. "Emma, are you all right?" I nodded, still mute. He sat up and leaned towards me, putting a hand on my arm. I didn't move. "What's the matter? Are you still upset about your father?" I couldn't tell him it was the room and his shirt and the champagne, so I just nodded again. "Look, they didn't have much in the way of food – just some crisps – but have a drink, it'll make you feel better."

"I don't want anything to drink, Guy, it gives me a headache."

"Champagne doesn't, does it? Have half a glass to celebrate your birthday then perhaps the rain will have eased off enough and we can get going again."

I looked up at him but his eyes were veiled as they so often were. He smiled. "You look quite beautiful."

I turned my head away. "That's not what you said earlier."

"No, well you do now you've dried off a bit. Your hair's longer than I remember and so red – Rembrandt red…" He put his hand out to touch it and I tried not to flinch. "It's still damp. Here, let me dry it for you."

"Don't, Guy." I stood and went to the window. If anything, the rain fell more heavily now, solid sheets of water driven by the wind. I heard the pop of a cork behind me.

"I've never seen you cry before. You haven't said what really upset you earlier. It wasn't just about the history, was it?" He came up behind and handed me a foaming, long-stemmed glass, almost full as the bubbles settled. I took a tentative sip to dislodge the tight lump in my throat before I answered.

"No."

"What then?" He stood so close I could hear his breath short and shallow as it stirred my drying hair. I drank again – a bigger sip this time – then another. It began to take immediate effect. "Well?"

"My grandfather… he said something about my grandfather." I swallowed to regain control and drank again.

"What about him, Emma? What upset you?" His voice sounded consoling now, softer than I had ever heard it before. Weakened by unfamiliar kindness, a tear escaped before I could catch it.

"He blames my grandfather for everything – *everything* – but he loved me, Guy. If it weren't for him I would never have wanted to be a historian. I would be… nothing…" I drained my glass shakily and he took it from me and refilled it.

"No one can stop you from being what you want to be, Emma," he spoke into my hair, putting his arm around me so that I turned into the cradle of it for comfort, my head already spinning. "No one can tell you what to do any more. You were born to study history – it runs through your blood." His words blurred a little and I swayed. He held me steady. I downed a quarter of my glass, feeling reckless.

"But my father doesn't understand. He won't stop… he just goes on and on and on… every time I see him…" My legs felt heavy and I rocked, nearly dropping my glass. He took it from me.

"Come and rest," he suggested. I sat down unsteadily as the bed waved beneath me.

"Every time, Guy..." He pulled me closer to him, his other hand holding my face still. "On and on..." He kissed my lips; they felt numb under his mouth. I pushed against his chest but he didn't move away. The room swam and all the sensations and emotions merged until I shook my head in confusion. "No, Guy, I don't want to... I hate him."

His mouth became insistent and his hand left my face and enclosed my breast through my flimsy shirt. I pushed at him halfheartedly, torn between giving in and hanging on. "No – I don't want to..."

"Yes, you do."

My mouth responded to his urgency and I kissed him back. He took his arm from around me and pressed me onto the bed with his body. I couldn't move; I didn't want to move. I wanted all the vacillation taken away and replaced by the conviction of his desire. But not like this, not drunk. I forced my eyes open but the ceiling spun and I closed them rapidly. His hand dragged my skirt up.

"Guy – no – get off me..."

"I've waited so long, Emma, you're so beautiful..."

His skin felt hot like flames; his mouth distorted my words. Too far gone to be afraid, yet not ready either. Pinned by his body, my head a mass of disjointed thoughts, I stopped struggling and gave up, the brash blue cover of the bed rumpling like folds of skin that moved with every motion he made.

He wasn't violent or particularly rough and it didn't hurt as much as I thought it would, or perhaps the alcohol made an effective anaesthetic, but it was an act empty and devoid of meaning. It lessened me.

I curled into a ball afterwards and I must have slept. When I woke, Guy stood over me calling my name. He had showered and dressed.

"We can make a move – the rain's eased."

That's all he said: "*We can make a move – the rain's eased.*" That's all it meant to him, a brief interlude in the storm.

I raised my head, my stomach queasy. I waited until the room steadied before shifting to a sitting position.

"If we hurry, we can get something to eat when we get back – I'm bloody hungry." At some point he had drawn the bedcover over me and it snagged as I moved my legs. I yanked it to free them. He flicked the switch on the kettle. "Water's hot if you want a shower."

Wordlessly, I moved to the edge of the bed and swung my legs over the side. He had righted the two cups and engaged in ripping open sachets of sugar, his back to me. The crumpled cover felt rough under my thighs. As I stood, a small dark patch glared accusingly from its surface where I had lain. I snatched the cover, dragging it off the bed and rolling it in a ball before he saw the evidence. A little blood – nothing in itself – it would wash out, but it was my blood and he had shed it without a second thought, as cavalier an action as his assumption that it was his to take.

Once showered, I hid the cover in the bath behind the drawn curtain and shut the door behind me.

"Ready? Better have this first." He handed me a cup with a tan-looking liquid in it. I drank it automatically, making no comment despite the lacing of sugar meant to disguise the tart contents.

He was uncharacteristically animated in the car on the way back. After a while he paused his monologue on a Jesuit text he had recently transcribed. "Are you all right? You're very quiet." Pewter clouds hung angrily on the horizon, threatening more rain.

"Yes."

"Bit hung over? You shouldn't have drunk so much."

"No."

We approached the suburbs of Cambridge, and the roads were empty except for the lights reflecting in the standing pools of water at the edges. He tapped his finger on the steering wheel waiting for a light to change. He hadn't looked at me since getting in the car. "Food," he stated, nodding in the direction of a takeaway.

When he climbed back in the car, he handed me a burger. "Have that; it's not gourmet but you'll feel better for it."

Better? Physically or emotionally did he mean? I stared at the unappetizing dome of bread with the charred meat protruding from it and wondered what on earth he thought it could do to make up for the void I felt inside.

He took me back to my room and left me there, eager to be away. I went straight to bed but did not sleep. I had expected it to happen at some time, but not like that. My choices were limited: if I accepted what happened as an act of coercion on his part, it would make me a victim – a role I didn't dare adopt in case it grew to be a bigger monster in my mind than the episode warranted. To ignore him and pretend it didn't happen was not an option. That left me with making the best of the situation, something at which I had become particularly adept over the years. To give meaning to the event and to imbue our relationship with some dignity, I dressed it to make it acceptable to myself: I chose to be in love with him.

For a time I made it work. Our affair placed him beyond the bounds of professionalism, illicitly tantalizing, so I believed him when he said he couldn't take me anywhere we might be seen, or home where his mother might gossip to her friends in the choral society. We met infrequently and in secret – less over the long summer holiday when he lectured abroad, more when I went with him to an international conference. We made love when we could because that is what lovers do, but as the weeks passed I grew to feel the emptiness of a relationship that was unfounded and without purpose. Above all, my hopes that I could find validity in marriage were to be proved baseless and void.

I poured so much of myself into my research and into our relationship that my other tutors complained as the standard of my work began to suffer. I thought we had been discreet, but not long before my finals, my personal tutor called me to her study.

We had met on a number of social occasions, but it was the first time she had asked to see me because of my work. She occupied a study in one of the old rooms of the college into which she had grown over the preceding decades. Books lined every available surface, interspersed with geological specimens: knobbly geodes and fossils acted as bookends and a spiky lump of quartz made do as a doorstop. She settled into her chair, light shining through her sparse grey hair, and studied me through her varifocals.

"Emma, I knew your grandfather." That wasn't what I expected to hear and my surprise must have shown. "He was an especially dear friend and I respected him greatly. If it weren't for him I would have made a very grave mistake and one that I would have regretted for the rest of my life. It is because of what he did for me that I offer you a word of advice – not, I am sure, that you will want to hear what I have to say." She folded her hands on the desk. "Emma, I know how hard you have studied to get here, but your work is going to the dogs. You are one of the most promising students we've had for a while and you are more than living up to your grandfather's hopes for you. However, if you carry on as you are, you're at risk of jeopardizing your degree, and I'd be failing both you and your grandfather if I didn't tell you as much."

A delicate mineral, the shape and shade of a pale pink rose, acted as a paperweight on her desk, soft dust gathered in its petals. I studied it as I thought about what she said. Her words didn't come as a surprise, which made it all the worse, because I had let my principles drift and betrayed my grandfather's faith in me. I still achieved top marks in Seventeenth-Century Studies under Guy's uncompromising supervision, but at the expense of my other courses. I couldn't fail now, not after everything I'd done to get here; I must get myself back on track. I made a mental note to talk to him about it.

"There's one other thing," she said. "Are you aware that Guy Hilliard is married?" The shock must have registered on my face because she took off her glasses and squinted at me. "No, I didn't think he'd told you." A bee buzzed frantically outside the open window.

"M-married?" I stuttered.

"Yes, I'm sorry."

"He can't be, it's a mistake. He... he didn't tell me."

"So it seems."

She said nothing as my heart withered and shrank. Married. Of course he was married; it made sense.

"Does he have a family?" I asked.

"I believe so – three children, I think." The bee's frenzied attack bore an accusation each time its soft body collided with the glass – thump, thump, thud – one for each child.

Hussy.

I stared at the spine of a book without reading it, as shattered thoughts coalesced. "He didn't tell me," I said again. She let the enormity of her revelation sink in as heat rose, then fled, from my face.

Harlot.

"Emma, is there anyone you can talk to about this? Friends, your parents?"

I had neglected my friends too much to be called one myself, and of those who might have been, Guy had effectively driven them away. As for my family I felt too ashamed to tell them, and I wouldn't give Dad either the satisfaction or the ammunition to tell me that he had been right all along.

Whore.

"Are you sure?"

She gave a little sigh as if she expected such a question, and proceeded to detail all the facts I needed to work it out for myself. When she finished, she replaced her glasses and repeated her earlier question. "Is there someone you can talk to?"

My head still reeled and her words didn't mean very much any more. "No, I don't need anyone. Thank you for letting me know." I rose to leave.

The older woman placed her hand on my arm. "I hope I've done the right thing in telling you. You can't live a lie, Emma – it's what your grandfather told me and he was right, although I didn't see it that way at the time. Of course, you're free to continue your relationship if you choose – I won't report it – but you have the right to put in a complaint against Dr Hilliard if you want. What he's done is unethical."

I would do no such thing, although that represented all I knew at the moment. "Thank you," I told her, "I'll think about it."

"Of course. You know where I am if you need me."

"Thank you, you've been very kind," I said mechanically, but I didn't hear her, I wasn't listening – I was miles away, planning what I would say to Guy.

***

I didn't shed a tear, not one drop did I let fall for what I had lost. I locked myself in my room and didn't eat or sleep until I had worked out what to do.

Guy was alone in his study. I closed the door behind me and leant against it without saying a word. He looked up from the essay he was marking. "Emma? We didn't arrange to meet." He did a double-take and put his pen down. "You look awful. What's happened?"

I continued staring at him, not sure how to begin because once I did, I couldn't be sure I would stop. He stood up and came over, and bent down to kiss me. I averted my face and he took a step back. His eyes widened momentarily as I saw the flash of recognition that something had changed. He dropped his arms, but kept up the act. "Are you ill? Is it the essay? For Pete's sake, Emma, say something..."

"You're married," I said flatly.

For once wrong-footed, he thought about denying it but saw it was pointless. "I... I couldn't tell you." He licked his lips nervously. "Things haven't been too good at home for some time. Sarah and I, we've drifted apart – it happens. Look, I've been thinking about getting my own place..."

"Does she know about me?" My voice sounded harsh and tinny in the space of the room.

"No – no of course not..."

"Then you've lied to both of us."

"I was going to tell you... tell her..."

I snorted with derision. "When were you going to tell us, Guy? When were you going to tell your children, your parents?"

"My parents?" He looked puzzled and I realized too late that they were just another fabrication. How many more had he woven to protect his lie?

"We can still be together, Emma. I'll get a place in town. We can..."

I cut in. "So you'll marry me?"

"Marry you?" A look of panic crossed his face. "I can't. I can't get a divorce; it's a sin."

"A sin? What do you call this? Since when has adultery not been classified as a sin? *'Grave sins and shameless vices...'* 1540 – Heinrich Bullinger – remember, Guy? You should do, you taught me. *'The reason for all this is that the vices no longer bear their proper names and therefore no one judges them properly as they are upon themselves and before God.'* Don't you dare talk about sin; don't you dare moralize with me."

"Nobody need know anything about us. Nobody need get hurt."

It took only an instant for the penny to drop. "You mean *you* needn't get hurt – your career, your precious job, your marriage. As long as you're all right, it's OK, is that it? Damn your wife, damn your children, and damn me. What was I – a quick screw, an easy lay as long as nobody knew? Too late – I know now and I'm not the only one."

For a fraction of a second he looked frightened. "What do you mean?"

"How on earth do you think I found out?"

He eyed me suspiciously. "Who have you been talking to? Who else knows?"

"Why?"

"What do you mean 'why'?"

"Why does it matter who else knows, Guy?"

"You little fool, of course it matters. My wife..."

"You already said your marriage is over."

"I did not."

I raised my eyebrows and lowered my voice, hearing it

drip with bitter irony. "Ah. So I was nothing more than an interregnum. How stupid of me, I should have known better. Let's just hope your wife doesn't find out, poor woman. At least I haven't a family to consider, only my honour – what's left of it."

"What is that supposed to mean?"

"It means, Guy, that you have so much more to lose than I have. Goodbye."

"No, Emma, get back here…" He made a grab for my arm but I shook him off angrily. "Why can't you do what you're bloody well told just for once in your life!"

I turned, opened the door, and left with as much dignity as I could muster, but inside I was no more than a beaten child: small, crumpled, and defeated. He had made a whore out of me, an adulteress, a marriage-breaker, and I let him. I hadn't heeded the signs: the hasty phone calls from behind closed doors, the sweet wrapper on the back seat of his car. He never once held me, never slept by me. A hurried affair – brisk and to the point – without tenderness, lacking in affection; a sham, a falsehood, a lie. And because I assented, it was as much my shame as his.

Two things happened as a result of ending our relationship: I threw myself at my studies with a new-found fervour, qualifying – as he had always assured me I would – with a First Class Honours degree. Secondly, I found within myself the reserves of strength to carry on. But I hurt; I ached inside because of what had been done to me and, by default, what I had done to this other woman.

Betrayal: a tangle of deceit where every step is quicksand, and nothing is what it seems.

I would never let it happen again.

1

Threshold

The hum the tyres made on the road changed as we left the highway. I sat up and rubbed sleep from my eyes. "Where are we?"

"Just coming into Howard's Lake. How are you feeling?"

I stifled a yawn. "Still tired. I can't seem to shake it off."

"I think you should reconsider and come back home with me, at least for the next few days. The college is no place for you to be right now and I'd be happier knowing you won't be alone."

"You mean so that Pat can force-feed me every four hours?"

He looked sidelong at me. "Among other things."

"Or is it because there would be at least one doctor on call all the time, if not three? I thought you said I'm going to be fine?"

"You are, but your heart ceased to beat for over seven minutes, Emma, and I'm not taking any chances. In the natural order of things you shouldn't be here at all and I don't want to tempt fate. I know I said there shouldn't be any complications, but I could be wrong and it's soon, too soon…" He trailed off; he wasn't only referring to my near-death during the last day of the trial.

"I know, Matthew, you're right, but it is too soon for me to come home with you now, not just for you, but for Henry and the family as well. We've been through this. You know how I feel. It wouldn't be decent somehow so soon after Ellen's death. Even if she said she'd understand, even if she never lived there with you, it's like crossing a threshold – it's significant."

"Emma, I've just buried my wife and I can't risk losing you as well. I appreciate your sense of propriety and, had these been normal circumstances, I would agree. As it is our lives go so far beyond the norm that the same rules cannot apply... what the... ?!" We had driven out of the screen of trees and into the gravelled forecourt of the college, narrowly missing a car parked half across the drive. The normally empty turning circle swarmed with vehicles. People waited in little groups on the steps and they moved towards us as they heard the sound of the powerful engine.

Matthew slammed on the brakes, simultaneously spinning the car in a tight arc before accelerating across the snow-covered lawns, slush ejected by the wheels. Once back on the drive, he checked the rearview mirror. "That was close and settles the matter – you're coming home with me."

Henry opened the passenger door when we drew up in the courtyard, his usually calm face crowded with worry. "Are you all right? I've just had a message from Joel – someone's tipped off the press that you're out of hospital and headed back to college. They'll be there now."

Matthew helped me out onto the crinkly ice. "That's where we've come from, the place is crawling. Henry, Emma will be staying here for a few days until things have settled down a bit."

I stole a quick look at Henry to gauge his reaction but he smiled down at me.

"It's good to have you back here, Emma, and Pat will be delighted to have you to fuss over. I imagine she will want to feed you up." I suppressed a groan and he chuckled. Despite my fears that it was too soon after his mother's death, Henry made me feel as welcome now as he did at Christmas. He steadied me as I rocked a little and his smile lessened. "I expect you need to rest. I think Pat's already made up the bed for you in your room just in case. I'll go tell her there'll be another mouth to feed." He walked back to the Barn, his light step more that of a fifty-year-old than the seventy-odd he was supposed to be. He might be the same age as my father, but that was the only similarity between them. Matthew put his arm around me and together we walked across the snow to the door to his kitchen.

"Do you think it counts if I cross the threshold through the back door?" I asked him, a yawn coming out of nowhere to catch me unawares.

"I think," he smiled, "that the only thing that matters at this moment is that I get you into bed – to sleep," he added, before I misconstrued.

It was all that I could do to keep my eyes open long enough to hear that my father's flight had taken off safely and that Harry was on his way back home from the airport. I wondered how much of the last few days' events Dad would disclose to my mother, or whether he would neglect to mention that she had nearly lost her daughter to a massive cardiac arrest brought on by an overdose of caffeine. At least he would be able to tell her that the man who had attacked me would probably be institutionalized for the rest of his life, and, even if my reputation had been tarnished by the trial, I was exonerated of any culpability. But although my father would no doubt let her know that Matthew had suffered a bereavement, he remained unaware that it was not his ninety-six-year-old grandmother that he had buried only two days ago, but his wife.

I shouldn't be here. I mean, I shouldn't be *here*, but circumstances dictated otherwise and – as Matthew drew the quilt over me before settling in the chair by the window to watch – I wondered not for the first time: where do we go from here?

* * *

"The Dean will never forgive me," I said gloomily as I read the local newspaper the next morning. "Shotter won't tolerate the college being brought into disrepute with scandalous gumpf like this." I waved the offending article in Matthew's direction. "That's another nail in my job coffin." I closed the paper, folded it, and chucked it on the bedside table. "Sorry," I said as he winced. "At least the story no longer makes headline news and has been relegated to page three. How fitting."

Matthew came over from where he had been standing with his face to the sun, and put the paper in the bin. "The Dean can go hang. Your year's secondment is up in the summer anyway and he won't terminate your contract before that; he wouldn't have the audacity after what you've been through. Besides, would you want to continue at the college if you had the choice of working elsewhere?"

I considered for a moment. Although I had come to the research college primarily to pursue a lifelong ambition to study the unique journal, I had grown very fond of my little group of post-graduate students, whose MAs I oversaw.

"I'd like to stay. I've enjoyed working with my group, despite all the interruptions we've had to put up with. Even if it hadn't all been ruined by Staahl and the trial, and Shotter wanted me to continue, I don't think it will be an option. There's my position at Cambridge to consider."

"It's a very long way to commute, I agree," he jested, "unless you were thinking of going back permanently." Despite his smile, I detected an undercurrent of uneasiness.

I pulled him down to sit by me.

"Only if I have no alternative. Of course, I might apply for another overseas position – Auckland, perhaps?"

He bent his head so our eyes were level. "Mmm, couldn't you think of something a little closer to home than New Zealand?"

"Birmingham Uni has an excellent Byzantine Studies department," I suggested, fighting the temptation to laugh.

"That would certainly be a change in direction for a Medieval and Early Modern historian, Emma. Anyway, when I said closer to home, I didn't mean England."

"You didn't?"

"No," he nuzzled my hair, "I didn't, as you know perfectly well."

Yes, I knew, but I wanted to hear him say it, to say, "Home – here in Maine – with me, Emma." I held my fingers against his cheek, serious for a moment.

"I don't like to take things for granted, Matthew; that way I don't get hurt."

His smile drifted and he took my face between his hands. "The one thing you are safe to assume, my love, is that I want you here… no – no that's not what I mean. I want us to be together, wherever that is. We don't have to live in Maine; we can go anywhere, including Auckland if you really want to. There are no ties here, not any more."

I understood what he meant; Ellen's death released him in more ways than just from the marriage vows that had kept us apart, but he was wrong if he thought himself entirely free.

"Your family is here, Matthew, and your research."

He played with the end of my dressing-gown cord, coiling it and letting it unwind a couple of times before answering. "We'll have to move in the next couple of years anyway when I can no longer conceal my lack of ageing. I can continue my research anywhere. As for the family, we will discuss it, of course."

They would discuss it, yes, but they would leave the final decision to Matthew as head of the family. If truth be told, for weeks I hadn't dared think beyond the next twenty-four hours. I hadn't risked hoping for anything more than getting through one day at a time. I felt as if we had been stuck in stasis forever although, in reality, I had known of Ellen's existence for less than a dozen weeks, and met Matthew only a matter of a few months before that. Yet it seemed an eternity – separated by his secret and his marriage. Now, with her death and the end of the trial, all that changed, and the possibilities were endless – so much so that I felt daunted by them.

Matthew looked apprehensive. "Emma, it's going to take me time."

"Yes."

"After so many years of being with someone – even if separated by Ellen's age and infirmity – we had a bond that was more than a marriage contract."

I glimpsed the pale tidemark left by his wedding ring. "I know you did."

"When you live as long as I have you carry so many memories, and with Henry living next door as a constant reminder of what Ellen and I shared, I can't just move on."

"I know you can't, I understand. I wouldn't expect you to."

"It's going to take me longer than I thought," he said again, looking dejected.

I smoothed the hair from his forehead and kissed the little lines of self-doubt between his eyes. "You have time, Matthew. You have as long as it takes."

He buried his face in my hair and for an age we sat like that until a light knock at the door broke through the insulated happiness which encased us. We sat slowly apart. The knock came again and this time Pat's cheerful face appeared around the door.

"I didn't know if you'd be awake. There now," she said as she came in, bearing a tray with something steaming and probably nutritious on it, "it's time you had something to eat."

I still felt full from my last force-feeding. "But Pat, I've only just had breakfast!"

"That was hours ago. You can't hope to get better on an empty stomach." She sounded like my mother, all bossy and jolly.

Matthew rose from beside me. "I'll take a walk; I won't be long." His smile meant to reassure, but he carried with him waves of grey-blue doubt and grief.

"That's OK," I said. "Take as long as you like. I'll still be here."

He took to walking by himself, only leaving me when Pat or Henry was within earshot and I could be relied upon to not develop some cardiac complication for the hour or so he spent crossing the frozen land. On his return, I would monitor his mood, intervening when I thought he might want to talk, and leaving him alone when he did not.

One afternoon, a week or so after the end of the trial, I watched Matthew cross the courtyard and disappear through the covered entrance, imagining him leaving light footprints on the compacted snow like his thoughts. Pat set a tray of tea and toast on the table beside the chair and, instead of decamping to let me eat alone as she usually did, sat down on the chair opposite. From a bag suspended from her arm, she drew her latest sewing project.

"You know, I was just so glad when Henry said you would be staying after all. It's been years since I've had anyone to look after. The children were never ill, and Jeannie hardly ever catches anything and when she does, Dan wants to care for her. I sometimes feel like making something up just to be able to nurse one of them. At least they eat now, so I can feed them."

"They didn't eat?" I queried, welcoming the interruption and rising to hunt for a sock under the bed before joining her again. The very thought of the gargantuan amounts of food the siblings consumed at Christmas made me pale.

She snipped at a cotton thread with a pair of dainty gold scissors. "They don't need that much; they eat because they want to, not because they have to as often as they do, or anywhere near as much. It's a sociable thing, like drinking in company. It's what's expected, isn't it? Matthew's always been very particular about the family appearing normal as much for their sakes as anything. I think he feels how different he is more than he likes to say." *Snip*. She cut a new length of thread, knotted it, and narrowed her eyes as she passed the end through a fine needle. "Henry was fine. Ellen got him used to eating plenty when he was young, so by the time I met him, she had him well trained, but the children were quite another case. Maggie was a nightmare to begin with, you can imagine. Being a step-mom isn't something I would have chosen. I never knew when she would eat from one day to the next, and she wouldn't talk to me at all – just cried for her sister and mommy. And when I had Dan, and then he had his children..." She wagged her head slowly. "It's quite a thing to get your mind around, this Lynes family, and it took me a while, I can tell you. I'm used to them now, of course, and I wouldn't want them any other way, but now that I have you to look after, well, *you* can catch cold as often as you like and I won't complain."

I pulled on the sock and eyed the mountain of toast she expected me to plough through.

"Pat, I'm sure you have better things to do with your time than nurse me. I wasn't planning on being around to be looked after that much."

She ceased stitching and gave me a keen, enquiring look. "You're not thinking of going back to England, are you?"

Partway through spreading homemade conserve, I replied steadily, "No, I'm not planning on leaving."

Her face brightened again and she picked up her patchwork and started on the next square. "Well, that's a good thing, because one thing I don't think any amount of my mothering could do is mend Matthew's heart if it were broken. I met him in the early years after the crash which crippled Ellen, when I started dating Henry. He never said anything, of course, but it was like a weight around his heart all the time. That's gone now. Even with Ellen's dying that load isn't there any more." She hesitated, and I could sense her weighing something before she spoke. "I expect you know what it's like to have your heart broken, don't you?"

For a moment I thought that she meant when I had fled back to England hurt and bewildered – before I unravelled Matthew's past, before he brought me back to the States, before he told me about Ellen. Then, I had breathed through only one day at a time. As I didn't answer immediately, Pat said, "I don't want you to think I'm prying, Emma, but it sounded to me as if you had a bad time with that man in Cambridge when you were a girl."

"Oh..." She meant Guy. I remembered her face when the prosecution revelled in the details of the affair, how she avoided my eyes, and the sniggers of the courtroom making me feel soiled and unclean. I had worried about what the family must think of me, and the memory of it still cut.

"Pat, I haven't thanked any of you for being at the trial. I know you were there for Matthew – and for Maggie, of course – but I really appreciated seeing you. It can't have been pleasant, especially with some of the things that were said about Matthew, and then there were the insinuations the prosecution made about me."

I prepared for the censorious pitch to her mouth, but she said, "It must have been very hurtful for you to hear."

"Quite honestly, I've tried to forget the whole thing that happened at Cambridge. It's not something I'm proud of, but nor was it what the prosecution counsel made it seem – it wasn't calculating or trivial at the time."

"I'm sure it wasn't. Don't think anyone is judging you, Emma. We all make mistakes and sometimes mistakes are made for us. Nobody in this family thinks any less of you for it." She smiled across the small table, full of warmth and affection. "It must have been difficult for your momma at the time."

I had a mental image of Mum standing by the telephone in the hall spitting nails as my father took another call from Guy, her normally placid countenance white with fury.

"It wasn't easy, no."

She nodded. "I know how I would feel if I had a little girl who found herself in the same situation. I'd find it difficult to let her go. I think I would want to wrap her up and protect her forever just in case it ever happened again."

"It might take Mum a while to get used to the idea of me being here, but she appreciates that Matthew is nothing like the man I knew at Cambridge, and I'm older and have my own life to lead, so…"

She patted my arm. "Chickadee, you will always be a little girl to your momma. I know that I still think my Dan's in Fourth Grade and getting into fights all the time."

"Did he?" I asked, surprised. Dan always seemed so mild-mannered I couldn't picture him fighting.

She hooted. "All the time. He didn't tell us that he was being bullied at school, and by the time he arrived home, all his cuts and bruises had healed, so we were none the wiser."

I remembered Joel's lacerated hand healing before my eyes at Christmas. "So how did you find out?"

"I didn't until one day he came back with his shirt all raggedy off his back. He begged me not to say anything, so I let it go. But later, when I found his books all torn up and some very unkind things written on his bag, I was beside myself. Henry was off in Europe and Maggie playing me up and I'd just about had enough. Dan hid the things in the storm cellar because he was afraid of what I might do and I would have given those boys a piece of my mind – and the school, too, for not taking them in hand…" She stopped and took a deep breath, her lips resisting the slight tremble that set up in them.

"What happened?" I prompted.

"Matthew came back from work – we were living in the south at that time – he heard all the commotion, sat Dan down, and had him tell us everything, all of it. Dan hadn't told me half of what went on because he didn't want to upset me. He was always such a kind boy." She smiled fondly.

I took a sip of tea. "What did Matthew do?"

"Well, he stood there very calmly and listened to everything Dan told him. When he finished, Matthew just said, 'I see,' in that way he has of saying everything without saying anything much at all. Then he took Dan's hand, and the next thing I knew my son was trotting off down the dirt track toward town, hand-in-hand with his granddaddy, quite happily like they were going fishing together. When they came back sometime later, Dan had a new bag and books and those boys never touched him again. He seemed much happier at school after that."

I conjured an image of the two of them in the rich light of the afternoon, crickets darting from their path, gold hair competing with the sun.

"Did you ever find out why they targeted him in the first place?"

"Because of his differences. Dan's clever and always learned quickly. His granddaddy taught him more than the school ever could and it was a small school, so he stood out more. He was never ill, he liked to study, and didn't roughhouse with the other boys. And then there's his looks" – her eyes strayed to my hair – "you can imagine." I could, all too well. "What he didn't let on was that he always gave as good as he got, but they outnumbered him and he didn't know how to fight or to get out of trouble before the fighting began, so Matthew took him in hand and taught him both. He's had not a peep of trouble since." I must have seemed very grim because Pat smiled unexpectedly. "It's been a learning curve for us all and never a dull moment from one year to the next. You can't get bored in this family."

"And Maggie?"

"It took Maggie a while to accept me – you know how she dislikes change – but she did eventually, although we've never been close. Now, *she* never had one minute's trouble at school – no one would have dared – but she didn't have many friends, either." Pat shook her head. "Her momma has a lot to answer for." She gathered her sewing into a neat bundle. "I must take an iron to this before I do any more and you look ready for another rest when you've eaten that toast. Can I get you some more?"

Curled up in the big chair in Matthew's study, I tracked the emotional landscape of the two men in the waves of colour streaming from them. Still new to me, this sensitivity to the emotions of others at times left me speechless and at once both amazed and disquieted. At this point, Henry displayed the colours of concern – no, not as strong as that, more misgivings – as they discussed his daughter Maggie's mental state. And Matthew? Although I knew it wasn't possible, he looked a little tired, or grey – yes, grey – and his eyes were the colour of smoke and not as clear as I was used to. He had spent months looking out for me, or looking after me, and we were both ready for a holiday. I raised the subject when we were alone.

"Where would you like to go?" he asked.

"I've always wanted to see New Zealand. I suppose you've already been there, haven't you?"

"Not since 1876. I expect it's changed a bit since then."

"I expect it has," I replied dryly.

"I have too many work commitments and not enough holiday leave to make it worthwhile until later in the year."

"It's a long time."

"It is," he agreed, "so I thought we could do with a stopgap, more of a break than a holiday. I have some business in New York…"

"I've never been," I bounced. "Can we go to the Metropolitan Museum? It has a superb collection of medieval artifacts and I've always wanted to see the Egyptian section; it looks wonderful in the photos I've seen."

"… and I was going to ask whether you would like to go too, but you seem to have already answered that question." He smiled at my exuberance. "One step at a time. First I want to make sure you're strong enough. How about a short walk this afternoon?"

The river flowed deep and silent next to us and we walked along the riverbank where the snow lay thinnest and red-stemmed dogwoods sprouted like whiskers, glowing in the sun.

I tucked my arm through his. "How are you, Matthew? Really?" We negotiated the safest path and I sensed he searched for the words to voice his deepest thoughts.

"It sometimes feels as if I've been grieving for forty-six years. Ellen's death has been a shock, but somehow it seems right; it was time. If I'm honest with myself," he smiled thinly, "and that's harder than you might think, she'd been ready for many years;

I just didn't want to see it. I'd persuaded myself that she wanted to live, and it was only during those last weeks when she knew I couldn't save her and that I wouldn't try, that I understood how I'd imposed life on her. She wasn't afraid to die; she had a better place to go and I'd been keeping her from it." He rubbed his forehead with the knuckle of his thumb. "I told you once how selfish I can be."

My foot slithered on the uneven ground and I gripped his arm. "I remember, but there's no point in castigating yourself for it. Isn't it part of being human that we cling to life and to all with which we're familiar? Ellen brought you love and a sense of normality; you were just hanging on to it for as long as you could."

"Mmm, that's as maybe, but I think of all the relatives I've had to tell over the years, waiting for them to accept that the life of the person they love is over and there's no going back. You would have thought that I'd be used to it by now – I've had enough practice – but it never gets any easier. Their grief is so tangible, so understandable – they mourn for what they've lost." He ducked under red-ribbed branches, holding them back until I passed safely beneath. "It's rarely the dying who voice their fears once the initial shock passes. They find peace more readily than the living. In the years after I realized I wasn't aging, I used to think that people used faith to comfort themselves as they faced death. But as society changed and fewer people looked to religion for answers, I came to believe that it wasn't so much they who sought comfort in faith, but that they were *being* comforted; they just didn't necessarily know it."

We watched the water tumble between rocks, free and easy and without restraint. The snow had gone from the steep face of the bank, revealing gnarled roots, and the first shoots of spring bulbs nestled in south-facing crevices.

I picked up a stray twig broken by a late frost. "I like the thought that, despite our frailties, we are still loved." I released the stick into the water and watched the current pick it up and toss it downstream. I noticed Matthew hadn't said anything. The stick vanished.

Eventually he said, "That is why I can finally let Ellen go not just physically, but emotionally as well, because I couldn't offer her what she wanted and needed most. I couldn't give her the peace she can find in God. There was nothing left to stay for."

Under the shelter of a tree, a small, unfamiliar flower had thrust its way through the lace-edged snow. I bent down to look at it more closely, fingering the veined petals. "It's a big step, leaving behind all that we are comfortable and familiar with and stepping into the unknown."

"Are you speaking emotionally or spiritually?"

"Both." I straightened and smiled when I saw his puzzled frown. "It's a big step for both of us." We had come to a kink in the river where a log had become jammed between two rocks. I rather thought that it was precisely how Matthew must feel at times – caught between Heaven and Earth and not going anywhere while life – and death – continued to flow around him regardless.

We stopped at a low-slung footbridge barely a plank wide, skimming the turbulent waters. He launched a twig at the river and I took a tentative step onto the bridge, teetered momentarily, then steadied and made my way to the centre. The plank had cracked and worn and the single handrail offered more in the way of hope than safety. He followed with a careless ease that made my caution seem clumsy. He looked fixedly through the shot-silk surface of the water. "Look." He pointed to where the overhanging bank sheltered a deeper pool. A shaft of sun lit the pebbly bed.

"I see it." A darker streak held its own against the current. It might have been a length of weed but for its speckled back as it swayed back and forth in the clear water. I wanted to reach out and touch it. I wanted to feel its slime-slick body move in my hands, and I recalled Matthew telling me how he had taught his great-grandchildren to catch fish. He must have been remembering too, because he calculated the distance between the overhang and the water.

"Was that one that got away?"

He grinned. "It must be; it'd better watch its step. I haven't forgotten I promised to teach you to tickle trout. Do you think you have the patience?"

I shifted slightly and my shadow danced across the water's surface. The fish darted deeper beneath the bank. "I think so. It was Granddad – that's *Dad's* dad, by the way – who didn't have the patience to hunt fish. If he could have intimidated them out of the water he would. Failing that, he would have resorted to explosives. He didn't have the finesse to woo them – bludgeoning was more his style." I remembered my grandfather's red-scowled face glowering at the water and the permanent anxiety I felt when with him. Those days were always overcast and grey in my memory – dank, dark days, marled with churned mud that glued itself to my boots so that I carried the weight and smell of it back home. "It was Grandpa who taught me to fish when I was very little. We had a duck punt and we used to stalk the fish, so Beth and I had to keep very still and quiet so we didn't frighten them. When I couldn't keep quiet any longer, Grandpa let me sing to the fish and they liked that. He used to call me his Lori Lie and place me in the bow to lure them." We had spent long, sun-soaked hours in the boat during the summer holidays, trailing fingers through fine filaments of emerald weed as Grandpa worked the stern oar, driving us slowly forward across the shallow lake. I became aware again of the restless water by my feet and of Matthew watching me, his lips parted.

"How could any creature resist such temptation?" he said and I smiled self-consciously. "They sound like happy memories." He pulled me closer to him. "I'm ready to move on. Thank you for being patient with me."

"I think that is the first time anyone has called me patient. You bring out the best in me."

He kissed my upturned face. "I would say we're a perfect match."

I flinched as the low sun dipped and bobbed under the waving branchlets, striking my eyes. He shielded them, his expression becoming wistful as he lifted a long strand of my hair to the light. "This is almost the same colour as those dogwoods – so beautiful – Rembrandt red." I froze and turned away. I felt his hand on my shoulder. "What is it? What have I said?"

"It's not you." I bent my head, burying the lower part of my face in my scarf.

"What in the name of goodness did I say to upset you?"

"You didn't say anything, it was... oh, it's so stupid," I floundered. "I didn't mean to react."

"Did somebody else say the same thing once? Sam?"

"No, not Sam."

"Guy?"

I nodded.

"He said you were beautiful and he upset you?" I glanced up and saw him frowning.

"It wasn't so much what he said, as how and when he said it." Merely remembering made me shudder. I felt exposed sitting under the arc-light of the sun, revealing something I thought I had dealt with and almost forgotten. But deep disquiet, as born from such an early, bruising experience, is not so easily put aside.

"It was your first time?"

I nodded again. "Yes."

"But something happened, something went wrong? Did he make you do something you didn't want to do?" Alarm spread through his voice. "Emma, did he force you?"

I hunched into my coat, grasping the collar tightly around my throat. "No, not really. I'd had too much to drink." I smiled weakly, but he looked aghast.

"He let you drink and then took advantage of you?"

"Something like that."

"Like what – exactly?"

"There's no point going over it, Matthew. It was a long time ago, it doesn't matter."

Appalled, his eyes flared. "Matter? Of course it matters. Whatever he did to you, this… man has hurt you. He's left scars as surely as Staahl did. Emma, I want to know what he did."

"Why, Matthew? Why do you need to know?"

He turned bleak, blank eyes on me. "Because right now I want to kill him," he snarled. Horrified, I stared at him, but the moment passed and he slowly drew his hand down his face and said more moderately. "I need to know so that I don't make the same mistake and say something to upset you again." Tentatively, he said, "Tell me what happened."

I found it hard to find the words to describe the impact that night had on me without it sounding banal or sleazy, but he waited patiently.

"I'd had an argument with Dad. Guy picked me up from home but it was raining so hard we had to stop before we reached Cambridge. He… he found us a room. I didn't want that, I didn't feel comfortable, but he said there was nowhere else and I was soaking, so…" Matthew became still. "He went to get something for me to eat, but there wasn't anything."

"He came back with alcohol instead," he said quietly.

How stupid, how naïve.

I nodded miserably. "Yes. He said it would make me feel better. I… drank it." I wondered whether he regarded me as the fool I felt.

"And…?" he said, not moving.

"He started kissing me and… you know."

"No, I don't."

I avoided Matthew's eyes. "He started kissing me. I didn't really want him to, but he wouldn't stop. I'd had too much to drink and he was too heavy, and I thought… I thought that I owed him for helping me with my work, f-for making him wait so long." I swallowed. "Anyway, it was over pretty quickly and it didn't hurt that much." I picked at the fringe on my scarf, remembering all too clearly how I felt that night. I looked up as an odd, rough noise came from his jaw as his teeth ground together. "Matthew, stop it!"

I heard the fractured agony in his voice. "He raped you."

"No! No he didn't, he can't have done!"

His face clouded. "Why not?"

"Because then I would be a victim. Don't make me into a victim, please – I haven't the strength to be a victim." I scrambled to my feet and edged along the plank to solid land, leaving Matthew with his eyes closed and his clenched fist to his mouth. For a long moment, he said nothing. Eventually, he swung his legs back onto the bridge and followed me. "And afterwards?"

"Afterwards? Afterwards he drove me back to uni."

"What did he say? Do?"

"Nothing – well, he talked about some research or something…"

He swore and whacked the trunk of a nearby tree, making it shiver from root to crown. "He said nothing about what he had done? No apology, no concern, no affection? And you had an affair with this man. He raped you, and you had a *relationship* with him?"

His accusation stung. "Don't. I know how it sounds, but I had to…"

"Did he compel you?"

"No, if anything I did. I had to make it into a relationship, don't you see? If I hadn't it would have made it so much worse."

"You had to legitimize it, you mean?"

"Yes!" All the years it had taken me to justify my actions and here I was again, with those same feelings of helpless guilt and tainted youth. I felt dirty. I turned my back on him. "I'm sorry."

"*You're* sorry?"

"I know how it seems. I was an idiot… I should have seen…"

I felt his hand on my back and he turned my face to his, and there was so much kindness there, compassion, and distress. "You were young and innocent, and an older man took advantage of a situation he created to take what he wanted. He raped you, Emma – there is no way it can be dressed up to be anything else, no matter what you did afterwards to rationalize it to yourself. You owed him nothing – he took everything. What he did was despicable; he's everything I hate in a man."

"He's not as bad as Staahl."

"No, he's much, much worse. Staahl had insanity as an excuse; this man has nothing to defend his behaviour. Where is he now?"

"Why do you want to know?"

He shrugged and looked away. "Curiosity."

I clasped my arms around me. "I don't know. I think he's left Cambridge, I'm not sure. I haven't asked and nobody's said. He kept trying to see me again when we broke up, but I wouldn't. After he tried to commit suicide I only saw him once – at a conference last April. I didn't speak to him. He phoned before Christmas when I was back at home, but Dad wouldn't let him speak to me."

"Does anyone else know what happened?"

I shook my head. "No."

His thumb stroked my cheek. "And this you have carried by yourself for all these years." Some of the tension left him and I detected regret in his smile. "Now how can I tell you how beautiful you are without it reminding you of him?"

"*You* can tell me – I believe you, I trust you." I rested my head against his chest and he caressed my hair.

"But not enough to tell me what he did to you. Were you ever going to tell me?"

"No, not if I could help it. I'd persuaded myself that it didn't matter and I didn't want it coming between us. It's over – another lifetime."

"It's left its scars, otherwise you wouldn't have reacted as you did. It won't come between us because the foundations of what we have go far deeper than he can reach. Remember the text you sent me during the trial – the quote from Donne? *'Who is so safe as we? Where none can do Treason to us, except one of us two.'* Do you remember how it continues?" I shook my head, soothed by his words and by the vibration of his voice beneath my cheek.

"*True and false fears let us refrain,*
Let us love nobly, and live, and add again
Years and years unto years, til we attain
To write threescore: this is the second of our reign."

He smiled. "Well, perhaps this is still our first year together, but the same principle applies. I understand why you didn't tell me, Emma, but it is not your shame; it's his. What you did was to protect yourself in the only way you felt you could at the time, and he doubly betrayed you because he lied to you about his wife, and took what little hope you had." His hand stilled on my hair. "I know that I didn't tell you about Ellen, and I can only trust that you'll forgive me in time, but what we have is richer and stronger than all of that, and we said 'no more lies' and I meant it – I meant it, my love." He bent to look into my eyes and saw I fought tears of relief because now he knew and he understood, and it couldn't sully what we had. "Marry me, Emma, be my wife." He lifted my face and with infinite tenderness kissed each eyelid in turn, then my lips, and we drew from each other our grief and with each kiss condemned it to the wastelands of the past.

From somewhere behind us, bird song rang sharp and clear, beckoning spring.

2

Eternal

The sun had skirted around the house and the study felt cold without direct light. Matthew lit the fire and pulled a cocoon of blanket around me. Now within his arms I felt warm – inside and out – and content. I stirred and he eased around until he faced me, and kissed my smiling eyes. I touched the curve of his mouth. "Are you real?"

"As real as you are." And to make certain I believed him, he took my hand and placed it over his heart. Beneath my palm the regular *beat*, *beat* confirmed the truth of it. I replaced my hand with my lips, and then burrowed against him, at ease and at peace.

"What are you thinking?" I asked.

"About us, Ellen, the family – life." Tucking my head beneath his chin, his steady breath stirred my hair. "In many ways it might be enough that we've made solemn pledges to each other. For centuries that would have been valid in the eyes of the law and the church, but things have changed, Mistress D'Eresby, and we have a wedding to arrange."

I groaned. The thought of arranging a wedding, of all the clothes, invitations – the food – seemed daunting enough for someone who had never organized anything more than a seminar, but the thrill of marrying him was liquid metal in my blood. "I can't quite believe it yet," I said, dazed at the very idea of it.

"Well," he extricated himself, "I might be considered a modern male in some respects, but in others I'm a traditionalist, and I won't believe it until I have done one other thing, so if you will excuse me..." He picked me up in my blue blanket and put me in the big armchair by the fire, then crossed to the desk and reached for the phone.

"What are you doing?" I asked, beginning to hum a few bars from *My Fair Lady*, the notes becoming song as joy burst from me. He dialled, waited.

"Colonel..." he said in reply to a muffled answer.

I squawked, clamping my hands over my mouth.

"Matthew Lynes, yes, Emma's fine, very well, in fact. No, I have no concerns for her health at all at present. The strange noise? Oh, I think you'll find that was Emma singing – yes, it was interesting, wasn't it?" I gesticulated wildly at him, and he laughed silently. "I trust the family are well? And Emma's grandmother? That's good to hear." I trotted over to the desk, dragging my jumper on over my head and Matthew pulled me onto his knees. I nestled contentedly into his neck.

"Really? That's encouraging. Look, Colonel, I phoned because there's something I would like to discuss with you. I have asked Emma if she would consent to be my wife, and she has said *yes*." I bounced, mouthing, *Yes, yes, yes*. "We would be very pleased if you would give us your blessing." I could hear the bass notes of my father's voice over the line, but couldn't make out what he said. I tugged at Matthew's arm and he put the phone on hands-free so I could listen.

"... splendid..." Dad was saying. I could hear a great deal of excited chatter from Mum and Beth in the background, with chirruping from the twins, and an occasional gurgle from baby

Archie. By the echoing sound their voices made, they were in the dining room. "… it's about time Emma had something to look forward to. I take it you will live in the States?"

"We haven't discussed our plans yet."

"No, of course not, and I expect it's too soon to have thought about dates for the wedding?"

"I think sooner rather than later." Matthew raised an eyebrow in question and I nodded wildly.

There followed an ominous pause. "There isn't a necessity for haste, is there?"

"Not at all, Colonel, but equally we see no need to wait. However, Emma will have the ultimate say in the matter."

"Well, good luck with that; you know she can be very strong-willed at times – a bit of a handful." Matthew took the opportunity to kiss my pout. "But I expect you already know that."

"I wouldn't have it any other way, and it's probably what's given her the strength to cope over the last few months."

Dad humphed. "I think you are probably right on that point. Your parents must be pleased. It can't have been easy for you losing your wife."

Matthew hesitated. "No."

"But Emma's a good girl for all her stubbornness. She'll be a loyal wife, and I have no doubt you'll look after her."

We both heard the implied threat. I scowled but Matthew just smiled. "I will."

"And I don't have to ask if you can afford to keep her, do I? She's quite low-maintenance in that respect – good, sturdy economy model." I heard his muffled laughter. He must have known I was listening. "I would like to have a word with my daughter, if I may?"

"Of course." Matthew handed the phone to me.

"Hi, Dad."

"Well, well, this is a turn-up for the books, hey, Em? And I didn't have to pay him much in the way of a dowry to take you off my hands." He guffawed.

"*Dad!*" I protested.

"Your mother and sister are delighted of course. No doubt you will have female things to talk about – dresses and flowers and all that guff. It's a pity you're so far away." I heard the slight catch in his voice and understood that for all his bluff talk, he would miss me. For the first time in my life I felt a wrench at the thought of not seeing him, and Ellen's forewarning about the inevitable separation from my family as Matthew's agelessness became apparent, materialized. I couldn't let the future cloud our present happiness – this was now, and we still had some years ahead of us before contact with my family became reduced to disembodied phone calls and the internet, or brief visits without him, and lies – always the lies.

"We're not that far away, Dad, and Matthew's going to teach me to fly."

"He's not going to let you loose in that jet of his, is he? Good grief, you'll be shot down as some rogue intercontinental missile. I've never forgotten that time Rob made the mistake of letting you ride his motorcycle – reckless, totally reckless. No wonder he sold it."

"That's because he had to buy a car when the twins were born. It had nothing to do with me and you know it."

He chuckled, "Yes, well," then sighed. "We're so pleased for you, Em; you sound truly... content." He meant that I sounded happy at last, because it had always seemed to elude me somehow.

"I am. Give my love to Mum and to everyone – especially Nanna. Tell Beth I have the perfect matron of honour outfit in mind for her: lovely big lacy frills, all fluffy and pink." I could hear an exclamation of horror in the background from my sister, and Flora's excited voice shouting, "Me, me, me!"

"I will, Em. Just take care of yourself." Again, the thick note that told me he needed to control his emotions. "Oh, and tell Matthew that he has my permission to marry you. I didn't think people bothered asking nowadays."

Matthew took the phone and replaced it, giving me a quiet moment in which he cuddled me. I let out a long breath. "Wowie."

"Wowie," he agreed, looking up as we heard a faint chink of china on glass.

"Pat?" I asked.

"Supper," he replied.

"Oh, there you are!" Pat exclaimed. "I couldn't find you anywhere. I didn't know what Matthew had done with you…" She faltered and I caught a glimpse of my bright, flushed face in the mirror between the windows, my hair in disarray.

Matthew took the tray from her. "This looks wonderful, Pat. I know Emma's hungry."

"Am I? Oh yes, I am." I jumped up and sniffed the steaming plate of beef and sliced potatoes in a rich gravy that made my mouth water. "It smells lovely."

"Now, I know you said not to cook for you but I came across this recipe from your own part of England and had to try it." Matthew and I frowned simultaneously. "You know, Lincolnshire hot-pot?"

I threw my arms around her. "Pat, you are so kind, and I love hot-pot, wherever it's from. You spoil me."

She beamed. "There now, I sure hope I do." She halted. "You are from Lincolnshire, aren't you?"

I laughed. "Yes, I am, but hot-pot is a Lancashire dish – not that it matters one jot. You've just invented another type."

"I wasn't wearing my glasses – when I read the recipe." She looked dubiously at the plate.

"Mmm, it smells fabulous."

"Have a fork," Matthew said, handing me one. "Pat, is Henry about? I have something to tell him."

"I think he went to the observatory. Do you want me to go fetch him for you?"

"No, I'll find him, thank you. Perhaps you wouldn't mind staying with Emma for a while, would you, please? I think she would like to talk to you."

"That was delicious," I said, putting down my fork and placing the tray on a little side table. "Perfect Lincolnshire hot-pot. Pat, I have something we want to tell you and I'm not sure how you're going to take this but..." I counted to three, "... we're getting married."

For a moment, the loudest thing in the room was the *tick-tick* sound of the cooling metal of the grate, and the noisy thumping of my heart, then she clapped her hands.

"Well, at last and about time too! I never thought I'd live to hear it. What took him so long?"

I stared at her open-mouthed. I had expected a reaction, but not this one. "Er, Ellen only died recently."

She flapped a hand. "Yes, yes, I know. This is so exciting. We haven't had a wedding since Dan and Jeannie's twenty-five years ago. Now, you British have a different kind of wedding cake, don't you? And then there's the wedding feast to arrange... there's so much to do." A thought struck her. "You are getting married here in Maine, aren't you?"

Still somewhat taken aback by her reaction, it took me a moment to reply. "I don't know, we haven't discussed it at all yet."

She tutted in her good-natured way. "Just like a man. It's the details that count. I'm sure your mom will have something to say on the matter." I rather thought she would. I had a vision of two clucking hens and me not having much say in my own wedding. She must have guessed what I was thinking. "Now, you won't want your future daughter-in-law taking over, will you?" I did my best imitation of a goldfish. She laughed. "It'll be just as strange for me, sweetie, believe you me."

"Golly, Pat, this is going to take some getting used to, isn't it?"

"Sure is, honey."

"How is everyone else going to take it, do you think? What about Maggie? What about Henry?"

Her smile faded. "Ah well, just let his papa handle that. It's a little soon, but Henry's always known you would take his momma's place one day and he's very fond of you. Matthew'll talk him round, and I'm as happy as a gopher in spring for both of you, and that'll help him accept it in the right spirit of things."

"And Maggie?"

"Well, Maggie's another question altogether. Let's just leave her to the boys to sort out, shall we?" I had an image of her seventy-year-old "boy" and my nigh-on four-hundred-year-old fiancé dealing with Henry's troubled and troublesome daughter, and silently wished them luck. Pat found a piece of paper and a pen on Matthew's desk and sat, poised and expectant. "Now, what about your wedding feast?"

In Plain Sight

"So, how did it go with Henry?"

"It went," Matthew said quietly. "He'll be all right." He leaned over and switched on the desk lamp.

I must have hoped that Henry would have been a little more enthusiastic about our news, but his grief was still raw.

"I suppose it's still so soon," I observed.

"Yes." He adjusted the shade. "How did Pat react when you told her?"

"She's already planning the wedding breakfast."

"Good, that will make it easier for Henry to come to terms with the idea. Pat is fairly irrepressible once she has the bit between her teeth." He gave me an oblique look. "And what about Ellie?"

Rather than prolong the agony, I had decided to tackle Matthew's great-granddaughter as soon as she returned from her shift at the medical centre. She sat in the kitchen of Matthew's home – his home, *our* home – neat brows drawn into a question.

"So you have something to tell me, huh?"

There could be no easy way to tell Ellie so I made it as quick and painless as I could. Her face flushed then paled as she fumbled her hands in her lap, and after a minute, her colour returned. "Oh, OK, that's great I guess."

"I didn't want you to hear it from anyone else."

"No, that's cool. It's really good. I'm so pleased for you." She didn't look it. "I didn't expect... I mean I thought that you might... just not so... soon."

"We don't think there's much point in waiting."

"Do Mom and Dad know?"

"I think Matthew's telling them now."

I gave her some time to think it through and went into the larder to fetch the tea. The room looked more used now, populated with all the packets and bits and bobs you would expect to find in any normal kitchen anywhere. Just looking at it, nobody would have guessed that I was the only person who ate in this household. When I went back in, Ellie had regained her equilibrium.

"This is so weird. For all my life Ellen was the sort of great-gran you would expect to have – you know, old, and kind of cranky now and again – but you..." she shook her head as if trying to sort the information in it, her honey hair swaying with her, "even if I try really hard, I don't think I can ever see you as my great-grandmother. You just don't fit into that category; you're more of a friend."

I left the tea on the table and went to stand in front of her. "You know, Ellie, that's one of the nicest things anybody has ever said to me." And before she could react, I gave her a hug, which made everything right between us.

On taking the mug of tea I offered, she added with a twist to her mouth, "I really am glad for both of you – and us. It could have been so much worse – he could be marrying Megan." And at the thought of Matthew's thwarted, permanently pouting Nordic blonde research assistant, we both had to laugh.

"So Ellie's accepted it?" Matthew sorted through some old papers he had taken from a concealed panel behind one of the bookshelves in his study. He had shown me how to locate the catch that opened it.

"Fine, and she's delighted I've asked her to be a bridesmaid." I nodded at the wall. "Isn't that rather an obvious place for a secret cubbyhole?" I ran my hand around the now empty space, the contents sitting on his desk in the lamplight.

"It is," he agreed. "Which is the whole point." He leaned inside the hole and applied pressure to the top left and bottom right corners of the rear panel at the same time, and the whole panel slid out of sight, revealing a deep space from which he took a large, battered metal box, with lifting handles either side of it. "The trick is to give them what they think they're looking for, and then they're less likely to hunt any further. The compartment is lined in lead, so shouldn't be picked up by a scanner as a void, but could be detected as a dead zone, so" – he rapped his knuckles against the wood lining of the outer safe – "this is also lined in lead and faced with wood..."

"To give them what they are looking for," I finished.

"Precisely. But as technology advances, so I have to come up with more effective ways of concealment. Soon, I reckon we'll come full circle."

"In what way?"

He smiled cheerfully. "I'll resort to hiding things beneath old yew trees again and hope developers haven't set their sights on a bit of real-estate, and start digging."

"You've done that before?"

"Oh, yes. That's when boxes like these come into their own." The metal thudded dully under the rap of his hand.

I pulled a face. "It makes you sound like a criminal."

"Well, I'm not, and I always try to stay within the law of whatever country I'm in and at whatever time I'm in it. Within reason." He took a small silver-coloured key from his desk. It looked innocuous, like any key to any cupboard whose contents needed minimum security.

"Watch." He placed the key in the lock of the box and I heard a slight click from inside. "That's armed the explosive device."

"Matthew!" I took a step back.

"Wait..." another click, "... there's a thirty-second time-delay. Now rotate anti-clockwise one-quarter turn." A whirring like the wing-beat of a small bird. It stopped. "Then turn the key fully and take it out. The mechanism is now deactivated and safe." He opened the lid. I half expected to see "Top Secret" written across the neat cardboard folders almost filling the box; instead, it looked like old documents. A frayed edge of a legal ribbon escaped from one folder; from another a glimpse of a wax seal. I drew in a deep lungful of one of my favourite scents.

"Yum, I smell vellum – and parchment – delicious. It's better than chocolate. What's in there and why do you need to protect these documents with explosives?"

He smiled at my sudden zeal. "It contains enough explosive to rupture these phials, which in turn sets up a chemical reaction that will destroy the contents irretrievably. It's crude in today's terms, but very effective, and it won't harm anyone inadvertently."

I surveyed the row of little glass bottles arranged within the lid and what must have been the detonator among them. "What happens if the phials break by accident?"

He flicked at one and I flinched back. The glass tinged, but no more. "They won't – not even if the box is dropped – hence the need for a detonator. But get the sequence and timing wrong with the key, or try to force the box open, then – *ka-boom*!" He grinned. "It's been an exciting life at times."

"Golly, Matthew, you certainly know how to get a girl's pulse racing. Most men would buy a bunch of flowers, but you, on the other hand, demonstrate Pandora's Box!"

He placed a finger against my neck. "Mmm, nope – your pulse is nice and steady. I think it'll take a lot more than an old box to raise your heart rate. Now, there's a challenge." His lips substituted his fingers against my neck, and a hand found its way beneath my jumper and caressed the skin of my back.

"Reprobate," I chastised softly.

"Wanton," he replied. My mobile rang. "Of all the saints…"

I pulled his face back to mine. "Ignore it." It rang again – insistent. I fished it out of my pocket, about to switch it off, but saw my sister's number.

Beth sounded too upbeat to be the bearer of bad news. "Em – it's Beth. Nanna's fine, don't worry, I'm not ringing because anything's wrong. Dad and I were just wondering…"

Frustrated relief broke through my initial fear. "Beth," I looked at my watch and counted on, "it's the middle of the night in the UK. What on earth do you think you're doing phoning now!"

"Oh, it's Archie's latest tooth. Rob and I have been taking it in turns to sit up with him. It's my turn tonight. I was really fed up but, do you know, it can be awfully peaceful at this time of night – I swear I can hear the daffs opening. They're quite fabulous at the moment, you should see the garden when the sun shines – which hasn't been that much lately. How's your weather? Still have snow? Ooo, I'd just love to see some proper snow for once." I thought I had huffed soundlessly but obviously not quietly enough, because she apologized. "Sorry, look, Dad and I wanted to know what you had in mind for your wedding breakfast – we're just talking some ideas through – you know, having a look at what you might like. I'm making a list now. What's Matthew's fave food? I bet it's not burgers…"

I put my hand over the microphone. "Can you hear this?" Matthew raised his eyebrows in assent and looked sympathetic.

There came a break in the monologue on the other end of the line. "I'm not disturbing you or anything, am I?"

"Yes, you are."

Beth whinnied like a schoolgirl. "Ooo, sorry! Really? At last! What's he like?"

"Beth!" The box with the explosive strapped to its lid winked at me. I averted my eyes.

"Sorry, Em, just wondering. So what about it? Don't tell me – he's vegan. He is, isn't he? I knew it. With skin that good he doesn't eat animal fats, does he? Do you remember those sisters at school – the youngest was in your class, she had buck teeth, remember? They were vegan and they had great skin. Shame about the teeth though. I wish I could be so disciplined, but you know I really like my food…"

I pursed my mouth. "Beth…"

"What?"

"Matthew and I haven't even discussed the wedding yet and I don't know where we're getting married, so please don't go arranging things. I'm going to need your help, but please, *please* let us sort ourselves out first."

"Oh."

"Please, Beth?"

Matthew was reading a time-worn document with interest. He picked up another one. Seconds passed. Finally, "Yeah, OK. But Flora thinks she's going to be a bridesmaid."

"Well, of course she is! And Alex my pageboy and, Beth, please will you be my matron of honour?"

"What, and wear pink frills and lace? Not on your nelly!"

"You get to choose the outfit: silk, fitted, flattering…"

"Oh, go on then, you've twisted my arm." She gave an impish laugh. "I don't suppose Matthew could come and fix it?"

"No, he can't. And by the way, he's not vegan. I'll let you have the date and venue and things when we know. Are you all right with that?"

"Yes, I suppose so. Can I think about the twins' outfits?" An Archie-shaped siren wailed plaintively in the background.

"Please do. I haven't a clue where to start."

Archie's pitch began to climb towards a crescendo. Beth had to raise her voice to be heard. "I'd better get back to him before he wakes the neighbours. Love to Matthew – have fun, play safe!"

"Yes, thank you, Auntie Beth," I replied with lashings of sarcasm, but she had already gone to her son.

Matthew flipped a piece of paper over, cast his eyes down it, and put it to one side. I sat in my chair opposite his desk wondering how much longer he would be. He didn't raise his eyes as he scanned the next document.

"How did Dan react?" I asked.

"Well. He's very pleased, he likes you a lot."

"And Jeannie?"

"She didn't say much, but she still thinks you're making the biggest mistake of your life, or rather your career, which amounts to the same thing in her eyes." He continued reading.

"What about Maggie – when are you going to tell her?"

"I'm going to wait until she's more stable. Any more questions?"

"Yes, what do you want to show me?"

He stacked the folders into neat piles and waited until I'd settled next to him before he lifted the first sheaf of papers. "These relate to this estate: the house, the land, goods and chattels. Henry owns the Barn, and Dan the Stables – those are in their names. Everything else is mine. This section, here" – he put his hand flat on a fatter pile – "is to do with various investments, also in my name."

I didn't want to know because my knowing made it seem as

if he thought he wouldn't be around one day to manage it all. "Why are you telling me this?"

"Concentrate. Everything to do with my current financial affairs belongs in the outer safe – you know how to access it. There is nothing in there that will, in any way, suggest who I really am." He held up a slim leather wallet, about A5 in size. "This document case holds my current passport, birth certificate, identity, the works – all right? Emma? Do you understand?" I nodded mutely. "This box," he tapped it once, "contains everything else. You know where it's hidden, and it stays there until such time as it's needed."

"Why are you telling me, Matthew?"

"Because soon you will be my wife." Despite the context, I felt the thrill of it roll through me. "Emma, I want you to learn the mechanisms to open and close these compartments and the box. You need to know them off by heart until you can do it blindfolded. Right, let's make a start."

It wasn't what I had in mind for an evening's entertainment but, by the time I mastered the box, I felt fairly confident that I wouldn't destroy the contents with a fumbled sequence. What I didn't know – and he did nothing to throw light on the matter – was why he thought it necessary for me to have this information, and in what circumstances he thought I would need to use it.

CHAPTER

4

Moon and Stars

I never went anywhere without it. The little triptych Matthew gave me at Christmas gleamed reassuringly beside my bed – the last thing I saw before I slept, the first thing when I woke. When it had been made, oh, centuries ago by an unknown maker in some north Italian state, its creator went to sleep each night in the sure and certain knowledge that he didn't know what the new day might bring, or whether he might live to see it at all. Over the last months, I too had witnessed the turmoil of uncertainty, and today, the box and its contents hidden in the wall served as a constant reminder of unquiet times.

We were in our own insulated world for those first days, and our world had changed. We were entirely our own and each other's. We talked and walked and made plans and, when I slept, he was there when I woke. It could not last; life intervened and by Sunday evening I steeled myself for the return to college and work.

Matthew watched while I emptied the chest of drawers. "There's nothing to worry about. Ellie says the reporters gave up and left. They're more interested in the big fraud case in Portland and I'm glad to say you're old news."

"I'm history – is that it?" I said, thrusting a delicate jumper into my bag. Matthew took it out and refolded it carefully before replacing it.

"As I said, nothing to worry about. Of course, if you stayed here, there would be no such concerns." He stood close behind me, his hands on my hips, his mouth to my ear so his warm breath tickled. Swallowing temptation, I freed myself from his embrace.

"And I wouldn't get any work done. I've so much to organize and you're too much of a distraction to have around. May, Matthew – that's only weeks before the conference. How am I supposed to get a wedding organized by May in a foreign country *and* finish my work for the conference!"

"May gives us plenty of time. Only yesterday you were complaining that you wouldn't have any say in the matter with Pat and your family getting involved in the arrangements. We can make a start next weekend in New York."

"Yes, but…"

"No buts, May. We agreed last night, didn't we – remember?"

I warmed with the memory. "You took advantage of me; you had me in a compromising position."

He caught me up, laughing. "Yes, I did, didn't I? No second thoughts?"

"None." I kissed him. "None at all."

There was still one outstanding matter I needed to confront before I left the security of his home and faced reality. Pat sat alone at her dining room table surrounded by books and magazines when I went to see her later that evening.

"My, you're looking better – quite recovered. I was just searching for some English recipes for your wedding feast. I'm so glad you've decided to get married here. We can make it such an occasion, although I expect your parents will be disappointed not to see you married from your home. How have they taken it?"

"I haven't told them yet, Pat."

"No? Will you soon?" By that she meant, "You will tell them soon, won't you?"

"Yes, I will, when I get back to campus." And I'd survived whatever I might find there. Notwithstanding reporters and my students, I had the potential Shotter problem to sort out. "Actually, Pat, I wondered if Henry might be about?"

She examined me over the rim of her spectacles. "Henry? Yes, why sure he is; he's in the observatory. You'll need a torch and a warm coat if you're going out there."

Tucked away to the south-west of the Barn and hidden by a rise in the land, I followed my nose and the faint imprint of Henry's footfall until I found the pale dome of his observatory glowing under the starlit sky. He must have heard the snap of my footsteps in the broken snow because he didn't look surprised when he opened the door to my knock. Either that or he had been expecting me.

"Emma, come in." Muffled in a deeply quilted coat, he looked warm, with only his fingers exposed at the tips in fingerless gloves. He smiled in welcome, but with an unaccustomed restraint.

"I'm sorry to disturb you, Henry."

"Not at all. It's not much warmer in here, I'm afraid. Come and sit down." He pulled out a stool on castors and waited until I sat before going over to a squat metallic tube on tripod legs resembling a mortar launcher, taller than him by a half-head.

I didn't know where to begin. I had rehearsed what I wanted to say, but now that it came to it, it sounded inadequate, so I rammed my hands in my pockets and said nothing. Henry squinted down the eyepiece. I had to start somewhere.

"I've never seen a telescope like that, Henry." *Wow, that sounded lame.*

He straightened. "It's a sixteen-inch reflector, the best I've had. This is a good place for an observatory – free of light-pollution and with a clear aspect. I'll be sorry when we leave." I heard resignation in his voice and I wondered if Matthew had already broached the subject with him, and whether he saw me as the reason for leaving. He bent over the telescope again. "Are you interested in astronomy, Emma?"

I studied the domed interior lit by subdued red light: the computer, the shiny surfaces, the glass – so far removed from the wood and brass of my grandfather's telescope and deep night skies smoked by the foxed glass of the lenses. "My grandfather had an old Ross telescope we used to take out into the Fens sometimes, though we weren't able to see much through it." It wasn't why I liked going. I could spend hours alone with him and away from home, when he would tell me all about the early days of the Royal Society and the astounding discoveries that had silently shaken the world. I smiled at the memory. "I'm more interested from a historical point of view and how people believed the planets influenced their lives, but I'm afraid I'm totally ignorant in every other respect."

"And what do the stars tell you about your marriage to my father?" His candid question caught me off balance and I found him looking at me with a cloaked expression.

"I'm sorry it's so soon after Ellen's death, Henry. We would have waited, but…" I chewed my lip, unsure how to continue now that it came to it.

"In the circumstances you didn't want to wait? No, I can understand that, and my father would want to do right by you in any case, but there's still a part of me that wonders if my mother's memory has been… discarded." I stared in horror and he smiled sadly. "I know that isn't the case, Emma; it's just my grief talking. Don't take any notice of an old man. I need a little time to adjust. I'd known my mother all my life, you see, and, although I thought I'd prepared for her death, I think a part of me believed she would never die. She'd been on the verge of it so many times, and so many times Dad brought her back. But not this time – this time he wasn't there to save her." No, he had been at my trial giving evidence for me.

"There was nothing he could do, Henry," I said quietly, but we both knew that Matthew could have been there, would have been there, but for me.

"He was where he needed to be, Emma, we all were. Ellen would have been the first to say it if she could. That's one thing of which you could never accuse my mother – there wasn't an ounce of sentimentality about her, always straight to the point."

"I remember," I said, thinking of the meeting we'd had in the weeks before she died, needle sharp to the point of cutting, stalwart – hard perhaps – and certainly not soft, but for all of that, not unkind either.

He grunted a laugh. "I'm sure you do; she's not easy to forget. You saw her after many years of struggling to maintain a family against some hard odds. She couldn't do that without adopting coping strategies. She wasn't always a tough old bird, Emma – life made her like that."

"Do you blame Matthew?"

Henry took longer to answer than I hoped he needed. He spent some time making tiny adjustments to the instrument in front of him. Finally he tapped at a computer keyboard on a bench. "Dad did everything he could to make things easier for her, but he couldn't change the circumstances in which they found themselves, or those that are peculiar to him. My parents stayed together through thick and thin. It wasn't easy for Ellen, especially after the war. You know about that, I suppose?"

"A little. Matthew mentioned it."

"Yes, I thought as much." A tiny whirr from the tripod

distracted him. He watched it for a moment. "That's the automatic tracking device, it saves fiddling about – not like the telescopes I was brought up with." I shifted and waited. "Ellen was an old woman when you met her – old and sick and tired – but she wasn't always like that. She had been young and vibrant until the crash that crippled her. She stuck by my father like glue, although it must have been very hard for her. She didn't shed a tear when he was away at war and not even when the news came of my Uncle Jack's death; she just went into herself and mourned alone. I suspect she didn't want to scare me. I wasn't very old at the time, but I remember it as clearly as I do yesterday." He raised his eyes to mine – his father's eyes but for the contact lenses he used to disguise their colour. "I've thought a great deal about those days recently. You know, I don't recall her crying until my father came home and she discovered he was just the same as when he went away. Those few months were the hardest – harder perhaps even than after the crash. I woke one night, a few weeks after he returned, and I heard her raised voice. I'd never heard her shouting before and I crept to the landing. I had to be so quiet or she would have skinned me if she'd caught me out of bed." He shook his head at the memory. "I sat there and listened. I could see her below and she was so angry – angry and upset – and wound up like a spring, shaking with fury. She kept saying repeatedly, 'Why didn't you tell me you're different, Matthew? Why didn't you tell me?'"

"What did he say?"

"He didn't say anything – not at first. He looked haunted, to tell you the truth, as if his worst nightmare had come true. I didn't know then that he still hadn't told her the whole truth. It wasn't until later that I learned that he'd kept it from her. He told her it was the effects of a new nerve agent."

"He was trying to protect her."

"Yes, I know. I've never known my father do anything maliciously and the truth would have been too much for her. I didn't understand that then, of course, and my first instinct was to protect my mother. In my childish simplistic way he had made her cry and I couldn't forgive him for that, not at first – not until I was older and he told me. I must have hurt him deeply and I haven't quite forgiven myself for that." I sensed a wash of remorse shading him plum. So that's what the colour of guilt looked like.

"He's never mentioned it. Matthew's so proud of you."

"And I of him. It's only as the years have passed that I've come to realize what he must have gone through, and even so, I wonder at times what he hasn't told me, what more there is to know." I held his gaze, wondering if he could read the obfuscation in my eyes, but he turned away at last and leant over the telescope. "I must have been a difficult teenager. I went through a rough patch at school. I didn't know why, of course, but the other kids picked up on my differences and I made my father's life hell for a time. I blamed him for everything. Then one night – a night not unlike this one – when I was being particularly foul, he took me outside and started to show me the constellations. He told me that they have been a constant through all the ages of Man and how, long after we have gone, they will be there still. Then he told me that he was different and that I had inherited those differences and that he was sorry for all the pain he put me through. *Him* causing *me* pain!" He bowed his head and I felt his palpable regret. I touched his arm and he briefly laid his gloved hand over mine. "For the first time in years I let him talk and was prepared to listen. He must have guessed I was ready to hear what he had to say and I only wish I'd been able to before. But, there you go – that's kids for you." He seemed to be finding something particularly absorbing through the telescope, or perhaps he found the subject of his youth difficult to talk about.

"Is that when you became interested in astronomy?" I rubbed my hands together to get some warmth to the tips.

"It took me out of myself, away from all that I thought I knew and understood. Dad opened a whole new world for me to explore. He bought me a telescope, taught me how to map the stars, to use them to navigate. I came to understand myself and to accept and respect him. It opened my eyes to how much he knew, and even now he sometimes surprises me with the breadth and depth of his knowledge. Heh, for years I thought he might be an alien! That was in the 'fifties when such things were all the rage the first time around. We still don't know what he is for sure, do we, Emma?" His voice dropped and I suspected he was asking me.

"No, I don't know why he is as he is, Henry. Nor does he, but he keeps looking, doesn't he? You all do – it's what he bases his research on. He wants to find a cure for his condition." I had allowed a harsh note to creep into my voice and Henry looked at me in surprise.

"But that's not the whole story, Emma. It's true Dad wants to know what made him that way, but his work goes far beyond helping himself. He's spent years working on ways to alleviate pain in patients and to halt the progression of certain diseases. He's used himself as a guinea pig more times than I can count. It's his research that's pioneered some of the most important breakthroughs. You won't hear his name in the news – you know why he avoids publicity at all costs – but he's behind it, you can be sure of it."

I had been so caught up in our time-limited future together that I hadn't looked beyond it. Matthew's work remained largely unknown to me, and I had made assumptions based on my fear. Could he have commanded respect from people like Matias and Sung if all that concerned him was his own mortality?

Henry broke through my ruminations. "Ah, now that's a rare sight indeed! Come and have a look at this." I joined him and looked through the eyepiece. What I saw stole my breath.

"That's beautiful! I've never seen a planet so clearly!"

"Isn't it wonderful? It's Saturn in a phase where the rings are at a very shallow angle and you can see the transit of the moons. Remarkable. Matthew will want to see this." He picked up a phone lying to one side, but didn't dial. "Emma, what I said earlier – I'm sorry how it sounded. I've known since Dad met you that he would marry you one day if he could, and a part of me still wishes that my parents could have had the same relationship you seem to have. It's as if he's been waiting for you all this time and that hurts as their son. But, for what it's worth, I'm glad he's happy and I'm glad it's you – despite the age difference." His mouth creased upwards, making him look like an older version of his father.

I returned his smile. "Henry, he loved and respected Ellen, as he does her memory. I'm not capable of replacing her even if I wanted to, just as the woman who will one day take my place will be a person in her own right." His eyes broadened at my frankness. "I couldn't ask Matthew to live on his memories alone; they are not enough to sustain him. He needs to belong as much as we do. I will die one day as surely as Ellen has. We might not like it, but history will repeat itself. However many years down the line it might be, perhaps my successor will be having this same conversation with my son or daughter."

Henry fell silent for a moment. "So you think he will live that long?" he said quietly, and I mentally thumped myself when I remembered that he believed Matthew to be no more than a century old and hadn't thought in terms of immortality and that, in his mind, his father's life was finite.

"Who knows, Henry? He doesn't."

"And you can handle the thought that one day he might meet someone else and you will become obsolete?"

How clearly he read my mind. For all my talk of not replacing Ellen, for respecting her memory, my life would pass and another would take my place as surely as I took Ellen's. I looked away. "I can't speak for the future; I only know what we have now." How fervently I clung to the notion because, despite what we had in each other, the future held no certainty.

I had said what I wanted to say, and Henry made it clear, in the way he embraced me as I left the observatory for the warmth of the house, that he did not begrudge our future together. My respect for him was matched only by my admiration for his gentle stoicism and the love he held for his father. For all of that he had not shied from the question which, one day, I would face as inevitably as my death.

Hors de Combat

Although only a few weeks had passed since I'd last been in my apartment, it seemed like decades. Elena must have been in to collect some clothes for me and had tidied the throw and plumped the cushions at the same time, but otherwise left it as she found it. After Matthew's home I saw it for what it was – empty, soulless, a place merely in which to sleep and pass the time. Only Mr Fluffy, my pot-bellied cactus, made the place more human.

"I'll see you this evening," Matthew promised as he put my bag on my bed. "You know where I am if you need me, just call." I nodded, missing him already, and he tipped my chin and kissed me as if he understood. "This evening," he said again and then left me alone.

I toyed with the idea of e-mailing Beth and letting her know our decision to marry in Maine, and then thought of the inevitable response, and justified putting off telling her until the evening on the grounds of self-preservation.

I unpacked slowly, heaving the pile of magazines Pat had given me onto my desk. Wedding magazines – lots of them – thick, glossy, and smug. I leafed through the top one. Brides of all shapes, sizes, and colours and not a freckle in sight. What did the world have against ginger freckles that we were so underrepresented? I noted a glorious redhead on page nineteen but it wasn't natural, with skin smoothly pale and perfect with not a speckle to mar it. I sighed and concentrated on what they were wearing: extravagant, buoyant concoctions in shiny satins or layers of net. Most were off the shoulder and gathered too high on the waist. Only plainer styles were labelled for the "mature" bride, and at twenty-nine I wasn't prepared to accept *that*. With a flurry of regret I remembered going shopping with my mother and sister for a wedding dress for Beth, and knew the same wouldn't be happening for me. What would Mum say when I told her of our plans? I shuddered at the thought of family weddings, friction, and the inevitable guilt.

I escaped to my tutor room in preparation for the day, burying myself in the comforting familiarity of the seventeenth century, surrounded by posters of flesh-eating monsters and a dead poet.

"So, what do you vagabonds have for me today, then?" I greeted my group cheerfully as they filed into my room.

Josh looked me up and down. "Hey, Dr D, we heard you were dead." He grinned jovially and I tried not to be taken aback. The events of the last day of the trial seemed so distant now.

"Er, no, not as far as I'm aware, Josh, thanks." They stared with open curiosity, and I supposed it unreasonable to expect that they hadn't heard the salacious details of the trial in all its humiliating glory. Only Aydin behaved as if I were relatively normal. He put his bag on the floor and held out his hand.

"I am much pleased that you are OK. These things are now over, *evet*? Yes, and we can work now and all will be good. The fire is out and you are not burned; your news is old news, I think." He beamed widely and shook my hand. The others looked bemused, but neither Aydin nor I felt like explaining his reference to our conversation after Christmas, when the campus had been awash with gossip about me. "The fire of rumour," he'd said, "will burn hot and fast and burn itself out without doing any lasting damage." He had been right – still a little singed on the outside I might be, but inside I remained whole and fresh and clean.

"Thank you, Aydin, it's good to see you. Let's get on."

They settled in their chairs and we slipped back into our routine more easily than I had left it only a few weeks before. By the time we finished the session, I had arranged to see each of them separately so I could go through their work in detail, and they fully accepted that I was not a ghost.

Half-way across the quad after lunch and wishing the snow would hurry up and melt, I found myself outside the medical facility without really knowing how I arrived there. The glass doors swung open invitingly. Would it matter if I took a peek just to make sure he was all right?

A familiar gravelly voice rose in greeting. "Well, look who's here!"

"Matias!"

He swung me into a crushing hug. "Who's back from the dead, hey? I can't tell you how glad I am to see you; Elena has been driving me insane these last weeks." He stood back and examined me closely. "You're looking remarkably well, I must say. I couldn't believe it when I heard what happened. I honestly didn't expect to see you back here before the spring break." His voice dropped along with his customary smile, and he clasped my hands in his. "Quite frankly, Emma, I didn't think we would be seeing you again at all. It sounded like…" He shook his head and he didn't need to finish what we both knew he meant.

"You can't get rid of me that easily, Matias Lidström. It takes more than that to put me out of action."

He managed a laugh. "Yes, that's what Matthew said just before he told me he has to marry you to keep you out of trouble."

"Beast!" I walloped him. "You could have told me he'd said. I've been very restrained – I haven't told anyone yet."

His face crinkled. "That's more than Matthew's been doing. He wanted to tell me the second I walked through the door this morning, I could tell."

"How?"

"Apart from the grin the size of Niagara you mean? He gave the game away when he asked me to be his best man. I said I'd have to think about it and let him know…" He took a rapid step backwards as I aimed a jab at his ribs. "… and then I thought about what Elena would do to me – or not do to me – if I didn't accept, so I told him that if I didn't have anything better to do that day, I might as well spend it eating and boozing at his expense. Hey, hang on there, you'll make the staff jealous!" The people milling around the foyer weren't paying the slightest bit of attention to us, and besides, I didn't care who saw me plant a delighted kiss on his stubbly cheek.

"What does Elena think?" I asked, once I had relinquished my hold on him.

"She doesn't know; I haven't told her. I thought you would have done by now and I'm not saying a word about it until you do. Can you imagine what hell my life would be if she found out without you there to answer all her incessant questions?" He made his fingers into a mouth and made it jabber away, making me laugh.

"Don't worry, I'll tell her when I see her. Light the blue touch-paper and retreat."

I spent the afternoon engrossed. Hannah had produced a fascinating initial response to her proposal, which required intense concentration on my part to unravel. Should her hypothesis be proved right, she could turn current thinking on its head. As it was, the facts just didn't stack up.

After struggling to make some sense of it for several hours, I welcomed Elena's interruption shortly before remembering I had something to tell her. If I had a chance. I hadn't seen her since the trial and she was bursting with gossip as she danced through my door, her face glowing with excitement.

"I have so much to tell you! Now, let me look at you first." She spun me around before I could say anything, then stepped back and scanned me up and down. "Yes, you are well, I think. I could not believe it when Matias said you were coming back so soon. He would not let me see you at Matthew's home. He said that you had to rest and that I would make too much excitement for you. I said to him that he is a man and he doesn't know what a woman needs, and he said that he thinks he does and that you didn't need me!" Her laughter rang out.

"Elena, I have something to tell you..."

She pranced across the room, her long arms waving above her head like saplings in a breeze. "And then there were all the reporters for days and days. Nasty rude men asking lots of questions and flash, flash, flash with those cameras in my face – like this..." and she illustrated by thrusting her hand towards me so that I ducked instinctively out of the way.

"Elena..."

"And I told them," she waggled her finger, "I told them that the things they said about you were not true – lies, all lies – and that you were nearly killed by that terrible man. And when they asked about Matthew..."

My head jerked up. "What did you say about Matthew?"

She stopped as she heard the edge in my voice. "I said he is a good doctor and he saved your life, nothing more. You said not to, Emma, do you remember? You said that no one must know how close you are."

I breathed again. "That's good. Elena, can I tell you

98

something?" She looked at me with her head on one side, which usually preceded some profound declaration. "Elena?"

"Do you know," she said slowly, "there is something different about you. *Da*, I can see it, you look alive. Yes, yes, alive and happy. Hah! Something has happened I think!"

"I survived a massive cardiac arrest, perhaps?" I suggested dryly.

She flapped a hand. "Yes, yes, of course. But this is something else." Her eyes narrowed. "You look, mmm – all warm and happy – yes, that is it – happy."

I couldn't hold back any longer. "That's probably because I am, you noodle. Good grief, I've waited all day to tell you."

"You must tell me *e-*verything. No, no, tell me nothing – I shall guess." She made herself comfortable on one of the armchairs and sat forward, hands on her knees, eyes bright with anticipation. "Matthew took you out to dinner and…"

I held up a hand. "Clichéd and pointless; I don't eat enough to warrant spending money on."

"Oh, so you lay there dying, and he took you into his arms and…"

"Unprofessional and far too public – we were in the courthouse at the time," I reminded her.

She pursed her lips. "In bed as you…"

"Nope."

She crossed her arms huffing in exasperation. "What then?"

"Well, that would be telling now, wouldn't it? Suffice to say he…"

"Swept you off your feet and asked you to marry him," she interrupted gleefully.

"Well, yes, he did as a matter of fact."

"*Da*," she whooped, "I knew it! It is written all over your face. This is such good news. You have mended his heart…"

"And he mine. We're getting married in May."

She became still and quiet. "Married? In May? But this is so soon. Matias and I have not even... we cannot..." She gathered herself. "There is so much to do first. What about the arrangements? What about your dress? Do your family know? Are you pregnant?" I spent the next five minutes filling her in on the details, then she wrapped her willowy arms around my shoulders. "I am so, so happy for you."

"Thank you," I returned.

"And now," she said, stepping away and using the back of her sleeve to dry her face, "I must tell Matias. This is such a good day and he will be so pleased for you both."

She produced her mobile and had lifted it to her ear when she stopped and squinted at me. "Why do you look like that?" I rearranged my face to look innocent, but too late. "He knows? Matias already knows about the wedding?" she asked. I nodded. "He did not tell me! Wait until I see him," she almost spat, her hands on her hips like a fishwife. I didn't know who should be more afraid – him or me.

"It's not Matias's fault, and anyway, I wanted to tell you first and didn't want him spoiling the surprise. I have a question to ask." She sneaked a look at me, curiosity roused. "I would love you to be a maid of honour – or matron of honour if you beat us to it and marry first."

Her face fell. "No, that won't happen."

"Why not?"

"There are difficulties." I waited for her to go on but she didn't elaborate. "I will be your maid of honour and interfere in your wedding instead, no?" she said with a small smile.

"Interfere to your heart's content," I said, hopping down from my perch and making for the door before Matthew could use his key.

"Well, hello there," he said, grinning at me. "Matias here is looking for Elena. Is she with you? He mentioned something about needing a bulletproof vest… ah." He came to a halt. "I see. Good evening, Elena."

"Incoming," Matias groaned behind him, as Elena glowered like a thundercloud.

"Good evening, Matthew," she said primly, then turned on her fiancé. "Matias, you did not tell me."

He grabbed her slender frame in a bone-crushing embrace. "I knew you would want to hear it from Emma first, my little sugarplum. I think this calls for a part – don't you, Matthew? A joint celebration in honour of our beautiful brides? What do you say, girls? How about a party?"

Elena forgot to be angry. "I will need a new dress."

He nuzzled her neck. "Of course you will, kitten."

"A party?" I said hesitantly to Matthew, thinking of all the food and drink he would have to avoid.

"Definitely. We have something worth celebrating with a few good friends, music, dancing… sounds like a plan. Matias and I will arrange it, as you have enough to do."

"Emma and I can go shopping this weekend," Elena suggested, already practising a few dance steps.

Matthew took the bag he carried through to the kitchen, calling back over his shoulder. "This weekend is already booked, I'm afraid."

"New York," I explained. "How about the one following?"

"New York," Elena said wistfully. "Matias, we haven't been to New York for ages…"

He growled, "No, we've been to Finland and St Petersburg instead; New York will have to wait. I'll have to look out my tux for the wedding. I'm a little more dignified around the waist than before Christmas. All that Russian fare Elena's mother produced – it would've been rude not to eat it."

Elena prodded his stomach. "All you did was eat, eat, eat and now you are getting fat. It is your own fault. Look, Matthew is not even a little fat," she said as he returned from the kitchen. Matias ruefully observed his newly acquired paunch.

"Well, Matthew is younger than I am and he gets far more exercise by the looks of it, though how he's developed muscles like those from picking up a scalpel I'll never know. Besides, he never eats anything much to speak of, while here I am, doing my best to support the agrarian economy of this country..."

"Single-handed." Elena tittered. "I like you just the way you are, like my little Russian bear, all round and furry and..." He put his hand over her mouth and she giggled from behind it.

"All right, I think they've got the idea; you don't need to show me up any further in front of Superman here." He pitched a look at Matthew, then at me. "I don't suppose I'll be able to rely on you to fatten him up and redress the balance, will I, Emma? Do you two compete to see how little you can eat? Abnormal, the pair of you."

My mind went into free-fall trying to think of something to say, but Matthew replied seamlessly. "It's all in the genes – nothing either of us can do about it, I'm afraid."

"You could darn well eat more for a start. Tell me which genes are responsible and I'll start a program of genetic modification and be the guinea-pig. How about it, Matthew? Take a break from all this blood analysis and geno-morphing and venture into adipose-reduction. We could make a killing on the open market, what with your brains and my looks – what a team!" He elbowed Matthew in the ribs and yelped, clutching his arm, the grin dropping from his face. "What the...? What've you got under there? Body armour?"

Now I felt Matthew tense. "Caught a nerve I suspect. Want me to take a look?"

"No, I don't think so, thanks." Gingerly, Matias rubbed his arm, eyeing Matthew in a way I hadn't seen before.

I soothed Matthew's ribs. "That'll teach you not to abuse my fiancé. Elena, keep Matias under control, will you? He's supposed to be his best man, not duffing him up."

Elena forgot all about compassion and rounded on him. "Best man! Matias, you did not tell me. How can you be best man like that? You will not be able to fit in your clothes! Stop making such a big fuss about your arm. Come, we have things to do and you have a party to arrange." She dragged him towards the door. Matthew winced in sympathy and Matias grimaced back, his elbow all but forgotten except for the element of speculation that remained in his eyes when he bid us goodnight as they left the room.

CHAPTER

6

New York

Days passed and with them the snow. Depressed grass, crushed by months of frost, now churned into mud under student feet as they ignored the "keep off the grass" signs dotting the quad. Everything looked grey or brown and lacklustre – life suspended – a long breath held in anticipation of an early spring. Then the sun shone. Within days, spears of green burst through the broken sward and pulsing buds erupted on the trees lining the paths. Heads lifted towards the sun, shoulders straightened, steps lightened and, like ants from a nest, the campus emerged into the light.

I had arranged to see members of my tutor group individually over the coming weeks, spending many hours every evening in my room pruning their initial work until the dead wood was cast aside and new growth lay gleaming and transparent on the page. It now became a question of bringing the research to fruition and that would be quite another matter. Not all would stand up to scrutiny and, until each piece had been honed to perfection, I would not, could not, let it pass muster. If Guy had taught me anything, it was to raise the game and maintain unassailable standards. My students would rise or fall on the work they presented at the conference and my reputation with them. I thought their research encouraging, but in no way complete.

By the time I put my pen down on Friday evening, I felt ready for the weekend. I yawned and stretched my legs out under my desk.

"If you're too tired we can postpone the trip for another week." Matthew massaged my stiff shoulders.

I rested my cheek on his fingers. "No, I'm up for it; *a change is as good as a rest*," I quoted Nanna. "Anyway, you said you have appointments to keep in New York. I'll get some sleep on the plane." We were catching a late night flight on one of the internal airlines from Portland, rather than taking his jet. "I'm all packed. I didn't know what to take so I'm playing safe."

He stroked my cheek. "Safe – that's what I like to hear. Anything you need we can buy when we're there."

"If we have time," I pointed out.

He tugged my plait like a bell-pull. "We'll make time if need be. Ready?"

Even in the early hours the city streets heaved. People spanned crowded pavements, meandering fluidly before melting into the darker side streets away from the biting illumination of the shop windows.

Spangled in light, the hotel's façade looked like a French chateau from a hundred years ago, and I wondered if I appeared as shabby as I felt after the flight, wishing I could be at ease in these polished surroundings. Still weary despite sleep, I had to remind myself that not so long ago the most I might have looked forward to was a long, slow recovery with a brain resembling a green vegetable, so – all things considered – I wasn't doing too badly.

I stood up straight and tried to assume an element of poise and composure as we fed through the revolving glass doors and into a foyer glinting glass and gold, the marble floor echoing our footsteps. I found it strange, disorientating, like being thrown from one world into another.

Matthew made arrangements with a man who greeted us by name. I became sidetracked by a sudden clatter as, oozing opulence, a middle-aged couple rolled through the doors, shattering the discreet hush in a bloom of alcohol. The woman lurched in our direction, flashing vulgar diamonds and neon teeth, jingling noisily as she wove past and leaving a florid scent as pungent as sweat. The man belched loudly. Wealth. It took people differently. I grew up with the vestiges of wealth left by generations of fading fortunes until it became no more than a distant memory in an almost forgotten past. Matthew seemed comfortable with money, wearing it neither to dress his reputation, nor to boost his esteem, but as a tool to secure the comfort and safety of his family and to ensure their means of escape, and its lack of hold over him endeared him to me all the more.

He declined an offer to show us to our room, and together we walked towards the lift. He seemed to know where we were going.

"Have you been here before?" I asked.

"Once," he said quietly, "when it was first built."

Now alone in a room the size of my entire apartment, with walls of panelled silk and ornately plastered ceilings, he seemed uneasy. He extracted a white rose from the extravagant arrangement on a table, smoothing a curled petal abstractedly.

"What's the matter?"

He wandered over to where I took in the lamplit view from the window and wound the flower through my hair. He smiled a little. "Nothing... only..." He took my hands in his, looking troubled. "I can't help wondering whether you would have preferred a room of your own."

"Why?" I asked, surprised.

"Two reasons," he wavered. "Does this remind you of what Guy did… at the motel?"

"No. Next?"

Patently relieved, he continued, "Your reputation – I didn't think to ask you how you felt about sharing a room so publicly."

"I don't think people care nowadays, Matthew."

"People might not, but I do if it matters to you."

I pulled his arms around my waist. "In my heart we're as married as if we'd already taken our vows. In true seventeenth-century style we are espoused before God, Matthew, and that spousal is binding. It's not as if we are going to be doing anything anyway, more's the pity." I wrinkled my nose and pretended to pout, but he laughed, and shook his head.

"We did agree to wait, and in any case, I think we should make our intentions clear, don't you?"

"How so?" I asked.

He tapped his pockets and began digging around until he found something that jangled when he removed it. "It's time you had these," he said, holding out a small bunch of house keys on a chain.

"Oh," I said, taking them from him. "Gosh, these make it feel very real somehow. Thanks." I examined them more closely, and the peculiar ring-shaped key fob in particular. Radiating light from its depths, a rectangular claret-coloured stone, simply cut, sat in a crown of gold between two lions, the bodies and tails curving to form the band. It looked old, the band worn thinner than the rest. I held it up, confused. "What's this doing here? It's an odd place to keep a ring."

"Do you like it?"

I nodded vigorously. "It's a brilliant copy; they've managed to make it look authentically old and a bit tatty. Even the stone looks real."

He rubbed the back of his neck, looking awkward and hopeful in equal measure. "It'd look better on your finger. Try it on."

"Like one of those Christmas cracker rings? I loved them when I was a tot – best bit of Christmas. Not that this looks like a ring from a cracker, of course," I added, undoing the keychain catch and releasing the ring. I popped it on my index finger and wiggled it under the side lamp, making it sparkle. "It really does look old. Where did you get it?"

With an amused shake of his head, Matthew removed the ring. "No, my love, it's for this finger," and he slipped it on my left hand. It sat snugly on my ring finger, and neither too big nor strident it felt at home at once. "It belonged to my grandmother, your namesake – Emma D'Eresby. My grandfather gave it to her on their marriage – those are Lynes lions there, you see?"

"Oh," I said again, this time feeling dazed and a bit light-headed. "I see."

His smile became uncertain. "I… thought you would like it."

I fingered the imperfections in the curly-maned lions, the slightly misshapen rich gold band, the vibrant pink stone with signs of age worn on its cut faces. "Your grandmother's." I looked at him, feeling oddly emotional, seeing the aching vulnerability in his eyes. "It's perfect, Matthew. I love it. I love you."

When I woke he was already dressed.

"Sweetheart, I'm sorry, I know you'd rather sleep, but we need to make a move if we're to make the first appointment."

I looked for a clock but couldn't see one. "What time is it?"

"Six-thirty. I've ordered breakfast. The first meeting is at eight."

I turned over, heavy with sleep, and pulled the cover over my ears. "That's very early for a business appointment and on a Saturday. I'll wait here if you like; I don't want to hold you up."

He rolled me back again and I shut my eyes against a stubborn streak of sunlight. "I would like you to come with me."

He said it in such a way that required my attention. I opened one eye. "To a business meeting? What do I know about business?" He looked particularly handsome this morning. I stretched and wound my arms around his neck and he smiled, hauling me upright and out of bed as I clung to him crab-like. "Ow," I moaned and went and had a bath in the most luxurious marble bathroom I'd ever set eyes on, which sort of made up for it.

"You look beautiful," he assured me as I checked my reflection in the mirrored glass of the elevator for the umpteenth time as it rose, floor-by-floor, to the top of a skyscraper in the heart of the business district. He wore a muted calfskin jacket that moulded to his shoulders in a way that made me gulp when I saw him. He made unconscious elegance effortless. He wasn't dressing for a city meeting, yet somehow it didn't matter. Perhaps centuries of life gave him the confidence. I had some way to go. I took off my quilted coat and slung it over my arm to see if it made any difference. My nut-brown jacket and trousers would have been fine for a day out shopping in London, but they weren't tailored enough for a business meeting.

"I feel decidedly underdressed for such *elevated* surroundings."

He smiled, acknowledging my feeble joke. "That's rather good for this time of the morning. What you wear to today's proceedings isn't important; you don't need to prove anything. Anyway, I don't think he'll know what's hit him; he won't be expecting anything like you."

"Who won't?" I asked in the velvet hush. "Why are we here?"

Matthew's eyes narrowed conspiratorially. "Why indeed. That is a question I frequently ask myself."

"Don't be so infuriatingly obtuse! What are you up to?"

I didn't have to wait long to find out. The lift opened directly into an anteroom. The PA's desk stood empty. In fact, I hadn't seen anyone else other than the security guard on the door since we'd entered the building at ten to eight. The double doors to an expansive office sat open like jaws. Modern and masculine, the exclusive room nonetheless had a faint aroma of mothballs. I thought it empty at first, but a man – possibly in his late fifties, but whose immaculate silk suit and handmade shirt were meant for someone younger – emerged from a chair where he had been waiting. Steel hair cut razor-sharp and manicured as a lawn sat on his head like a wig, while a smooth face inclined to fleshiness made him look sleek and pampered. Gold cufflinks winked as he held out his hand. He assessed Matthew with shrapnel eyes. "Dr Lynes, I have not had the pleasure; we spoke on the phone."

Matthew shook his hand. "We did. Emma, this is George Redgrave – his family have looked after my family's financial affairs for the last century."

Mentally, I readjusted the time scales we were working to and made a note not to let anything show on my face. I needn't have worried – I hadn't registered with the man. Smiling without conviction he dismissed me, and turned back to Matthew. Irritation prickled before I could stifle it. Redgrave's voice creaked on the low notes as if about to break, an old voice, resonant with success and as superior as a cat. Used to being listened to, he articulated slowly. "My father always spoke highly of your family, Dr Lynes; in particular your grandfather, with whom he met on one occasion before you were born. I understand he is no longer with us. I regret not having the pleasure of making his acquaintance." The man smiled again, this time displaying expensive capped teeth. "You didn't say what it is you wish to discuss. How might I be of service?" He gestured towards two chairs in front of a broad partner's desk behind which he proceeded to sit like a judge.

Matthew waited until I settled on my chair before he also sat down. "Dr D'Eresby and I are to be married in May. I would like to make some financial arrangements prior to our wedding."

I think my surprise showed. Fair enough if Matthew had things he wanted to sort out, but if I'd known it would involve me, I'd have worn a suit. Or perhaps not. Redgrave cast a cursory glance at me and smiled fulsomely at Matthew, smelling money.

"Of course, and congratulations on your forthcoming nuptials, Dr Lynes. This is rather short notice to draw up such a complex agreement, but I will see to it immediately. I trust the young lady accepts the need for a prenuptial contract?"

Matthew put his hand on my arm as I began to react, addressing Redgrave without raising his voice. "No, there'll be no prenuptial contract between us; that is not the nature of our business here today."

Like a headmaster about to reprimand a recalcitrant boy, the man folded his hands on the leather-topped desk and looked very grave. "Dr Lynes, given the nature of your considerable assets" – he drooled over the word – "I trust you will be making arrangements to limit your financial liabilities in the event of an unfortunate cessation of your marriage?"

Matthew remained impassive. "That will not be necessary."

"I'm afraid that I don't understand your thinking here. You intend to contract a marriage without protecting your substantial estate?" He made it sound as if only a fool would do such a thing. My hackles rose.

"Not at all; that is precisely why I'm here."

George Redgrave sat back in his chair and nodded slowly. "Very commendable. I thought that I must have misunderstood." He picked up a heavy gold fountain pen and pulled a piece of embossed paper in front of him. The pen lid slid off the barrel with a soft sigh. "Now, if I may take the young lady's details..." He trailed off as Matthew held up his hand.

"There is no misunderstanding. There will be no requirement for a contract; however, I would like you to arrange for Dr D'Eresby to have complete access to my estate, to take immediate effect on our marriage. In the event of my death or disappearance she is to be given control of it and..."

"No!" Redgrave and I said simultaneously. My head swarmed: death, disappearance. If he wanted me to have a heart attack he was going the right way about it. Redgrave went puce. He took out a blue silk handkerchief used only for show and mopped his forehead.

"Dr Lynes, I must insist that you reconsider this line of action."

I hated to admit it, but I agreed. My voice shook slightly. "No, Matthew, you can't, you mustn't."

In the subtle shades of his voice I detected telltale signs of obstinacy. "I can and I will."

"I don't want your money," I objected. He sucked his teeth, and standing, led me to the window, where his back became a barrier to Redgrave's curiosity. He lowered his voice.

"Emma, listen to me. This is to protect your future – our future – and that of any children we might have."

I strove to find the words I needed. "I don't want a future without you. Money is nothing; life would be pointless. You said you might die, Matthew. Why did you say that?" I saw signs of distress as he put out his hands to comfort me, but I shook him off. "Don't, just don't," I choked.

"Or in the event of my disappearance, Emma. I have to put it in unequivocal terms to ensure there is clarity in law. If I need to disappear I will know that my wife is provided for until my return. And I will return. You understand that, don't you?" I heard the urgency in his voice. "Don't you, Emma? You know that I will always come back." I couldn't look at him, so I just nodded, biting my lip until it hurt. "That's my love," he said gently. "Trust me."

He waited until I had blown my nose and sat down before he turned towards Redgrave, who had regained his composure and been straining to hear our conversation. I stared bleakly at a paper clip half-buried in the deep pile carpet.

"Dr Lynes," Redgrave drawled, adopting a paternalistic tone he must have found particularly effective with stubborn young clients in the past, "it is highly irregular to place such a fortune so casually at the disposal of any young woman without some guarantee that assets will be protected. Please allow me to make some enquiries on your behalf. For example, has she been married before? Are her family, shall we say, of solvent means, trustworthy, reliable?"

Furious, I flashed crimson, but since it seemed he rated me as no more than a slug under a rock it made no difference. He made me feel grubby and cheap and I ground my teeth to prevent my temper flaring, no longer upset, but angry and defensive. I sat on the edge of my chair and fumed quietly.

Matthew crossed his legs in a seemingly casual movement, but his normally quiet blue aura had lost its equilibrium and red ire tinged it purple. "Nonetheless, that is what you will do." His voice became eerily calm and I recognized the signs, but the other man didn't.

"Just a few discreet enquiries as to this young lady's suitability to manage such an estate, at least," he pressed.

"My decision is final. Have the documentation drawn up and ready for signatures by the end of April. There will be a substantial incentive involved in the satisfactory completion of my request. The alternative is not an option." Matthew had come to the limits of his patience. The man heard it this time and flustered, dabbing at his face again.

"I understand. And if the young lady should, er… decide not to remain in the marital home, or makes an alternative emotional attachment? This is, after all, a very great deal of money and any young woman – especially if not accustomed to great wealth – might be tempted to… well to… abscond, so to speak. I'm sure you understand."

A muscle in Matthew's jaw contracted sharply. He leaned forward and tossed a leather portfolio he had brought with him onto the desk. It slithered to a halt. "You will need these to complete the documents. They are all in order. All investments, bonds, holdings, stocks, and shares are to be transferred on my wife's request to the accounts listed. All property – including our home in Maine – land and businesses will transfer immediately to her, either on her demand, or automatically should I disappear. All monies held in any of my accounts are at her disposal. She will have complete access to all aspects of my investments, do you understand?"

Redgrave's gullet rose and fell. "*All* investments, Mr Lynes?"

"That is so."

"I don't know anything about investments," I said numbly.

"The family will help you if need be. You'll have nothing to worry about," Matthew said kindly. He stood, ending the meeting. "If you have any further questions relating to my instructions, you have my contact details. I expect to hear from you shortly. And, Redgrave…" the man looked up at his changed tone, "your remarks show a marked lack of respect towards Dr D'Eresby. Do not ever question her integrity or that of her family again. Should she need to contact you I will expect you to show her the same degree of courtesy you reserve for me." He hadn't altered the volume of his voice yet Redgrave started as if hit, and stuttered out a response that we didn't wait to hear.

Matthew was still seething when we reached the street. Once outside, he took a deep, slow breath. The city air smelled clean compared with the sanitized fug of the office. A car horn barked and was answered by another. "Emma, I'm so sorry – I had no idea the man's a misogynist. His father was quite different, completely charming, and he would have been ashamed to hear his son speak as he did in front of you."

I still reeled from what he had done to be too concerned about a condescending, self-satisfied, patronizing bigot. "Matthew, how could you? I don't know the first thing about investments. I always thought they were something priests wore. Stocks, shares, bonds – and businesses – what businesses? I didn't know you had any. Ugh, it's too much! How did Ellen handle knowing she had responsibility for all that money?" I scrabbled my hands through my hair thinking I would wake at any moment.

"Ellen? I didn't do this with Ellen. She had her own resources; things were different between us, you know that." He tamed my insubordinate hair with his fingers. "The money is only there to protect us, Emma. As you said, it is nothing if we don't have each other or our family. To whom else can I entrust it, if not you? Who else will benefit from it, if not you?"

I thought that fairly obvious. "Henry? Dan? Your grandchildren and great-grandchildren. Your family must come first, not me. I have enough to live on." A car sped by, kicking up a stone that bounced harmlessly against the rock-clad wall of the building. I toed it into the gutter, not looking at him.

"Emma, married yet or not, you are part of that family. You are my priority now. It doesn't lessen those bonds of kinship I have with my son and his family any more than adding a brick to a wall weakens it. Henry doesn't need my money and nor do the rest of the family. They are already very wealthy. Ellen was an heiress; she left Henry everything."

I knew she had inherited her parents' farm after her brother died, but that didn't constitute a fortune or warrant the designation "*heiress*". "I thought her parents owned a ranch?"

His mouth lifted into a slow smile. "They did, but it's now part of an extensive oil field." He waited until the information permeated my frazzled brain.

"Oh!" I said. "OK." I frowned. "I see. Well, then… yes, but you could have warned me."

He turned my collar up against the chilly wind and used it to pull me closer. "And have you making a fuss and probably refusing to cooperate point blank? I know you better than you think, Emma D'Eresby."

"Don't you bet on it. I've only ever been after your money and don't you forget it."

I giggled as he grabbed me around my waist and blew in my ear until I begged him to stop. A matronly woman in tweed with a resplendent bosom, upon which pearls bounced, made disapproving grunts as she passed.

"She thinks we should act our age," Matthew chortled.

I tweaked his scarf. "Yours or mine?"

We walked arm-in-arm along the tree-lined pavement under the naked branches. "It makes what I earn so piffling paltry," I mused. "Peanuts, poverty-stricken penury…"

"I take it you are referring to my financial affairs again?"

"… penniless, impoverished, impecunious…"

"All right, what's the matter?"

"It makes my income irrelevant. I feel redundant in the face of such wealth."

"Mmm, do you indeed." We walked on a few paces. "It's true

that we don't need your income any more than we need what I earn, but that's not the point. It's fair remuneration for our efforts. Besides, you want to work for your own sense of self-worth, don't you? As do I. It's part of who you are."

After a lifetime of arguments with my father it came as a welcome change not having to explain. I remembered Elena saying how she longed to bake cakes and make a home for Matias, and how work was something she did until she married. Not for me – my work had always meant more to me than a means of passing the time.

"So you're happy for me to work when we're married? You don't want me to stay at home and twiddle my thumbs and cook?"

He snorted back a laugh, for which I gave a reproving look. "Sorry, that was uncalled for I know. I'm sure you could cook if you wanted to. No, I don't expect you to stay at home and keep house – what century do you think I come from? If I wanted a housekeeper, I'd hire one, although the thought of you in nothing but an apron is quite appealing..." He raised an eyebrow and was only saved from my scathing reply because we needed to cross the road and I had to concentrate.

"What are you doing?" he asked when we reached the other side.

"Avoiding the cracks between slabs," I said, doing just that.

"And the reason being...?"

I let go of his arm and hopped a few paces. "Ooo, you had a deprived childhood." I spied a lovely clear stretch of pavement, free of pedestrians, perfect for playing hopscotch. "Haven't you heard of the bears?"

"Am I going to regret asking what bears have to do with the sidewalk?"

"Probably." I started to hopscotch down the pavement. "For the sake of the uninitiated, the corners of London streets are crowded with bears waiting for anyone silly enough to step on the lines between the slabs."

"Are they indeed," he said, amused.

"Oh yes. Masses of them waiting to gobble you up." I jumped a few more steps, then spun around to face him. "Didn't Henry grow up with Christopher Robin and Winnie the Pooh?"

"I'm afraid he didn't. He's obviously suffered as a result. I take it you did?"

I made it to the next road intersection without knocking anyone over and waited for him to join me. "It's a fundamental part of childhood – that and Peter Rabbit and Jeremy Fisher. Did you have anything like them as a child?"

We crossed the road to a line of glossy shop windows, all halogen lights and monochromatic minimalism. I couldn't see any price tags.

"Expectations of childhood were quite different. My mother died when I was nearly three and my father said she had a lot of sickness with her second pregnancy. I was quite lively and probably a handful, so I spent much of the time with my grandmother." He stopped outside a window with faceless manikins sporting extravagant wedding dresses. "We have plenty of time to look at dresses if you would like to," he offered. Frankly, I thought his childhood more interesting, but I would have to wear something for our wedding and at least this shop looked as if it avoided flounces.

"Five minutes," I conceded.

Well, that was a joke. It took over two hours to disengage from the exceptionally helpful assistants. I stood in front of one of those mirrors designed to reflect an unrealistically positive image and felt my heart sink as the two exquisitely dressed women fussed and preened around me. There were an awful lot of off-the-shoulder designs that made the most of my freckles and not enough of my bust. Others were made more of pearls and sparkly bits than fabric and weighed a ton. I quite liked a long, slim dress in a delicate wild silk that took in my curves and ended with a modest train, but then I saw the price-tag and nearly had a fit. *Less is more*, I thought, and in this case, a very great deal more. The women twittered and swooped between us, flattering and gushing, but all the while I felt acutely aware that it was Matthew's approval they sought, not mine: they assumed he was paying, and that was galling. By noon, I'd had enough.

"Time for lunch," he said cheerfully, sensing my fraying mood before I said anything.

"You thought that funny, didn't you?" I asked as we escaped into the sunshine.

His attempt to conceal his mirth failed. "It was quite amusing, yes. I thought the one with the black stripes looked... striking."

"You mean the one that made me look like a zebra with a ten-foot train? Yes, wasn't it just," I said without any effort to disguise sarcasm.

"However, the plain one was very elegant. I thought you liked it?"

"I did."

"But not enough to buy it?"

Not at that price. "No, not really. Golly, I'm hungry."

"Really," he said, unconvinced, and we went in search of somewhere to eat.

We ended up in a quiet park underneath a lace-work of trees, watching small children play in the sun-dappled shade.

"So, you were telling me about your childhood," I reminded him, munching through an apple to make up for the chocolate and bagel already consumed.

"My childhood, yes. Well, as I said, my grandmother – your namesake – helped bring me up in those initial years after my mother died and before I went to school. I had a tutor of course, so from a very early age I had formal lessons."

I licked my fingers. "In what?"

"Latin, Greek, and French, History, Geography, Mathematics, Music, Rhetoric – and formal lessons in Scripture – that sort of thing – a typical gentleman's education you could call it, except..." A child fell over and he watched and waited until she scrambled to her feet without obvious injury before continuing. "Except my father was always interested in science – or science as we knew it then – so he encouraged me to take an interest in the natural world: to observe, to think, and to draw conclusions based on those observations."

"But what about *cracks* and *bears*?" I asked, remembering the snugly times at bedtime with my mother or Nanna as they read me comforting stories from pastel-coloured picture books. "What about cuddles?"

"Expectations of childhood were different then..."

I humphed, interrupting him. "I know that, but still..."

"... and I was going to say that although it was different, I still felt loved and wanted, if that is what's bothering you. I used to sit next to my grandmother as she worked her embroidery and she would tell me stories of her childhood and that of her parents. And she would sing and sometimes play the cittern or lute if her fingers weren't too stiff – I liked that. She had her solar in the south wing and it was warmer there in winter than anywhere else."

"So you have happy memories of your early childhood?" A football rolled towards us, bumping into my foot. Matthew bent down and threw it back to the waiting boy before answering.

"It was strict and quite regimented, but I found security in that and I always knew where I stood. And there was a certain amount of freedom many children don't have now. There were fewer pressures and I had the run of the estate and no rules on safety apart from not getting myself killed. So there was freedom, and yes, on the whole my memories are happy – perhaps more so than yours because I didn't have the friction with my father that you did."

I didn't want to think about the incessant rows with Dad when he was in one of his black-dog moods. "I was just thinking – can we go to the museum now? Do we have time?"

He shook his head, smiling. "No, we don't – and we don't have to talk about your childhood either, if you don't want to. The Met will take a whole day to do it justice, so I thought we could save it for tomorrow."

7

Waiting Room

"Hurry up!" I all but jumped up and down in the lift but it stuck stubbornly to its sedate descent to the lobby. "Come on, come on," I urged.

"We have all day, there's no rush," Matthew reminded me. "The Met doesn't shut until five-thirty and you'll be dead on your feet by then. Pace yourself a bit."

"But it's already nine…"

"Yes, and it doesn't open for another half-hour; slow down." The lift came to a halt with a refined thump and I shot out as the doors opened, poise and refinement put on hold. "And you haven't eaten enough to keep you going," he called after me. I waved the remains of the muffin I had secreted from breakfast as evidence to the contrary as I crossed the lobby, ignoring Diamond Woman sprawled conspicuously on a gilt sofa. Golly, was that *fur* she wore? It clashed with the fake tan.

I writhed impatiently as Matthew exchanged unhurried pleasantries with our butler (butler, for goodness sake!) who escorted us to the waiting car, but it took only minutes to reach the Metropolitan Museum.

"Where to first?" Matthew asked as I scanned the list of galleries in the entrance foyer that reminded me a bit of the Natural History Museum.

With so much to choose from, I almost salivated. "Well," I began, reading down the list, checking each off on my fingers: "First things first – all the early galleries: Egyptian Art, Greek and Roman Art, then the Middle Ages – this is agony, there's lots – European Paintings, the Textile Center. Where's the Cloister Collection? It's not housed here, is it? Will we have time to see everything? And what about you? What would you... like... to see...?"

Matthew held up a hand as I stuttered to a halt. "Right – stop – I understand your desire to feed your obsession and encapsulate world history in one day, but we won't be able to see everything and you will need to eat at some point, so let's prioritize and we'll go from there." I must have looked horrified at the suggestion that we leave something out, because he grimaced and shook his head in resignation. "All right, but don't overdo it. You had a long enough day yesterday as it is."

"And night," I reminded him.

"And night," he agreed, grinning now, "but it was a great evening. Let's just take today one step at a time."

By the time we had viewed American culture, skimmed Japan and China, and lingered among Arms and Armor, it neared noon. After a sit-down lunch, where he kept me in my chair until I had eaten enough to satisfy him, we headed for the European galleries. He became progressively more reflective as we toured the portraits, until we came to a painting of a thoughtful young man. After a while, I became conscious that his mood had changed perceptibly and a milky-white colour permeated the air around him, like mist, but enveloping, comforting. It wasn't a colour I had seen around him before. My hand found his. "What are you thinking?" He contemplated the picture a moment longer before answering.

"I was thinking that this was a contemporary of mine. We didn't know each other, but we breathed the same air, we ate the same food – yet here I am and there he is – centuries apart, and the only thing that separates us is that he is dead and I am not."

"Does that upset you?"

"Not any more." And he raised my hand and kissed the ring on my finger.

"I love portraits," I said as we moved on to the next. "I like the way they form a tangible bridge with the past, more so than any other art form."

"Perhaps, but they were often painted with an agenda in mind, be it political, spiritual or whatever, nearly always projecting an image of themselves they wanted us to see. It's the ultimate form of hypocrisy. Take this man…" He indicated the image of an Italian banker from the late fifteenth century, his hands together in prayer. "His business was making money, yet to look at him here, he appears more like a priest than a businessman. Where's the honesty in that?" He frowned at him. I thought he was being a tad harsh.

"But that tells us just as much about him in another way. He wants us to remember him as a righteous man, whatever the nature of his livelihood. To him that is more important than being remembered as a merchant. Whether he lived his life as he wanted us to think he did is another matter, but he thought it important enough to commit it in paint." I recalled Matthew's parents' tomb lying against the south aisle of the long forgotten church far away in Rutland where he had been born, of his disfigured image – his face smashed beyond recognition – an outcast in his own community. I thought then of his likeness captured in glass with the rest of his family, immortalized. I shook my head to clear my mind of the memory and moved on to another painting.

"What about this chap?" Matthew said. "It's clear he's a monk and from that we are supposed to determine the man, but do we, other than he's a Carthusian with a dodgy beard and shifty eyes? Is he being any more honest than the banker?"

"Probably not if you put it that way, but who would want to be remembered for their faults? I wouldn't." I wondered how Matthew would want to be remembered by the world if he had a choice: as son, father, surgeon, betrayed nephew to a jealous uncle? Or as a glitch, a misfit, a survivor? He beat me to it.

"Emma, how would you want to be portrayed?"

The question took me by surprise. "I really don't know. It would presuppose anyone would be interested, unless I do something earth-shattering or useful in the future. Having my portrait painted would be pointless, don't you think?"

"Why? Isn't your work worth remembering you for?"

"Not really, no."

"What about your descendants?"

I laughed until I realized he was serious. "Children – you want us to have children, Matthew?"

"Why not? Don't you?"

That was something else I hadn't given any serious thought to. For the time being, the museum galleries were forgotten.

"I don't know. I've never considered myself to be very maternal, and besides, wouldn't it add yet another layer of complication to our already complicated lives and one we could do without?"

"How so?"

"Eventually it would bring more outsiders to the family, more people to know your secret, more risk of exposure to the world."

"Perhaps, but isn't that a risk worth taking and didn't we agree to call them *newcomers*? Isn't it one of the greatest legacies we can leave: our children, and our children's children – people we have loved and nurtured who can bring something good to this world?"

Put that way, he had a point, but he overlooked one thing: Archie's little red face screwing into a full-throttled scream the moment he saw me came vividly to mind. "But Matthew – me, a *mother*?"

He caressed my hair with an expression he wore when he wanted to tell me how much he loved me, but couldn't. "Yes, you. Who better than you?"

We had been alone in our corner with only the watchful eyes of the past to witness our conversation, but now a family of four rounded the corner as if on cue, a tot of about two bouncing on his father's shoulders. The mother lifted the older boy to have a look at a fine Holbein, pointing out the detail on his clothes. The boy jiggled up and down excitedly, and I found myself trying to hear what he said, imagining what I would say if I were his mother and attempting to engage his interest. I smiled.

"I rest my case," Matthew said softly. The family passed us, the older brother now tugging at his mother's hand, impatient to finish with these dead men's faces, irrelevant in his world. We continued our perambulation.

"Have you ever had your portrait painted?" I asked him.

"Once, a very long time ago, shortly before my... *resurrection*." Pain lay behind the word; it still sat uncomfortably after all this time. "My father wanted a portrait in case something happened to me. He never said so, of course, but war had broken out and Death is unpredictable in whom he takes."

"Where is it now?"

"I don't know. Lost – destroyed probably. When I realized I wasn't aging I went back for it some time after my father's death to cover my tracks, but it wasn't there any more. I expect the servants burned it in the hope they would dissociate the household from the taint of my memory – a purge, if you will – a cleansing fire." His mouth twisted.

I hated to see it, to hear the hurt in his voice, and my army of sprites took up arms inside me. "I detest what they did to you and what they had been prepared to do."

His eyes widened. "No, Emma, don't blame them; they were afraid. They lived in fear. It was all around us like a hidden enemy – we never knew when it would surface."

"But you said they purged you, Matthew, like some disease."

"Yes, but I don't blame them. Their reaction was symptomatic of the time. They were ordinary people caught up in it all. You know as well as I do how it was then; you've made it your life's work."

"They had choices, Matthew, just as you or I do. They chose to disown you; they didn't have to."

"And you know what might have happened to them if they didn't. Where would you draw the line to protect yourself, your parents, your children?"

"Loyalty, Matthew – they had a duty to you as their lord. What do we have unless we can depend on those around us? My ancestors' motto was *Loyauté Me Oblige*, but some of them didn't and they betrayed the trust placed in them. Treachery is never right, whatever the circumstances."

"Even if faced with torture and death?" he asked soberly.

"Yes."

"You can be so uncompromising sometimes; would that it were so simple." We had caught up with the little family, the toddler creased with laughter as his brother played hide-and-seek behind his father's legs. "Faced with a choice between protecting your lord, to whom you owe fealty and your livelihood, or your family and children, with whom you have bonds of love and kinship, who would you really choose when it came to it? Don't tell me it would be your master, because I won't believe you. It's an age-old dilemma and I don't suppose it's any easier now than it was then, or a thousand years before that."

An uncomfortable truth, made more so because he had lived it and asked me to understand and forgive those who had betrayed him. I didn't answer and he didn't press me, because we both knew what that answer would be, so I could only stare at my feet and mumble, "I would rather die than betray you."

He tipped my chin with his finger. "Well, let's just hope it's never put to the test. Come on, this is far too serious and melodramatic a conversation for a museum, and we still have to get to The Cloisters before it shuts or I am going to have to work very hard at earning your forgiveness."

As it was, we had a mad rush to make it to the Medieval European section at The Cloisters with barely enough time to do justice to the collection. Occasionally, I would find Matthew lingering near an exhibit lost in thought, and I would wait patiently until he looked up and came back to me, back into our world from wherever he had been. Then he would return my smile and take my hand and move on. Sometimes he told me what he had been remembering, and sometimes he wouldn't and left it to my imagination to work out. There was a tantalizing moment when, with the briefest sideways glance, he tried to whisk me past a display that caught my eye. I dragged him back to get a better look, squinting at the brightly coloured rectangular cards with rounded ends and strange little symbols. "I've never seen anything like these fifteenth-century playing cards, Matthew, a complete set – and the suits – they're different but quite recognizable. I had no idea cards were being played in this form at that date. Did you?" He wasn't even looking, so I tugged at his arm. "Did you, Matthew?"

He almost seemed embarrassed. "Misspent youth," he confessed. "Well, part of it. It's not something of which I'm particularly proud. Home could be very quiet, and my uncle, he... well, despite everything that happened and the inevitable tensions that left between the brothers, despite all that, he was lively company."

I shifted weight from one foot to another. "You were bored," I stated bluntly.

"Yes, I was," he admitted. "It wasn't my father's fault and I don't think it was just my mother's death that made him so. He was a modest man, very temperate in many ways, and my uncle didn't have his responsibility…"

"And was more fun?"

"Yes, and prepared to take risks that seemed immensely adventurous to me at the time – until I grew old enough to see him for what he was: empty, shallow, without thought or regard for anyone else. I must have given my father many a sleepless night."

I lifted a foot off the ground and rotated my ankle to ease the aching. "Like Henry did to you?"

Matthew made a face. "In a manner of speaking."

"Did your father reprimand you? Were you beaten soundly and left chastened and repentant, never to gamble again?"

He gave a short laugh. "Oh no, he was far more subtle than that. He let me make mistakes, find my own way, discover my conscience so that I had nothing to fight against but myself. It must have taken singular strength to do what he did, when he did it. My aunt, Elizabeth, would have taken a rod to me if he had let her. I remember her berating him for spoiling me, saying he would let the Devil take refuge in his son unless he drove him out with daily beating. She mistook his wisdom for weakness. She always had a sharp tongue and she actually crowed when the rumours about me started. We didn't see much of her after that; she didn't want to be *infected*." He shook his head. "Anyway, that was much later. I must have put my father through purgatory before I went to Cambridge and sorted myself out."

"Matthew, do I detect a twinge of guilt?" I didn't need to hear it; I could see it clearly enough.

"Is it that obvious? Believe me, you don't know what you put your parents through until it's done to you." My face must have fallen because he quickly added, "I'm sorry, I didn't mean you; there's also the law of cause and effect. Your father didn't handle you with any great subtlety, did he? You were a sensitive little girl and he gave you reason to rebel. Would you have done so otherwise, do you think?"

"I don't know. I can't ever remember a time when we didn't argue. Would you have handled me differently?"

He brushed my cheek with the back of his fingers, his smile warm. "Absolutely."

I thought it strange that, generationally, he had more in common with the creators of the contents of the displays next to us than he did to me, yet he had more insight into parenting than my own father, who had seemed only a shade off despotic at times. There had been moments when I fancied that Dad had more in common with a Gauleiter.

By the time we arrived back at the hotel, my appetite for antiquity satiated at last, my feet had become leaden blocks and a nagging ache worked all the way up from my legs to my hips and settled in the small of my back. It was at times like these that I seriously envied Matthew's stamina, and opted for dinner in our suite and respite in a hot bath.

I hadn't heard the phone ring.

Screwing the last drops of water from my hair, I emerged from the bathroom. Matthew didn't need to tell me something was wrong. He held my mobile in his hand. I let the towel drop.

"What is it?"

He took what seemed like an age to answer as he came to me and placed his hands on my arms, his eyes dark with distress. "Emma, that was Rob."

My pulse beat raggedly as my breathing shortened and my chest tightened in response. "It's Nanna, isn't it?"

"I'm so sorry. She died a few hours ago; he's been trying to reach you ever since." He still held the shiny mobile. I hadn't thought to take it when we went to the museum. "She died peacefully in her sleep without pain or discomfort."

"Mum... what about my mother?"

"He said she's coping. She was there at the end so had time to say goodbye."

How many times had he broken similar news to grieving families, trying to make the shift from this life to the next easier for them, as he had when he told me Nanna was dying? We had visited her that sleet-laden evening in December and he sensed her approaching death and tried to prepare me. The waiting room – the antechamber to a better life beyond the only one we knew.

I waited for the tears to come, for the overwhelming grief to surge in a black tide, to submerge me as it had when Grandpa died. I waited for the growing awareness, long anticipated, that something so beloved and perpetual as my Nanna had come to an end. Despite her illness, she had always been there. She had been there until a few hours ago and now she was not. She was gone. She was nothing. She was memory.

Matthew said something and put his arm around me, but I couldn't feel it; I couldn't make his words join up. He tried to get me to sit down because I shook, but my knees locked and I couldn't move. I could see the concern in his face, his lovely face, and I didn't want him to worry.

I disengaged his arm. "I'm all right. I just need a few minutes."

I didn't look at him, but sightlessly returned to the bathroom and closed the door.

Lavender's blue... The marble floor beneath me felt as hard and relentless as the throbbing melody pounding my veins, the one Nanna used to sing in the sunny garden days of childhood, when Grandpa was still alive and with a lifetime of song to look forward to. *Lavender's green*... I rested my head against the soft fabric of my bent knees and let the song cycle around and around until it became a wordless stream of images, the images melting into emotions and the emotions, pain. *When I am king, dilly, dilly*... But the pain didn't touch me; it was somewhere else, a separate part of myself – boxed in, contained, controlled. *You shall be queen*... I had to cry; it was the least I could do for her in recognition of all that we meant to each other, of what she meant to me.

In an attempt to feel something, anything other than this nothingness, I dared to conjure Nanna's face, her flyaway hair, her blue eyes glinting with mischief behind her sensible granny specs, the laughter bubbling just below the surface ready to burst from her with the least provocation, the scent of summer flowers she always wore because it reminded her of sunshine and picnics. I reached out and grasped the pain and made it mine, and I felt it – a grief that pierced the very heart of me and became real.

Lavender's blue, dilly, dilly, lavender's green... Nanna, my Nanna – her song was over.

I could feel Matthew's anguish from behind the closed door and he hadn't moved from where I left him. He said nothing but searched my face when I emerged, touching the tip of a finger to the last tear clinging to my eyelashes that I had missed. "End of an era?"

I nodded because it was safer than speaking, and leant against him, welcoming his arms around me now that I had found my grief and made it my own.

8

Happenstance

The sudden shower from the clear sky caught us all by surprise. Matthew moved in closer behind, sheltering me from the squall. Sunlight struck the diamond drops as they fell on the coffin.

"Foxes' wedding," I said, "a sun-shower; Nanna would have liked that."

Beth smiled wanly. "She would have told us to catch the raindrops for luck."

"And make a bridal necklace for our wedding," I added, remembering her laughter as we danced in the falling rain, our hands outstretched and our grandmother clapping in glee. Beth sniffled into her hanky and wiped her eyes and we both looked over to where our mother stood, palely brave, with Dad beside her struggling with an umbrella.

Behind us stood several dozen people who had come to the cemetery to see Nanna safely laid to rest. I had imagined a quiet ceremony. I didn't know how many people she knew, but it was gratifying to see the number who wanted to mark her passing. She would not be easily forgotten.

I leant towards my sister. "Nanna would be sorry to have missed the party."

Beth blew her nose and her voice wobbled. "She would have hogged all the salmon sandwiches." Rob raised an eyebrow, but we either cracked jokes or else we cried, and we both knew which Nanna would have preferred.

After a short silence the vicar resumed the interment. The rain stopped and the sun shone on the upturned cups of lilac crocuses scattered between the graves. I shook the sleeves of my black coat free of the last drops of moisture. I had hoped not to have worn it again so soon after Ellen's death. Listening to Matthew's quiet and steady breathing, I wondered what recent memories this resurrected for him. I found his hand and held on to it tightly.

A small group of sparrows flocked and gossiped in the bare branches of a nearby tree, drowning the vicar with their voices. Beth blew her nose again, distracted. "It's a good thing Archie isn't here. Can you imagine the commotion he would make with such an audience?" She almost giggled. She found this harder than she expected and her emotions were all over the place. She fought more tears and, to prevent my own, I bit my lip until it stung and Matthew tightened his hold on my hand.

It was all over in a few minutes. Most people drifted away after a few words spoken to Mum, eager to be off, not sure what to say but needing to say it anyway. I watched as she responded to each in turn with a little nod, a part smile, and nobody else could see how bleak she felt inside, how angry, how abandoned. One of our neighbours latched on to her. Her head bobbed up and down as she spoke, tight, iron-grey curls bouncing about her perpetually rosy cheeks. I knew her to be devout with a well-meaning enthusiasm that spilled over into every conversation and, whatever she was saying now, Mum's emotional status turned from confused blues into fuming resentment the colour of damsons.

"Wait here. I'll be back in a moment," I said hurriedly as I headed towards them.

"… rise again and be reborn like a butterfly from a chrysalis," our neighbour was saying, fluttering her fingers when I intervened before Mum exploded.

"Hello, Jackie. Thanks for coming; Nanna would have appreciated it. I think Mum's a little tired now and we should be getting home. Would you like a lift?" I put my arm around my mother's shoulders as they vibrated with fury. "Mum, Dad's gone to organize the cars so he won't be long." The woman declined the offer and smiled sympathetically, still nodding happily, her world all sunshine and eternal love.

My mother scowled after her. "Bloody woman – who does she think she is?"

"It's all right, Mum, she means well. The car's on the way. Let's go home."

Her eyes stared and she gripped my arm, her fingers biting through the thick fabric. "Bloody, bloody butterfly – what does she know? What does she know?" Her voice became shrill, and several faces turned to look at us. Her thin frame encased by my arms quaked violently, her face paler than white – bloodless – almost blue.

"It's over now." I sought Matthew for help, but he was engrossed in conversation with Rob, then looked more desperately in the opposite direction to see if Dad might be ready with the car. A number of people walked at a respectably funereal pace down the slight slope towards the gates, but one figure, striding against the tide, steamed towards us. I stopped short, my stomach crunching in recognition.

"Blast," I said before I could stop myself. Mum looked at me in dismay, her anger momentarily forgotten.

"What's the matter, darling?"

I should have foreseen it; I should have known. Making his way purposefully towards us I saw the stringy, grizzled form of my parents' friend, Mike Taylor. Heart racing, I glanced rapidly at Matthew. He had his back towards us and Mike hadn't seen him yet. What were the chances he wouldn't recognize Matthew after all these years?

Don't turn around! I yelled silently at Matthew's back, but too late; he was already turning as he caught the panic in the ether. Instantly wary, he saw the expression on my face. I adopted as genuine a smile as I could manage as Mike reached us, but all he had to do was raise his eyes. I tried to block his line of sight. "Mr Taylor, it's lovely to see you," I began, frantically.

Coming to a standstill in front of us, Mike focused over my shoulder. His jaw slackened. "Good heavens! It can't be..."

I broke his field of vision, pulling Mum with me. "We need to get Mum back home; she's not feeling very well."

"It's impossible," he exclaimed, still staring over my shoulder.

"Emma, darling, what is it?" Mum's voice trembled with spent emotion. "Mike?"

It was out of my hands and I could see no point in bluffing now. Beth and Rob were looking our way, confused, but Matthew was crossing the ground towards us, his expression indecipherable, so I couldn't tell if he recognized Mike or not. He didn't look at him as he approached but offered Mum his arm, and she placed a fragile hand on it gratefully as he spoke quietly to her. "Mrs D'Eresby, the car is ready."

Mike studied him without speaking and, for a second, I thought the charade had worked as Matthew began to lead Mum across the soft ground towards the path.

"Matthew Lynes?"

Matthew stopped, turned, and met the eyes of the older man.

"Matthew Lynes," Mike said again. Matthew assumed a polite smile.

"Yes," he said.

"You don't remember me?" I could tell from the taut line Matthew's mouth made that he did, but his expression remained ambiguous. Rob and Beth joined us.

"Is everything all right?" Beth asked, looking from one man to another.

"I'm sorry, I don't believe we have met," Matthew replied evenly, ready to walk away.

"Do you know Matthew?" Beth continued brightly.

"No, he doesn't," I said too quickly, kicking myself.

"I never forget a face." Mike shook his head. "Thirty years ago, on a video link. You talked me through a heart procedure you pioneered and saved that boy's life – and my career."

Matthew frowned as if trying to remember. "No, I'm sorry; you're mistaken. Excuse me, I must take Mrs D'Eresby to the car." He turned away, but Mike called after him.

"Mike Taylor – thirty years ago – I never forget a face. When Emma mentioned your name, I thought it must be a coincidence, but seeing you now..." He took several steps towards him, studying his features. "You look just the same. You haven't changed."

Blood pounded in my ears and the knot in my stomach tightened until I felt sick. Matthew needed to get away; he needed a distraction. Why didn't he go, leave, run? But he just stood there, calm and composed while he had his identity laid bare before my family.

Matthew – go! I pleaded, and his eyes flicked to mine before he looked back at Mike, and smiled. "It's an extraordinary coincidence, but I suspect you spoke to my father, Mr Taylor. We are very alike and he specializes in cardiology."

It seemed abundantly clear that Mike struggled to accept the story, piecing together his memory until, bit-by-bit, the puzzle would be complete.

Mum's brow furrowed. "Matthew, I thought Hugh said your father's name is Henry. It is Henry, isn't it, Emma? Yes, I'm sure that's what he said."

I opened my mouth but Beth jumped in before I could think of something to say. "That's daft – you would have been about two at the time, Matthew, wouldn't you? Honestly, and I thought Em's maths was bad." She scraped her thick brown hair behind one ear. "Golly, I'm famished. Isn't it lunchtime?"

Heavy feet snapped a winter twig. "Mike," Dad's voice boomed, "I didn't think you could make it." He took Mum's arm as Matthew relinquished her to his care. "Penny, I'll take you home and put the kettle on."

Her peaky face looked up at him. "Matthew's father's name is Henry, isn't it, Hugh?"

He looked nonplussed. "Henry? Yes, it is. Mike, you've met our future son-in-law, Matthew Lynes?" He might have added "the one who messed with my daughter's head", but he didn't need to because Mike remembered perfectly well from our conversation before Christmas when he had been asked to assess my mental state and before I discovered Matthew's true identity.

"I was just saying, Hugh, that I swear I spoke to Dr Lynes some thirty years ago. Either that or he has mastered cloning. And the man I spoke to *was* Matthew, not Henry. A bit of a coincidence, don't you think – same name, same face, same profession?"

I sensed Dad's quickening interest. "Really? That is a coincidence."

Matthew shook his head, and to my surprise, a broad smile replaced the frown. "I'm afraid there's no mystery – my father and I share the same name as well as the same calling. Matthew Henry Lynes: like father, like son – a tradition among some of our families in the States. The confusion was bad enough when I was young, but when I qualified it became impossible. He adopted his second name to preserve his sanity. It's quite understandable how we could be mistaken for one another; we are so similar after all." His voice dropped and smoothed as he spoke, the persuasive tones slipping out woven deceit among willing believers. Everyone stared at him as if mesmerized, the last notes lingering in the silence.

An early bee hummed, breaking the spell. Dad cleared his throat noisily. "He is too," he agreed, "and a damn good surgeon to boot. I expect we're all ready for something to eat. Will you join us, Mike? Penny didn't want a wake so it's just the family."

To my relief Mike took the hint even though Dad hadn't meant it as one. "Thanks, but I won't impose on you." He took in Matthew's distinctive features again, before conceding defeat. "My mistake, Dr Lynes. I'm afraid age is uncompromising; it has a habit of playing tricks as one gets older. As Beth said, it would be ridiculous." He then smiled, wished us luck and, kissing Mum fondly on both cheeks, bade us farewell, taking with him the cloud of suspicion.

"What happens when the lies catch up with you, Matthew?"

We had consumed the simple lunch prepared the evening before by Beth and Rob, and now Matthew and I finished the washing up. My sister was putting Archie down for a sleep, the twins were out with Dad and their father to run off excess energy, and Mum was resting. We had the kitchen to ourselves.

Shirt sleeves rolled up his forearms, his fair skin glistening with soapsuds, Matthew handed me a tureen to dry. "They don't, not very often. It takes two to dissemble, Emma – one to deceive and another to believe the deception. Give people a convenient truth and, more often than not, they'll believe it."

I handed him the old, stapled tureen lid with its worn gold top-knot, remembering, with a wrench, the last time I had seen Nanna lift it off steaming vegetables a year ago – a year ago this Easter. "How many times have you been recognized like Mike did today?"

Sweeping the sponge over the crazed surface, he rinsed the lid and gave it to me. "Not often, but enough to know what is a passing curiosity I can deal with, and what's not."

"And when it's not, what then?"

"Then my choices are limited: to remove the obstruction, or to run."

Obstruction?

The door swung open as Beth, cheerfully replenished by a second glass of wine at lunch, came in with a stray fork. "Is someone going for a run?" She leaned between us and plopped the fork into the water. She picked up a tea towel. "Want a hand? Rob's gone to the café to get things ready for tea. Everyone's always hungry after a funeral – I know I am." Her breezy act fooled no one except the twins; inside she hurt. She wanted to keep busy, but I needed clarity from Matthew.

"No thanks, we're just about finished here. Do you want to see if Mum is up yet?"

She flicked the towel at me. "I know when I'm not wanted. I'll leave you two love-doves alone, shall I? Not for long, though," she flourished a finger. "Dad and I have been plotting, and then there's your dress – I want to know what you're wearing."

I groaned. The wedding. With Nanna's death there hadn't been the opportunity to tell them we were getting married in Maine. This was going to be fun.

"You can't escape, Em; come on, we have to have something to look forward to."

I smiled weakly. "Later, Beth, OK?"

"OK," she shrugged and left us alone.

* * *

"*Obstruction*, Matthew?"

He gave me the fork without meeting my eyes. His arm felt slippery wet under my hand, ominous strength in the unyielding muscles. "*I could kill you so easily*," he told me once. "*I could squeeze the life out of you and no one would know; my secret would be safe.*"

"Remove an obstruction – how?"

He looked at my hand on his arm, and touched the stone of my ring. "In the last resort I will do whatever I have to, to protect those I love."

"You would kill?"

He let the water out of the sink, took the fork from me, and dried it.

"We're done here," he stated, and with that ended the discussion.

I tried not to brood on it and, having watched him ease my mother's grief through gentle conversation, I found it hard to believe him capable of ending someone's life. This considerate, compassionate man, who strove to relieve the suffering of others, was no killer and yet was prepared to kill. I had seen how close he had come to killing Staahl. What would drive him to such extremes again? Where would he draw the line and, once crossed, would there be any way back for him to healing, to acceptance and forgiveness? My fingers sought my cross and, with a sough, remembered its loss. I found a strand of hair instead, and wound it around my finger. Matthew had been a soldier once – he had received orders and, in turn, commanded others in war. He killed in the line of duty; would he do so again autonomously?

"A penny for them, Em?"

"Hmm?" I came to. "Do you think Dad is capable of killing someone, Beth?"

She choked. "Dad? Where did that come from?" She coughed again and I leaned forward to thump her back.

"It just occurred to me that having been in the Army he must have accepted that one day he might have to."

"Yeah, but only under orders, Em. He wouldn't just go out and... kill someone... randomly."

"Does being under orders make it any more acceptable? Isn't it abrogating responsibility?"

Her brow puckered. "I don't think so. Golly, you pick your moments. Look, for what it's worth, I think there are exceptions to the 'thou shalt not kill' rule and one of them is defending what you believe in and your right to believe it. That's what Dad was doing when he was in the Army. I'd kill if I had to."

"You would?"

"I'd kill to defend my family, Em. Wouldn't you? Wouldn't anyone?"

The twins rolled the baby on his back and attacked him with tickles. Who wouldn't want to defend them if push came to shove? But at what cost?

A resounding crash, followed by a string of mild oaths, emanated from the room next door. Beth wearily levered herself to her feet. "That'd be Rob; I'd better go and see what havoc he's wrought this time."

"I'll deal with it, Beth; leave it."

She waved me back. "You look after Arch, I'll clear up. I know who has the better deal."

The baby and I regarded each other warily from across the room. I smiled – he frowned.

By the time Rob called us in for tea, Archie and I had come to a mutual understanding: he wouldn't wail if I didn't try to entertain him, which suited us both. He spent the intervening time beaming at Matthew, which was pretty annoying, but very convenient. He hauled himself unsteadily upright and batted Matthew's knee for attention in much the same way our old cat did to me.

Matthew bent down to pick him up in a movement so natural, so unconsciously normal, it made my attempts to bond with my nephew appear clumsy. The baby snuggled against him, playing with the buttons on his shirt, his eyelids fluttering as he drifted towards sleep.

Archie had just dropped off when Alex accidentally decapitated Barbie against a chair leg. Flora scowled at the mutilated torso, contemplating the choice between exacting biblical revenge on her brother or playing for sympathy from the adults. Clasping the severed head in one hand, Alex eyed his sister, weighing up his chances of survival. I leant over from where I sat and extracted the head and held out my hand for the body. "This reminds me, Flora," I said, scooping the enviably shiny hair from the neck of the doll, "of something Sir Walter Raleigh said just before his execution." Immediately intrigued by the mention of a violent death, Flora forgot to be cross. "He said, '*So the heart be right, it is no matter which way the head lieth*.'" I popped it back in place and viewed the result. "Which is just as well, because I've just put her head on back-to-front." Flora giggled and twisted the doll's head until her chin pointed over her exorbitant breasts.

"That's OK, Emma, her heart and head are in the right place now." She gave me a kiss, then turned around and whacked her brother with the doll.

Yes, I thought, watching the siblings tussle, *for the first time in my life, that's how I feel – my head and my heart are in the right place*. I smiled quietly, realizing the truth of it, and looked up to find Matthew watching me over the baby's sunset hair with an expression of absolute tenderness.

* * *

I went to see Mum in her room and her brittle smile seemed as fragile as eggshell, but her rest had helped even out the dips and bumps of bereavement and now, with the funeral behind her, she had discovered a sad equilibrium on which to ride out her mourning.

"I can't explain how it feels," she said in the few moments when we were alone in her room sitting on the edge of her bed, the old-fashioned eiderdown still rucked from her rest, "but the closest I can come is to describe it as desolation. I feel so alone, Emma – I feel orphaned." Her careworn face crumpled and my heart ached for her because I remembered how it had been after Grandpa died and my world imploded. It hadn't mattered that my parents were still alive, my sister, my family – he had been my glue, and when he died I came unstuck and no amount of fixing could make me whole again. Those cracks had been as evident as fault lines in the earth, scars that only time would erase from the surface, but still apparent in the deep fissures of my psyche. I understood and, as she leant against me and wept, without thinking I reached inside her to where she was drowning, and fed her the new hope I had found.

"There now," she said after a few minutes, wiping her eyes on a little linen hanky and sitting up, "what would Nanna say if she saw me being so self-indulgent?"

"She would say that it's time for a cup of tea and a little something to set the world a-right."

She gave a broken laugh. "She would too, and she would be quite right. I feel much better now, darling – almost back to normal."

"It's OK to be sad, Mum; it'll take time."

Tucking her hanky back in her sleeve, she stood briskly.

"Yes, that's all very well but we have your wedding to prepare for. There's nothing quite like a wedding to keep one's mind occupied. First things first – tea and then plans."

9

In the Dog House

The children stared goggle-eyed. "We didn't know what to do so we did a bit of everything," Beth explained as we scanned the heaving table. "A trad afternoon tea, Lincolnshire-style – for Nanna," she added.

Mum's eyes welled. "Nanna would have loved it, thank you, darlings." She sat in her usual place with her back to the French windows. "I'm not sure if I can do it justice."

Beth adopted her efficient, motherly voice. "No, but you can give it a good go. Places everyone, please. Alex, Flora – wash hands."

Nanna might as well have been sitting there with us, surrounded as we were by all that she loved: her mother's Coalport tea service as dainty as she had been, the silver teapot with the ebony handle and a little dent in the side where Grandpa had dropped it. The Victorian sugar bowl with lion paw feet had been a peace offering, and Nanna had laughed when he had given it to her and said that he could drop the teapot anytime he liked. And one of her favourite pieces – the three-tier cake stand in vibrant pink Beth and I thought she would like one year, when I was about six. We had bought it in the market one Saturday morning and it had taken all our pocket-money. I cried when I chipped it on the way home, but Nanna seemed so pleased and she never failed to use it. She always used lacy doilies, she said, because they looked so pretty against the pink, but I suspected it was to hide the chip. It was covered now in an assortment of delicate cakes and sandwiches – smoked salmon sandwiches with cream cheese on buttered bread cut as thin as cloud and as white. Flora's hand darted out.

"Flora!" Beth remonstrated. "You must wait until Granny says."

Mum stroked Flora's curls. "Poor darlings, you must be so hungry. I wonder if Matthew would mind if we started? Would he think us awfully rude?"

"He said not to wait, Mum. He won't leave Archie until he thinks he's settled."

Beth snorted. "Golly, won't he? I certainly would, little monster. I swear he does it to wind me up. I hope he's not mucking Matthew about. Rob, perhaps you ought to go and check, then he can come and have tea. You can have yours when Arch is asleep."

Rob rolled his eyes and deposited the napkin he had just unfolded back on the table. "Thanks," he said, his soft Scottish lilt now heavily laced with good-humoured sarcasm. "And there was I thinking Matthew could do with some practice with kids and I could do with something to eat." He pushed his chair back from the table, but I blocked his exit.

"Matthew's fine, Rob. He'll join us when he can. There's no point both of you missing tea and he said he's not that hungry."

Rob sat down and picked up his napkin again. "Matthew didn't have any children with his first wife, did he? That would make you a stepmother." He obviously found the idea amusing.

Mum offered Flora a sandwich as the child's hand wavered over a petite lemon-iced cake. "Sandwich first, darling; there're no crusts, so your wobbly tooth will manage quite nicely. Poor thing, to lose his wife so young."

"He's used to children; he has two nephews and a niece," I dodged, wondering if I could change the subject. "Great sandwiches; did you make them last night?"

Beth tutted. "Honestly, Em, you haven't a clue, have you? Rob made them this afternoon. They'd be stale otherwise."

I found it exhausting fielding questions and still felt drained after the flight the previous day. It was bad enough having to keep up the deception over Matthew's peculiarities, but keeping the details of his family, the trial, and my sudden near-fatal encounter with the coffee played havoc with my brain. Like elastic, tea in our family traditionally stretched endlessly. I peeked at my watch. I envied Archie, now probably fast asleep. Matthew would only be able to stay away for so long.

Rob asked me a question.

"Sorry, I didn't catch that, Rob."

"I said, what does Matthew drive?"

I smiled artlessly. "A car." Alex and Flora went into fits of giggles.

"Right, OK, Miss Quick-Wit, I suppose I asked for that. What sort of car?"

I cocked my head, thinking. "It's quite small, dark shiny red – and has two doors..."

"Sounds like a Fiat Panda, Em," Beth guffawed.

"It might well be for all I know. It's a dee-bee-something or other." I could see Dad eager as a boy to tell him. "Ask Dad. He knows." Rob swapped chairs with me so that he and Beth could discuss cars and engine capacities with Dad in tones usually adopted by religious adherents.

"Beth," Mum called, and reluctantly she joined us in a cohort at one end of the table. Mum grasped each of our hands. "Girls, while the men are otherwise engaged – Flora and Alex, this concerns you as well… Some time ago, before Nanna became ill, she gave me a few things to give to you in case anything happened." She held our hands more tightly and we smiled in support. "They are just little things, but they meant a lot to her and she wanted you to have something to remember her by." She let go and bent sideways to a crocheted bag by her chair and took from it small, regular-shaped packages, wrapped in cheerful paper with a tag. She handed us one each. I read my name in Nanna's careful writing, a little spindly with age, as she had become. "Open them now, darlings. She had a message for each of you."

"What about Archie?" Alex asked.

"There's something for him too, for when he's old enough not to chew it."

Alex nodded, justice deemed to be served, and opened his parcel. A slight movement of air caused me to look up as Matthew slid into the chair next to me. I pushed my empty cup and a plate with a partly eaten sandwich in front of him for appearances' sake.

"We're having presents from Nanna," I told him, then more quietly, "You were an age getting Archie to sleep – how long did it take, one minute or two?"

He grinned. "Thirty seconds, if that. I was making a couple of calls. I seem to have missed tea."

"So you have. What is it, Alex?" My nephew had become very quiet. Dark eyes peeped through floppy hair.

"It's a medal – look." He held it out. It was Grandpa's Victoria Cross.

Mum lifted it from its case and held it in her palm. "He won it for trying to rescue a young sapper when they came under enemy fire as they bridged a river. One of the soldiers became stuck in the mud. It was very slippery, you see, and the boy kept sliding back into the river and was becoming weaker by the minute. Shells were landing all around them, but Grandpa went back for him. That's when he was wounded."

"What happened to the soldier?" Alex wanted to know.

"Grandpa couldn't save him. He was always very sorry about that, but he stayed close by until he died so that he wouldn't be alone. Nanna wanted you to have his Victoria Cross because she said that you would always do the right thing, Alex, and you reminded her so much of your great-grandfather." He sat back in his chair, fingering the medal, lost in thought. "Now, Flora… goodness gracious, what are you doing!"

"I'm a warrior princess. Daddy, Matthew – look at me, I'm a princess!" Flora announced, flashing a large silver letter-opener with a mother-of-pearl handle over her head like a sabre. Alex ducked just in time.

Beth grabbed her hand. "Put it down before you kill someone!"

"But I'm a warrior," Flora moaned.

Mum smiled indulgently. "Nanna always used this to open her letters in the morning, just as her mother did before her. It was given to her by your great-great-grandmother, and it was very special, so she wanted you to have it."

Flora's lower lip quivered. "Nanna was a princess too," she snuffled. "Can you be a princess in Heaven?"

Rob ruffled her hair. "Of course you can, Bubble. You take the best of yourself to Heaven."

"So I can take Barbie?"

Her father grimaced. "I'm not sure that's quite what I meant, Flora."

"No, I know," she said primly, "but I thought I'd ask anyway."

Rob refilled our cups as Beth opened the brown leather box. "Isn't that Nanna's pearl necklace?"

"Grandpa gave it to her when I was born," Mum said, "and she always wanted my first-born to have it. You know what it meant to her, don't you, Elizabeth?" The string of pearls, like little moons, gleamed against the silk lining. Mum stroked her hand. "There, it's all right, don't get upset. Do you have a hanky? I have a spare one. Now, Emma, what about your present?"

I had already opened mine, easing open the lid of the box when no one was looking and wordlessly slipping the elegant watch over my wrist. She had worn it up to the day she became ill.

"Grandpa gave it to Nanna on their wedding day and she wanted you to have it. She always knew you would find someone special one day." Her eyes drifted to Matthew, resting briefly on his wheat-gold hair, the exact colour of her father's, and then back to me. "Well now, that's enough of the past. There's the future to consider and a wedding to arrange. Have you decided on St Mary's or St Martin's? You've left it rather late; May is such a popular month for weddings. What are we going to do if the churches are fully booked?"

The change in conversation wrong-footed me. All I could do was flounder as I lined up excuses ready to be fired in our defence.

"Hang on, Mum, you don't even know if Emma and Matthew want a church wedding."

"Well, of course they do, Beth – don't you, Emma?" Not waiting for an answer she rushed on. "Matthew, you're not Catholic, are you? It gets awfully complicated, but I'm sure something can be sorted out. Oh," she suddenly thought, "you don't belong to one of those peculiar sects Emma used to tell us about – you know, darling, the ones who left after the Civil War and started new colonies in America."

"No, I don't," Matthew said, trying to keep a straight face, "nor am I Catholic. I'm nothing more exotic than an Anglican. However, we…"

"Thank goodness for that," Mum butted in. "Mixed marriages can work of course – Rob's Church of Scotland, after all – but it can place an additional strain on a relationship and there are enough of those in life as it is. Oh dear, I'm prattling, aren't I? I'm so sorry, it's just this is so exciting after everything else." She tailed off, smiling apologetically and making me feel even more guilty, if that were possible.

Dad replaced his cup and continued the mugging for her. "The thing is, Emma, it took months to organize Beth and Rob's wedding..."

"Nearly a year," Beth amended.

"Nearly a year, and leaving it this late might mean we have to make certain compromises about the venue."

Matthew frowned and leaned forward. "Emma and I have decided..."

"... to marry in the States," I finished, to deflect the flak from him. "I'm sorry, I meant to tell you before, but the time never seemed right. I'm sorry," I said again, becoming scarlet. A silver spoon rattled as it fell on the table.

Mum broke the silence first. "You can't possibly!"

Dad's eyebrows gathered. "Daughters should marry from home, Emma. All the D'Eresby women have married from home." He rounded on Matthew. "Young man, this is out of the question..."

"But I want to be a bridesmaid!" Flora wailed.

Beth shook her head. "We can't afford the air tickets for all of us. I think Arch might travel free, but the rest of us..."

Dad barked over the rising commotion. "It's bad enough you living in the States, but marrying there... this is inconsiderate of you both, especially you, Matthew. I'm sure you're quite aware of this country's traditions even if you are from America."

I jumped to my feet in burgeoning temper. "Dad, that's unfair, leave him alone. Listen…"

"What would Nanna say?" Mum quivered, dissolving into tears. "We've been so looking forward to this."

Dad brandished his finger, the old tyrant back again. "You haven't thought it through; it's totally selfish."

Flora began to cry and Beth tried to comfort her and Mum at the same time. Rob stood behind them, bewildered. "Why can't they decide where they want to marry?"

"Quiet, Rob," Beth snapped. "Emma, it's not practical."

"It's your duty to your family. It's a disgrace," Dad scowled, leaning on his knuckles, his shoulders hunched to his ears. Matthew rose to defend me.

"No, Matthew, leave it, please," I cautioned him. "Will you all listen…"

Flora sobbed and Alex drew up his legs, hands over his ears, and started rocking back and forth. Emotion the colour of bitter chocolate choked the air. Enough was enough.

"SHUT UP, *ALL* OF YOU!"

Beth gasped. Alex ceased rocking.

"This is my decision, so don't blame Matthew. He wanted us to marry here but I persuaded him to get married in the States."

"Why, darling?"

"Because…" I couldn't think of any cogent reason that would explain my decision. "Because I want to, Mum." It wasn't much of an explanation, but I couldn't tell them the truth. I couldn't tell them that I wanted Maggie to be there, that it wasn't right that Matthew's granddaughter wasn't part of the family event and that marrying from home as I'd always wanted would exclude her because she was too ill to travel that far. I couldn't explain that I was taking the place of her beloved grandmother, and that it was the least I could do to offer this token of peace and to lay some foundation on which to build a future relationship for all our sakes. I had found it hard enough to explain to Matthew, who at least knew the circumstances, but to tell my family was nigh on impossible. I made him promise not to tell, and he stood by the table now, struggling to keep his word in the face of the criticism being flung at me.

Mum wavered. "But your family…"

"Matthew has a family too. Besides, the arrangements have been made."

"But…"

"And I won't change my mind," I added just in case anyone thought I might.

"I want to be your bridesmaid, Emma. You said I could."

"And you will, Flora, but it will be in America, not here, that's all. And you don't have to worry about the tickets or anything, Beth, because that's all taken care of."

It was Rob's turn to sound doubtful. He had his pride even if he found it difficult to make ends meet sometimes. "I won't have you paying for our flights."

"No, of course not, but the jet needs to be flown regularly, so this is as good an opportunity as any."

My father eased his neck in his starched collar. "The jet?"

"Yes, Dad."

"And the church has been booked?"

"All done."

"What about the reception? And guests – what about invitations?" Mum asked.

I sat down, sensing the worst was over. Dad sat too. Matthew remained standing, his fingers tense on my shoulder. I put my hand over his. "We were wondering if you would mind helping with those? And Dad, we really would like a traditional wedding cake, but they're difficult to come by in the States."

His face slowly returned to its more normal buff. "And you thought we might make you one?"

"Please."

"I'll have to look out your grandmother's recipe, and there's barely enough time for it to mature, but for you," he relented, "we'll see what we can do."

Beth's disappointment still leached from her. "We were so looking forward to organizing the food, weren't we, Dad? Who's going to do that now?"

I crossed my fingers under the linen tablecloth, then as an afterthought crossed my ankles as well. "Pat – Matthew's mother," I barely wavered at the lie, "has all that in hand. It'll be a joint effort between you."

"Oh."

"What I really need help with though, Beth" – she looked up hopefully – "is my dress."

Feathers were gradually settling back into place although, now and again, Mum shot a wounded look in our direction. Dad and Beth were finishing some of the food and packing away the bits they couldn't eat, and Rob had gone up to check on Archie, when Flora sidled up to Matthew. She regarded him shyly, with Barbie in one hand, a pink cupcake in the other. "Matthew," she lisped, offering the cake, "I've saved this one for you."

He knelt down and took it from her outstretched hand. "Thank you, Flora, that's very kind of you. Will you mind if I keep it for later?"

"That's OK," she said, "I know you won't eat it; you never do."

10

Going Home

Matthew wasn't next to me when I woke the next morning, nor could I find him downstairs. He had put away the bedding he was supposed to have used and by my cup on the breakfast table had left a cryptic message: *gone fishing*.

I was still puzzling over it when Mum came in with her cereal. She looked weary, but had lost the desperate, haunted look of the day before. "Matthew's an early bird, isn't he? He'd already finished breakfast when I came down this morning at about six. He's very thoughtful, Emma, I must say – he'd put his things away." It was her way of saying she accepted our decision, even if she didn't like it. "It took your father years to learn to tidy up after himself. He was always leaving cupboard doors open. I feel sure it was his way of rebelling against Army discipline. I only wish he had rebelled a little sooner and got it out of his system. I found the egg rages most difficult." She smiled regretfully.

Dad and his rages. He had raged over the colour of his morning egg, and over the brand of sausages she bought. He raged if his egg was too runny, or a mite too firm. But most of all, he raged at me. Mum bore the brunt of it, caught in the crossfire with Nanna. Together they acted as mediators, interpreters, and between them kept a smouldering peace.

Mum added milk to her bowl without looking up. Trapped in the sheltered courtyard, the wisteria unveiled its first lilac frond. Each year Nanna would say it was the harbinger of spring and we would all chorus that she said that about every spring flower. All around us were poignant reminders of her vitality.

"I miss her too, Mum."

"I know Nanna hadn't been at home for months, but she was always *here*, and now she isn't. I'm finding that hard at the moment; it's so silly of me. No, stay there, darling. I don't think I can handle any sympathy this morning. I need to get back on track." She found her hanky, holding it to her nose until the urge to cry passed and I sat back down feeling superfluous. "I'm sorry if I overreacted yesterday, Emma; I'm just disappointed. I think we were all looking forward to getting busy with the wedding arrangements and it would have made her passing a bit easier. If only she could have lived a little longer and seen you married she would have been so happy for you." Her voice quavered. Finally she squared her shoulders and her resolve. "There now, it can't be helped."

No, it couldn't. If anyone could have swayed me it would have been my mother, but I had thought long and hard over my decision and, try as she might, I wouldn't change it now. I would, however, do what I could to make it easier for her. "I've been racking my brains who to invite, Mum. Any ideas?"

She needed no further encouragement and rattled through a list of names of distant relatives I had barely heard of, let alone met. "… and then there's Cousin Betty from Lytham St Annes. She moved away donkey's years ago. I wonder if she's still alive? What about Matthew's side? You'd better make me a list."

A list. That meant committing the lie to paper. She looked behind me as I debated the wisdom of such an action. "There you are, Matthew; we were just discussing your family."

"We're making lists for the invitations," I clarified quickly. He bent down to kiss me, smelling of sharp Fenland air. Mum continued writing names on the back of a gas bill. She ceased, pencil poised in transit.

"Darling, what about Joan Seaton? She was such a friend to Nanna. She sent a lovely letter – have you seen it? Here…" She went to the high mantelpiece and fished out a letter folded in thirds from behind the row of consolation cards. "*Consultation cards*" I used to call them when little and before I knew any better. I opened it, visualizing the spry sparrow of a woman as she unwittingly revealed Matthew's story to me in the fragmenting realm of her home.

In writing as fragile as gossamer, she apologized for not attending Nanna's funeral, blaming extreme age and her unwilling son in equal measure in terms that made me smile. Matthew read it with me. I let my finger rest under the address – Old Manor Farm, Martinsthorpe – and he nodded once, briefly.

"Mum, I think Mrs Seaton would find the journey to the States a bit much."

"Oh, yes, probably." She sat back and put her pencil down. "I'm afraid that's going to be the case for most of the family. There are so few of us left now, and what there are, are mostly too old or ill to travel. That's what comes of an only child marrying an only child – the slow extinction of a family. You girls are the last D'Eresbys, and I am the last Chapman. Such a shame. Still, I've never dwelt on it; that's more your father's line. Matthew, do you have the list for me?" He handed her another envelope, his graceful copperplate dignifying the scruffy edge. She read it. "Is Daniel your brother? And Joel and Harry are your nephews and Ellie your niece? Your father must be so pleased to have grandsons as well. How lovely." I steeled myself. I could see where this was going. "Perhaps you'll have children one day…"

"Mum," I cautioned.

"Your father would be so pleased. Nowadays it's quite usual, you know, to give the children the mother's name..."

"That's it, we're off," I said, standing rapidly and grabbing Matthew by the hand. "No baby talk, Mum. You promised."

"Did I?" she was saying as we left the room. "I don't seem to remember..."

We reached the stone-flagged hall suppressing laughter. "Are you sure you want to marry me? Just think of it – daughters are supposed to turn into their mother."

He grinned. "Your mother's just a bit anxious at the moment and, don't forget, you're half your father."

I buried my face in my hands. "Don't remind me. What a combination! It's not too late to change your mind."

He trapped me against the wall, making his intentions abundantly clear. "Oh, believe me, it is. You know how seriously I take my vows," he said, kissing down my neck and raising goose-pimples on my arms. The smaller of the two stuffed pike frowned down on us. I pushed halfheartedly at his chest, trying not to laugh.

"Not here. You don't know who might be watching! So where did you go this morning?" I asked as a key turned in the front door and Dad came in with the newspaper and a bunch of daffodils. Tiberius dashed past him and up the stairs, where he stopped to wash a white paw.

Matthew ran his hand through his hair. "I went for a walk."

"Old haunts?"

He narrowed his eyes. "That's one way of putting it. And then I went to church."

Dad took his time hanging up his coat. I drew Matthew into the sitting room out of earshot.

"Which one?"

"All Saints – does it matter? It has different glass and the pews are new, but that's about it. Not much has changed since I last went," he calculated, "three hundred and sixty-six years, six months and fourteen days ago, depending on which calendar system you're using."

"Not that you've been counting."

"I've had time on my hands. Anyway, I had a chance to reflect, which brings me to what I want to ask you." He still held Mrs Seaton's letter. He looked at it now as if it contained some great revelation – or burden. Dad passed through on his way to the next room, accompanied by Tiberius, ever hopeful for food, and Matthew waited until the door closed behind him. "Emma, I want to go home... I mean, I want to go back to Martinsthorpe – before we leave for the States, before it's too late." He stood there stripped of certainty, suddenly defenceless. "Please, Emma, I need to see where it happened, where it all began."

Sometimes we cannot move forward without going back. How circumstances had changed. Mine. His. Who would have predicted it; who could have known how topsy-turvy our world would become. That little twist of fate that brought me to the same road down which I had driven four months before, and in circumstances so different that I hardly recognized the person I had been then. Only the landscape looked familiar: brown ploughed fields and blunt hedgerows, and trees ready to green. He sat quietly in the seat next to me, a moment waiting to happen.

"I'm not sure how close we can get."

He didn't take his eyes from the land. "Close enough. It's about a mile and a half from the church, with farm tracks that'll take us near the river. We can walk from there."

He folded the map he had been studying and tucked it inside his coat pocket and resumed his familiarization of the surrounding countryside. He had become increasingly pensive as we left Stamford and joined the main road west of the town and headed towards Oakham. He barely queried the expansive new reservoir but, as we entered Oakham and drove slowly through the old centre, past the school, and through the market place where the stocks raised in him a wry smile, his expression changed as he found landmarks he recognized. We headed south, turning down the road through Brook and towards the extinct hamlet that had been his home.

The day felt damp after morning rain, but the sun now shone thin and clear in the unfurnished sky. I parked the car in an indent of the narrow track and waited until Matthew found his bearings. Winter wheat stubbled the field around which we edged until we met the contorted line of the river where decades of tractor wheels had cemented the ground into an incidental path.

At first we kept a measured pace, the only sound our breathing, but then his stride lengthened until I almost ran to keep up. He waited for me. "I'm sorry," he said, as I caught up with him, but all the while his restless eyes searched. "It's not far now."

"It's all right," I said, drawing air and waving him on. "You go ahead, don't wait for me."

We came to a moderate slope rising from the river towards uneven ground. I heard his sharp intake of breath, sensed his sudden hunger. "Matthew, go!" I insisted, and long-limbed and fleet as a deer, he covered the field to the crest of the slope and in seconds, was gone.

When at last I made the rise, he stood as still as the withered bushes on the banks below. Loss bled from him like treacle. He turned when he heard my approach, hollow-eyed, adrift. "There's nothing left, Emma; it's all gone."

"I know, darling." I enclosed him in my arms, holding him, his face concealed in the folds of my hair, until his dejection melted into mere sorrow and from sorrow to resignation.

"I didn't know what to expect – ruins, rubble even – but not this." He kicked at a lump of masonry. It dislodged from the mud and rolled sullenly to a halt in the young wheat, fringed in green. He bent to retrieve it, brushing soil from the soft grey-gold of the stone. Smooth on one side, the mason's saw marks were still evident on the cut face of the stone. "Even in winter the walls were made of sunshine," he remarked, laying the stone to rest among the broken remains of his home. He swept his arm along an imaginary line. "This marks the outer walls, and over here…" – he strode to a section of uneven ground – "… must have been where the gatehouse stood. Yes, look…" He jumped from a deep ripple in the ground long years of ploughing had failed to erase and along the dent it made. "This was the moat; it leads all the way around and joins up with the river and fish ponds. Come, I'll show you." His face brightening, he began to rebuild his memories. "The road approached the house from over there. It meant that anyone nearing could be seen from the gatehouse from a quarter of a mile away. We kept the ground free of trees and undergrowth so we had full view of all the land between here and our cousins, the Seatons – over there." He pointed in the direction of Old Manor Farm across the fields. I could see the tips of the trees that surrounded the building, but nothing more. "Well, we could from the top of our walls anyway. When my forebear originally built the house, the course of the river ran further to the east. A body of men would be forced by the moat and the river to make the approach no more than four abreast. It made them easier to pick off that way." He smiled grimly. "As long as you knew they were coming, that is."

Shading my eyes, I circled slowly, taking in the lie of the land and the subtle swellings over which the young crop grew, bearing testament to what lay beneath. "And you didn't have enough time the night you were attacked?"

"No, the gatekeeper was an old man, a loyal retainer my father kept on. He had fallen asleep, and by the time he raised the alarm it was too late. Enough of my uncle's men had crossed the squeeze-point and gathered along the moat over here." He stood with his back to the sweep of land and opened his arms to encompass the moat and bridge, with the gatehouse rising in his memory beyond. "There wasn't much room for them to manoeuvre, but there was enough." He held out both hands to me and I leapt the little distance across the collapsed moat to be caught securely by him. "We had gates, but no portcullis, and the bridge was designed to be raised in the event of an attack but, as it was, by the time we had manned the walls the weight of men on the bridge meant we couldn't lift it."

I took in the distance between the bumps of the fallen walls and the far side of the moat.

"But they were within range, surely, and they had burning torches. Didn't that make them easier to pick out?"

"Torches? Yes, they had a few, I suppose, but not enough to make them easy to identify."

"But Nathaniel said the sky was alight with them."

"Did he? It's not how I remember it, but I was too preoccupied at the time to take much notice. They were easily within range, but we were loath to open fire. William was my uncle after all, and this had been his home. If we could have come to some peaceable arrangement, we would. We didn't know he would attack – it wasn't clear at that point. I had the household maintain defensive positions here..." he pointed to his left, "... and here," to his right, "and we placed the falconet – the small cannon – at this point, here." He stepped into a clear area of ground. "We had a small arsenal and I had the staff trained to a fair degree. I'd seen what happened to undefended manors and I wasn't prepared to let that happen to ours. But... but then we always thought we would know our enemy. We never suspected... we never thought... damn it, Emma, my own uncle – my father's brother!" His agitation spread in the keening wind that lifted my hair like a pennant around my face. I tamed it brusquely.

"The enemy within, Matthew."

He smiled bitterly. "Quite."

A harsh cry like a klaxon rose above our heads as a ring-neck pheasant took flight. We followed it until it dropped from view beyond the river. It had given him time to compose himself and he resumed the conversation.

"When I was wounded, they brought me through here" – together we passed under the imaginary arch of the gatehouse – "and then into the courtyard and across to the main house." We walked the short distance together, "... through the great door, past the buttery and pantry to our left, towards the stairs, and up into the wing of the house where my quarters were. Of course," he added, "I was unconscious at the time and... well, you know what happens next."

"You live long and prosper," I said softly.

He half-smiled at the quote. "If you can call a life spent largely alone and forever on your guard prospering, then I suppose I did."

He spent a moment studying the humps like mole tunnels that marked where the walls once stood. His hand traced a shape in the air next to him. "When I was a boy, I used to imagine that the lion carved on the stair newel supporting the family shield – about here – would come alive at night and pace the grounds on guard like our dogs." He looked thoughtful. "I think my father might have had a hand in fostering that idea. Anyway, it was a comforting thought. I used to pat the lion every time I went past. I don't think I was the only one – he had a wonderfully glossy mane."

"Like yours." I reached up and touched his hair lightly. He captured my hand and pulled me towards him and over the crumpled ground. "Let me show you the Great Hall, Mistress D'Eresby, if you will."

Standing in an open field, a carpet of green beneath our feet, he conjured the walls and windows around us, the arras behind the dais, the table at which he sat with his father and grandmother, and it felt as alive and real as he did, and as vivid. For the moment, his uncle's betrayal lay forgotten and lost in happier memories. Finally, he took one last look around over the rolling land and the outlines of his home buried beneath it. "I wish you could have seen it. New Hall was modest, but fine in its way, and my home. And I wish you could have met my father – you would have liked him and he would have loved you as his daughter." And he bent and kissed my brow, bestowing his father's blessing in that one, simple, archaic gesture.

"That wasn't as bad as it might have been," he said philosophically as we reversed down the track until I found a gate in which to turn. I wasn't so sure. If finding his obliterated home had shaken him, how would he react when it came to seeing what waited for him in the church?

"Matthew, are you sure you want to go to the church? It's not as you remember it; some things have changed – things you might not like."

"I have to do this," he said quietly.

We followed the deeply rutted road as it curved, displaced water spraying the tattered vegetation on either side. The gates to the old house came into view as we rounded the bend.

"Emma, look out!"

As I slammed on the brakes, the steering wheel span out of my hands. He grabbed it and the car skidded to a halt, my heart racing with the engine. Mere feet away the deer looked at us calmly, shook her russet flanks, and nimbly leapt through a gap in the hedge.

"Shoot!" I squeaked.

He raised an eyebrow. "Possibly, but I think you'll find you need a gun rather than your father's car. If you wanted venison, you only had to ask."

"Oh ha, ha," I grumped, angry with myself for my lapse in concentration.

"The unexpected happens, Emma. It wasn't your fault."

I shoved the gearstick into first and nosed the car around until it was more or less straight, letting the wheels find a purchase before easing us forward again. "That was stupid of me. I should have been more careful."

"Well, as I said, the unexpected happens." Somehow I didn't think he was referring to our near-accident.

We passed through the stone gateposts with the iron gates lying haphazardly aside, and down the long drive now graced with daffodils bobbing and curtseying as we passed. We drew up in front of the remains of the gatehouse, giving him time to remember. After a minute I asked, "Ready?" and he answered by opening his door and climbing out. *He might think he is*, I thought, *but am I?*

On the doorstep next to last summer's bedraggled pelargonium, of which now only a brown stump remained, I placed the bowl of shining narcissi I had bought that morning, and knocked on the gnarled oak door. Matthew examined the exterior. "This is close to what I remember, though that part of the wing looks different and this oriel window is new." By "new" he meant it was four hundred years old, rather than six. "The range of barns we saw has been expanded as well. It looks like they extended the original barn by quite a bit. The manor must have gone through a prosperous phase after the war."

I knocked again and stood back. "Did you visit often?"

"Quite a bit. We were on good terms with the Seatons and we came to church here regularly as well, although it stood apart from the house then, of course, and the village was bigger." He disappeared around the side of the new wing to investigate just as the door began to open.

Her silvered hair a little awry, Joan Seaton's wren face popped around the edge of the door, her cautious smile becoming bright as she saw me. "Emma, my dear, how lovely to see you again." She opened the door wide and stepped over the threshold, her long necklace of jade beads swaying as she moved. "You look much better than when I saw you last; you have some colour in your cheeks. Oh," she said, disappointed, "but you're all alone. I thought you were bringing someone to see me. No matter, come along in anyway."

"Hello, yes I have, but he's exploring. I'm sure he won't be a moment. Thanks for letting us come over at such short notice."

"My dear, you know how few visitors I have. In the last few months since you came, I've only seen the postman, that lovely young man who delivers my groceries – he always stops for a chat on a Thursday – and that other one." I waited for her to expand on "the other one" but she didn't. "And my son, of course, when he remembers he wants something." Whereas when I had last seen her she had been nimble and quick, today she leaned on a silver-topped cane for support, and her movements were hesitant. She saw me looking. "I had a little fall in the snow. It has quite put me out of sorts, but I'm on my feet again." She laughed. "Oh, gracious no, only one of them. Our roles are reversed since last time, it seems, and now I'm the fragile one. Do you think this young man of yours will be very long? Only I'm not quite the woman I once was, you see, and... oh, my dear!" She gasped and I pivoted to see what had made her eyes shock open, to find Matthew materialized behind me.

"Mrs Seaton, I apologize for keeping you waiting." The sun struck his hair as he bowed low over her hand. "Matthew Lynes, ma'am."

Eyes fixed on his face, her pulse visibly beating under the thin skin of her neck, she pulled herself together enough to answer, "Yes, but of course you are." She continued to stare, then straightened her back. "I'll lead the way. Don't trip over the cat."

We entered the dim outer hall, Matthew taking in the details and steadying me as I nearly tripped over the bundle of fur lying by the door. I took the opportunity to say, "You old charmer."

He looked surprised. "I believe it used to be referred to as *courtesy*."

The inner hall felt hollow somehow, and not just old, but shabby. Even the spring sun appeared drab as it struggled through the stained glass of the stair window. Dust delineated where the inlaid marble table once stood in the centre of the worn stone flags. It looked abandoned and unloved, and the Gurney radiator sat stolid and cold to one side.

Her hand flitted towards the void. "I'm finding myself a little short now and again, so my son, Roger, sells some family things for me – just a few to tide me over until such time as I no longer need it." She smiled with regret. "They never seem to fetch as much as I would hope, but there – times have changed and you young people don't always like old things, do you?"

I suppressed a welter of dismay at the pillaging of her world.

"We certainly do," I countered, noticing that the fine Georgian long-case clock no longer stood where it once did.

We entered the great hall and behind me I heard Matthew's subdued exclamation as he recalled it at once, although cobwebs formed curtains over the windows and only a small fire burned in the grate.

"Mrs Seato..." I began.

"Joan, my dear, please."

"Joan, do you have anyone to help you?"

"Roger says I can't afford it, so I have to make do and I haven't been able to do as much as I would like since my fall. I know it is such a mess, but I don't look at it, you see, and then it isn't there."

Behind me, Matthew muttered, "I know what I would like to do to her son."

"Shh, she'll hear you."

"Then at least she'll know someone cares," he growled, but quieter this time.

Joan still rambled as she shuffled over to one of the pair of sofas and sat carefully down by the fire. "Roger says the paintings will fetch quite a bit, but they are family, and I can't find it in me to let them go – not yet, anyway. Once the furniture's gone, he wants to start on the silver. Some of it is quite old, you know. My husband was very proud of it – it's been in his family for generations." She looked into the flames with an expression of longing. "For generations," she said again. "Now, come and sit down and tell me what it is you wanted to see."

We sat opposite her, avoiding the broken springs in the sagging sofa, and described how we wanted to research Matthew's family.

"I can certainly see the family resemblance, my dear; it's quite remarkably strong. And all this time my husband thought the Lynes family had died out. From whom do you say you are descended?" she asked Matthew directly.

He reverted to the cover-story we agreed before we came, more comfortable steering as close to the truth as we dared. "I believe the family's been traced back to Matthew Lynes of New Hall."

"But that's just a few miles from here, although I'm afraid little remains of it now. It was a fine house in its day, I believe. My husband had a picture of it from the 1680s, I think… or was it? It was after the Restoration anyway. Would you like to see it?"

"Very much," he replied.

"So for all these years the Lynes have been alive and well in – where did you say you come from?"

"I live in Maine."

"Do you? It's strange but you don't sound like an American to me; perhaps that is Emma's influence. You know what happened to Matthew Lynes in 1643 and how his uncle betrayed him?"

"Yes, Emma's told me."

"And how he survived, but rumours circulated about him – rumours that spread until it was no longer safe for him to remain, and he left?"

"Yes."

"But no one knows where he went and it was supposed that the family died out. Well," she tapped the arm of the sofa in triumph, "now we know better! So, you say that he went to America? What my husband would have done to have met you! Oh, and your dear grandfather, Emma. Those two spent endless hours secreted with papers and such things, researching, researching until goodness knows what time of night – and sometimes into the morning as well. Your grandfather, Douglas, even brought a research assistant with him one time – one of his students – I don't remember the name, but then I don't remember as much as I used to." She shivered, and pulled the knitted jacket around her shoulders. "I feel the cold more than I did. Getting old isn't much fun, my dears, as your Nanna used to say. I'm so sorry I wasn't there for her funeral yesterday. How is your mother getting on?"

"She's coping," I said. "I think it's more difficult for her because it's her second parent. She feels lost, but she has Beth and the children and that helps. They've been marvellous, and she really appreciated your letter, thank you."

"Did she? I'm glad. I expect she's looking forward to the wedding?" Her eyes twinkled. Although we hadn't said anything, my ring had probably been a bit of a giveaway.

I felt myself colour. "Oh, yes."

Matthew built up the fire with the meagre supply of logs he found next to it. He put the fire irons back in a place where she could reach them easily, and she watched the lithe grace with which he moved, and it seemed to jog her memory. "Thank you, my dear. I expect you would like to see the church now – what remains of it?"

With his back to her, she couldn't see his face dim, but he had formed a strained smile by the time he turned around.

"That would be most kind."

This time, she let him help her as they led the way through the abandoned rooms of the original house, along the passage of the new, to the decorated arch of the church of St Martin's embedded in the outer wall.

"Matthew, are you sure?" I asked when we reached the ancient door as Mrs Seaton went ahead into the body of the church.

He took in the chevron carving curving over the doorway, the worn faces of the saints either side, and the seated figure of Christ in the centre. "It's what I came for." He went inside, but I didn't follow immediately.

"Come along," Joan Seaton chirped, popping her head around the door, "and please don't faint again, Emma – the first time was quite enough, thank you."

I smiled wanly and entered the sepulchral gloom. The single lightbulb had blown since I'd last been there. As my eyes adjusted, I found him standing facing the empty space where the altar once resided. Expressionless, only the tension across his shoulders gave him away.

"This is what you're after," Mrs Seaton called to him from the remaining aisle running along the south wall. When he didn't reply, she said a little querulously, "My dear, the Lynes family monuments are over here…"

It reminded me of seeing a film where you know what is going to happen next and you're too frightened to watch but you have to anyway. As if drawn by some compulsion, Matthew walked slowly to where Mrs Seaton stood beneath the high memorial window, and looked up.

"There, you see – isn't that you?" she said, pointing to Matthew's image captured in the radiant colours of the glass. For a ghastly moment I thought she meant it literally and waited for his reaction, but he remained mute. She continued, "Now that I see you here, you look just like twins. Wasn't he a dish! I know where you get your looks from. I always rather admired him, although I didn't tell my husband of course, though I'm sure he guessed." She clapped her hands in delight. "That's his brother – he died in infancy; and their mother – such a pretty thing. The father always struck me as being a touch dour, but now that I look at him, he has the kindest face. But not the uncle… yes, well, probably the less said about him the better! At least he got what he deserved." I looked at William Lynes next to his older, sombre, brother – handsome in his way, but history had soured his image as far as I was concerned, and the phrase "handsome is as handsome does" seemed to suit him perfectly. Joan pointed to the window with her cane. "And there are the grandparents – Henry Lynes senior and his wife, Emma D'Eresby. How remarkable," she trilled happily, "and here you are now, a D'Eresby and a Lynes marrying. You must be related, you know – distantly, of course. How my husband would have loved to have met you, Matthew." In her budding enthusiasm, she didn't seem to notice the shroud of silence clinging to him. I wanted her to stop, to cease – to acknowledge his need to be quiet and to be alone. But she'd had months of silence in which to dwell, and she expended every ounce of energy she had stored on reliving his story. "And I'm sure you'll want to see this," she said, stepping to one side.

His eyes dropped to where her hand rested on his parents' tomb, and the colour drained from his face, the wave of emotion flooding from him becoming so potent it consumed me. I braced myself against it. "Matthew... please," I choked. Dazed, he looked around and, as realization flashed across his face, he let me go, a release so tangible that I stumbled back against a column, breathless.

"Take care, my dear, the floor is rather uneven," Mrs Seaton said, oblivious to Matthew's turmoil as she circled to face him again, beating the ground with her stick, *tack, tack* against the cream and red tiles, the knights and their horses eternally ready for battle. "I always thought it such a tragedy how they treated him. By all accounts they regarded him highly until then, but to do this to someone's memory is simply desecration, quite unforgivable. My husband was very proud that the Seatons never went with the crowd, although it meant trouble for them at the time." She lightly touched Matthew's defaced marble form, then looked up at him, faltering as she took in his expression. "Perhaps you would like to be alone. I'll go and find the picture; there's no rush."

His voice shook as he broke the silence at last. "Did they really hate me so much?"

I let go of the column. "No, darling, they didn't. They were frightened – you said so yourself."

He stabbed in the direction of his stone image, his shattered face bearing witness to the frenzy of fear in which he had been caught. "Fear did *this*?"

"Fear drives people to many things they wouldn't do otherwise. It's what they thought you were that they feared – not you, but what you represented…" The look on his face cut me short.

"Had I known," he said, "what they thought of me and what my father had to endure until his death… Our own people did this. Christ forgive them because I'm not sure if I can." He turned his face from me, his fingers gripping the side of the tomb. Nothing I could say or do could ease his hurt. "Emma, please…"

"I'll go and help Mrs Seaton," I said before he needed to, and left him kneeling, head bowed, by his parents' monument.

I found Joan struggling to fill the kettle in a kitchen smelling of damp and decay. Pale green gloss paint peeled in patches from the walls and worn lino from the floor. I took the heavy kettle from her and filled it. "What does your son do, Joan?"

"Roger's a merchant banker – quite an important one, I believe. We had hoped he would run the estate of course, but he was never very fond of the country and he couldn't have the bother of it all when my husband died." She perched on an old wheezy vinyl-topped stool by the stove like a finch. The tap dripped incessantly.

"Does he visit often?" I asked casually, looking for cups and saucers.

"You might need to rinse those, my dear." I tipped a spider out of one; it scuttled under the crack between the sink and the draining board. "He visits when he can, but it is quite a way for him to travel from London, and he doesn't like to leave the City because he always has a meeting to go to. He works so hard," she added, but a bit defensively I thought, as if she were trying to convince herself. "He would come more often, but times are difficult for bankers these days, not at all like they were."

But not that hard, I thought, crossly scanning the dilapidated kitchen and the thin, frail old woman sitting in it. *Definitely not that hard*.

"Your fiancé seemed a little quiet in the church, if you don't mind me saying so, Emma my dear."

"I think he found it more difficult than he expected; it's quite an emotional journey for him." Clichéd, but I couldn't think of a better way of putting it.

"Families are emotional, aren't they?" she agreed. "There's no getting away from them – it's in the blood, so to speak. Matthew is astonishingly like his forebear, so very handsome, don't you think? When I was a girl and not yet married a year, my husband spent some time restoring part of the fabric of the church, as it had got into quite a shocking state in his parents' day. I helped him sometimes – just little jobs, like cleaning the tiles or the brass inscriptions – and I used to imagine the Lynes family stepping down from their memorial window and what I would say to them and especially to him." She looked out of the window into the stone-walled courtyard, and it seemed to me that she warmed a little at the memory, and her peaked face softened. "It was all such a long time ago," she said, and I wasn't sure whether she meant her youth, or his.

The kettle finally boiled and I made tea under her exacting eye. I carried the bent tray with the rattling cups through to the great hall as she recounted tales from her girlhood as a young bride at the manor. The sun shone in her voice as the years melted away in her words, and I thought how loved Nanna and Ellen had been in their great age, and how this old woman wasn't, and the neglect she accepted when she shouldn't.

Matthew joined us sometime later. I looked up anxiously as he came and sat down beside me, and I couldn't tell whether his smile was to reassure me, or a sign that he had found some peace within himself.

"Did you find what you came for, my dear?" Joan asked, offering him a cup. "I'm afraid your tea will be rather tepid. Emma will make you a fresh cup, won't you?" She eased herself with some difficulty into a more comfortable position and Matthew winced.

"Have you been given anything by your doctor for your pain, Mrs Seaton?"

"Dear, how clever of you to notice! Dr Crawford said it's to be expected at my age and paracetamol upsets my stomach, so I just have to put up with it."

Matthew's brow knitted. "You need to keep warm," he said, pulling a rug from the sofa and folding it over her knees.

"Roger said he would order some wood at Christmas, but then I had my fall. There's some left from last year which will see me through to summer." I imagined her struggling with a few sticks at a time from goodness only knows where she kept the wood pile.

Matthew must have been thinking along the same lines. "I'll see to that before we leave. Do you have any heaters of any kind?"

"Just the one in my bedroom – oh, and another in the solar, which I don't use any more. But Roger says…"

"Hang Roger," Matthew muttered sourly, safely out of earshot and already on his way towards the hall and the stairs to the first floor. I hoped she wouldn't notice that he knew where to go.

"Roger is always worried that I won't have enough to live on," she explained.

"I'm sure he wouldn't want you to be cold," I said, coming to sit by her and thinking that he probably didn't care one way or the other as long as she didn't spend his inheritance.

Matthew was soon back with an electric heater. "You need to keep this on all the time, night and day, so the room is warm when you come down in the morning. It's much more efficient that way." He looked about him, at the high ceilings and tall windows, the stone floors barely covered by threadbare rugs from another century, then at the modest heater giving out an insubstantial heat. "Night and day, Mrs Seaton, without fail – doctor's orders. I'll get some wood in before it gets any later."

Her hand fluttered to her face as she watched him leave the room, then she turned to me, old again. "It is such a big house to heat. Roger says that I should think about going into something smaller, but I really don't want to leave."

"It's your home; of course you want to stay for as long as you can." I remembered how Nanna had felt the same way. "It's a lovely house, so full of sunshine. I think it's one of the finest medieval manors I've ever seen, and I've seen loads. I did a research project on them once."

She lit with delight. "That's just what that man said – the finest moated manor in the area, he thought. I was so pleased because it must be difficult to see it through all the dust." She sighed, looking around her. "He was very attentive and most interested in the history of the area."

Matthew came in with a load of logs, and disappeared again.

"Have you eaten, Joan? Can I make you something?"

I heated some soup and buttered bread for her. When I brought it in, Matthew had completely filled both sides of the cavernous fireplace with logs, protecting them from sparks with two fire-screens he found somewhere. Joan was telling him about the row of shields carved on the stone surround. "You can see the Seatons quartered with the Lynes coat of arms, and here – with the Harringtons." I placed the tray on a small table next to her. "Thank you, my dear, but I'll see you out first; it takes me an age to eat nowadays."

She walked us slowly to the door, still chattering away happily. As we stood on the threshold, she cocked her head, looking more like a small bird than ever. "What a couple you make; how pleased your grandparents would have been to see you, Emma, and so proud. They would have loved this young man of yours." She smiled up at Matthew. That was the best thing she could have said to me. I carefully placed my arms around her thin shoulders and embraced her gently, wishing so much that she had someone to care for her.

She lifted the jade beads from around her neck and, with hands shaking from the effort, placed them over my head. "There," her sharp eyes sparkled, "my mother-in-law gave these to me when I married. They are such a lovely green and they look so well against your hair."

"Oh, Joan, no really, I couldn't…"

"But of course you can – they are for the young and I have no one else to leave them to. Roger never married and I only have some distant cousins and they wouldn't appreciate them. I believe," she said, looking up at Matthew, "that you are the closest living relatives the Seaton family now have. How strange, how very peculiar." She reached up and tentatively touched his face. He smiled and bowed his head.

"It would be an honour to be so, ma'am."

"Emma, my dear," she said without taking her eyes from him, "it could almost be him, he is so very like."

"Yes, he could, couldn't he," I said. We left her with the

fragrant narcissi glowing in a little patch of late sun as we returned to the car.

We were both quiet as I drove with a greater degree of caution down the lane and towards the main road home. "Is there nothing we can do to help her? She's so frail – more so than when I last saw her."

"She's strong enough in herself, but she's in a fair amount of pain and it would help if that were under control. I'll phone her doctor and suggest a new type of pain relief that won't irritate her stomach. I know it's not ethical to interfere with another doctor's patient, but…"

"Ethics didn't stop you looking after me in your own rooms after Staahl's attack, if I remember correctly."

"There are times," he replied, "when common sense and humanity take precedence. Anyway, in this case, I'll say I'm a relative over from the States for a visit, which should explain my lack of protocol. But it shouldn't be necessary to intervene." He stared fiercely at the fields beyond the hedge-line. "It makes me so angry, Emma, this attitude to the elderly. It's as if someone reaches a certain age and then they're… written off as a mere inconvenience. And when there's no one to care for them, to protect them…" He lapsed into a brooding silence as we passed the shores of Rutland Water and headed towards Stamford.

"Is that what happened with your father?"

Agitated, he bit his knuckle. "No… yes… probably," he admitted. "Seeing her like that and the house, the church, my parents – at least Nathaniel did what he could to look after my father, but I should have been there; I was his son and it was my duty to look after him, Emma. I failed him."

"Did he say that when you went back to visit him?" I slowed

as the traffic built up. Cars – with fractious children, and dogs panting in the back – queued to leave the reservoir.

"No, of course not. He knew as well as I did what would have happened if I'd been caught. It was safer for him as well as for me to stay away, but it doesn't alter the fact that he needed me."

"It was better that than seeing his son accused under the Witchcraft Acts and hanged." I shuddered. "Much better."

"Well, it's a moot point because I wasn't."

I didn't think it debatable at all, but he sounded in no mood to discuss it now, and I let the matter drop.

We were nearing Stamford when I remembered lunch. "I'm starving," I remarked to no one in particular. I heard a grunted laugh next to me.

"Then the venison had a lucky escape."

And I knew that, whatever his misgivings about his actions in the past, he had concluded there was nothing he could do about them now.

11

Dining Out

We didn't mention it again. Beth and Rob had invited us to their home so that Mum and Dad didn't have to cook, nor rely on my dubious attempts to sustain them. Now, more than ever, I wished I'd had the patience to learn to cook when young, and when Nanna had been there to teach me.

My sister lived in a tight stone terrace. They bought the house when they first married and it was too small for a family with three children, but buying the coffee shop had taken up any equity they had earned and they would have to stay put until the business broke even – or broke the bank. In the case of the latter, they might be obliged to move in with our parents, and Rob did everything in his power to prevent *that*.

Herded by Beth, we squeezed down the narrow hallway. Rich, meaty smells drifted from the kitchen at the back.

"Dinner won't be long – go on through," Rob hailed us from the kitchen, bottle in one hand and a half-peeled parsnip in the other. We filed into the tiny sitting room area, filling it at once.

"Darling, where are the children?" Mum asked, joining us on the sofa.

With Archie's chewed bunny in one hand, Beth waved in the general direction of the stairs. "Arch is in a straightjacket in his cot and the twins are getting ready for bed. They've been promised a DVD if they're quick, but they couldn't decide between *Dracula* and *Aliens* last time I checked."

Dad did his neck thing, looking like a turtle. "I'm not sure if those films are entirely suitable, Elizabeth. If I'm not mistaken they are both rated eighteen." To be honest, I think we were both surprised he'd heard of them. Beth gave me a sidelong look and I kept a straight face as I considered the children's choice.

"I reckon there's not much to choose between them, Beth. For thrills, perhaps Newt and Ripley trapped in the med lab with the alien just about outdoes Lucy Westenra's gallons of blood."

Matthew laughed. Mum looked aghast. "Oh dear, that really isn't appropriate, darling."

"Beats *Bambi* any day," Beth mused.

"*Bambi* gave me nightmares," I agreed, before we couldn't keep it up any longer and burst into snorts of laughter at the look on our parents' faces. We hadn't played that trick for a long while, and the previous few days had been spent with our emotions reined in so tight that the least provocation had it bursting from us in laughter or in tears.

"Girls, really," Rob admonished, coming to join us and adopting a broad Scottish brogue for the scolding. "A little decorum, if you please. Matthew, keep your woman under control; she's leading mine astray."

"I wish that were possible," Matthew retorted. Beth and I hooted with laughter and Rob grinned until Beth took pity on our parents, whose expressions of opprobrium were almost Victorian.

"Don't worry, they've decided on *Babe* – again – and that's nothing to do with teenage sex, Dad, in case you were wondering. Anyway, the kids'll be down to say goodnight when they've done their teeth. I'd better take Arch his bunny or we won't hear the end of it. Want any help, love?" she asked, as Rob left for the relative sanity of the kitchen.

Rapid light feet flurried down the stairs and the twins bundled into the room smelling of bubble bath and toothpaste. "We've come to say night-night," Flora announced grandly, looking all pink and fluffy in her dressing-gown. "Night, Granny, nighty-night, Grandpa." She flung her arms around her grandfather and he gave her an affectionate hug.

"Goodnight, Bubble, sweet dreams."

I felt a sudden flush of envy at their easy relationship. I had been lucky to get a grunt from him when Flora's age. I saw Alex watch them, his finger in his mouth, and I knew with a stab that he felt it too. Quiet and reserved, he needed a patient touch and insight to draw him out, and Dad had neither. In a flash it was forgotten as they launched themselves at us.

"Hey, kids!" Matthew laughed, catching Flora before her knee landed in my stomach, and swinging her to one side. "I think this Clone gun is yours, Alex," he said pulling something angular from where it embedded in my thigh.

Alex took the piece of Lego from his outstretched hand. "Thanks! That's really cool. I've been looking for that for ages! Will you play Clone Wars with me?"

Rob came back in, his dark hair sticking to his forehead from the steamy kitchen. "Bed, you two."

"But we want to stay for dinner!" they wailed in unison.

"This is grown-up food. Bed!"

"'That's *cool*?'" I said to Matthew as footsteps thundered up the stairs. "You're a dreadful influence, Matthew Lynes, and how on earth do you know what a Clone gun looks like anyway? I thought that plastic thing was a miniature sink-plunger from a Dalek – or possibly Barbie's into DIY now, or something."

"It pays to keep up with the times," he said lightly.

"Not in my line of work," I shot back.

Dad interrogated his plate. "This looks interesting, Rob. What is it?"

Rob picked up the now empty serving dish to make more room on the crowded table. "Boar in a port wine and cranberry jus."

"We're compiling a file of new recipes," Beth explained, "so we want to try them out on family before we poison our customers."

"Gee, thanks," I said, wondering how I could manage my sister's generous helpings. I pinched a baby broad bean the colour of my jade beads, ignoring Mum's reproving glance. "What customers? I thought you only have planning permission for a coffee bar."

"We have," Rob said, passing around a dish of aromatic creamed parsnip scattered with nutmeg and parsley. "But one day, God willing…"

"… we want to open a restaurant," Beth finished for him.

"And I bet you didn't see my lips move, did you?" He threw a look at his wife.

She blushed a bit. "Well, we do."

"Since when have you wanted a restaurant?"

"Since about six years ago, Em, but you were never around to tell and you never asked," my sister said a touch tartly. It was my turn to redden.

"What sort of thing are you aiming for?" Matthew asked.

They set to discussing covers and profits while I concentrated on the food and kept my head down.

"We've worked out the suppliers, turnover required, profit-and-loss forecasts – the works, but, well, you know – the banks have been a bit chary about lending recently."

Beth rolled her eyes. "Tell them, Rob, for goodness sake; they're family."

He sat back, puffing his cheeks like a skinny lizard. "The banks won't lend without five years' worth of books, and the last three have to have turned a profit. We spent a heck of a lot on the initial refurb costs, which we've only covered recently. We don't have enough equity to form a decent enough deposit, and the housing market's taken a tumble so we're not likely to recoup what we've already sunk in the café. Business is good, but, for the time being, we're stuck."

I helped distribute tall glasses filled with layers of foamy chocolate and a velvety dark sauce. My mouth watered.

"Now these," he said as we placed them down, "we concocted in your honour, Emma – complicated, tricky, and need careful handling, but well worth the effort, hey, Matthew?" He raised a glass in token salute, interposing a smile and saving himself my retort. "They need to be eaten quickly, though, because the layers collapse as they warm."

Dad held his glass to the light. "Ingenious" – he sniffed the contents – "smells good too."

"Nanna would have loved it, Beth. She always enjoyed your cooking."

"I think Nanna would have found this a bit strong, Mum – it packs quite a punch. It's not one for the kids." A thump shook the floorboards above our heads. "Talking of whom…" she groaned.

Matthew stood up. "I have to head that way. Can I put this in the fridge?"

"Surely," Rob said. "Do you know where it is?"

"So where did you two go today?" Beth asked, plomping down in Matthew's chair between Mum and me, and pulling her glass in front of her.

"Towards Oakham. I wanted to show Matthew some of the

area." My spoon sank into the chocolate and small bubbles burst with little pops, releasing a heady aroma. "I always forget how pretty it all is around there with the spring flowers and wildlife."

"We nearly had venison for dinner." Matthew slipped into Beth's place. "All's well; it was Alex's head."

"Oh…!" Beth started to get up.

"But he's fine," Matthew assured her, "and so's the wall."

"Venison?" Dad pursued, much to my annoyance.

"Matthew, you promised not to say," I said, as he ignored the ferocious looks I gave him.

"A fine roe hind. I should say we came this close," he held up his hands with a sliver of a gap between them, "to an insurance claim and enough meat for a year."

"Darling, this is quite delicious. I can't make out that flavour; what's in it?"

"It's quite simple, really, Mum," Beth explained, "but you have to use the finest grade chocolate…"

"That's a gross exaggeration, Matthew. We were nowhere near that close; we missed her by at least… that much." And I widened the span generously.

"… egg whites and double cream…"

I lifted a spoonful of chocolate, savouring the anticipation. "Do you like venison, Emma?" Rob asked before I could get a mouthful.

"She certainly did this morning," Matthew chuckled. I sighed and lifted the spoon at last to my mouth.

"… and then there's the secret ingredient…" Beth was saying, leaning across the table to top up Dad's glass. "You add an extra, *extra* strong cup of espres…"

"Emma! Don't touch it!" Matthew yelled, lashing out across the table and knocking the spoon and glass away from me. The glass soared into the air, spraying the dark morass across the table and shattering against the wall. Chocolate oozed like blood. Everyone stared at the wall, then at Matthew, and finally at me.

Beth gulped. "Strewth!"

"R-ight," Rob stated, but Matthew had his hands around my face, wiping my mouth with his thumb.

"Did you eat any... Emma, did you eat *any*?"

I pushed his hand away, not sure whether to laugh or be cross. "No, you didn't give me the chance."

Relief swept over his face, and he dropped his hands, but Dad, grey and sweating, stood shakily. "I didn't think there was any coffee in it. Are you all right, Em?"

"I'm fine; don't fuss, please. Beth, Rob, I'm so sorry – it looked delicious. I'll get a mop." I started to rise but Matthew pinned me to my chair.

"No, you won't; you'll stay away from it until I've cleared it up. I don't want any getting on your skin."

Mum had gone very pale. She hadn't said a word, but now, slowly, she rose to her feet. "What, may I ask, was that all about?" This was usually the point at which, as children, Beth and I made ourselves scarce as we sensed the calm before the storm. Her voice trembled. "Why is Emma fine? Why shouldn't she be *fine*?"

I could attempt a lie, but Mum could sniff out a falsehood quicker than I could chocolate, even if all I wanted to do was protect her. I realigned a stray knife without looking at her. "I'm a bit allergic to coffee, Mum, or... or something in coffee."

Her voice became steely. "Define 'a bit' for me, Emma."

I hawed. "Well, a bit more than a bit, I suppose – quite a lot really."

"Emma!" she barked.

"It can kill her if she ingests it," Matthew said calmly. I stared at the tablecloth and waited for the reaction.

Beth gaped. "Golly Moses, Em, you should have said."

Mum levelled a look at me that could cut ice. "And how long have you known this?"

I peeked at her. "Since the trial. I was unwell during the trial."

"How unwell?"

"Uh…"

"She nearly died," Matthew said, really choosing his moment for complete honesty. I frowned at him, and then at the dark stain making glacial progress down the wall.

Dad adopted his best military stance intended to show he had everything in hand. "Now, Penny, she's fine. There is really nothing at all to worry about, it's all under control."

She rounded on him, her lips drawn back over her teeth, anger like a whip. "You knew? And you didn't tell me? How could you, Hugh? And you, Emma, I thought I could at least trust you to tell me the truth. I have just buried my mother and now I find out that I nearly lost my daughter as well."

Dad twitched, I cringed, and Beth cowered. Rob made a quick exit to the kitchen with the remains of the desserts. He returned with dustpan and brush. Guilt-ridden, I took them from him, but Matthew promptly removed them, and I went and sat down in the corner, feeling useless and stupid in equal measure. Normally so even-tempered, there were times when Mum could keep her rage simmering for hours, and this looked like one of them. She was still blazing when she turned on me. "What else haven't you told me, Emma? What else are you keeping from me?"

I flinched as, from the corner of my eye, a shard of glass sliced Matthew's finger, his skin instantly healing before the blood seeped through. I looked up at her and wondered what – if ever she were to find out – her reaction would be if she knew what deeper secrets we guarded.

12

Entente Cordiale

Mum had been decidedly frosty over breakfast the next morning, so when she said she wanted to talk to me after lunch, I thought I might be in for an ear-bashing at the very least. Dad retreated to his potting shed to tend his tomato seedlings, so I knew something must be up.

Drizzle misted the windows of her bedroom and we huddled around the electric fire glowing in the redundant hearth. "Darling," she began, looking fearfully earnest and proper with her hands clasped in her lap, "Matthew's been very sweet and he says his parents would like to help pay for the wedding." *So far so good, but she could be lulling me into a false sense of security.* I smiled. "I know they are well-off, but there is the matter of family honour. However, apparently they will be offended if your father refuses." I nodded heartily. "So he's pleased to accept. Now, you and I have one or two things to sort out ourselves." *Gosh, she looks like Nanna when in one of her forthright moods.* "Darling," she said again, "I have something I want to say." *Here we go, brace yourself...*

"I found it difficult at first to accept you wouldn't be returning home, and most disappointing when you told us you were getting married in America, and you and your father both know my feelings about being kept in the dark about your... *mishap*... last month. I trust that it is now all in the past and we have so much to look forward to without any other surprises."

I nodded solemnly.

"Good." Her face softened and she allowed a smile to creep through. "I don't know whether you remember the veil." The veil. How could I forget? "Beth chose to wear a short veil when she married, which was her choice of course, although I don't know why." I did; she had said the long lace veil swamped her, making her feel *dumpified*. It had been the source of one or two chilly moments between them. "Now, I don't know whether you have thought about your veil yet, but…" she slid a large, flat box from next to her chair where she must have kept it in waiting, "both Nanna and I wore it, and it's for you and Flora – and any daughter you might have in the future – to wear it if you would like." From the box she lifted lengths and lengths of gossamer cream net, a delicate border of lace scalloped around the edge. "It's very old of course, and very long, and I don't know whether it will go with your dress, but…"

"It's lovely, Mum; it's perfect. I'd love to wear it."

"Oh," she dimpled, a rare sign of delight, "I'm so pleased. I don't know whether you realize, but Nanna had all her marbles right up to the day she died. I told her you were getting married and she remembered Matthew. I think it made her passing that much easier knowing how happy you are." She pulled her hanky from her sleeve and dabbed her nose. "Nanna knew how close you were to Grandpa, my darling, and she wanted you to have this." In the palm of her hand she held a single, heavy band of gold, distinguished by a narrow rib of platinum running flush around the centre; I recognized it at once.

"Grandpa's wedding ring." I took it. "Thank you." I enclosed it tightly within my fist.

"I think Matthew reminded her of Grandpa. Oh, and before

I forget," she said, jumping to her feet, "I meant to give you this." She fished under her bed and came out with a small, brown leather suitcase little bigger than a flight bag. It had seen better days: the chrome fittings were tarnished and the corners were knocked and scuffed. "I had quite forgotten Nanna wanted you to have Grandpa's case when she died. I've no idea what's in it – some of his old diaries I expect."

It was one of those objects that had always been there, sitting on the floor by Grandpa's desk gradually gathering dust, and I never thought to ask what he kept in it. My hand hovered near the clasp, but Mum made busy noises. "There now, it's time for tea and then I suppose you'll be off," she said, a little too brightly for it to be genuine.

Several hours later as the plane nosed through the blanket of cloud, I let go of Matthew's hand and retrieved the case from the overhead locker.

"The case your grandmother referred to?" he asked, as I settled into my seat with it on my knees. I rested my hand on the cracked surface and stared out into the reddening sky.

"Yes," I said, fingering the tarnished metal initials D. A. C. "This was Grandpa's for as long as I can remember." But although I longed to see what had been so specifically willed to me, part of me wanted to let it lie unopened and its contents undisclosed, as if knowing what it contained would break its spell.

CHAPTER
13

Party Beast

I double-checked the reference number Hannah had used; it didn't tally. "I'm trying to work, Elena."

She thrust the list under my nose. "This cannot wait; we have to send the invitations by the end of the week."

"Yes, and I have to get this done in time for the conference."

The piece of paper hovered menacingly. "Emma, if you do not look at this list, I will invite *everyone* to the party."

I sighed and put my pen down and took the list, resigned to the fact that, until I did, she would bug me without mercy. "Well, definitely Siggie Gerhard and Saul Abrahms – we've been trying to meet up for ages." I gave the list back to her and picked up my pen. The paper reappeared in front of me.

"More," she demanded. "Matias and Matthew need to know how much food to order."

"Bothersome wench," I said, running a finger down the list. It was all very well, but between one thing and another, I hadn't managed to meet many people on campus and, of those I had, there were some I didn't particularly wish to see again. "You can forget about inviting Madge for a start – I swear she's first cousin to a spitting cobra, she's so venomous. I don't know him... or her... Megan! Whose idea was it to invite Megan?"

"Matias said she is one of the principal researchers on the project, and as part of the team she should be invited."

"Yes, but have you ever met Megan, Elena?"

She put her finger to her lips, thinking. "No," she said at last.

I believed it my duty to enlighten her. "About twenty-five, lots of shiny blonde hair, big baby-blue eyes, skin of an angel, and long, long legs Megan?"

She didn't require any time to think about *that*. "*Nyet!*" She grabbed the pen from my hand and slashed an angry line through her name and handed it back to me.

"OK, let's look at the rest. Sung is a must, so's Dawson... good grief! What's Sam doing on this list? And don't play the innocent with me, Elena Smalova – I know a setup when I see one." I crossed his name off and scribbled it out with a thick, black line just to be on the safe side.

Elena pouted her disappointment. "It is time you two made up and were friends."

I toyed with the idea of telling her about Sam's attempt at *friendship* before Christmas, of my resulting bleeding nose and his broken jaw. "And have you told Sam this?"

"Yes, I said that he is being so stupid and that it is time to be nice, like he used to be before..." she wavered.

"Before he met me, by any chance?" She looked apologetic. "And what did he say to that?"

"He did not say much, but he rubbed his chin like this – a lot." She massaged her jaw in imitation.

"That figures," I said tartly, regretting it as her expression lost its hopeful tenor.

She retrieved her kilim bag from the chair, stuffing the list back into it and slapping the flap back into place. "I do not understand why you are still angry with him. He accepts you are with Matthew now and he will not try anything again."

I didn't doubt it. After Matthew had broken his jaw, and I threatened him not to tell anyone, Sam wasn't likely to risk another confrontation. Part of me wanted her to know what had happened, but I didn't want the inevitable interrogation that would follow nor, it would seem, did I hate Sam enough to sully the friendship between them. "You're right, Elena. It's time to let bygones be bygones, but I still don't want him at the party. Trust me, it's not a good idea."

"OK, let it be-gone. I have work to do, so I must go too." She hoisted the heavy bag onto her shoulder and opened the door. "I forgot to say, the Dean was looking for you earlier. I did not think you wanted to talk to him so I said that you were still recovering and have to rest."

I grinned. "Too right – thanks."

She waved a hand over her shoulder. "You're welcome," and as the door began to close, "but, I do not think he believed me."

I knew I shouldn't be worried about Shotter, but that didn't stop me brooding. Matthew suggested I contact Human Resources at Cambridge to make sure they were in receipt of all the facts, but as I laid out the details of Staahl's attack, the trial, and subsequent cardiac arrest, the voice at the other end of the phone became increasingly reticent, and I sensed that I was not the first to have contacted him. By the time I replaced the receiver, it sounded like all I had offered was a list of excuses, and I felt more gloomy than when I began. Now Elena's offhand comment confirmed my suspicions that the Dean had me in his sights; all I waited for was the fatal shot. And, if that wasn't enough, Eckhart was becoming an increasingly frequent visitor to my tutor room.

"Ah, Professor!" He popped his head around my door, hair sticking out in a frenetic fuzz. He tumbled into the room in his brown velvet jacket and thick corduroy trousers looking like Mole before I could invite him in, and drew up a chair. He thumped a clipboard in front of me, knocking my iPod flying. I caught it before it hit the floor. "I have a list of delegates I thought you might like to se... see." He had taken to discussing, in minute detail, every and any aspect of the conference. I rather suspected he found the responsibility of organizing it overwhelming, and his levels of anxiety steadily escalated the nearer to June we came. I, too, had plenty of things on my mind, and quite frankly, apart from my students' role at the conference, the administration of it wasn't one of them. But I found him totally benign and completely conscientious, so I hadn't the heart to turn him away.

I smiled in welcome. "Good morning, Professor. How might I help you today?"

"The... the delegates?" he addressed the bookshelf over my shoulder.

I skimmed down the list; there were some pretty impressive names and I questioned, not for the first time, my wisdom in placing my four untried MA students so publicly in the limelight.

"Professor, does the Dean know you and I discuss the conference?"

Using a stubby finger with the nail bitten flush, he pushed his glasses further up his nose. "N... no, but I'm certain he would be delighted."

I wasn't so sure. "Is there anything you would like me to comment on specifically?"

He blinked, owl-like. "There!" He poked at a name in triumph.

It hadn't registered. "Oh, Antony Burridge." The plagiaristic self-publicist. "That's quite a coup. Gosh... yes. Well done."

He beamed. "I knew you would be pleased. He's just brought out another book. Per... perhaps you've seen it?"

Seen it. Read it. Identified a lot of it. "Yes, I have."

"Quite brilliant," he enthused, arms flailing. "Refreshingly different, I thought – very well researched."

"Thanks," I murmured, making a grab for my desk lamp as it toppled near the edge. Eckhart's attention wavered. "Professor?"

His eyes tracked my hand and I hid it self-consciously. He refocused, fumbling in an inside pocket of his jacket and producing a small box from which he pulled a peculiar eyepiece. Through the lens, his eye bulged alarmingly. "Ma... may I?" he said, holding out his hand expectantly and, when I looked at him nonplussed and a little apprehensive, he blinked in the direction of my ring.

I removed it reluctantly and he took it without a word, examining it from every angle. Then he looked at me directly for once. "Where did you get this?"

"It's my engagement ring..."

"Yes, yes..." he said impatiently, "but where did you get it?"

Taken aback, I shuffled in my chair. "Why? Does it matter where it came from?"

Eckhart rotated the ring in the light from my desk lamp with an expression of complete absorption. His lips moved continuously but without making a sound, until I worked out he said "provenance, provenance, provenance" repeatedly. "Provenance," he said out loud, fixing me with a giant orb.

"I really couldn't say. Why do you ask?"

"This," he said, holding my precious ring between finger and thumb as if making an accusation, "belongs in a museum."

"No, it doesn't," I said quickly, taking it from his surprised hand, "it belongs on my finger."

"It's remarkable, very fine. You can see the transition between the Gothic and the Renaissance... and the stone..." he gazed longingly towards it, "... signifies constancy, wards off sadness, counteracts poison – cut like a… an elongated octagonal bezel – very hard to cut at this date – almost impossible, in fact. And the clarity… yes, yes, and an exceptional colour. The workmanship of these lion heads is outstanding. And open at the back, see? To allow contact with the skin to… to focus the power of the stars into the wearer to heal, to protect. Possibly influenced by Simon Forman's theories – it's the right date. If so, it's a rare jewel indeed. Very rare." He removed the lens, fumbling slightly as he folded it and slipped it back into its box. "But I haven't seen this ring before," he said, almost to himself. "It's not from a known collection and I know all the collections – all of them, you understand. Per… perhaps you will permit me to do some research…?"

"I don't think that's necessary, but thank you."

"Ah, well, pity, pity. If you should change your mind…"

"Then I'll be sure to ask you, Professor."

Pondering Eckhart's comments on my way to meet Matthew at the lab, I caught sight of Shotter's bulbous form making its way towards the history faculty across the quad. I darted behind a group of students and used them as cover until I made the safety of the medical building, and slid in through the doors. Matthew waited by the reception desk, reading loose notes in a file.

"Hallo," I said, checking over my shoulder. "Can we go now?"

"Thank you." He handed the notes back to the receptionist who had adopted a coquettish stance in vain. He noted my flushed face. "Problem?" he asked, as I threw another look at the doors when they whisked open.

"No, no. Can we go the long way round? I need a walk; it's a lovely day."

He surveyed the graphite sky. "Who are you trying to avoid – it's not Sam again, is it?"

"No, I haven't seen him in ages. It's Shotter. I think he's on the warpath."

Matthew smiled without mirth. "Then he better not cross mine. I won't allow him to bully you, Emma; no job is worth that. I'm happy to go and see him with you if you want me to, and get this sorted out."

The coward in me thought it was exactly what I would like, but I had my pride. Besides, I'd faced bullies successfully before, and the Dean should be no different. If the worst he could do was to rap me over the knuckles for the amount of time I'd had off over the last two terms – whatever the cause – then I could weather it and put it down to experience. Seen in that light, it wasn't so bad.

"I'll be fine," I reassured him. "We're both grown-ups. What could possibly go wrong?"

I managed to avoid Shotter for the next few days, but I only forestalled the inevitable. I was halfway down the cloister mulling over the joint problem of Hannah's lecture notes and a birthday present for Harry, when I heard someone calling my name. I turned around to find the bursar hurrying towards me.

"Professor D'Eresby, if you have a moment." I waited for him to catch his breath. He blotted his neck with a neatly pressed hanky. "I'm not as fit as I should be." He looked closely at me. "You're looking very well, Professor, I must say – much better than I would have expected. How are you?"

"Quite recovered, thanks," I said, curious to know what it was that had him chasing after me. "Did you want to speak to me?"

"No – yes, rather the Dean would like to see you, if you can spare the time."

Blow, I wasn't ready for this. "When?"

"Now, if you wouldn't mind." From the way he said it I didn't have much say in the matter. I liked the bursar; he came across as being a straightforward, no-nonsense type of man with a kind streak that softened his businesslike approach to matters. I always thought he felt uncomfortable in the presence of the Dean, or rather, that he didn't share his perspective on life. Now, from the expression on his face, he would rather not be delivering this message.

"I see – of course. Is the Dean in his study?"

Despite the brisk nod, I saw regret in his eyes as I held them momentarily. He didn't need to say why I was being summoned, the only question being what excuse Shotter would use to reprimand me. It seemed worse than being sent to the Head's study after the unfortunate incident at school. Dad had been furious, Mum disappointed, and I narrowly avoided expulsion largely on the grounds of being a scholar and the Head also having red hair and therefore inclined to understand my reaction. The bursar held out his hand to show me the way as if I didn't know already.

Shotter must have been waiting by the door because he opened it almost immediately. "Ah, Professor D'Eresby, please come in and sit down. I would like us to have a little chat." The bursar turned to go. "Bursar, if you would be kind enough to stay."

I sat on the edge of the sofa as Shotter settled his frame in his chair. Buttons on his waistcoat strained; his short, thick neck barely cleared his collar, making his resemblance to a toad all the greater. Little time had passed since I last sat opposite him in those initial days at the college. Not much time in terms of hours and days, weeks and months, but eons in how my life had changed since then. I had been so certain of my future – a different future – one filled with the journal and books and learning. A different hope, a different fulfilment.

The Dean interlaced his fingers across his stomach. "I hadn't anticipated us having this conversation quite so soon, my dear, but you seem to have made a remarkable recovery." I heard the insinuation. I didn't bother responding – I saw no point – we both knew why I was there. "However," he continued, "I have been advised that in the circumstances, a period of recuperation is necessary to ensure a complete recovery..."

"How long?" I interjected.

The Dean didn't like being interrupted. He fixed me with small, ice-pick eyes. "To avoid the risk of complications I believe at least three months is recommended, followed by a further three months of light duties."

Risk of complications? For whom?

"Three months would mean I couldn't supervise my students' work."

His smile became smug. "Professor Eckhart would be pleased to take on the duty for you."

"Eckhart?" I said too loudly. "It's not his area of expertise, Dean, and I'm perfectly well enough to carry on my teaching duties." That wasn't the point, was it? I'd been such a blasted nuisance since I'd arrived he couldn't wait to be shot of me. But my students were a different matter; no one else at the university specialized in my area and a change of tutor this late in the day would endanger everything we had worked towards. Even if they could find someone else to take my place at such short notice, my group wouldn't be able to present their papers at the conference. Our plans would be scuppered, drowned in their infancy.

Shotter leaned back in his chair, the gold watch chain slung taut across his waistcoat like a rope-bridge. "Professor Eckhart is very experienced, my dear, and complete rest has been recommended."

"By whom?"

The bursar coughed uncomfortably and the Dean's eyes hardened. "I have taken medical advice on the matter." Behind Shotter's head, the row of academics' portraits gazed deadpan from their positions on the wall. Staahl's had been replaced by the glacial beauty who had pursued Matthew at the New Year party, and mine was still there, hanging on in; but for how much longer?

"Dr Lynes is the most senior medical member of staff on campus, isn't he?" I asked, already knowing the answer.

"He is," the bursar confirmed before Shotter replied.

"Shouldn't you ask his advice?" I tried as a long shot.

His voice dropped. "This is not just a matter of your health, my dear, it is also a question of reputation."

At last, the truth. "Whose?" I asked, caustically.

Shotter's jowls multiplied as he lowered his head and focused on me with his blue-coloured splinters. "This college has a reputation to maintain. Your unfortunate accident brought unsavoury details to light that migh…"

"Accident?" I jumped to my feet. "I was attacked by one of this college's senior academics. It was no accident…"

"… unsavoury details that might bring this college into disrepute, which I cannot allow. It is for the best that you take medical leave of absence until the end of the semester, when you will return to your own university and no more need be said on the matter."

Like heck I would. "And if I choose not to?" I challenged.

The Dean's tone became menacing. "I can make life difficult for you. You might find the opportunities you enjoyed at Cambridge not as forthcoming as they once were. I would advise you to take care of what you say, my dear; we don't want things getting out of hand and damaging your career. If you decide that an extended period of sick leave is preferable, however, I'm sure I will be able to recommend your work most highly." As I weighed the threat behind his words, a haze developed around him: angry hues of dark greys and reds like tumescent clouds of volcanic ash. But if he was angry, I was furious.

"And I'm expendable, is that it? And my students? Hang the truth, damn justice – they are no more than inconveniences where the reputation of the college is concerned." I grabbed my bag. "There are men like you scattered like flies throughout history, Dean, breeding maggots of expediency at the expense of truth."

Shotter heaved to his feet. Short, fleshy fingers gripped my arm. "I strongly advise you not to do anything rash. Take your time to think about what I have said, but don't take too long."

Once outside, I wiped my arm free of the feel of him, quelling the nausea of anger, loathing, and dread. It didn't matter, it shouldn't matter, but I had striven all my life to build my reputation as a historian and I was damned if I had survived Staahl and the trial only to have that loathsome man destroy me. I became aware that a young couple were watching me curiously, and I hid my shaking hands behind my back, determined that no one – *no one* would threaten me ever again.

I was still outraged when Elena came to see me before the party.

"So what are you going to do?" she asked when I could contain myself no longer and told her the whole story.

"I don't know." I whacked my mug into the sink and washed it roughly. "It's so unfair; I knew he would have a go at me, but I didn't think he would get *rid* of me." The mug chinked ominously as I all but threw it in the cupboard and slammed the door. "It's not that I need the job, but I want one, and it's the fact he's prepared to damage my reputation unless I do what he wants."

"Can he do that?"

"I think he's already started. The HR at Cambridge sounded

dodgy when I spoke to them. Another phone call from Shotter could really sink me." I looked at her in despair. "You know what academia is like, Elena. Gossip spreads like wildfire and before you know it, no one will touch me with a barge pole." Her forehead drew into a puzzled frown. "I'll be unemployable," I clarified.

Elena's dark eyes grew round. "You cannot let this happen. You must do what he says. It does not matter if you take leave of sickness now; you will still be paid and it is only a few weeks and you will be married…"

"But it does matter. A lot. First," I counted on my fingers, "Eckhart isn't up to speed on my group's theses and he's not a specialist in my field. Secondly, my students and I have something planned for the conference which he doesn't need to know about but which is really important for their futures." Elena raised an inquisitive eyebrow and I hurriedly went on before she asked. "Thirdly, he's… well, he's Eckhart…" – she nodded in tacit understanding – "and fourthly, blast it, Elena, they're *my* students. I've let them down enough as it is and I want to see them through to the end of the year."

She extracted the tea towel from my hands before I wrung it to death, and looked earnestly into my face. "Emma, you must talk to Matthew; he will know what to do. And even if he does not, Shotter will think that he does. He is a little afraid of him, I think."

"Shotter's afraid of Matthew? Are we talking about *my* Matthew? Why?"

Elena went through to my bedroom and adjusted the strap of her dress. I followed her, but it looked to me as if she struggled to find a way of saying something diplomatically.

"The medical centre and science fac are very important to the college, and Matthew had them built, yes? But Shotter took the er... the... I do not know what it is called." She looked at me for help.

"Credit?" I suggested.

"*Da*, he took the credit." She wandered over to the mirror on my chest of drawers and began fiddling with her hair.

"Yes, that sounds plausible, but you said he is *frightened* of Matthew; that's very specific, Elena." She took a lipstick from her glittery clutch-bag that matched the trim of her dress, and pouted at her reflection. "You look gorgeous; tell me what you meant."

Lipstick in hand, she spoke to the mirror. "Matias told me that when Sung first came to the college, there was some little... trouble – I do not know what – and he was going to be deported." I recalled Sung mentioning something about Matthew getting him out of North Korea, but nothing about keeping him in the United States. "Matthew went to see Shotter and persuaded him to let Sung stay."

"So...?"

"So, Matias says that Shotter is careful around Matthew."

"That still doesn't amount to being frightened though, does it?"

"No, but it is perhaps the way Matthew looks, as if he can see right through you, and you do not know what he is thinking." She reapplied her lip colour as if she had explained everything, snapped it shut, and spun round to face me. "Now," she declared, "what shall we do with your hair?"

I couldn't give a fig about my hair, but I did want to know what Matthew had over Shotter, and why the oily Dean should be frightened of him. I wasn't in the mood for a party. Shotter had managed to get under my skin as effectively as he no doubt intended, and the irritation he set up threatened to spoil my whole evening. What I had to ensure, however, was that I didn't ruin it for anyone else. "Elena, about what I told you earlier – don't say anything to Matthew, will you? Nor Matias, either."

"But you must tell Matthew!" She looked up as a series of raps announced their arrival.

I stopped her as she went to answer the door. "No, I want to deal with this myself. Promise me, Elena, not – a – word."

Tossing her head and tutting she pulled away. "All right," she agreed reluctantly, "I will not say anything, but I think you are wrong."

It wasn't the first time I had been told that and, no doubt, it wouldn't be the last. Rightly or wrongly I thought it for the best, so I let my head rule my heart for once, and smiled as Matthew came to collect us, determined to enjoy the evening.

The Barn had been transformed. Every ledge held candles that guttered each time the door opened to let someone through, throwing dancing figures on the white walls. Even the heavy open beams had candles in little glass pots balanced along their length and, wrapped between them, the strings of clear fairy lights from Christmas. Harry finished lighting the last of the candles, swinging from the beam and hanging like a monkey for a second before landing neatly beside us. "Hey, Emma, how are you doing?" Enveloping me in a hug, he almost lifted me from the ground. "Engaged, huh? This is the best news ever; I'm so glad for you guys. And don't worry about remembering who's supposed to be related to who; it gets easier after a bit." A plain silver cross swung on the chain around his neck; he found the artifice as hard as I did, despite what he said.

"Lying, you mean, Harry?"

He grinned. "I'd call it an alternative form of reality."

Nerves fluttered as the strains of music filtered down the spacious room and the first of the guests drew up outside. I took a deep breath and steeled myself for the evening ahead. I turned to Matthew. "Tell me again why you wanted to hold the party here and not somewhere inconspicuous and totally devoid of anything whatsoever to do with the family? I thought we had to keep a low profile. Having a party here is like waving a big flag – with bells on – saying, 'Here we are, look at us.'"

Matthew's hands circled my waist as we moved to the music. "Do you remember what I said about the box in the wall and about how one of the best ways of keeping something safe is to make it obvious?" I nodded dubiously, putting my arms around his middle. "Well, here we are, in my parents' home, throwing an engagement party, surrounded by friends and family. What could be more normal? What do we have to conceal? Hiding away when we should be celebrating would raise more questions, and there are some things we want people to see. Now when we talk about home and family, people will visualize this – we're giving them the story we want them to believe."

"But you didn't before."

"I didn't have *you* before. People accepted me as a bit of a recluse because of my alleged bereavement. I have no such excuse now." He smiled, his eyes warm, the corners lifting into the tiny crinkles I loved to see. "Come on," he said, "we have guests to greet."

By the time a lull formed in the dancing as our guests investigated the tables laden with food, the combined effect of bodies and candles had my skin glowing. Fanning myself with a tablemat while Matthew went to get me a drink, I went to stand by the door, breathing in the night.

"Hello, my dear," Siggie Gerhard greeted me with a kiss. "This is spectacular."

She didn't say whether she meant the building or the party, so

I just said, equally ambiguously, "They've made a wonderful job of it," to which she agreed.

"You know, Emma, I was delighted to hear of your engagement. It seems fitting that two of my favourite people should marry. I haven't had a chance to catch up with you. You owe me a chat, and I owe you dinner, remember? No, I don't suppose you could forget," she went on as she saw the look on my face. "I was talking with Saul about what happened at Staahl's trial."

I ceased fanning. "What about it?"

"The peculiar relationship between Matthew and his sister." No doubt she saw the instantaneous loss of colour as my face paled. I lifted the mat to fan my cheeks again where spots of heat rose to blaze. "It was very unpleasant for you, wasn't it? I'm sorry; I shouldn't have brought it up."

Matthew seemed to have been sidetracked by Dawson and his wife and I wanted him to hurry up, yet curiosity burned. "What about their relationship, Siggie?"

"Are you aware that I know Margaret Lynes professionally? For some years now we have attended the same committees. I'm on the board at the local hospital's psychiatry wing."

"No, I didn't know."

"Do you need to sit down?" she asked with solicitude.

"No, thanks, I'm just a bit hot." Dawson was now deep in conversation, while his wife clung to Matthew's arm.

"Saul and I were saddened to hear of her breakdown," Siggie went on. "I visited her shortly afterwards."

"Matthew didn't say…"

"He wouldn't have known – no visitors were allowed at the time. I went in my formal capacity as part of the initial assessment. She was quite lucid, you know, but the way she referred to her family intrigued me." The track changed and a few couples began a slow dance to "It's a Mad World". I choked back a laugh and she smiled in surprise.

"Yes, I thought it funny, or rather, odd. She obviously has a deep regard for Matthew, despite what I believe happened in the trial, but it came across more like deference than sibling affection, and this I found strange. And she was articulate yet confused about your relationship with him." At last, Matthew had managed to detach himself from Dawson. "Margaret was very shaken by the death of her grandmother, and did you know she had an older sister who died when they were very young?"

Hurry up! I urged Matthew, but Matias waylaid him. Matthew cast an apologetic look in my direction, then frowned as he read my expression.

"Yes, I believe she died in a car crash," I replied, enunciating clearly. Worry passed over his face as he read my lips.

"It was what we would refer to in the trade as a *life event*, and it has influenced the way she views relationships ever since. I hope you will believe me when I say that I wouldn't normally discuss a patient with a third party, but in this case, what she said has a direct bearing on you." Matthew was making his apologies to Matias.

"On me?"

"Yes, she kept saying that you were taking her grandmother's place."

The floor moved beneath my feet. Siggie put out a hand to steady me. "Emma? Are you all right, my dear?"

Matthew's arm slipped around my waist. "Hello, Siggie. Emma, drink this – it's warm in here." He handed me the cold glass and I drank thirstily. The room steadied and I managed a smile.

"Siggie was just telling me that she's seen Maggie, Matthew." His arm tautened perceptibly. "She says that Maggie thinks

I'm taking her grandmother's place." Try as I might to appear unconcerned, my agitated pulse beat unevenly and I felt sure Siggie would detect it. I put my hand nervously to my neck in an unconscious movement, but Matthew captured it and held it within his own.

"I'm afraid my sister is quite unwell. She's been deeply troubled by our grandmother's death of course, but it's more than that. Working with Staahl put an enormous strain on her – she's been saying some very odd things. I think we have to be looking at a diagnosis of a delusional disorder – possibly cyclothymia, would you say, Siggie?"

"What's that?" I asked.

"It's on the bi-polar spectrum," Siggie answered. "A mild form, triggered by a variety of things, and a stressful event can be one of them. It is something I have suggested in my initial report, but it can be difficult to diagnose. I'm relieved I seem to be on the right track." She regarded him speculatively. "Would you say you have a good relationship with your sister, Matthew?"

"On the whole, given she still grieved for her sister throughout much of her childhood, yes, I think you could say we do. I have a great deal of respect for her."

"That's odd," Siggie said. "That is precisely what she said about you."

The conversation wandered onto more general topics, allowing the jitters to dissipate into nothing but an unpleasant underlying sensation – a reminder that she had strayed very close to a truth that should have remained hidden. Pat helped by insisting I try each of the dishes displayed before me. The food and her affectionate enthusiasm warmed the cold fear in my tummy and, by the time Elena located me, I had become fully engaged in wedding conversation. Pat spotted an empty dish that needed filling and excused herself.

"Emma, he's lovely," Elena mooned in Harry's direction. He waved genially when he saw us and I waved back. "I had forgotten how gorgeous he is. Doesn't he look like Matthew?" She finished her wine and looked for another.

"He's only a boy, Elena, and you're spoken for. How much have you had to drink?"

"Not much." She spread the fingers of one hand, tucking her thumb in clumsily. "Gorgeous," she hiccuped.

"Somebody call my name?" Matias wandered up with another plate of food. Pat's caterers were obviously going down a treat. Elena pinched a delicate piece of bread-wrapped asparagus from his plate and bit off the end. "He's, mmm, so lovely," she hummed.

Snatching the plate from Matias, I pushed them towards the couples slowly rotating around the cleared centre of the floor. "For goodness sake dance with her, Matias, she's driving me nuts."

Elena snorted. "Emma's nuts..." She fell against Matias. "Gorgeous," she slurred happily.

"I think you are better at this than you give yourself credit for," a voice said from behind me. "Feeling better?"

"And I think you've been listening to other people's conversations," I replied, turning to find Matthew leaning against the wall, thumbs hooked in his pockets. He pushed himself away, whirling me into a waltz then slowing to a swaying glide on the outside of the circle of dancers. "I didn't know you could dance," I smiled up at him.

"Remind me to show you a more contemporary one when we're alone."

"Would that be contemporary to your time, or mine?"

"Mmm, I believe that my time has the edge on romance, but I'll leave that for you to decide. Talking of romantic assignations, are you still happy for me to arrange our honeymoon?"

"As long as we can go to New Zealand."

"Where else!" he laughed, swirling us effortlessly through the other couples like water between rocks. One of the boulders rolled into our path. "Excuse me," Matthew apologized automatically as they bumped shoulders.

"An 'excuse me' dance, is it? Well, in that case, I'll have this one with Emma," Matias grinned. "Swap?"

Although still inclined to giggle, Elena had sobered considerably. "I love dancing!" she cried as she tottered from her man to mine.

"Behave yourself," Matias cautioned, obviously thinking along the same lines.

"I will," said Matthew.

"It wasn't you I was worried about," Matias grumbled, as Elena gazed in evident admiration at my fiancé, before they moved away.

"I must say," he said as he snugly settled his arms around me, "what's sauce for the goose is sauce for the gander. What a fabulous dress – electric blue, would you call it?"

"No, I wouldn't, and a certain gander will get his goose cooked if Matthew catches you, let alone what Elena will do to you."

His hold loosened enough to be respectable. "Still a fab dress. Fab party too, don't you think?"

"You've done a grand job between you – thanks."

"We couldn't have done it without Matthew's parents. Great couple – they obviously adore him. I met his brother Daniel as well; had a long chat. They're a close family, aren't they? Lucky." There was a touch of envy in the way he said it.

"Elena told me about your situation, Matias – about your parents not wanting you to marry Elena because she's Russian. I'm sorry."

"Yeah, well, the damage done during the war has deep roots. It's a relief at least now they know we're engaged. It was hard keeping up an act before and it wasn't fair on Elena. She deserves my respect, even if my parents aren't willing to accept her."

"How's your mother?"

He grunted. "Alive. What sort of son does that make me that I look forward to my own mother's death?"

"It's not her death you're looking for, Matias, just her acceptance."

"In my family, we say that old wounds run deep. Do you know what I fear most?" I shook my head. "That I won't be able to forgive my mother, and she'll die knowing it. How would that be for a wedding gift for my bride, hey?" He looked to where Elena chatted away to Matthew.

"Elena said that your father is less opposed to the idea. Could you not work on your mother through him?"

He raised a hand in greeting as we passed Sung with a girl I didn't know. "He's as crippled by her illness as she is. He can't think beyond her next dose of medication or hospital appointment, and she's immovable. Hell'll freeze over before she gives in." His face creased into deep ridges and I sensed years of acrimony.

"Perhaps that's what she wants to do more than anything else."

He frowned. "What is?"

"Give in. It must be hard to put up so much resistance when you love your child as much as she does you. She must be so frightened; she's dying and she's terrified she'll lose her son as well as her life. I would put a bet on it that all she really wants to do is to be able to say *yes* to you, but she doesn't know how." We stood as the other dancers continued around us. I don't think I had ever seen him so troubled, and his hurt angered me because it seemed unnecessary, and all he wanted to do was the right thing, but he felt thwarted at every turn. "You could just get married," I said, already knowing his answer. He shook his head, dislodging the woolly waves he had so carefully tamed, and we began dancing again.

"I can't explain it, Emma, but we have to start our marriage right. If my mother doesn't approve then we'll have to wait; otherwise it's like having a rotten cherry in life's bowl. You can't make the fruit whole again and the rot can only spread. So," he shrugged, "we remove the mouldy fruit before we start to eat." He didn't look at all happy about the idea.

"Matias, try again before it's too late. Go and see her. Be completely honest and tell her how you feel. Give her the chance to make things right between you before she dies, and forgive her for both her sake and yours."

"You're probably right," he said as we slowly covered the floor. "I'll talk it over with Elena. Where is she, by the way?" I caught sight of Matthew and Elena as people passed between us. They had stopped dancing, and she seemed to be explaining something. Matthew looked worried, then his expression became flint, followed by swift anger as he sought me among the other couples, and met my eyes.

"That's done it," I said under my breath, anticipating confrontation as she anxiously followed Matthew across the room towards us. I could cheerfully have throttled her. "You said you wouldn't say anything," I accused, ignoring Matthew.

"If you'd told me yourself she wouldn't have needed to," he fumed. "What did you think you would achieve by keeping this from me?"

Matias asked, "What's happening? What's she done?"

"Snitched," I growled. "You promised you wouldn't, Elena."

She opened her mouth to answer but Matthew intervened. "Don't take it out on her. She told me because you wouldn't."

"Why? What did she say?" Matias demanded.

"Ask Elena, she'll tell you," I snapped, glaring at her. Several faces turned to watch us. Dancing with Siggie not far from us, Henry gave us a cautionary look.

"Not here," Matthew said. "Next door."

"Fine," I retorted, leading Matthew to the end of the Barn and through the adjoining door to his home, taking every ounce of self-control to plaster my face in a smile.

Once in the privacy of his drawing room, Matthew turned on me. "What did you think you were doing keeping something like this from me? Why did I have to hear it from Elena? Is this how it's going to be between us: you're threatened by that excuse for a man and you decide – in your wisdom – not to tell me?"

By now, feeling belligerent, the rancour I stored from earlier in the day threatened to breach my thin reserves of patience. "I told you weeks ago that I wanted to sort this out myself."

"That was before he tried to blackmail you. I mean, how bad does it have to get before you involve me?"

"I don't want to come running to you every time I have a problem, Matthew."

"Why not? I'm going to be your husband in a matter of weeks – doesn't that warrant a level of trust?"

I faced him squarely, refusing to give an inch, yet sensing the hurt I'd unwittingly caused. I folded my arms across my chest in an attempt to bolster my defences. "Will you tell me every little thing that happens? Because you certainly haven't in the past."

He threw an incredulous glare in my direction. "Little? You call your career *little*?"

"Stop prevaricating. You know what I mean. Would you involve me?"

He stopped. "Of course I would!"

Bingo. I reduced my voice to no more than an accusation. "Why is Shotter afraid of you?"

He whirled round. "Who told you that?"

"Elena did."

"And you rely on Elena for accurate information?"

I stuck out my chin. "You did. Matias told her you went to see Shotter when Sung was going to be deported. He said that Shotter is afraid of you."

He looked at me sideways. "Did he say why?"

"No, he didn't know. Elena reckons it has something to do with Shotter taking the credit for the med fac and knowing you could expose him…" Matthew gave a derisory snort. "But I don't think that matters to you, does it?" Hooded, veiled, I hadn't seen an expression like it since the cabin – one I didn't think I would see again.

His voice had an edge to it. "So what do you think I did?"

"You tell me." From the set of his shoulders, he had no intention of telling me anything. I resisted the urge to goad an answer from him, and instead used my own silence as a weapon against his.

His rigid stance loosened. "So, you didn't tell me because you thought I would threaten Shotter. With what – violence?"

"No, but if you had, the maggot would have jolly well deserved it."

That raised a pencil-thin smile. "'Maggot', I like that. Why, then?"

"Because I need to know that I can sort it out for myself, Matthew, for my own self-esteem. I know that the weaker part of me would love you to walk in there and duff him up…"

He gave me an arched look. "Crude, immoral, but possibly effective."

"But I don't want to always be hiding behind you. I want to be strong in my own right."

He came over to where I stood defensively entrenched. "There might come a time," he said slowly, "when you need my help." I saw how deeply he wanted me to trust him.

"Then I will come to you and ask for it. But remember, you're second in the line of reference and I doubt I'll need to go beyond the first."

The stubborn line to his jaw relaxed. "As long as you rely on Him you won't need my help, but in case you do, or in case I'm part of the solution, will you promise to tell me if you have a problem with *Calliphoridae*?"

"What-ids?"

He smiled. "Maggots of the common blow-fly – unpleasant opportunists like Shotter. Will you tell me if I promise not to intervene unnecessarily?"

That still left too much scope for misinterpretation. "Not to intervene unless I ask you to," I clarified.

He shook his head. "Too restrictive – give me more credit than that."

"All right, you're not to intervene unless we've talked it through first and I agree that we tackle it together."

"That seems... reasonable," he conceded. "Let's just pray that it doesn't come to that."

Sobered by my outburst, Elena eyed me with a degree of caution a few minutes later, but, as Matthew intimated that she hadn't broached the subject of Shotter first, I gave her the benefit of the doubt. I suspected he was being chivalrous and that her semi-inebriated state played a greater role in the event than he admitted, but I loved him the more for that, and her none the less. So, by the time we entered the Barn and rejoined the party, we were both smiling.

Matias greeted us with his usual tact. "Took your time," he drawled, loading as much innuendo as he could into those three words and ending with a meaningful smirk. "Hey, Elena told me about Shotter, the slimy sod. Going to have an accident involving a tree, is he, Matthew?" We both frowned at him and he held up his hands. "Just kidding. Nasty though. But you're going to sort him out, are you?" he directed at Matthew.

"No," we both said together. "I am," I added.

Matias whistled through his teeth. "Good luck with that."

Elena was making odd faces at me. "I had too much to drink; it made my tongue like this." She wiggled her finger up and down. "But you have made it up now?" She cast her eyes from my heated face over my hair and back to my slightly crumpled dress. She beamed. "Yes, I think you have definitely made it up." And she let out a peal of laughter.

CHAPTER

14

Security of Tenure

He thrust the paper in my face, his eyes black with contempt. "Don't think I'll accept this from one of my students. I'm disappointed in you, Emma. You've failed me; you've failed him."

Words stumbled from my mouth. "But, Guy..."

His lip rose in a sneer. "Your work is mediocre, you are overrated, and you don't belong on this course. You don't belong *here*." The faces of the other students echoed his disdain, enjoying my humiliation, my fall from grace.

"I did my best. I did everything you told me to, everything. I'll do anything you want, anything at all, but don't fail me, don't send me home."

"Your best isn't good enough. There is nothing in you that raises you above the pedestrian. Let's face it, Emma, you have nothing I want." And with that he turned his back on me.

"Emma, wake up – come on – we'll be late." Guy shook me until I opened my eyes and rolled over. Remnants of the dream clung to the fringes of sleep. I didn't recognize the room. Guy dragged on black trousers and did up a belt with a buckle made of silver. I had seen it before. He was impatient.

"Come on, hurry up. The water's hot if you want a shower."

Something wasn't right. I rubbed my eyes. "Where are we going?"

"The car'll be here in a minute. Your father's downstairs waiting."

"Dad?"

He buttoned his shirt, a burgundy shirt stained darker in patches, like blood, where the rain had fallen. I didn't like his shirt.

"What's the matter with you? Get a move on, will you – your dress is on the back of the door."

"I had a dream…"

He whipped the blue cover from me, revealing my vulnerability. I tried to cover myself with my arms.

"Here." He threw the dress bag onto the bed beside me.

I looked at it. "Why are we here?"

His look became disparaging. "You little fool, why do you think?"

I pulled the dress bag towards me and slowly unzipped it. A stark, white dress with a cheap lace trim and layer upon layer of net lay crumpled in the bag. I stared at him in disbelief. "I'm not marrying you!"

Grey eyes, dead eyes, eyes that never blinked. "Of course you are; it's what you want."

"No, it's not. I'm marrying Matthew. Where is he?" I jumped from the bed and ran to the door, half expecting to see him behind it. "Matthew!" I called, but found nothing but the empty corridor and blank-faced doors stretching into the distance. "Matthew!" I cried, my voice rising in despair. "*Mat–thew!*"

I don't dream. I daren't dream.

I shot upright in bed, gasping. Fear threaded my veins and into the drumbeat of my heart. I listened: nothing in the room except darkness and the rhythmic *tschk*, *tschk* of the battery-powered clock. I reached over and fumbled for the bedside lamp, driving the terror back into the night. The triptych waited patiently. "I'm marrying Matthew, I'm marrying Matthew," I repeated over and over like an invocation until my heart steadied its restless beat. I climbed out of bed and went to make a hot drink. Sleep wouldn't return tonight.

It neared the end of April, and the nights were still cold, even if the warmest of days held a promise of summer in between the frequent showers. I pulled my blue blanket around me and settled on the sofa with my students' latest batch of work and my own paper I needed to complete. Work and tea would offer the best solution. My mobile sat next to my steaming mug. I stretched out a hand, then made a conscious effort and picked up the tea instead.

Matthew sometimes worked during the night. Not leaving until I slept, always there when I woke, he mostly covered staff absences at the medical centre, but occasionally, as tonight, it was so he could complete an investigation into something thrown up by his latest research. Once, I asked what he had found in the samples of blood taken after my cardiac arrest, but he had looked thoughtful and said that the tests proved inconclusive, except that I needed a little more zinc. Always there when I went to sleep and when I woke – except for tonight when I needed him to reassure me he wasn't a dream.

I scrambled out of the blanket and went into my bedroom and found my engagement ring, slipping it on and feeling immediately within its warm band the security of tenure it offered. Back on the sofa, I sorted the papers in order of priority, sending a prayer of thanks that I was now in a position to do so.

After our engagement party I had paid Shotter a visit, and that it was unexpected showed in his surprise when he opened the door. He removed the napkin covering his waistcoat. The remains of his lunch waited on a tray on his desk.

"Dean," I said more brightly than I felt, "I'm so sorry if this is inconvenient; we need to have a little chat." I walked past him and waited until he closed the door.

"Professor D'Eresby, I was in the process of having lunch…"

"Yes," I stated, without moving.

Interpreting my mood, he wiped his mouth and threw the napkin beside the tray. He didn't ask me to sit down. "I expected you to take more time to consider my proposal…" he began.

"Did you?" I interrupted, and went on before my courage failed. "I've had a good think about what you said, and we talked it through and concluded that it doesn't matter anyway, as we're both looking forward to a change of scene."

Despite his irritation, he asked, "Both?"

"Yes, Dr Lynes and I. We had been contemplating a move in a couple of years or so; however, if you insist that I take extended sick leave there's no point waiting. This has just brought our plans forward. Matthew will miss the college of course – especially after the huge personal investment he made in it – but he won't find it difficult securing another position, not with his reputation. We come as a package, you see: where one goes, so does the other."

Shotter understood the implicit threat. In the intervening seconds as he calculated his options, the temperature plummeted. He made his way to the window overlooking the grounds and stood with his hands behind his back. A ride-on lawnmower hummed across the grass, leaving a pale swathe in its wake.

"And you have discussed all of this with Dr Lynes?"

"Yes, of course. We both believe in complete honesty; it's integral to a good marriage." His back stiffened – so he didn't know. "Matthew would have come with me today, but he's making some final arrangements. He wishes to make clear that he doesn't want there to be any misunderstanding." Actually,

Matthew had said nothing of the sort, but I let the suggestion hang in the air.

The Dean's fingers twitched. He turned around. "Your visit is quite fortuitous, my dear." A stench of hypocrisy displaced the fresh scent of cut grass. "Just this morning I received assurance from a senior medical advisor that, given your miraculous recovery, you will not require leave of absence." I said nothing. "Your position is secure," he added.

"Marvellous," I said, "and Matthew will be so pleased. He does hate having his medical opinion questioned. I'll leave you to finish your lunch; I hope it's not cold." As the door began to close I remembered one last thing. "Oh, since we're staying, if I'm too late to intercept it, please disregard Matthew's letter of resignation, won't you?"

The insincere smile on the Dean's face evaporated, but I didn't hang around long enough to see what replaced it.

"How was it?" Matthew asked as soon as I entered the refuge of his office.

"Horrible, but for some reason he's had a change of heart. I've had a reprieve." I paused and decided I had to confess. "But I'm afraid I used your name as leverage. I didn't know what else to do."

"Come here," he said, enfolding me in his arms. "That's my clever girl, don't worry." He kissed my hair and I breathed in his clean scent to rid me of the foul taste the exchange had left.

I was under no illusion that Shotter wanted me to stay to retain Matthew. I didn't like the thought that I had nothing to offer professionally that Shotter considered worthy of keeping, but more than that, I didn't want to use Matthew as a threat.

* * *

So here I sat at three in the morning, afraid to sleep, with a pile of work to keep me company and a mug of tea to keep me warm. We were on a tight schedule to get the presentations complete before the middle of May. Thereafter, once back from our honeymoon – *honeymoon*, the mere thought of it sent wiggles of pleasure to my very core – my students would be on independent study and we would have a few weeks in which to iron out any wrinkles that might become evident before the conference. So far, they were on track. Three of them at any rate. Hannah was proving to be a problem.

I had always suspected that the determination that had served her well to date might one day thwart her ambition. I had followed her research closely: groundbreaking it might be, but it was also flawed. Our last meeting in my tutor room had been tense.

"I understand what you're saying, Hannah, and there are aspects here with which I agree, but your theory is not borne out by evidence."

She clamped her overshot jaw. "But, Professor, you said that this was a good line to take. You said it's under-researched. If Abbott argued that the establishment of the system can be dated to 1648, I can't see why I can't use the same argument to assert that it was established a decade earlier."

We had already covered this ground at length.

"Because you have no evidence, Hannah."

"But I can prove it."

I clapped my hands. "Great. How?"

The stubborn chin again. "I *know* it's right, Professor."

I did my best not to let my exasperation show, but she pushed her luck taking this line. "Hannah, come on, that's not good enough. Knowing it and proving it are two completely different things. You have to maintain your integrity and the only way you can do that is to be completely honest with the facts. If you make a statement, you must be able to back it up with hard evidence; otherwise it will take just one snipy student in five years' time to come along and discredit you. One wrong move and it can ruin your career. The short-term gains aren't worth it, believe me; I've seen it happen."

"But if Abbott can do it..."

"You're not Abbott. You don't have his decades of experience and knowledge to back you up. You're letting your theory drive your research, and it's a classic mistake to look only at the facts that support your hypothesis. If you present your paper based as it is on selected evidence, there will be a dozen historians in that audience ready to take you down." I pushed my laptop to one side and leaned forwards on my desk. "Look, the research you were doing before you went off on a tangent was good, solid, and above all, provable."

She thumped her folder down. "Anybody could do that."

I closed my eyes and counted to ten before opening them. "I know it's not going to set the world alight, but it'll stand you in good stead. It's no mean feat to produce a paper based on original research in a year, Hannah."

She snorted. "Yeah, well nobody's going to remember me for it, are they?"

"More to the point, you won't be remembered for the wrong reasons, either."

"Neither will you," she snapped back.

Ah, now that I wouldn't accept. I sat back and observed her dispassionately. We had always rubbed along fairly well. She came across as being self-contained – that was something I understood – but she could also appear rather superior towards her peers, a status she had not earned. True, I would rather not be associated with poor research and a weak argument, but my own stood up to scrutiny, and had done so for nigh on a decade. By the time I completed my undergraduate study, I had already tackled independent research, had it authenticated, and seen it published to some acclaim. Guy might have been a bastard in some respects, but he made sure that the execution of my work met the exacting standard of his own. It was the least I could do to ensure that my students benefited from the same level of expectation, even if it meant breaking Hannah on the rack first. I opened my laptop and switched it on. "Right, Hannah, that will be all, thank you."

"But," she started to say, "what about my work?"

I thought about what Guy would say in such a situation, then decided I couldn't be that cruel. "As you said, Hannah, it's your work, it's your choice. I've told you what I think; now I have work to do of my own."

Watching her surreptitiously as she packed her bag, I clicked on a random link without paying much attention. She was crimson. Perhaps I'd been too soft. Guy would have stamped all over her by now, but then I wasn't Guy, and I believed there were ways of nurturing students without crushing their will to live.

I heard her sniff, and she might have wiped her eyes before leaving my room, but if that was the extent of her suffering, I would have done her a favour. The humiliation she would otherwise face in front of hundreds of seasoned historians didn't bear thinking about.

Three-fifteen. Time stretches at night. I wondered what Matthew was doing now – not this, I bet. I flicked through Hannah's latest effort, pleased – no, relieved – to see she had taken my advice after all. Something caught my eye. I sifted back through the pages searching, then slowed down and went through them one by one. I might have made a mistake; I hoped I had made a mistake. I hadn't. There it was: Hilliard.

Ugh. Even seeing his name revived the cold repulsion of my dream. What on earth was she doing referencing him? I began reading in earnest. She hadn't referred to him once, but a number of times, drawing on several works plus a more recent one with which I was unfamiliar: *The History of Belief: C17th Popular Culture in Counter-Reformation Europe*. Very now, very Guy.

She had returned to her original thesis, with a few amendments, but on safer ground. Except now she took it a step further and closer to my own area of interest: *Coven or Covenanter? Witchcraft Trials and the Act of Uniformity, 1662*.

Right up my street – and his.

I was still reading when Matthew returned as the sun made an appearance from an overcast sky.

"Good morning!" he said, coming over and kissing the top of my head. "Have you been up long?" He went through into my bedroom, taking off his sweater.

I came back from the seventeenth century, always a bit of a struggle at the best of times. "I couldn't sleep. I thought I'd get some work done."

He came back in, unbuttoning his shirt. "Anything interesting?"

I would have to get a copy of Guy's book to cross-reference her sources. "Act of Uniformity."

"I remember it well. I'm having a shower."

Where was Guy? What poor deluded student had he in his sights now? And why should I care? After a moment, I looked up. Matthew still stood where he had been, his shirt over his arm. "Are you all right? You're very quiet."

I remembered to smile. "A bit tired, I didn't get much sleep."

"Oh?" He came and put a hand on my forehead. "You're

running a low fever. Bed, now. I'll get you something to reduce it."

"Am I?" I said, genuinely surprised.

He returned from the kitchen with a couple of tablets and a glass of water. "Are you still here? Bed."

"Bully," I halfheartedly objected, but recognizing the first signs of a temperature. "I'll be OK with an hour's sleep." I gathered my work into a pile, which he promptly removed from my hands.

"Sleep – not work. This will wait for a few hours."

By noon I entered the hush of the library having slept the temperature off, and made straight for the history section without pausing to greet the librarian.

Thief.

I heard the echoed whisper in the sigh of the automatic doors. The last time I had been here I had taken the journal. That very same night Staahl nearly killed me, and the journal had been in my possession ever since, pricking my conscience. I had always planned to return it – it just became a case of when. Today, though, I had another reason to visit the library and one that wouldn't wait. Hannah must have borrowed Guy's book, so it would be here somewhere.

His name jumped off the book's spine long before I registered its title. I snatched it from the shelf and stuffed it between a couple of textbooks I didn't want and wouldn't read. *Infantile*, I berated myself, but noted that I didn't change its position nor touch the cover. *Afraid of contamination?* I asked myself wryly.

Throughout the afternoon tutorial with Aydin, all during Eckhart's customary visit, the book played on my mind, until at last, I could bear it no longer.

I slid my chair back from the desk and stood up. "I think it's a fantastic idea, Professor. I'll let you get on now; you must have loads to do."

Eckhart nodded enthusiastically, his glasses sliding down his nose until he peered short-sightedly over them. "Yes, yes, I'm exceptionally busy. Now, I have s... some details of the accommodation I would like to discuss with you."

My heart sank. "I'm very busy too, Professor. Perhaps we could look at it tomorrow?" I pulled the books from my bag and put them on the desk skew-whiff where they spilled perilously close to the edge.

He pushed his glasses back up his nose. "Ah, yes, you must want to get on with your work..." His eyes fell on a book on my desk. "Professor Hilliard! My, my, well, well! Is this a new work? I must read it." He reached for the book but I placed my hand firmly on it. I'd forgotten Eckhart held Guy in high esteem.

"I'm sure there'll be another copy in the library, Professor."

Nodding wildly and hunting in his pockets to see if he had his library card, he left the room without saying goodbye.

Once alone I picked up the book. Seeing Guy's face again after so long had shaken me. The photograph had been taken in an office – not the one at Cambridge, but I remembered some of the titles on the bookshelves behind him and the cavalry pistol and mortuary sword mounted on the wall. He sat obliquely to the camera but stared directly into it. His dark brown hair – now flecked with grey – looked thinner, the style shorter, but his body still had the lean vigour, his stance the intense purpose, his expression the same arrogance in which he held the camera's eye. And he wore a burgundy shirt. It was as much as I could do just to read the biography: "Foremost in his generation... academic rigour... intelligent narration... brilliant autopsy..." *Yeah,*

yeah, blah, blah. "Revealing a unique perspective and profound understanding of this turning-point in history."

That had me hooked. Despite myself I read on, hearing his voice, his turn of phrase, impaled by a single word when he made a point. It seemed to be one in a series of books he was producing, a combination of revising extant works and new research. Blast him – whatever my personal feelings, I couldn't fault his professionalism.

Dusk fell, had grown and darkened by the time Matthew came to find me. I threw the book in my desk drawer and slammed it shut as the door opened. I could see the worry in his eyes.

"It's late – you weren't answering your cell."

I vaguely indicated Aydin's notes in front of me. "Sorry, I got carried away. I didn't keep a check on the time. What time is it?" I started to pack my things away. He came to help.

"Past nine. Have you eaten?"

Had I? "I don't remember."

He frowned. "You seem a little preoccupied." He stroked a stray strand of hair back from my face. "I understand you have a lot to do, but it seems more than that; something's bothering you."

I stopped then because he worried, and he worried because of me, and that wouldn't do. If truth be told I felt uneasy. Much of what Guy had written I instantly remembered from ten years before. But there was new research here as well and, more significantly, his perspective had changed, bringing him closer to my own area of specialism. If that wasn't bad enough, the path he followed brought him straying too close to home. When I discovered Matthew's identity it was by no random chance but through a systematic search. Even so, I would not have looked for him had I not a personal interest and a series of incidents emphasized the differences he so carefully concealed. The chances that anyone would hit upon a trail that led to him were remote beyond the realms of reality, but then, as I had proved, reality often depends upon the angle from which it is viewed. I couldn't risk anyone stumbling across his trail. I couldn't risk the journal's absence from the library being noticed. Like the box in the wall, the safest place to hide it was where it might reasonably be found.

Matthew tipped his head on one side and took his time to assess me. "Perhaps what you need is some fresh air and a little sunshine. Come home with me at the weekend; I would like to introduce you to some friends of mine."

The last thing I wanted to do was to be sociable. "Can't we stay here? I want to get this finished."

"Humour me; your work will wait until Monday, and I have to go home to meet my guests. You won't find them taxing conversationalists and you might even discover you enjoy their company."

I didn't want to – I wanted to put the journal back before any more time passed, but the library would be shut now. "All right," I said less than graciously. "How formal is it going to be and what's the order of dress for these guests of yours?"

He smiled. "I really don't think they'll care one way or the other. Come as you are."

I looked down at my jeans and boots, then up at him, and wondered what he found so amusing.

15

Rogues and Vagabonds

Where once snow lay, now dunes of spangled grass swept before us, lapping at the shores of the white house in its lake of malachite. In the early morning sun, drops sparkled after the night rain. I leaned out of the car window and breathed in the clear air as we drew up to the house. Better rested than the day before, I had a sunnier outlook on life, and felt less inclined to grump.

"Hi, Emma!" Ellie sang as she crossed from the Stables. "Matthew, I managed to swap that duty with Dr Ellis and he'll cover the whole weekend. Have we an ETA?"

Matthew shut the boot and checked his watch. "Any time after eight. Is everything ready?"

"Sure. Gran said if you can spare some time, Emma, she'd like you to have a look at the menu for the wedding breakfast. Oh, and she said to ask if you've eaten." She laughed at my expression, tossing her long ponytail over her shoulder as she made her way towards the garage.

"If you see her before I do," I called after her, "tell her Matthew force-fed me at some ridiculous hour this morning."

"Will do!" She waved in acknowledgement. She seemed very chipper. I don't ever remember looking forward to guests this much when her age.

"What do these visitors do for a living?" I asked Matthew as we went inside and into the kitchen.

He put my bag down by the table and went to the fridge. "They're... athletes."

"I didn't think you were still involved in athletics."

Seemingly satisfied I wouldn't starve, he leant against the work surface with his arms folded. "I'm not much, but I like to keep up to speed." He laughed quietly. "Would you like a cup of tea?"

"No thanks, you made me drink two this morning, remember? We looked up as we heard a vehicle rattle along the drive and past the Barn's east face. Any moment it would appear in the courtyard.

"That'll be them," he said, suppressed excitement making his eyes glow. "What are you waiting for? Come on!"

The courtyard remained empty. "What *are* we waiting for?"

Like a puppy straining at the leash, he urged, "Emma, come on, this way!" He led across the courtyard and out beyond the range of buildings and under the open sky. There, where the land dipped away towards a slow bend of the river, Ellie and a rough-coated man were unhitching the tailgate of a large trailer. The man disappeared inside and a moment later came out leading a bay stallion.

Matthew accelerated, unable to contain the excitement that had been waiting to burst from him all morning. Tugging to free itself from its lead rope, the horse saw him. It neighed, its large eyes wide and staring, and reared away, the rope flying out of the man's hands. A handsome horse, deep russet and shining in the sun, its neat head held high and long mane flowing, it trotted fearlessly towards us. Matthew put out his hand and the animal thrust its nose into his palm as he caressed its neck and talked quietly. The horse whinnied. Matthew looked over to me. "Would you like to meet one of our guests?"

I walked cautiously towards the horse, not wanting to spook him, but he stayed still until I reached him and touched his velvet nose. "He's lovely," I breathed.

He ran an experienced eye over the stallion. With the flat of his hand, he felt the horse's neck, down his long, fine legs and across his flank. He checked his back, his hooves, and his mouth, finally patting him, satisfied. "I've always kept horses. He's in good shape, aren't you, boy?" he addressed the horse. "He'll be ready for a ride when he's settled later on. His name's Oliver – Ollie. Would you like to ride him?"

I looked at the strong, muscular body, flanks quivering with unspent energy, nostrils flaring as he caught the scent of freedom in the breeze, and thought that, as much as I would like to ride this magnificent animal, I would probably end up with a broken neck if I tried.

"We'll ride him together, if you'd prefer," Matthew offered.

"Can he take both of us?"

"Morgans are very strong; they're resilient and good-tempered as well. He won't mind, there's nothing to you anyway."

"In that case, I'd love to."

"Good. Hang on to him for a moment, I need to check out Ellie's mare." He handed me the lead rope, and the horse and I assessed one another.

"Hello, Ollie," I said softly, and rubbed the short star blaze on his nose, easing my fingers under the band of his halter. He gauged me with lustrous eyes fringed with long, dark lashes and at that point, I think I fell in love.

After speaking to the man, Matthew was back. "Do I need to be jealous?" he asked as I gazed at the horse.

"Absolutely," I sighed. "How can you bear to be parted?"

"I miss him all right, but we overwinter them in boarding stables by the coast. It suits them better over there where it's less harsh and I know they're well looked after."

Ellie led her mare, with its ivory mane and a coat the colour of pale apricots, towards us. I had never seen her so animated. "Lizzie's so pleased to be back. I'll take her out later; she's desperate for a run. Isn't she pretty, Emma? Matthew gave her to me."

I stroked the mare's long blaze. "She's adorable," I confirmed.

"Lizzie and Ollie love each other, don't you?" Ellie kissed each one.

Oliver and Elizabeth: that sounded familiar.

"Oliver and Elizabeth?"

"Sure, why not? Matthew named them."

"I bet he did. Haven't you told Ellie who Lizzie's named after, Matthew? That's very remiss of you. How sloppy. Or slapdash."

"Then you'd better tell her since it's your subject," Matthew shot, grinning, removing Ollie's halter as the horse smelled water. The stallion trotted to the trough, dipping his nose towards the surface and drinking. Lizzie joined him.

"There, what a fine couple they make," I said with some irony. "You're looking at Mr and Mrs Cromwell, Ellie." She looked puzzled. "Oliver and Elizabeth Cromwell: English Civil War landowner, Parliamentarian, Lord Protector. Demoniacal despot or enlightened leader – depending on whose history you read. Anyway, it was a happy marriage by all accounts – they had nine children, so it better have been."

Ellie watched the horses drink. "Why did you give them names from English history, Matthew? Why not call them… George and Martha, or something American? I didn't know you were that interested in English history."

Matthew gave me *I'll get you later* looks behind Ellie's back.

"It seemed like a good idea at the time, Ellie. You know what I'm like," he said, looking over her head at me. "I enjoy *strange* and *obscure* things, especially if they're *English*."

"British," I corrected him.

"Are you?" he asked. "How so?"

"My great-grandmother was Scottish."

"Really? I thought I was getting a thoroughbred for a wife. I didn't know I'm marrying a mongrel."

I whacked him for that – not that it made any impression on his rock-hard body, but I gave it my best shot. "Cheeky inbred ingrate, you can't talk..." I stopped even before he flashed a look. Too late – Ellie had picked up on my slip.

"Inbred? What do you mean? We're not inbred at all, though we don't know that much about the family, do we, Matthew?"

I linked arms with her and we started to head back to the house. "I'm just trading insults, Ellie. Don't take any notice of us. Where I come from, families like mine often intermarry over many generations; that's why we're all a bit loopy I suspect. Saying someone's inbred is a common slur – I don't mean it literally." It sounded a plausible explanation to my ears, but Ellie didn't look convinced.

"Gramps has always wondered where the Lynes came from. He thinks the family must have originated in England – it's an English-sounding name, isn't it? He's been trying to trace the family for years but he keeps coming up with dead ends. You're a historian, Emma, couldn't you help?"

I could, but Matthew kept a tight lid on his origins on the grounds that what the family didn't know couldn't harm them. As far as Henry knew, Matthew came from the East coast of the States around the turn of the last century, and his parents had died when he was too young to remember them. No wonder Henry found it hard to track them down, and Matthew wouldn't be helping. He kept a steady pace behind us as we waded through thick grass.

"Sorry, Ellie, I'm not a genealogist and it's a minefield. It's not something I've ever studied."

She seemed disappointed. "That's a pity. Gramps is kinda sad about it all. He'd like to know where the family comes from, and Gran can trace hers back two hundred years."

"Has he said so?" Matthew asked, and I heard the unmistakable signs of anxiety. We reached the covered entrance to the courtyard, leaving the bright light for sudden dark, our voices and footsteps echoing.

"No, but he doesn't need to; you know how he goes quiet when he's talking about something he's not comfortable with. He sort of trails off, like a car running out of gas."

We both glanced at Matthew because we knew exactly where Henry had inherited that from, but if he registered what she'd said, he didn't show it. Instead he was looking back the way we had come, twisting his ring. Ellie must have thought she had upset him because she said, "It must have been tough on you not knowing your parents. I can't imagine what it was like."

"It was a long time ago, Ellie, and I'm beyond remembering." But the colours that stalked him were not the deep shades of sadness; they were the leprous hues of guilt.

The horse started forward, then settled again to a well-mannered walk.

"Steady there," Matthew soothed, patting Ollie's neck. "Try not to squeeze with your legs, sweetheart; he thinks you want him to go faster. I won't let you fall."

I gripped a chunk of dark mane instead, trying not to tug, and recalled my riding lessons from childhood. "I think I'm getting used to riding without a saddle. It's not easy, is it?"

"No, but it's a useful skill to have at times. You're doing very well and he's a good horse – intelligent and very dependable – you're quite safe."

Warmed by the sun, the crushed young grass beneath Ollie's hooves smelled sweetly fertile. Breathing deep lungfuls, I relaxed as Matthew had taught me, feeling my balance improve. "I'm sorry I landed you in it earlier. That was careless of me."

"It's easy enough to do; you covered it well though, so no harm done."

"Except to you, perhaps?"

"What do you mean?" Matthew tightened his hold around me as Ollie negotiated an uneven rise of ground, but he allowed the horse to find its way, and his own body remained relaxed and fluid as if horse and rider were one.

"I sensed how guilty you feel about not telling Henry the truth."

"Guilty? Yes, I suppose I do feel guilt, or perhaps remorse is closer to it. It's never felt right lying to him. I can justify it, but it's not the same as creating a public lie – this is at the very heart of the family and of who we are. I've wondered, over the years, whether I should have told him the truth a long time ago. Now I think it's probably too late. When you've lied to someone for so long, how do you go about telling them the truth? How could he ever trust me again?"

I couldn't begin to answer that one so I didn't. Matthew clicked his tongue and Ollie turned right, heading towards the river.

After a while I asked, "Don't you think Henry would understand if you explained why you never told him?"

He took a moment before replying. "Would you? How would you feel if you were in his place?"

I thought about being Henry, then how I felt when I'd

discovered Matthew had consistently lied to me: the sense of betrayal, the anger. Even when he explained why he had done it, I found it difficult to forgive him, until my love for him overcame my hurt, and compassion defeated resentment.

Ollie's hooves chinked metal on stone as we neared the gravelly banks. The river ran thick with melt-water, deep pools of turgid green, silt-bound and dangerous. Matthew clicked once and the horse came to a standstill. He slipped off his back, landing lightly, and held up his hands to guide me to the ground.

"Thanks," I said, flexing sore muscles. "I should think Ollie could do with a rest as well." The horse wandered a few feet away to a lush patch of grass and started grazing, unperturbed. Matthew hadn't pressed me for an answer, but he waited for one nonetheless.

"I think that if I were Henry, I would love and respect you, and know you well enough to understand that whatever you did, you did in my best interests, despite my initial reaction and however long it might take to come to that conclusion."

"As you did?" he said quietly.

"Yes, as I did. There are several major differences though; he has known you all his life and so the hurt might run deeper because he will think that you should have trusted him enough to tell him at the outset."

Matthew's mouth twisted. "And secondly?"

"And secondly, he has known you all his life and he respects and loves you above all else and will forgive you anything."

"As you did?" he repeated.

"As I did," I confirmed. "And I hardly knew you, nor did I know the circumstances surrounding your deception at first."

"The fabrication is there for a purpose, Emma. While the threat still exists, should I not continue to protect him? And not just Henry, but the family as well. Where should the lie end and the truth begin? Do I tell everyone – Jeannie, Maggie? The more people who know who I really am, the more chance there is that I'll be discovered, and all those associated with me. At the very least, by telling him I might risk losing my son."

"But would he run the risk of losing you? What are the alternatives?"

"That I let him live out his life in the lie, until…" His mouth pressed into a line, smothering the words.

"Until?"

"Until time relieves me of the responsibility." Bitterly, he swept the head off a long-stemmed flower growing proud of the surrounding grass. Ollie lifted his head and shook his mane. "Sometimes I'm so tired of this burden of knowledge, of carrying this pretence."

"At least I can share it with you for the time we have together."

"Do you think you should have the responsibility as well, that you become part of the invention – help me sustain it?" He ground the toe of his riding boot into the flesh of the earth and it bled darkly over the leather.

"It was my choice to do so, Matthew. You didn't choose to be the way you are – you're just trying to make the best of it, and I'm happy to help you do so. If you decide to tell Henry one day, I'll support you in any way I can."

He put his hands behind his neck like open wings and stared skywards into the brilliance of the sun. Minutes passed in which he seemed to be thinking, then, shaking his head once, he said, "Not while the threat exists."

When would it ever end for him? Not on Henry's death, nor on mine. For him "eternity" had a completely different meaning.

"Eternity?" he queried.

I didn't realize I'd said it out loud. "I was just remembering Vaughn's lines: *'I saw Eternity the other night, A Ring of pure and endless light.'*"

He took off his slim-fitting riding coat and spread it over the ground, inviting me to sit. "And?"

"And I was thinking that for you, stuck as you are, eternity is less certain than it is for me, but no less timeless."

"Possibly; however, I haven't had a day's illness in over three hundred years, I still have all my hair and my own teeth, and above all, I have you." And to prove it, he nibbled my ear.

"And the sun is shining," I laughed.

"Why, yes, ma'am, so it is, and you need to rest your weary bones," he drawled, glancing around. "The grass is soft and there's no one hereabouts…" His hands whipped about my waist and he had me on my back before I could blink. "Hush there now, or you'll frighten my hos'." Ollie swished his tail lazily, paying no attention. "Now that sure is a pretty sight," he hummed, pulling my hair free of its plait and spreading it out around my head. His voice dropped, becoming honey. "The colour of embers." He touched my lips with his, then my eyes. "*… Then fire be set within my flesh, And brand thy name upon my heart…*' Here is one fire I wouldn't mind being consumed by, my love. What a conflagration you set within me."

I didn't want to think of flames and death; I wanted to listen to the sound of his voice among the grasses and the rush of the tree-fringed river. I placed my hand over his mouth. "Shh, don't talk of fires. Tell me about… horses, instead."

His eyebrow rose in eloquent disbelief. "Horses? I speak of love and you want me to tell you about horses. Now I know I have competition for my affections. I should never have introduced the two of you. As for you," he addressed his horse with false ire, "how base is it to steal my maid's heart when my back is turned!" Ollie pricked his ears and walked over to his master, bit rattling, nudging his face until Matthew pushed his head away with a laugh. "Off with you, vagabond. There's laws against your sort."

"I think they've been repealed." Plucking a broad-bladed grass, I trapped it between my thumbs and blew steadily. It gave a satisfyingly raucous rasp. Ollie shied and stamped. "Sorry," I apologized and set to plaiting stems together instead. "Did you have a horse in Rutland?"

"It would have been a bit difficult getting around without one. I had a very fine courser – Arion. My father gave him to me as a colt when I reached my majority. He took a lot of training, but it was worth it; he served me well. He was fast and strong, like Ollie." He removed bits of grass from my coat and from my hair.

I knotted the grass plait and circled it around his wrist, tying it into a bangle of green. "Arion sounds familiar; it's a classical name, isn't it?" I selected three more long blades, nipping them off at the base. The sun warmed my back; I wriggled pleasurably.

"Arion was the son of Demeter and Poseidon, renowned for speed, and… he was immortal."

I laughed. "That's ironic."

He rotated the rope of grass, the twisted stems bruised. "Quite."

I started work on a matching braid for me. "What happened after you changed? Did he still recognize you? Ow!" The stem razored my thumb. Matthew took my hand and examined it. Blood beaded my skin.

"No. He was already dead then." He put my thumb to his mouth and sucked gently. "He was shot from under me at Ancaster Heath in April 1643." He made it sound matter-of-fact, but I knew it to have been a short, bloody skirmish. "There, that'll heal more quickly."

I looked at my thumb; there was barely a sign the skin had been sliced at all. "That must have been soul-destroying."

"It was, but at least I despatched him myself rather than letting some cack-handed field-butcher do it. I expect you know about Ancaster Heath? It could hardly be called a battle – more of a rout. The whole event was a fiasco from beginning to end and not something to be proud of."

"But you survived," I said.

A wry smile tipped his mouth. "Evidently."

"Who did you serve under?"

"Lord Willoughby, initially. I was in the Lincoln Trained Band at first, then joined Cromwell's Horse for a brief while."

"I thought you were in the infantry. I'm sure Mrs Seaton said something about that ages ago. You trained the household staff, didn't you?"

"I did, but cavalry was my greatest strength. It was my father who taught me to ride but my uncle who taught me to fight, as soon as I could hold a practice sword. Now that's ironic, isn't it? He also insisted we had some firearms to defend the house, but that was before I went to Cambridge – when we were still on good terms." He seemed to be tracking something towards the mountains too small for me to see. "I increased the arsenal, updated it, and trained the staff. It seemed like the most prudent course of action. My father would have us trust to God's mercy to protect us, but at that time, I'm afraid, I looked to iron and powder."

I sat up to look at him. "He protected you in the end, didn't He?"

"He certainly did, though only He knows why."

I laid my head on his chest. "That's OK, you don't have to have the answers to everything." I closed my eyes and let the warmth bathe my face, although I would regret it in the evening when I looked at my speckled skin in the mirror. From somewhere far off, a bird of prey pierced the air with its call. "So you were a *'godly and honest*' man, were you? Otherwise Cromwell wouldn't have had you in his troop. What I don't understand is why you were at home in July. Why did you miss the Gainsborough skirmishes?"

He fingered his shoulder where the long line of his silvered scar lay hidden beneath his clothes. "I was wounded at Grantham in May."

"When Willoughby was routed at Belton?"

"No, later in the day when Cromwell led the charge against the Royalists. I returned home to recover and found my father in ill health and with no one else to manage the estate. Besides, there were quite radical elements within the ranks with which I couldn't, in all conscience, agree. And I wasn't the only one. I had a great deal of respect for Cromwell – for his personal conviction, his energy, his attention to detail – but some of those he attracted didn't have either the education or the balance in their approach to their faith."

"You mean they were bigoted and intolerant?"

"I wasn't going to be quite as uncharitable as that, but yes, basically, quite a few of them were, and the war gave them a greater voice than they would have had otherwise. Reform was needed to a degree but the danger was in…"

"… throwing the baby out with the bathwater. From what I've seen of your fighting prowess you've had lots of practice and if that wasn't during the Civil War, when was it?"

"Afterwards."

I gave him one of my best withering looks. "Matthew, I think I had gathered *that* much."

"The problem I find with you," he said, sitting up so that I was obliged to roll away or get a damp patch from the grass on which he had been lying, "is that you are never content with a little information; you want the lot."

"That's not true!" I protested.

"And that whatever I tell you, you want to know more. You are never satisfied until you have bled every last drop of information from me."

"I like to have a complete picture."

"So, you can understand my reluctance sometimes to give you any information because I never know where it's going to lead."

He made light of my obsessive streak, but time and again he drew a veil over his past – whether to obscure it from me or from himself sometimes wasn't clear. Each time I learned a little more, piecing together the strands of his life until gradually I might weave a picture I could understand. But it was slow, and I impatient, and sometimes I pushed too hard and he baulked like a stubborn horse and had to be coaxed instead.

"Sorry," I said, standing, brushing my legs free of grass and regretting getting my kneecaps wet as my trousers stuck damply to them. "It's just that you represent a huge temptation and I've always been a teensy-weensy bit impatient..." He raised a sardonic eyebrow. "All right, quite impatient, and I promise that I will try my very best to restrain my curiosity."

"Really? Expecting you to refrain from asking me questions is like giving an alcoholic a bottle of booze and telling him not to drink it. Talking of which, we must be getting back. Ready for tea?"

We spent the weekend riding, first bareback together, then further afield with me riding a saddled-up Lizzie, whose placid demeanour made Ollie look positively dangerous. We rode beyond the river and into the foothills where once we travelled on snowmobiles. How quickly the land had changed and how I changed with it until I could barely recognize either. It was a weekend spent in the sun and at peace in the knowledge that Monday might bring with it an entirely different turn of events.

CHAPTER

16

Power of Knowledge

Monday.

I had always liked Mondays. When young, Monday usually meant school and a day spent doing what I liked best – studying – and not being at home with Dad. Later, Monday meant lectures and tutorials and time alone with Guy winkling out facts from an obscure document overlooked by previous generations. Monday was an invitation to the week to which I looked forward as surely as almost everybody else did to the weekend. But not today.

Today I stood in front of the library with a book in one hand, my bag in the other, and, tucked away where nobody but my conscience could see it, the journal. I looked into the library's accusing eye and wondered how on earth I could get the journal back without being caught.

Still early, what sleep I'd grasped had been fitful and scant. My eyes felt scratchy and so did I. I had been so preoccupied that morning that I even forgot to put on my ring. My pretext for going to the library – not that I needed one – was to return Guy's book. I had finished it and it had lain festering under benign others until I could stand it no longer and felt obliged to take it back. "Here goes…" Seeking strength from my resolve, I marched towards the door.

Like the morning of the last day of October on which I had taken the journal – the day Staahl attacked me and everything changed – the library seemed empty and, for a moment, I thought my entrance went unnoticed. The air moved behind me.

"Professor."

I spun round. "Oh, good morning!" I tried not to look guilty.

The librarian's patient smile broke the plane of her flat face into brown creases at odds with her tight, smoothed black hair. She had materialized from the lines of shelves, from the very books she tended as guardian of their secrets. "It's a while since we last saw you here, Professor; have you come to return the book?" *The* book. Not *a* book, or the book*s*. Did she know? Had she guessed? Had she, in the rumour of the night while the campus slept, come across the empty box where the journal once lay?

"The book?" I hedged, perspiration gathering beneath my arms and the journal's thick presence wedge-like against my side. When I moved, it dug into my ribs, *nudge, nudge – here I am, here I lie – the thief took me.*

Her face continued to smile but her dark eyes betrayed little. "Yes, the book."

I shifted nervously and something fell to the floor. I looked down – Guy's book. I hoped my relief wasn't evident. "Oh, the book – yes, I have." I bent awkwardly to stop my coat swinging open and revealing what I hid beneath, but the librarian retrieved the book from the floor. She looked at the front, then at the back where Guy stared from the cover.

"Did you find it interesting, Professor?"

"Uh, yes – yes I did. Thank you," I added, because it seemed the polite thing to say. I was desperate to get a move on before I dropped the journal and gave the game away. The door to the library opened, but she didn't go to her desk nor did she look away from my face.

"Timeless," she said.

"I'm sorry?" I queried.

"Knowledge is timeless. It unlocks many secrets we thought were forgotten and some we would choose to forget." I looked doubtfully at the woman whose skin was the colour of dry oak leaves and as ancient as a living wood. Her flimsy, moss-green blouse rippled briefly in the breeze from the doors. "Men will go to any length to protect the knowledge contained in these books, and any length to obtain it. Any lengths." Her hand rested over Guy, stroking the silky cover as she talked, the only movement in her otherwise still body.

Why did she feel the need to tell me this? Did she want me to agree – or did she know what I had done? In any other circumstance I would have gladly enjoined a lively debate on the power of knowledge and how the pursuit and acquisition of it had shaped the world in which we lived, but now I could only offer "Yes" for want of something more insightful to say, because I knew only too well the lengths to which *I* had been prepared to go.

"I'm sure you'll be wanting to get on. I'll put this back for you." Tilting her head, she assessed the photograph. "An intelligent face, but there's something else – ruthless, perhaps, and subtle. Honesty cannot be hidden, but then neither can vice. You can see it in the eyes – he hides what he truly is, but then I expect you already know that." She looked at me directly and I flinched from the canyons of her pupils.

"Um…"

"It must be clear in the way he writes. Do you remember the code or would you like me to remind you of it?"

"The c-code?" I stuttered.

"For the security door downstairs. You are going downstairs, aren't you? For Richardson's journal. That is why you're here, isn't it, Professor?"

Bluff or not to bluff? If she'd sussed Guy in seconds from a photograph, what lie had she detected in me? And then it struck me that I didn't have to lie or complicate; I had to tell the absolute truth, so I did. "Yes, that is precisely why I'm here. And thank you, I remember the code perfectly well."

She nodded, smiled, showing tiny teeth as blunt as tree stumps and brilliantly white, and turned back to her desk, leaving me standing there like an idiot. I remembered to move.

Once beyond the coded door in the secluded vacuum of the vault, I came back to life. I let my heart rate subside to a steady beat and went to find the archive box in which the journal belonged. Yes, *belonged*, or at any rate resided. It had never been mine to take in the first place; I was not its heir. If any, Matthew might claim it, and, until we knew what to do with it, his secret would be safest here, hidden from the world as conspicuously as he lived in it.

I replaced the lid and slid the box back into place and the weight – the burden of trespass – lifted and I felt free of it.

Sometime later, when I emerged from the bowels of the library, the librarian looked up as I passed her desk. "Did you achieve what you came for, Professor?"

I didn't hesitate to answer this time. "Yes, thank you, I did."

She closed the book she had been reading, her hand partially obscuring Guy's face. "Congratulations on your engagement. 'May happiness be your companion and your days together be good and long upon the earth.'" It sounded like a blessing.

"Thank you," I said, looking at my ringless finger, smiling in return. I didn't ask her how she knew, nor did she offer an explanation.

At the end of April, Matthew drove us to the courthouse to sign the documents giving me Power of Attorney over his estate and equal access to all that he owned. As out of place in his city suit as a courtier in a Quaker meeting, George Redgrave took him to one side and none too discreetly tried to persuade him to change his mind. I couldn't hear Matthew's reply, but no doubt it ran along similar lines to the one he had given me when I attempted to do the same earlier, except Matthew's answer left me glowing with pleasure, not subdued and thwarted as Redgrave now was.

I took the opportunity to make an appointment to seek Duffy's advice. A week later, and barely hours before my family arrived, I was again in my defending attorney's office surveying the all-too-familiar scene from the window as she drew up a chair. "I didn't think to see you back here anytime soon. What can I do you for now, honey?"

I put my bag on the floor next to me. "I didn't know who to ask, Duffy, but I need some advice. Do you remember the prostitute who was killed back in October?"

She flicked her hair back from her shoulder. "The one you thought Staahl killed after that time he followed you to the diner?"

Golly, she had a good memory. "Yes. She had a little girl. I think she's living with an aunt now. I would like to set up a trust fund, or something like it, to help provide for a college education when she's older."

Duffy laced her fingers together in a way I felt sure lawyers were specifically taught. "Well, now, that's a mighty fine thing to do and you can afford it."

"No, I don't want to touch Matthew's money."

She held up a hand, rings glinting. "It's yours too, Emma; you're going to be a very wealthy woman. That sure was a sudden turnaround from being *good friends*." She laughed. "Now why am I not surprised you two are getting wed, huh? You just tell me that."

I couldn't help but smile. "Well, we were – we are – the best of friends; isn't that the basis for a good relationship?"

"Sure is, although I'm not sure the court would have accepted your definition of it. Still, justice was done and you're looking very well for it, I must say. Now, this child – it's an education fund you want? It's not something I know much about, but I have a friend who does. Would you like me to contact him for you?" I nodded. "OK, so this fund'll be in your name alone?"

"Yes, but I don't want her to know who it's from. Can it be anonymous?"

Duffy's thin, dark eyebrows rose. "It can, I believe. You'll need to give me your banking details, how much you want to give, that sort of thing."

I handed her a brown, sealed envelope. I'd been taking lessons from Matthew with his meticulous organization. "I think this is everything you need."

She opened the envelope and scanned the single sheet of A4. "Can I ask why you're doing this, honey?"

"The little girl lost everything to that man, Duffy; call it natural justice."

She gave a slight shrug and put the sheet of paper back in the envelope. "I'll see what I can do and get back to you. In the meantime, good luck – you're deserving of it."

That had been the morning. I raced back to my apartment to find Matthew waiting for me.

"I'm not late, am I?" I asked, dashing past him to the bedroom, already taking off my jacket. "I've left the car in the car park – here's the keys." I chucked them vaguely in his direction, hearing him catch them as I pulled my long-sleeved top over my head, dropped it on my bed, and began to rootle for a clean shirt in my chest of drawers.

He came to watch me, an amused expression on his face. "Successful?"

"Mmm?" Bother, the shirt needed ironing. I found my espresso-coloured top instead.

"Your appointment – was it successful?"

I stuck an arm through and pulled the slim-fitting sleeve over my wrist. "Oh, yes, I think so, thanks."

"Good." He hadn't asked why I needed the car, and I hadn't told him. "Dan's just called to say they'll be here in about twenty minutes. There were no problems; it was a smooth flight."

"Twenty minutes! That's sooner than I expected." I struggled to find the polo neck. Matthew located it and I pulled it over my head, emerging feeling scruffy.

"No, that's precisely the time we said. Here..." He smoothed my hair and freed my ponytail from the confines of the tight neck. "Emma, before your family arrive, I wanted to tell you..."

I cast around me, barely listening; there was so much to do. "Have you seen my hairbrush?" He picked it off the end of the bed where I'd left it that morning. "Thanks. You were saying?" I dragged the brush through my hair; it stuck stubbornly in some knots.

"Emma, listen – you need to know that Maggie's back at work and she's coming to the wedding."

My heart sank. "You told her?"

"Henry saw her last week. He gave her the choice of whether to come – we thought it better that way – and she took some time to think about it, but yes, she'll be there."

I wasn't sure how I felt about that. It was what I wanted and why I'd said we should marry in the States after all, but part of me had secretly hoped that she wouldn't come so that I didn't have to face her and feign an affection she wouldn't want, and I didn't feel.

"OK," I nodded slowly, "that's good."

"It's a first step," he said. "I know it won't be easy for either of you."

"For any of us," I acknowledged.

"I think perhaps you should meet before the day, just in case." Just in case she went bananas at the very sight of me. Despite trying to sound positive, little pucker marks running across his brow said otherwise. I reached up and kissed the telltale lines.

"I think that's a very good idea. She's your granddaughter and she needs to be there."

His forehead smoothed. "I won't let anything happen, I promise." But we both knew that Maggie's resentment of me went back further than our first meeting, deep into her childhood from which her recent breakdown stemmed, and nothing – or no one – could begin to guess how she might react.

My future home remained out of bounds to me until the wedding, but not the Barn. Having greeted my family and seen them settled into the house they were borrowing for the week, the following morning I was already under siege with Pat on one side and Ellie on the other.

Pat had a selection of blooms on the table awaiting my decision. A last-minute hitch with the flowers meant I had to select an alternative at short notice. Unfortunately, I was also trying to get some work completed before the wedding, and the two things were mutually incompatible, but equally demanding.

"Perhaps the orchids then, Emma; they will last and go well with your dress." She held a piece of silk next to the creamy orchid.

"That's lovely," I agreed, with half an eye on the computer screen.

"But peonies are more romantic." Ellie thrust a blush peony between the laptop and my nose.

"They are; I like peonies," I concurred, peeking around the blowsy flower-head looking for the *shift* key. "I just need to send this e-mail and I'll be with you." I clicked *send* and waited for the sent confirmation message.

"Emma, this is for your wedding," Pat said in exasperation, "and it's a rush order."

I closed the lid and looked attentive. "Sorry, Josh needed his work back ASAP."

Pat adopted her best schoolmarm voice. "Well, Josh isn't getting married."

"Yes, sorry," I apologized again. "I like the peony best – it's more British and sort of pallid and fluffy around the edges."

Ellie laughed and Pat tried not to smile in case it encouraged me. "Right, I'll get these ordered for the tables. So, you're happy with your bridal bouquet?" Roses and peonies and tiny, sweet-smelling flowers in creams and apricot with little green tongues of unfurling ferns. Yum. I nodded with enthusiasm. "Now, seating arrangements for the church," Pat said firmly, placing a list in front of me.

"Golly Moses, Em," Beth said, looking up at the expanse of the Barn as she scooped Archie from the baby seat. "You're going to live *here*?"

I kissed Archie and for once was rewarded with a smile. "Er, no, we're around the corner." Archie grabbed my finger. "Hello, Archie." We shook fingers.

"The big house? The b-i-g white house?" She used her free hand to exaggerate. "So, who lives here?" I wrinkled my nose at the baby and he tried to wrench it off. Beth prodded my arm.

"Oh, Matthew's er... his parents."

"You don't sound very sure."

"Of course I'm sure; I'm just stunned by my nephew's sudden acceptance of me. He cried yesterday." I blew a raspberry at him.

Beth reached inside the car for her bag. "He was tired from the flight, Em, and I think it's more likely to be the other way round. Rob!" she called to her husband in conversation with Dan. He looked up. "Can you bring Emma's dress in for me, love?" She closed the car door. "Hey, Em, you've caught the sun." My hand went instinctively to my face, visualizing skin as speckled as a thrush. "You should get out more; it suits you – you look quite glowing. Unless it's the sex of course."

"Beth!" I hissed, glancing around, relieved to see we were out of earshot. "We better get inside before you totally embarrass me in front of the family."

She grasped my arm. "Look, before we go in, what are Matthew's parents like? I can't help thinking... you know."

I was at a total loss. "No – what?"

"Well, Matthew is so... so I don't know..."

"Handsome, kind, intelligent?"

She gurgled, sounding like her son. "He is too. No, I mean he's very proper, very correct, old-fashioned, I suppose you could say, though I don't suppose you'd notice, Em – you belong in another era. I was just wondering, are his parents very patrician? Only," she went on hurriedly, "the twins can be a bit of a handful and they might forget their Ps and Qs. Alex gets so shy he won't say boo to a goose let alone look at one, and Flora – well, you know what Flora's like – I never know what she's going to come out with next. And they've been squabbling more recently, which can get embarrassing. We were in the café the other day and they started up this ridiculous argument about nothing and they were at it hammer and tongs. I swear we won't see those customers again." Archie patted her mouth and she kissed his little fat hand.

"I wouldn't worry; there's nothing intimidating about Pat and Henry."

Pat had plied the children with food before they'd stepped through the door. She had even managed to overcome Alex's natural reserve and he was chatting away happily with a glass in one hand and what looked like a muffin in the other. Flora had shown Joel her new tooth and was now finding his crewcut entertaining. She kept bouncing the flat of her hand on the straw stubble as he squatted in front of her beaming, and she threw her head back laughing. I had been momentarily stunned when I learned he had taken the jet to the UK to collect my family. When I said as much to Matthew, he had shaken his head and smiled as if every twenty-three-year-old could fly a private jet. Mum, on the other hand, stood awkwardly to one side watching them, seemingly unsure whether to intervene.

"We'd better rescue Mum," I said to my sister. "She's looking very formal and British."

As I watched the two families relax, I began to appreciate how accomplished the Lynes were at projecting the image of a conventional family, and how adept they had become, adopting – like a mantle – the illusion of normality. So, by the time Matthew joined us, I could almost believe it to be true. Almost.

Later that afternoon, as the children exhausted their quota of "being good" and their tempers, and those of their parents, began to fray, Matthew and I took them down to the paddock to meet the horses. Ollie lifted his head when he heard Matthew's voice and trotted over to greet us, thrusting his nose into my outstretched hand as an awestruck Flora gaped at him. She shoved past Alex to touch Ollie's mane. Alex hung back.

"Carefully, Flora – no sudden movements or you might

startle him," I told her, but Ollie nuzzled her hair in return and she giggled.

"I'm going to have riding lessons in the summer, Mummy said," Flora announced with a degree of self-importance, now stroking Ollie's nose, but more carefully, despite the eagerness in her face. "I wanted to before but she said I was too little and I'm not now because now I'm bigger."

"Yeah, you'd bounce if you fell off, chunky monkey, chunky monkey..."

Flora scowled at her brother. "You're jealous because you're not having lessons like me."

"No, I'm not! Riding is for sissy girls. I'm learning to fence, like Emma did."

"Emma's a girl."

"No, she's not, she's grown up, it's different." Friction crept like sea-mist, chilling the air. This went beyond simple sibling rivalry and jet lag. As Alex and I watched Matthew show Flora how to saddle Lizzie – helping her tighten the girth straps of the glossy saddle under the horse's belly, praising her all the while so that she grew with it, and blossomed – I asked him about his fencing lessons. All the time we chatted, he didn't take his eyes off his sister, and it seemed to me that he tensed inside where a knot of envy bound him. I remembered all too well the rancour it had caused in Beth and me, and the years it had taken before we found friendship and parity. I didn't want the children to go through what we endured, but neither did I know what could be done about it.

"Is she going to be safe?" Beth asked as she joined us, and Matthew lifted Flora high enough so that she could swing her leg over Lizzie's back and settle into the saddle.

"Don't be daft; you know he wouldn't take any risks with her," I carefully chided to drive away her doubt. I had to admit – albeit silently – that my niece looked awfully small on the animal's back as Matthew led her away into a slow, wide circle, a beam of delight across her shining face.

"Don't you want a go, Alex?" Beth asked her son.

He turned away from her. "Riding is for sissies," he snarled, and a coil of bile green escaped from him and wound into the ether.

"Oh Alex," Beth said, but she had no more an idea of what to do than I had.

"Do you remember how we were?" I asked her quietly.

"Yes," she said, "that's what's worrying me."

We were alone once the children had been herded towards the Barn for tea before returning to their house. Matthew removed the saddle and slung it over the fence rail.

"He's jealous," I said, "and it's eating him up inside."

Matthew drew his hand over Lizzie's flanks, checking for abrasions before letting her loose to join Ollie as he grazed the far paddock. "It reminds me of Harry and Joel when they were about the same age. Do you know what's making him envious?"

The day's warmth lifted dew from the evening grass, and the earth smelled fresh and clean. I leant against the fence as the low sun enriched the western sky and wondered how resentment could blind someone to so much beauty.

"Everything," I said finally. "Everything – and nothing. I feel so helpless. I want to do something, but it's like history's repeating itself."

He hoisted the saddle and together we walked back towards the tack room. "History doesn't repeat itself exactly though, does it? The problems might remain the same, but it's the individuals who determine the outcome, and they're always different."

Perhaps. Perhaps not. Whatever the case I couldn't bear the thought of sitting back and watching spite spiral into rank hatred.

Making Amends

Ellie left for a double shift at the med centre that would take her through the night. It was something she was accustomed to doing, and she would have worked longer if her unusual stamina hadn't attracted comments. So now she did the occasional extra shift and feigned tiredness. Gradually, I grew used to the differences in the family, but every now and again I forgot because they looked so normal, until one of them did something that reminded me how very different they actually were.

On form after a good night's sleep, the children were drawing on their father's reserves of patience at a rate exceeding its replenishment. He growled, but the twins continued to jostle each other around the heavy picnic hampers packed and waiting by the Barn's back door.

Matthew shouldered a couple of the baskets and looked around. "We need to keep an eye on the children. The river's high at the moment and I don't want them near it alone. Joel, did I hear you won't be joining us?"

"Meeting with Mom and Dad first," Joel grunted. "I'll get this stuff down there – by the willows, right?"

"If you would, thanks." Matthew glanced at Beth, who struggled to balance a wriggling Archie on her hip. "Henry, perhaps you could take the baby; it's quite a way to walk."

"I'd be delighted." Henry held out his hands, and Archie, having gazed solemnly at him, broke into a broad smile. Beth stretched her arms above her head to relieve her aching back as Archie began investigating Henry's beard, scrabbling his fingers through it much to Henry's amusement. I wondered whether the baby saw through his disguise more easily than adults, who saw only what they wanted to see.

"Come on, you two." I held out a hand each to the twins. "Quick, march. Let's see if we can beat everyone down there. What shall we be – legionary soldiers in Hadrian's army, or Caesar's invasion force? *Venite – Sin... dex... sin... dex...*" We marched out of the Barn, around the corner of the house, and down the slope towards the river, where we had feasted on spit roast pig that winter night in the snow.

We heard the river long before we saw it. It chewed the banks, frothing around rocks that stood in its path, rumbling as it churned the stony bed.

Several folding chairs already waited by Joel's basket about a hundred yards from the river, where a bend made a promontory on which grew lush and inviting grass, thickly studded with flowers.

Matthew eased the baskets down. The bruised grass smelled fresh and clean under the clear sky, and I inhaled deeply. "Mmm, this is de-*licious* – better than food. Who needs to eat when you have all this?" I opened my eyes. "Where are you two off to?"

The twins had drifted away, picking long-stemmed flowers they held in bunches. Every now and again they darted looks towards the trees where the river called. Matthew watched them as he unpacked the basket. "Alex, Flora, the river is dangerous; keep away from it unless there is someone with you, do you understand?"

"OK," they sang. Flora added, "We're picking flowers for tea."

She waved her bunch at him as they danced back through the grass, before handing them to me. "These are for you, Emma, 'cos you're the bride."

I kissed her sun-warmed cheek, all round and rosy. "Thank you, darling, they're beautiful."

"Are there fish in the river?" Alex asked, handing me his bunch and receiving my hug shyly. "Daddy said he would take us fishing at home, but it was raining and we didn't go."

"He said the fish would get wet." Flora pulled a face. "That's silly. Will you take us, Matthew? Emma said you would."

I pursed my lips at the blatant fabrication. "Actually, Flora, I don't believe I said any such thing. Nice try."

She adopted a superior pout. "No, but you would have done if you'd thought about it. You didn't think hard enough."

"Cheeky minx," I reprimanded, amazed at her sheer gall.

"You told a lie," Alex accused, his eyebrows drawn together in a black line. "Mummy said you mustn't tell lies, Flora."

Flora stuck her tongue out at him. "Neagh, neagh, I did not. I just said that Emma would have said it if she'd thought about it. That's not telling lies."

Alex shook his finger. "You're too stupid to know. Stupid, fat bubblehead."

"Alex!" I cried as Flora's eyes widened in hurt. Her teeth clamped angrily and she raised her fist. Matthew caught it before it engaged with her brother's face.

"That's enough – both of you." He put his hands on Alex's shoulders and turned him around to face him squarely. "Alex, that was unkind. Whatever you believed your sister to have done, she didn't deserve that remark; it was hurtful." And to Flora. "And you, young lady, don't play games with the truth. Always be honest when you can – especially with your family. They must be able to trust what you say because one day it might be really important. Now," he said, standing up as their parents approached, "I believe I told your aunt that I would teach her to tickle trout one day. How about it?"

"That sounds fun," Beth panted as she flopped into a chair.

Flora screwed up her face. "But I want to go fishing."

"It is fishing, dumm... Flora," Alex quickly corrected himself. "Ben's grandpa taught him – he told me so. Isn't it, Matthew?"

Matthew riffled the boy's dark hair. "It is indeed. Are you two going to help me set this up so our womenfolk can have somewhere comfortable to sit?"

"Well..." said Alex.

"Um..." Flora hummed, and the children's eyes slid hopefully towards the river.

"As knights would have done for their ladies," Matthew pointed out, "before they went fishing for trout."

"O-K!" Alex shouted.

Flora plopped onto the grass. "I'm a lady and you have to look after me, Alex."

Matthew hauled her to her feet, laughing. "Not yet, you're not, and not if you want to go fishing later. Here, catch..." and he threw her a cushion to put on a chair for her grandmother.

Between us we spread the rugs on the ground and made a corral of the chair legs and baskets to prevent Archie from escaping. He practised his unsteady walking from one adult to the next, clapping his hands every time they applauded, his sun-gold hair shining. Pat and Mum soon fell to discussing knitting patterns as Beth and the twins helped sort through the baskets.

Quieter than usual, Matthew watched the children from where we sat on the outskirts of the circle. Finally, he leant towards me. "How can I tell Flora not to lie in one breath, when every other I take is a fabrication? I'm such a hypocrite – it's worse than the lying." Archie tottered towards us over the rumply rugs and

Matthew caught him, waiting until he found his balance again before letting go. "You do understand, don't you?"

"Of course I do," I reassured him. "It's not the same at all. I couldn't love a liar and a hypocrite, and I certainly wouldn't marry one."

The light breeze stiffened, lifting my hair, and his expression softened. "Marry one – and you're marrying me. Just two days, my love." He lifted my hand to his lips and kissed first my ring, and then my finger. "Two days before you are mine." My tummy squiggled in a mix of warm anticipation and a flutter of nerves. He smiled, and I remembered that he could feel what I felt as clearly as I could sense his elation. "There's no escape, no quarter given," he teased.

"None needed, none sought," I replied, leaning my forehead on his. I looked up as something tugged my attention to find Beth looking at us, and I understood that what I felt was wistful energy riding on silent waves as tangible as water, as invisible as air. There were times now, when the boundaries between physical and ethereal blurred, each becoming as substantial as the other, and I had to remember not to let it show.

Mum and Pat were beginning to hand out napkins. I still felt full from lunch, but the twins were sitting in front of the food basket like expectant puppies on their very best behaviour. Holding a sandwich in one hand, Archie headed towards Matthew, dropped onto all fours, rolled over onto his bottom, and sat stolidly in front of him.

"Hello, Archie," Matthew said. "What do you have there?" Archie stuck his fist out with the crumpled sandwich. "That looks… delicious. Are you going to eat it?"

The sandwich remained stubbornly aloft.

"I think he's offering it to you," Rob said from the other side of the circle.

Archie waved the sandwich at Matthew, frowning now. "Da, da, da."

"Take the sandwich to Daddy, Arch," I encouraged, seeing where this was leading.

Beth passed a plate with several sandwiches on it to Matthew. "Here, you'd better have these; Arch can be very persistent, but he'll be fine if you eat something."

My nephew wouldn't be swayed. "Da-dy," the baby said, staring at Matthew with unswerving blue eyes.

Rob called, "Daddy's here, Arch."

Matthew took the sandwich from the chubby fingers and Archie squealed in delight. "Thank you, Archie," he said, but the baby couldn't be bought that easily and, climbing to his feet, snatched the sandwich from Matthew's hand and tried to force-feed him instead.

"*Widge...*" he insisted. "*Widge!*" With everyone now following Archie's antics with interest, Matthew's reluctance to play his game became increasingly obvious.

"Heavens above!" Pat exclaimed loudly enough so that the baby was momentarily forgotten. "I've forgotten to pack the tea," she declared, surreptitiously slipping a small packet into the pocket of her denim skirt. Matthew jumped up. "I'll fetch it. I won't be long."

Archie was not amused. There was a finely balanced moment when he gazed after Matthew, deciding whether to make an issue of it.

"*Archie's* sandwich," I reiterated. He gave me a disdainful look, stuck his bottom lip out, and sat on his nappy-padded behind with his back to me.

"That told you," Beth laughed, passing me a napkin.

A fly made a nuisance of itself. I swatted at it absentmindedly whilst nibbling one of the sandwiches. The day would have been too warm but for the insistent breeze that blew the sound of the river towards us, at once both lulling and inviting. I stretched out along the edge of the blanket, leaning on one elbow and listening to the conversation. Archie forgot to be cross and helped himself to the sandwiches Matthew had left, one in each hand for good measure, and poddled over to his father.

The fly buzzed my ear, making me flinch, and landed on the rug. I aimed to flap it away but it rose lazily into the air, dodging my advance. I heard the sound of voices and looked around to see Matthew, Dan, and Joel strolling towards us. Tossing a packet of tea to Henry, Matthew settled beside me.

"You're safe, Arch is asleep," I said.

Matthew smiled, then just as suddenly stopped. "Where're the children?"

"What?"

Rising again, he scanned the area. "The twins – where are they?"

"They were here a minute ago," Pat said, but Rob and Beth were on their feet, searching the surrounding levels with anxious eyes.

"Alex, Flora!" Rob called.

Long grass sighed in the breeze, but the sward remained untouched.

"Could they have gone back to the house?" Mum asked.

"Flora!" Beth filled her lungs. "Alex!"

Dan shielded his eyes from the glare. "We've just come from there; we would have seen them."

Fear swept through the party. Sound-scented air, as beguiling as water and as treacherous, rose from the river. Matthew and I turned as one.

"They'll be by the river," I said, dread welling.

Matthew was already moving. "Dan, Henry, take the southern

section down to the paddocks. Joel – the levels." There was no caution in their speed now, but no one counted how long it took for them to cover the ground. A call, the faintest of sounds carried by the wind and so brief it might have been no more than the suggestion of our hope, had Matthew veering through a fringe of saplings towards where the little bridge crossed the river.

Beth looked on the verge of collapse. "The river..."

"Stay here with Arch; we'll find them." I pushed her back towards Mum and Pat, as Dad followed Henry, and Rob and I ran as fast as we could towards the river where Matthew had been moments before.

Distended with melt-water, the rabid current roared and foamed. I looked up and down the banks, but could see no sign of the twins or Matthew. Cutting the river like a knife, the bridge was under water. Further away, I could hear faint calls as the men searched downstream.

Rob despaired. "They'll drown if they fall into this! FLORA! ALEX!" he began calling again, his voice cracking in anguish as I began running along the bank upriver. Where was Matthew? I stumbled on uneven ground, falling and feeling my skin scrape on rough rocks, not caring, and up and running again, my breath coming sharp and shallow, short and harsh. Nothing but the water and the wind, the rocks and the fury of the spate. And then a sound – a cry. Alex. Around the bend in the river where the willows hung close to the water, I saw him. "Alex!" I almost wept with relief. Wet hair black against his frozen white face, his body shaking, but alive – so alive. I fell to my knees and held him to me. "Alex, where's Flora? Where is she?" He stared at the river, eyes dark as the water. "She's in the river? Alex – is Flora in the water?"

He nodded. Rob came up behind me, his breathing noisy. I thrust Alex into his arms.

"She's in the river. Flora… FLORA!" Only a few dozen yards away on the opposite bank and half hidden by the trees, a dark shape moved. "Matthew!" I yelled, but he didn't look up as he searched the churning waters. Within a split second he halted, stiffened, and with a movement as fluid as the water, dived into the river. He surfaced once, disappeared again. I stared fixedly at the point where I'd last seen him. Seconds passed into a minute, then another.

Rob clutched Alex, watching the waters. "Where is she? For pity's sake, where's my little girl!"

Nothing but river, and wind and fear.

I pointed. "There!"

Fifty yards downstream, battling the current towards an overhanging tree, Matthew clawed the water in an attempt to reach land. The water bucked around him, the current too strong. I couldn't see clearly. I ran, hearing Rob's heavy footfall behind me, catching glimpses as Matthew swept downstream where the banks rose sheer.

"Matthew!" In and out of trees, ducking their treacherous branches, feeling them whip against my face, staggering into iron trunks until I could see him clearly this time. He fought the water using only one arm. Why only one arm? Then I could see – a small golden head held above the river.

Rob saw her too. "Flora!" he howled, dropping Alex to his feet and sprinting to the nearest overhang. "Emma, I can't swim."

I hunted frantically for a branch, anything that we could use, but the ravenous river – swollen with greed – would devour them if it could, so I lifted my head and with the full force that desperation gave me, bellowed, "JOEL! DAN! HEN-*RY*!" and let the river carry the plea downstream.

Wrenching a snow-damaged branch from a tree, Rob reached as far as he could over the water, but the leaping river tore it from his hand. Desperate, he stretched towards Matthew at the same moment as I yelled, "Watch out!" and Matthew turned in time to see the partially submerged rock. Bringing his arm around to protect Flora's head, he took the full force of the blow on his shoulder. Over the roar of the water I heard the gunshot crack of bone shattering. Rob moaned in horror, but Matthew managed to wedge himself between two boulders. With an almighty effort, with one arm he lifted Flora's limp body free of the water, punching her through the air towards her father. Rob's fingers grasped the little jacket, but she was too heavy, the current too strong, and she fell against the bank, her legs dragged by the water until the thin fabric began to tear. From my left, Dan raced to the riverbank, flinging himself on his stomach and reaching as far as he could until he seized her arm, bringing her to shore.

Henry arrived seconds later. He rounded on me. "Where's Dad? Emma, where is he?" Searching the waters, I couldn't see him. Fear closed my throat.

"Flora isn't breathing," Dan said over his shoulder, starting compressions. "Help me, she's not breathing!"

"Henry, you're the only one who can help her," I said, gathering my wits at last. "Joel, come on, we must find Matthew."

Together we ran downstream, Joel soon outstripping me. "The bridge! He'll be cut in two!" I yelled as Joel sped out of sight. Please God, help him! I was fast losing my breath and with it speed. Count – one – two – three – *run, damn it, run* – four – five – six – *faster* – seven – eight… each step pounding until there, on the bend, I saw Joel reaching out over the river. He grabbed something and hauled. Seconds later, his clothes clinging to his body, his shirt shredded where the rocks had torn it to ribbons, stood Matthew. His arm hung at an odd angle, his face colourless, but he was alive.

"Matthew!" I managed as I reached him.

"I'm all right, Emma. Where's Flora?"

Out of breath and overwhelmed with relief, I couldn't speak. Joel answered, "Gramps is with her – she's not breathing."

"Stay with Emma and make sure she's all right," he told him, and then sped off upriver, retracing the path we had followed.

I bent double, drawing air into scorched lungs. "His arm, Joel. I heard it break." I attempted to straighten and follow him, but Joel held me back.

"Wait up, Emma, give yourself a moment. Matthew's OK. He'd swum to the bank when I got there."

"But his shoulder…"

"He's fine," he said, and this time I detected an edge of authority to it I had never heard before.

"All right, but at least let me begin to walk back."

On his knees, Matthew bent over Flora so that all I could see were her little white legs in bright pink socks with one sandal missing. On the ground next to her, Rob cried soundlessly and Alex stood by his shoulder staring at the motionless body of his sister. Dan had gone, but Henry knelt by Flora, and as I neared, I could see him holding one small hand in his, his other against her neck. Father and son trying to save a life. It was like witnessing my own death. I felt sick.

Matthew started compressions again. It was at this point in some hospital drama that someone would invariably say, "It's too late, Doctor, she's gone," and the doctor would draw a hand across his face, defeated by death, disillusioned by life and his own failure.

Pump, pump, pump – breaths, one, two – *pump, pump, pump*, on and on until I wanted to scream *Stop!* and let the agony of waiting end. What would I tell my sister? What would I say to our mother, our father? How could their lives continue when one so beloved had been lost? A strange noise rose from beside me, and something touched my hand. I looked down and Alex whimpered. My heart breaking for him, I held him close. "Alex, it's OK. Flora's fine now." What ridiculous things we say to the very young; what lies we tell them about death to save us from the yawning truth. As I said it, I could almost believe it to be true, repeating, with my face pressed against his wet hair, "She's OK, she's OK, she's fine…" as if saying it would make it so.

Joel put an arm around my shoulders. "Emma, come on; let's get Alex back to the house."

Pushing him away, I dropped down next to Matthew. He didn't break the steady rhythm of breaths and compressions. "Flora's going to be all right, Joel. Look after Alex."

Henry looked up. "Emma…"

"Just give her a moment." I put my hands around her head and closed my eyes. She felt as cold as the fish I'd caught as a child and not my golden Flora, warm like the sun. I could not feel her life, but I could see it. I willed her to live, to breathe again. *Please – help her.* Raising my face, I fought the layers of darkness shrouding her to find her colours. "She's in there."

"I know," Matthew replied between breaths. "I'm trying to reach her."

"Come on, Flora," I urged. "Come on," I begged. There it was: a pulse of colour, like an explosion, fading again, then another – longer this time – ripe and full and ready to burst into life. "Matthew…"

"I feel it."

Her head jerked beneath my hands. I let go. She coughed, her body rising to expel the water and Matthew rolled her onto her side. Her first breath. She hacked again, then promptly threw up.

In tears, Rob wiped her mouth, calling, "Flora-bell, it's Daddy. Flora. Flora…"

She coughed weakly. "Daddy."

Matthew checked her eyes. Joel returned with a blanket as Beth ran up, deathly pale. She tried to tear Flora from Matthew, but he began walking rapidly towards the house. "We need to get her to hospital."

"But she'll be all right, won't she?"

"I'll run some tests. We should know within a few hours." And he broke into a sprint, reaching the house as Dan drew the car up at the front.

"What does he mean? Why does he need to run tests?" Beth gave a frightened gasp. "She's going to be all right, isn't she?"

Henry offered her his arm. "I'm sure she'll be fine, but he'll want to check there's been no lasting damage to her lungs and that she's fully responsive. Let's get back to the house and I'll take you straight to the hospital."

Beth was saying that she wanted to be with Flora, and Henry explained that she could stay with her when I remembered that in all the panic we'd forgotten Alex. There he stood, staring at the crumpled damp patch his sister had made on the thin, stony grass. He shook slightly. Putting my arm around his skinny frame, I tried to draw him away. "Come on, Alex. If we hurry we can go to the hospital too and see how Flora is."

He pulled back. "I don't want to."

"That's all right, we'll stay at the Barn. It's warm there and you can have chocolate milk."

He didn't say anything, nor did he move. I removed the hair from over his eyes and my fingers came away wet. He was crying. "Flora will be coming home, Alex."

His whole body shuddered. "I... I didn't mean to."

I didn't like the sound of that. "What, darling?"

"I didn't mean fo... for her to fall in."

I checked, but Beth and Rob were almost at the house now,

and there was nobody else close by. I knelt in front of him. "Alex, tell me what happened."

"We… we thought we would have a look at the river. Matthew said we couldn't go alone, but we weren't alone, were we? We were together." I said nothing; I didn't need to, he knew well enough. "Flora wanted to see the fish, bu… but I said she would have to go down to the water and she said she mustn't but I said it was all right, so she did. And then I said she shouldn't get too close but she thought she saw a fish and she tried to touch it. I tried to stop her, but she fell in. I did try, Emma, really I did." His shoulders sagged miserably.

"I think you need a hot drink. Mummy and Daddy will want to go to the hospital, but Granny and Grandpa will need someone to help look after Archie and you are the very best person to do that, Alex, because you're his big brother."

He fixed me with eyes dark like his father's. His voice quivered.

"Why don't they want to stay with me?"

"Because they know you're safe and they need to make sure Flora is safe as well."

He nodded and, letting me take his hand, together we walked back to the house.

Pat and Henry insisted we stay the night with them as we waited for news. Jeannie joined us around the long kitchen table with a big casserole she had cooked, and we ate it in preoccupied silence.

Rob and Beth stayed at the hospital while Matthew ran tests and monitored Flora throughout the night. By midmorning, the car drew up and Flora bounced out as if nothing had happened, followed by her parents, looking exhausted but relieved. She chatted away to anyone who would listen and nobody saw Alex's subdued look. Finally, as the fuss died down, Flora skipped up to him.

"Matthew rescued me," she sang, "but you tried to save me first; you're my hero," and she flung her arms around her brother.

"Flora, why did you want to touch the fish?" he asked.

She regarded him with wide blue eyes. "I wanted to tickle the fish and make them laugh," she said simply. "Do you want to see my bruises?"

Flora was indeed fine. The icy mountain water probably helped save her. She had been unconscious for no more than a few minutes before resuscitation began, but it had been a close call, as Matthew confided when we were alone.

He removed his watch with some difficulty. It had survived for so many years since Ellen gave it to him at their wedding. "I'll get it mended," he said, when I saw that it had stopped working. He had donned a jacket when he went to the hospital, but underneath he still wore the remains of the shirt from the previous day. He unbuttoned it, his movements unusually awkward.

"What is it?" I asked, reaching out to help him, then choked, mortified, as the fabric slipped from his back, revealing his right shoulder completely misaligned and bent like a misshapen bough.

He smiled ruefully. "It set before I could get it back in place."

I ran my hand cautiously over the unnatural undulations. "Does it hurt?"

"No, not now. I'll ask Henry and Ellie to set it for me."

"How? Surely you can't do that without…" Realization hit me. "Oh no, you can't, Matthew; you'll be in *agony*!"

"It's the only way to get it straight and it can't be operated on. I heal too quickly and anaesthesia doesn't work. Henry will break it and Ellie can set it – she needs the practice. Sorry," he apologized, when he saw I didn't find it even remotely funny. "It won't take long."

I bit my lip. "I can't watch. I can't see you in pain."

"I wouldn't want you to; there's no need." He lifted my chin with a finger. "It's really not as bad as it sounds."

Yes, it was, and I felt physically sick at the thought of it. He didn't tell me when the realignment was scheduled to take place and I couldn't ask. Only later, when everyone else slept and I sat restlessly on one of the Barn's big sofas, did I hear the front door open and guessed where he had been.

Ellie came in first, followed by Henry, then Matthew. Even in the soft light of the side lamp, Ellie looked a ghastly colour, and Henry not much better. Shooting me a look as she crossed the room, wordlessly she left by the back door to go home to the Stables. Henry slumped into one of the chairs, having aged a decade over the course of an hour. Matthew filled the kettle and switched it on. I broke the silence. "Is it over?"

Still wan, Henry smiled. "Emma, I leave it to you to ensure my father isn't so irresponsible in future. I don't want to be doing *that* again in a hurry. Dad, I don't think tea will be quite up to it, though thanks for the thought."

"The tea's for Emma; this is for you." Matthew handed him a glass of a rich amber liquid.

Henry attempted a laugh. "Cheers, I need this."

"And I don't need anything," I said. "Show me," I demanded, already easing the jacket away where it hung loose around him, not sure what to expect. His shoulder looked perfect and strong, his skin smooth and only the faintest smudges where the bone had been re-broken. Even as I watched, they faded and disappeared altogether. I kissed his shoulder, and laid my cheek against it.

He slipped his other arm around me. "You need your beauty sleep. Maggie will be here first thing in the morning and I know how much you're looking forward to seeing her again."

I prodded him ever so carefully and he kissed me back.

"You're welcome to stay here," Henry offered, but I thought that perhaps he and Pat could do with some time to themselves after the last forty-eight hours, so I declined with thanks. I looked hopefully at Matthew, but he shook his head. "Your bridal home is out of the question for another twenty-four hours. I'll take you back to campus."

"Can you drive?" I asked doubtfully. He answered by swinging his arm right around as if bowling for England. "OK," I allowed, "let's leave Henry in peace."

Matthew knew exactly how much I looked forward to seeing Maggie again. I tried not to think about it when Elena nattered away, waving nail-varnish colours in front of me long before any normal human had the right to be awake. I tried not to think about what Maggie might say when we drove away from campus as students began to stir. And, as we walked in through the Barn's kitchen door, I made every effort to be thinking about something completely different in case my nerves failed me and it showed.

She sat at the table flanked by Henry and Dan, mugs steaming in front of them in an attempt at normality. Her steel hair had been allowed to grow longer, and the boat-necked sailor top she wore over stone linen trousers was navy, not black. An element of compromise existed in the clothes she wore, a concession to femininity in the necklace half-hidden by the carefully chosen toning silk scarf. When she saw us she rose stiffly and waited until Matthew shut the door. She greeted him first, before turning to me. "Dr D'Eres..." she began, her eyes lowered. "Emma," she corrected. She raised her eyes to meet mine. I didn't know what I would see, but I would have been deluded if I expected warmth. I detected her usual chilly reserve, but the pungent hate seemed to have gone.

"Maggie," I responded, taking a mental step forward. I offered my hand. "I'm so glad you've come."

It was one of those moments when you don't know which way it will go – neither, by the expressions on the faces of those watching, did anyone else. Maggie regarded me for a moment as if calculating what lay behind my response. She shook my hand. I say shook – all it amounted to was the merest touch of my fingers before she withdrew, but it was enough.

"I'm pleased I was able to be here. We are having... tea." She avoided sneering the word, but only just. "Would you care to join us?"

I smiled. "Thank you, that would be most kind."

Good grief, what a charade. The atmosphere vibrated as Maggie and I enacted a ritual tea ceremony while plotting each other's demise. All we needed was an obi or two and cherry blossom and the scene would be set for a Samurai showdown. She set a mug of tea on the table opposite her and I perched on the stool. Matthew sat next to me.

Henry cleared his throat. "I was telling Maggie what an exciting few days we've had."

She took the cue. "I hope your niece is quite recovered. I believe near-drowning can have unforeseen side-effects some time afterwards."

Now, did she do that on purpose or did the cattiness come naturally? I didn't need to say anything because Matthew answered. "In this case, you'll be pleased to hear that Flora will make a full recovery. She's a robust little girl and very brave."

Maggie's face cracked a smile; it was the first time I

remembered seeing one and it didn't look natural. "I'm relieved to hear it; there'll be no need to postpone the wedding after all."

"None at all," Matthew said steadily.

There was a few minutes' respite as Matthew discussed transport arrangements with his son and grandson for the following morning. Maggie sipped her tea while watching me over the rim of the mug. "What a lovely ring," she said out of the blue. "It looks very old. Is it?"

For once she appeared genuinely interested, so I told her what I knew of it, leaving out the fact it belonged to her great, great grandmother four hundred years previously, which might have been a bit of a giveaway. Her stare never wavered. Even when I finished, her cold cat eyes continued to watch me: my mouth, the way I used my hands to illustrate a point. Eventually, I dried up. Searching for something to say, I returned the compliment. "That looks like an interesting necklace, Maggie. Have you had it long?"

One hooked eyebrow rose higher and, with a slow smile, she lifted the silk scarf to reveal the necklace. A gold snake coiled around her neck, each scale perfectly articulated, the head – with its brilliant ruby eyes – clasping the tail in its mouth. I had last seen it around the neck of Matthew's first wife. A chair scraped noisily as Henry left the table, throwing an angry glare at his daughter.

"Ellen left it to me," she said smoothly, watching her father's back. "Do you like it? Not a day goes by when I don't wear it in her memory." Her eyes slid to mine and then to Matthew. I wouldn't rise to her challenge, and I couldn't let Matthew be provoked. Henry ran the tap as he washed his mug with serrated movements.

"I remember her showing me," I replied evenly. "It was her favourite piece, wasn't it, Matthew? I'm sure Ellen would be delighted to know how much you treasure it."

We all knew the meeting to be futile. We had done our best

to build bridges, but this was one where the foundations of the association were flawed through to the very bedrock, and no amount of concrete could render the structure of the relationship any more solid than a tenuous fabrication.

"Well," I said, standing and relieving us all of the agony of further artifice, "I have a lot to do before tomorrow. It's good to see you recovered, Maggie. Dan, thanks for everything you did yesterday." I picked up my mug and went over to the sink on the pretext of washing it up. "Henry?" I said quietly, putting my hand on his arm. "Thank you, and I'm sorry."

Once in the courtyard and out of hearing, I let out a long breath. "Well, we tried."

"Yes," Matthew said, "we tried."

It was the only blot on the day because, shortly afterwards, Matias, Elena, and my family arrived for the rehearsal, and there was no time to think about Maggie, only getting things in the right order, and remembering who did what and stood where. Beth felt better for a long sleep and Rob, though drawn, had regained his humour. Only Alex still seemed quiet.

After the extensive practice in which I thought it would be a miracle if it came together on the day, Matthew had a brief word with Rob, and then disappeared with Alex through the adjoining door at the far end of the Barn and into his own home. I hovered by the door, indecisive. I waited for a few minutes and, just as I made up my mind, saw Matthew and Alex cross the courtyard to the garage block. Curiosity burned.

"Em, we're going upstairs to do our nails, OK?" Elena called from the stairs. "Then it will be your turn – don't go away."

"Yup – OK," I called back, half-listening and, when no one was watching, stole through the door and out into the courtyard and the fine drizzle that dampened it.

An oddly familiar noise came from the garage block – *tchink,* *tchink* – short and sharp like metal on metal. I edged towards the wide swing doors standing partially open. *Tchink*. I craned my neck, but a beam obscured my view and all I could see were two pairs of legs – one long and strong, the other short and thin, moving in an odd circular dance around the centre of the garage floor.

Tchink. Tchink, tchink.

"Good!" I heard Matthew exclaim. "Keep your head up, that's it, but stay on guard and don't let it drop. Well done, now parry... and again."

Parry – they were fencing?

I left them to it. Later, Matthew said that Alex found it hard to compete for attention with his sister and younger brother, with two overworked parents, so he wanted to give him some dedicated time and a chance to be himself.

So simple, so obvious, I thought. "Genius," I declared.

"Hardly," he grinned, shaking his head at my admiration. "It's what comes of living through three generations of children. Even then, I don't always get it right. Far from it," he murmured as an afterthought.

"Maggie has to want to be helped, Matthew. It seems she's determined to dislike me come what may. I think the best we can expect is a truce."

"A truce is only ever good for as long as it lasts and I'm not willing to accept her antagonism towards you, especially now when she has no excuse other than her sheer pig-headedness. If she rejects you, she rejects me. There can be no half-measures."

That was not what I wanted to hear. His family meant everything to him – all of them – and I never wanted to come between them. But it appeared that she was as resolute as he seemed determined and so it would remain until some compromise was found, or one of them yielded.

"Now," he said, pulling me towards him, "tomorrow is our day – your day – and nothing can spoil that."

"Only me forgetting my lines," I said ruefully, "or tripping on my dress."

He laughed. "You won't and even if you did it wouldn't matter because a bride can never be wrong. Look, the weather will be fine on our wedding day." The setting sun had broken free of cloud and burned the horizon. Matthew's face glowed, but the light came from within and, as we watched the last of the light fade from the evening sky, his eyes took on the heat of the sun.

Wedding Day

It had been so long in coming.

Dawn broke and I woke to see the sun defeat the night. I had spent the previous precious evening with my sister and my friend, the pair of them swapping innuendos as they painted my nails, until I begged them to change the subject and Beth started telling Elena as many tales of our childhood as she could muster to embarrass me instead.

Now alone as I watched the long shadows gradually shorten, it was my mother who pierced the silence in which I wrapped myself. "It's strange, isn't it," she said, giving me a fright as she sat on the window seat beside me and put her hand companionably on mine, "that you think the day is never going to arrive and then, when it does, it takes you by surprise. Nervous?"

"A little," I admitted.

"No second thoughts?"

I smiled. "None." We watched the growing day together for a few minutes until a snuffling cry from the children's room alerted us to a waking Archie. We went through to find he had kicked himself free of his blankets. The twins slept on. I tucked the soft cotton sheet around him and he wriggled contentedly in his confinement.

Mum reduced her voice. "This is a lovely house. It was so kind of Henry to arrange to let us have it – such a beautiful area." She took in the full-figured land smothered in trees, and the mountains I loved so much.

"I think Henry said his friend's in Saudi for a year and he's happy for it to be used. It certainly beats being in a hotel, doesn't it?"

She didn't answer and I waited for her to tell me what was on her mind. "Matthew's parents are super, aren't they? They seem very fond of you, and I know your father gets on with Henry – although I expect Henry gets on with most people. They were very supportive during the trial, weren't they? And Matthew seems to have a wonderful relationship with them – very close." She paused long enough for me to glance at her, but she wasn't waiting for a reply. "Emma, I know that this might be a strange thing to say, but I can't help feeling that the family revolves around Matthew."

"He's getting married; he's bound to be the centre of attention for a bit." Archie grizzled and Mum stroked his cheek until his eyelids drooped.

"I don't think it has anything to do with him getting married. It's the way he behaves and how his family treat him…"

"There's nothing wrong with the way he behaves," I said, a little too quickly.

Mum hushed me with a darted look at the children. "Darling, I didn't say there was," she said calmly, "but I watched him the other day at the picnic and he was very much, well, in control, one might say. Don't you notice? He calls Henry 'Dad', but he doesn't treat him like one. When he says something everyone listens – including his parents." The baby moved in his sleep. His eyelids fluttered open, then closed again and his thumb found his mouth.

If I sounded cross it was only because I didn't know how to respond. "Are you saying he's spoilt or something?"

"I'm not saying anything of the sort, so you needn't be so defensive. I'm just saying that I think Matthew is… singular, but I couldn't tell you why."

She wasn't the first to have said so and, no doubt, she wouldn't be the last. There was a chasm between thinking him different and identifying what made him so, and then a huge leap between that and knowing who he was. It wasn't the sort of thing you'd stumble across: "*Ooo, you're not quite the same, are you? That's odd, you must be four hundred years old.*" So why did a random comment like Mum's send insidious unease creeping through me? Why, instead, could I not laugh it off and tell her not to be so daft? Why indeed. Perhaps because I had no answer for her.

"Yes," I acknowledged, after a moment's consideration when I could find nothing more to say than how I felt. "He is different. He is everything I want and admire, and I love him more than my life."

She smiled at my earnestness. "Well, my darling, that's good to hear since you're marrying him today. For what it's worth, he might be different, but the world would be a better place with a few more like him in it, so don't be so jumpy or I might think you're hiding something from me."

I grimaced sheepishly and made a note to myself not to be so woefully reactive. "Sorry, I'm a bit nervy I suppose." We left the three children sleeping soundly and made our way back to my room.

"That's not surprising. You've come a long way and waited many years for this."

Yes, I had, but in this instance neither of us was referring to the States, or to the wedding, now only hours away. "Guy was a long time ago – a long time ago and irrelevant."

"It was a long time ago, darling, but he's far from irrelevant. Does Matthew know about him?"

"Yes."

"Does he mind?"

"Mind? Why should he?"

"Some men don't like the thought that their wife has been in a previous relationship. Does he know how serious you were?"

"Mum, as far as I'm concerned, Guy didn't exist. He has nothing to do with now, and now is all that I care about. Today, now, and the future. Guy doesn't figure."

"Darling, of course he doesn't, but you know as well as I do that our secrets are ghosts that come back to haunt us unless they're dealt with, and you don't want to start your marriage with any of those now, do you?"

I couldn't tell her that I suspected Guy would become a ghost sooner rather than later if Matthew had his way. "There are no secrets between us, Mum. He's aware of everything there is to know."

"And do you know everything about him? It works both ways, you realize."

Didn't I just. "I think so – all the important stuff anyway."

"Including his first wife?"

"Yes, including her. There are no skeletons there." Not any more.

She hugged me. "I'm so glad; that always worried me a little. At least he's a widower and didn't turn out to be still married like Guy. I don't think I could have coped with all that again."

I smiled feebly. "No, there's no fear of that now." I stood up and stretched. "I'd better get started if I'm to have a chance of disguising these freckles in time."

Years dissolved with her smile. "My darling, do you know I have always loved those freckles; they suit you. Don't try to hide them, just be yourself."

* * *

I stared at the woman in front of me, her eyes wide and bright with anticipation, skin flushed over high cheekbones. I took in the upturned mouth eager to smile – and I didn't recognize her.

"Do you not like it?" Elena asked anxiously, the make-up brush hovering in her hand.

"Come on, Em, say something!" Beth enjoined.

I shook my head. "What have you done? What have you both done to me?"

They exchanged looks. "If you don't like it…" Elena began.

"Like it?" I burst out. "You great ninny! You're miracle-workers – you should both be canonized." I turned to look at my rear reflection. "Oh, and just look at that train! Beth… Elena, I just… oh…" And I ran out of words to describe how I felt.

"Don't you cry," Elena warned. "Your mascara will run."

"And don't hug us, for goodness sake!" Beth added, backing away. "You'll crease your dress and your hair will unravel. Golly though, Em, you do look something."

I hadn't exaggerated; in the weeks in which she had to make my dress, Beth surpassed all my hopes. She had taken my sketchy designs and photos of portraits and turned them into the dress I had longed for since teenage daydreams of being a bride.

"It's perfect, Beth." The wide neckline revealed my collar bone, sculpting into a tight bodice that ran into a long, slender panel down the front of the dress and into a "V" below my waist. Embroidered in delicate shades of cream, seed pearls formed the heart of each Jacobean flower flowing in sinuous form down the panel.

"They were from Granny's necklace – you remember the one we broke donkey's years ago when we were dressing up? Mum thought you would like them."

I did. The same tiny pearls sprinkled across the wide sleeves, which faded into long, tight-buttoned cuffs. Where the rich oyster silk rose smoothly over my hips, it gathered in many layers into a short train, leaving my silk pumps just visible beneath. It was beautiful – it made me feel beautiful – and it was a style Matthew would recall from his childhood in a secret reference between the two of us.

Beth stood back to admire her handiwork. "What about jewellery?"

"I'm wearing Nanna's veil for something *old*, and my sapphire earrings for something *blue*."

Elena looked mischievous. "Yes, and I know what you're wearing underneath that is *borrowed*, but what about something *new*? How about a necklace; you look naked without one." She and Beth giggled. They both enjoyed a similar lewd sense of humour which they had plied liberally at my expense ever since they met.

I felt the empty space where my cross had been. "No, I don't think so, and anyway, my dress is new."

Ellie came in with Archie tottering beside her, clasping her hand. "Look at Archie, isn't he clever! And doesn't he look adorable? Your father wants to know if you're all ready. The cars are waiting outside and the twins are getting restless. Oh!" she said, looking at me for the first time. "Wow!"

"Thanks," I smiled, "and you all look gorgeous, and Arch here is going to steal the show."

As I watched the cars disappear from view, a soft *hurrumph* sounded behind me. I turned to find Dad standing looking very formal in his dark morning suit, the waistcoat buttons straining a little.

"Dad, you look very dapper."

He took in my dress, my hair, my glowing face. "Is it really nine years since Beth's wedding? And now my little girl is getting married."

His hands trembled slightly. I tried to lighten the mood before I became sucked in. "Rid of me at last, hey?"

"Don't say that, Emma. Whatever differences we might have had, you have always been my little girl. How ironic that now we seem to have sorted things out you move overseas. It can't be helped, but we'll miss you. *I'll* miss you."

"As you said to Mum, we're only a plane flight away, and I think that perhaps now we'll be closer than we've ever been, even than when living in the same house."

He laughed his gruff laugh. "How true, how true. Now, we had better make a move before Matthew sends out a search party. Before we go, I have something for you." He put a long, slender box in my hands. "Open it now; you won't have time later." Inside, on a double-link chain, was a small, plain gold cross. "It's as close to the one you lost at the trial as I could find, and the chain's much stronger, so no one can take it from you this time. I know how much it means to you and I wanted you to have something... I want you to remember how much..." His colour deepened, but he held my gaze. "If I don't have time to tell you later, I want you to know that I have always been very proud of you, Emma – always." He leaned forwards and carefully placed a kiss on my forehead. "I love you, my darling. I wish you every happiness."

I didn't care about my make-up; it had taken twenty-nine years for him to tell me, but only seconds for me to respond. "I love you, Daddy," and I clung to him as I had always dreamt I would, and he held me close, surrounding me in his scent of aftershave and humbugs.

The pretty, white-spired church sat on a knoll overlooking a broad lake on the outskirts of town, and new lime-green leaves hustled the silvered papery bark of slender trunks surrounding it. My bridesmaids waited in the sunshine, each lovely in their striking individuality, while to one side, Alex darted among the taller grasses trying to catch grasshoppers. A gentle wind lifted the edge of Nanna's veil, and nervous butterflies fluttered in my tummy as I caught the first strains of music from the open door.

"You look beautiful," Dad said, lifting the veil over my head. Offering his arm, together we went into the light-filled church and down the aisle flanked by familiar faces blurred by my nerves. They evaporated like mist when I saw Matthew waiting; my heart sang, my breath catching in my throat, and then it was just us in that moment of time between worlds. And when I said "I will" in a clear voice ringing with certainty, and the priest pronounced us man and wife, Matthew broke into a delighted grin, swinging me high in an arc before kissing me to a chorus of whoops and applause.

"My bride, my wife," he glowed amidst the general euphoria, but I was too full of our happiness to reply, too enchanted by the moment and by our promises to each other before God and our families to do anything but bathe in his elation. Holding hands, we led the procession as I all but danced back down the aisle, the children containing themselves no longer and dashing ahead of us, bursting out into the sun under the wide velvet sky.

By the time we arrived back at the house – *my* house, my *home* – Mum and Pat had long-since dried their eyes and were in full bustle mode organizing staff. Matthew and I stood at the doorway to our new life and greeted our guests – not many – just our closest friends and colleagues from college, and only those who had known the family for the span of the last decade.

Pat had transformed the house: garlands of green ferns and ivy studded with fragrant cream blooms hung in swags from the galleried landing and swathed the banisters. Simple vases as tall as Archie bore extravagant displays – not tight and formal, but loose and airy with a deliciously zesty scent that made me want to bury my face in the lax, wayward fronds, and inhale. No wonder I hadn't been allowed to see it all before the wedding – one look and I would never have wanted to leave.

I left Matthew's side and caught up with Pat in a brief lull and thanked her so profusely I managed to make her blush. "Why, that's my pleasure. I haven't had so much fun since... well, since I don't know when. I have to thank your mom for letting me make the arrangements. I'm not sure I would have been so accommodating." Mum hovered nearby, so she heard the comment as had been intended and now Pat softened her voice. "I've given Matthew strict instructions to make sure you have plenty to eat."

I laughed. "Rumbled. You know me too well!"

"I think I'm getting to," she agreed. "Now, have you seen the dining room yet?"

I hadn't, but before I had a chance, excited voices distracted us. "Photos!" Beth called, echoed by the twins – high-pitched and overexcited. Pat's face fell as she looked towards Matthew, talking by the staircase.

"Photos! Photos!" the children clamoured, bumping into one another in their eagerness to grab my hands and drag me outside. Laughing, I started to follow them.

"Emma..." I looked around; Matthew hadn't moved.

Dad's voice rose above the rest of the hubbub as our guests flowed towards the door. "I thought we were missing something; where's the photographer? Emma, come on..."

"Wait, Dad." Like flotsam on a beach, Matthew and his family held back, waiting as the house emptied around us. He appeared worried. "Is there a problem?"

"Sweetheart, I'm sorry, but I can't be in the photographs. I can't risk it."

Beth flurried back in. "Emma, Matthew, c'mon, everybody's waiting."

"In a minute," I called, and more quietly to the family so I couldn't be overheard, "it hadn't occurred to me. What can we do? It's something people expect at weddings. If we don't, our guests will take some – there're enough cameras between them to fill albums and that would be worse because they'd be beyond our control."

"We could ask them not to," Ellie suggested tentatively and without conviction.

Joel, transformed by his dress uniform, grunted, "Tell them, more like."

Henry shook his head. "I don't think either will work. Dad, what did you do when you married Mom?"

"I wasn't so concerned then as now. We had just the one photographer and not many shots were taken. Anyway, the plates were, er... accidentally broken and only the one survived." I knew the one; he had kept it with him always – a little tattered photograph of Ellen gazing up at her new husband, and something I couldn't now have. A smattering of disappointment must have shown because he said again, "Emma, I'm so sorry."

"It doesn't matter, but it won't stop people wanting to have pictures." I thought rapidly, trying not to chew my lipstick. "Perhaps if one of the family takes some photographs and we tell everyone we'll send on copies, then no one else need take any. We can edit out what we want – digitally master some of them – delete others. Might that work?"

"It might," Dan nodded. "I have a camera we can use."

Henry agreed. "Worth a try. Dad, shall we give it a go?"

We all looked at Matthew and he acceded with a touch of regret. "It's worth a go."

We posed for shots as any other couple would as Dan joked to make us all laugh. When my father mentioned his surprise at the lack of an official photographer, I told him that Dan had wanted to study fine arts and architecture in his youth, and he seemed to accept my explanation, which I believe might have been more to do with the mollifying effects of the champagne than the logic behind my answer.

Beth was doing her best to engage Maggie in conversation and I lurked nearby, thankful she hadn't noticed the disdain on the woman's face that had my toes curling. Maggie might hate my guts, but she could at least make some effort with my sister. Beth tried again. "What an unusual necklace. I don't think I've ever seen anything like it." Against the smoke-grey silk of her dress, the gold gleamed.

Maggie fingered the snake's head and her gaze slithered towards me. "Do you like it?"

"Yes, I do. I don't know much about antiques, that's more Em's thing, but it reminds me of the sort of jewellery the Duchess of Windsor wore in the thirties – you know, like her panther bracelet. Hey, Em" – reluctantly, I joined my sister – "have you seen Maggie's gorgeous necklace? You like anything old, don't you?"

I managed a smile for appearances' sake. "It's very fine."

Beth took a dainty canapé of lobster from a passing tray. "Mm, where did you get it, Maggie? Are those rubies?"

The woman undid the tail from the snake's mouth and lifted the necklace from around her neck. The articulated body coiled sinuously over her hands as she held it out for Beth to see. "My grandmother left it to me; it was her favourite piece. My grandfather had it made for her and she always wore it. She said it symbolized love. I believe it was a reference to Norse mythology, where the serpent Jormungand encircles the Earth for all time with his tail in his mouth. Only when the circle is broken will the world come to an end, as death breaks the bonds of love. Isn't it beautiful?" A thin smile curled her sharp mouth, reminding me of Monica and the cold mist of the cemetery.

"What a lovely idea – might I look at it?" Beth reached out to touch the head, but Maggie withdrew it and placed it back around her neck. Beth tittered a little nervously. "Golly, and I always associate snakes with deceitfulness. Emma, do you remember Grandpa reading us Poe's story – what was it?"

"'The Cask of Amontillado'."

"That's it. Wasn't that something to do with snakes? Didn't what's-his-name plot to kill Fortunato and trick him or something?"

I recalled Grandpa with a tartan rug over his knees, and my sister and I, all rapt attention, as the tale of deceit unfolded. "Something like that. Montresor was petty and vengeful and lured Fortunato into a trap." Maggie and I stared at each other with undisguised hostility. It had become a duel between us, an unspoken contest of wills.

Beth looked from one to the other. She took a hasty bite of another canapé, followed by a swig of champagne. "Oh, uh… that's it, I'd forgotten. So your grandfather gave your grandmother the necklace, but you didn't say what happened to him, Maggie. Is he still alive?"

With a quick, slick smile, Maggie challenged me to intervene. "My grandfather? He loved her to her last day." She dropped her voice and took Beth by the arm as if revealing some great confidence. "He would still love her, were it not for the duplicity of another."

Beth's eyes rounded. "What do you mean?" Before Maggie

had a chance to widen the gulf between us, she suddenly straightened, her eyes losing the sly look and becoming tame. I felt the welcome touch of reassuring hands on my shoulders.

"Yes, Maggie, what do you mean?"

Beth hadn't seen him. "Matthew! Ooo, you made me jump. We were just admiring Maggie's necklace. She said it was given to your grandmother to represent undying love. Isn't that romantic? Perfect for today. Something to do with a Norse snake and eternity."

Maggie blanched under Matthew's stare. "Really? I hope not, because according to legend, Thor will slay Jormungand before he himself falls victim to the snake's venom. That would be a pointless reference for a gift – worse than pointless – it would be barbed. I always understood that the necklace was given to commemorate their first meeting."

Maggie's interest quickened despite herself.

"Their first meeting?" I prompted, overcome by curiosity.

"Yes, I believe Ellen had gone to check the horses in the stable on her parents' ranch – apparently they had been restless all day. She saw one of the horses rearing and trying to break from its stall and a snake about to strike, but she became trapped between them as she tried to release the animal. Her brother, Jack, had brought a friend to stay, and when they heard the commotion, they ran into the barn and killed the snake."

I looked at him sceptically. "What, just like that?"

"Well, no, not quite," he admitted. "Jack managed to get the horse out before it killed anyone, but the snake was big and very aggressive and it bit the friend before he could break its neck."

Beth wiped her fingers on a white damask napkin. "So the friend was your grandfather. It wasn't a poisonous snake then?"

"On the contrary; it was deadly, and he... fortunate."

I tried not to laugh. "Mmm, he must have been." He smiled

down at me. I had almost forgotten Maggie. Now she looked with puzzled disbelief.

"She never said. Why didn't she tell me?"

Matthew said soberly, "There are some things that remain secret between husband and wife, Maggie. There are many things Ellen didn't tell you; things she didn't want you to know."

Maggie's face soured, but Beth chipped in brightly, "So how come you know, Matthew?"

"I was in the right place at the right time. Ellen could be selective in the things she revealed, and to whom. Now," he said, turning on his heel and searching the crowded dining room, "it must be nearly time for speeches. Where's my best man?"

From my interpretation of their gesticulations and judging by the amount being consumed with an air of Bacchanalian self-indulgence, Matias, Dad, and Rob were eulogizing over the food. While Beth hurried away to check on the cake, Matthew took me to one side. "Maggie's up to her old tricks I see. Don't let her get to you. Just remember you're her step-grandmother and pull rank if you have to." The idea was so ridiculous I couldn't help but laugh, and he relaxed into a smile. "Well, it was just a thought. Have you eaten?"

"Uh huh."

"I see. Perhaps I can persuade you to have a bit more before the champagne and toasts begin..."

"Toast?" I said hopefully.

"Toast*s*, Emma," he said, trying to appear serious and not succeeding. "And I wasn't planning to spend any time cooking this evening."

Now that was downright tantalizing. I rolled my eyes in exaggerated delirium and he took advantage of my weakened state to snaffle several exquisite concoctions from a passing waitress to feed me.

"OK," I managed between mouthfuls, "I'm fortified. What's next? Oh, yes – speeches. Rather you than me."

Matias's hair had come unstuck and curled in rebellious tufts which Elena failed to subdue. She gave up and came over to me. "Do you know where you are going for your honeymoon?" she asked.

"I do."

"Come on, tell me," she urged.

"All I can say is that it's somewhere mountainous."

There was a moment of confusion as Beth and Rob herded the twins and cautioned them to submission. Ellie managed to procure Archie, and he played happily with the pendant we had given her as a bridesmaid gift.

"Mountains," Elena mused. "The Andes? Alps? The Himalayas? Yes, yes, that will be good. Say it's the Himalayas."

"Nope."

She would have tried to coax more out of me but Matias called for everybody's attention, and she tutted as another tuft of hair liberated itself as she watched. Yes, I knew where we were going and it couldn't have been more perfect in the circumstances. My pulse fluttered keenly.

"Ladies and gentlemen," Matias announced, and silence fell over the gathering.

I have to admit that I hadn't been looking forward to the speeches. Dad's went on a little too long for comfort, and he needn't have referred to the embarrassing incident with the head of music, the trombone, and the cream puff, although he did remember to say that it hadn't been held against me. Nor did he have to mention my stubborn refusal to compromise on my career path and how it had led me to where I was today. I would have preferred it if he had refrained from enlightening the company about my experiment with my hair and the chemistry set I'd been given one Christmas, but I was grateful that, as he drew to a close, he turned to where Matthew and I stood together, and raised his glass to toast a beloved daughter and her new husband, to whom he owed everything.

Matias, on the other hand, obviously relished the opportunity to apply his satirical wit, alluding to some eye-watering anecdotes with glee. He just about spared my blushes, and his comments, whilst acerbic as ever, were couched in terms of the deep esteem in which he held his friends.

And then Matthew spoke and a deep hush fell on the room. In gilded terms, but without flattery so that every word counted tenfold, he thanked all those who had contributed to our relationship – for their support and their love – and it was clear from the faces of those around us that each person heard within his words their own name proclaimed loudly. He turned at last and I flushed under the intensity of his gaze as he thanked me above all others and, bowing low and raising my hand to his lips, resolutely declared, "My lady, my wife."

He went to fetch something to cut the cake.

"Have you seen it!" Elena exclaimed. "It is like a fairy-tale Kremlin in snow."

My mind boggled. "The Kremlin?"

"*Da*, come and look."

Already our guests were gathering around the table on which stood a cake of many snowy tiers and delicate webs of spun sugar, interwoven with apricot roses. "And you and Dad did all this between you?" I asked Beth when I'd recovered enough to voice my delight.

"Actually, Rob did the roses; he's a heck of a lot better than I am." Beth swatted Flora's hand before she explored the fragility of the flowers and gave me a wicked grin. "There's one tier for each of your children."

I snorted. "Five children? I think not!"

"Emma'll make a great mom, won't she, bro?" Harry beamed.

Joel slid Alex from his broad shoulders. "Yeah, their kids'll know all the kings and queens of England before they can walk. They'll be the freak-geeks of the school."

Jeannie's voice cut in. "Joel!" He put an arm around his mother's shoulders. "Emma's cool about it, Mom, aren't you, Aunty?"

I screwed my eyes at him. "Less of the aunty, if you please."

Somebody I couldn't see piped up, "I'm surprised the cake's not made of chocolate."

Rob grinned. "Who said it isn't?" Laughter circled the room.

"We'd better find out then, hadn't we?" Bodies parted as Matthew appeared brandishing the rapier that usually hung above the fireplace.

"That's an odd sword to cut a cake," Dad commented with a hint of censure. "I could have lent you my dress sword if you'd asked."

I tucked my arm through his. "No Dad, it's perfect." The ornate basket of silvered metal incorporated a coat of arms I knew instantly, the pommel terminating in a lion's head. Quillons curved either side like an elongated "S", and the fine long blade, darkened with age and lack of use, was notched. I touched the roughened edge.

"A musket ball," Matthew said, watching my reaction.

"It doesn't look very clean," my mother said doubtfully.

"It's just very old, Mum. About 1643, I should say."

Matthew smiled. "1638, or thereabouts. I've cleaned the blade and it'll do the job." A bit of an understatement, I thought, if it could sever flesh and bone. A peaceful end for such a weapon – how fitting.

Alex's eyes rounded like marbles. "Has it killed anyone?" Everyone laughed as they do when children say such things, but I noticed Matthew didn't reply. Glasses were refilled and, as Matthew placed his hand over mine and together we cut the cake, a contented sigh emanated from our families and friends.

Henry's voice rose above the rest. "At this point, and with Hugh's forbearance – on behalf of us all, I would like to welcome Emma to the Lynes family." He raised his glass and his eyes so that he looked directly at me, and if I'd had any doubts about him accepting our marriage so soon after his mother's death, I had none now.

The cake was taken away to be divided and I touched Mum's arm lightly as she directed one of the waiters. "Mum, please will you do something for me? Can you make sure that Mrs Seaton gets a piece of the cake – and this?" I slipped a little envelope into her hands.

"Yes, darling, of course. I suppose she was a good friend to Nanna."

Yes, she was, I thought, *and to me.*

Archie bombed around, slamming into people's legs, laughing as Ellie pretended to chase him. Beth took advantage and had become happily sloshed as the afternoon wore on. We stole a few quiet minutes in between things to catch up.

"Thanks for everything – for the dress, for coming to the States, for the children, for being you. I don't think I've ever said, but I think you're amazing. I've always looked up to you."

"Have you? Golly, Em, you've been drinking."

"No, I haven't. I'm perfectly sober, which is more than I can say for you, so don't go and forget this, will you? I know we've had our moments – all right, quite a few of them – but if it weren't for you I think I would have gone off the rails, especially after Grandpa died. You're so grounded, so solid... don't look at me like that, you know what I mean – and I wished I could have been more like you, so… thanks."

She wasn't so tipsy that she didn't understand what it had taken for me to say all that. She looked around us in deliberate, exaggerated misperception. "Gosh, you've got all this, and you wanted to be like me? I'll do a swap if you want?"

I hugged her, regardless of squishing my dress. "You are priceless, you great wallaby, and you really didn't need to laugh at the '*all my worldly goods*' bit in the service, did you?"

"No, sorry about that, but cripes, have you ever seen so much silver! I'm glad one of us is filthy rich. Dad was mooning about the family jewels again. I don't think he saw the funny side of it, although" – she cast a quick, admiring look in Matthew's direction – "I'll bet Matthew's well endowed… Ow! You didn't need to do that!"

"Shh! I think I probably did and you," I removed the glass from her hand, "have had enough to drink. You'll be fit for nothing later on."

She giggled. "*I* don't have to be fit for anything – you do." She roared with laughter and was still laughing when I steered her in the direction of her husband.

People were making those "time to go" noises. Lengthening shadows and mellow light predicted sunset, although still some hours away.

"We need to make a move," Matthew said, glancing towards the window.

"I'll get changed," I agreed, and went through to the flower-scented hall. It was quieter here and the fragrant green made it an oasis of calm. My feet were killing me. I took off my shoes and made my way up the broad stairs to the room I had used as a guest.

I don't know what made me look towards her door – perhaps the deadening presence I always felt near her like a light-absorbing black hole, or the movement of air, like a breath. Either way I stopped at the top of the stairs and turned around. Maggie didn't bother with a preamble; she launched straight in. "I know what you did that day in court."

I eyed her with caution, remembering our last confrontation in the study and what it led to. "Do you?"

She left the confines of her doorway. "I know exactly what you did. Don't think I'm grateful."

"I didn't do it just for you," I said. "I had to protect Matthew."

Sarcasm dripped. "Did you really?" She oozed resentment. Good grief, she resented me for helping her! A waitress carrying a heavy tray banged the kitchen door open, letting it swing shut behind her. Maggie sneered. "What did you think I was going to do that required *your* protection?"

"You tell me," I retorted, swinging one hundred and eighty degrees and heading for my room. A sharp *rat-rat* of hard heels on wood told me she followed. She put out an arm as I opened my door, blocking my way.

"Tell you? I don't need to; you were in my head." Voices below echoed up the stairwell as people gathered.

"Not here," I cautioned. She withdrew her arm and followed me into my room. My going-away outfit lay spread-eagled on my bed. I winced; Elena and Beth had left an additional item of clothing I hadn't expected and didn't want Maggie to see. I scooped it up and hid it under the jacket.

"You were in my head," she repeated, as if I had committed a violation. "You had no right to be there. I won't let you in again."

"Then don't give me a reason to," I replied brusquely. "I have to get changed." I started undoing the long row of silk-covered buttons that stretched like my spine all the way up my back, and hoped she would take the hint and leave. She didn't.

"I was ill; I can see that now. Working with Staahl, seeing you with my grandfather, my grandmother's death – pushed me too far. But I'm not ill now. I didn't like you then; I don't like you now."

I gave up struggling with the buttons. "That's fine by me, as long as you get one thing straight: granddaughter or not, if you do anything – *anything* – to harm Matthew or your family, you won't have the protection of insanity to stop me next time, believe me."

She drew herself up, adding inches to her height as she leered over me. "Oh, I do believe you. I wondered how long it would take for you to show your true colours. Do you really think he will believe you over his own granddaughter, his flesh and blood? You know nothing about us, nothing about what we have been through together. I only hope that one day he sees you for what you are – a jumped up gold-digger out for anything she can get. How long will you give it – six months, a year – before you file for divorce? I bet he didn't get you to sign a pre-nup, did he? I told him he should. I said that he was bringing an unknown into the family, a Trojan Horse." There was no confusion in the air around her. Even if I hadn't been able to read the colours, I would have felt her hate as manifestly as flesh-eating ants. How could she do the job she did so effectively and yet get me so wrong?

This was getting tedious. I managed a button, then the next. "Believe me? Matthew doesn't need to believe me. He *knows* me, Maggie, and he knows I will do nothing to hurt him and everything to protect him. Will you?"

She stepped forwards suddenly, catching me off balance against the side of the bed. I put out a hand to steady myself as she leaned towards me. "Will I what?" she all but spat.

I shoved past her. "Will you protect him, or is your spite so potent that it overrides all else, including his happiness? I don't know what you think you'll gain from all this, but Matthew and I are married now. It was what Ellen anticipated and accepted. There's no point you holding this grudge any more; it's too late."

Giggly laughter and the sound of running feet reverberated down the corridor. Maggie brought her face close to mine until all I could see was her doll-smooth skin and the black pits of her eyes.

"It's never too late," she said and left in a hiss of silk as the twins flung into my room.

"Look what we have!" they shouted in unison, bouncing onto the bed and waving their presents for me to admire, but all I could see was the loathing in her face and hear the threat behind her words echoing in their laughter.

19

Point of Fire

Many are the stars I see
But in my heart no star but thee.
From a seventeenth-century posy ring

"I could have taken you anywhere in the world," Matthew stated, "and yet you wanted to come here."

I joined him by the wall of glass that stretched across the entire side of the house. "Yes," I said simply. He lifted his arm and I leant against him and together we watched the last of the sun illuminate the still-white shoulders of the highest peaks. "We can go anywhere we want to in the future, Matthew, but we needed to be here at the cabin today. You owe me," I reminded him, bending my head back and looking at him upside down.

"Yes, I do," he said softly, "in more ways than one."

"How did you explain the broken window to Henry?"

"I didn't need to. He didn't ask and I didn't explain. It cost me a small fortune to have replaced." He smiled a little guiltily, but I thought it wasn't so much at the memory of the shattered glass, but what had prompted him to smash his fist into it in the first place. The window wasn't the only thing that needed mending the last time we had been at the cabin together. The revelation that he was still married almost caused a rift between us that nothing would have healed.

He rested his chin on the top of my head. "Talking of breakages, Maggie left in a foul mood. Whatever happened to the truce between you?"

"You did. It's what results when a treaty is based on an unequal peace – it breaks." It had been a perfect day which even Maggie hadn't managed to spoil because the lines of demarcation had been made clear, and I found a strange security in that. I pushed back against him. "Maggie can wait. By the way, I have a wedding gift for you, but I've left it back home."

"That's a coincidence, because I have one for you." I caressed the side of his face, and he nuzzled my palm, then kissed each fingertip in turn.

"It's been a wonderful day, Matthew, thank you."

"You made it so," he said, and what I had taken to be a reflection against his dark pupils was nothing of the sort, his eyes alight with an inner fire. He leaned close, a smile touching his lips, his dulcet voice low. *"Come lie with me, and be my love, and I forever thine…"*

It was as if I looked at him properly for the very first time. Not the surreptitious, furtive glances I gave him when we first met, nor the remorse-tinged looks when I learned of his wife. Now when I saw him the veil of guilt had been replaced by unadorned love and desire, no longer fettered by the assumptions and preconceptions we placed upon ourselves. The effect of his closeness raised a storm in my blood that I wanted him to tame. Flecks of radiating light appeared to move and dance within the intense indigo of his eyes that had fascinated me from the moment I met him – an ocean of blue circled with black. Through them, I could watch his changing moods as clearly as I could read the colours of his heart and, when he looked at me in the way he did now, I became lost as

I charted the tiny flames. And it seemed to me that they were real, not an illusion, but infinitesimal lights, the spark of flint striking stone. I felt their pull, compelling as the silken thread that bound us soul by soul, as strong as steel and incorruptible as gold. Had I wanted to, I could not have resisted him. I leaned against his strength, smelling the mountains in the scent of his skin, saying his name, feeling the shape of it on my lips, barely able to breathe. Heat swelled and his eyes flared bright for the briefest moment and then the lightest touch, a sable brush across the surface of my skin. His lips traced the line of my neck to the dip at the base of my throat, slow kisses, a lingering warmth where his mouth touched. Fingers echoed, pushing back the silk of my top, feeling it slide from my arms, leaving me exposed to his gaze.

He pulled his shirt over his head, leaving his hair in soft sheaves I smoothed with my fingers. His skin on mine, my breath came quicker now, little breaths as hands skimmed, negotiating curves, and I found the silvered scar on his shoulder, feeding tiny butterfly kisses with my lips, feeling him shudder. Mapping his chest over taut muscles until his hand joined mine and lifted it to his mouth, kissing deep into the palm, inhaling – his eyes closed – a moment in time before he found my lips and drew their softness into his own. There was no Guy and I had no past, but the present only, and my future that lay in him. For a moment his eyes held me with soft fire and I felt it within me, beyond describing, beyond this frail body of mine – honeyed heat and flames – and any moment without him would be too long. It was not in the mere act, but in the oneness we made together, flowing between us in sinuous waves lapping and undulating in time with our bodies, fluid until we were one movement, one entity, one whole.

At last we were still and at peace. We lay very close facing each other, his hand resting on my waist and mine lightly against his chest, binding us, the fulfilment of our hope more than the realization of desire. Gradually, as my breathing eased and my body cooled, I became aware that he smiled at me. "I've never felt anything like that before," I confessed, feeling a little self-conscious.

He drew me to him and I warmed immediately at his touch. "Neither have I," he sighed, in a mixture of contentment and release.

Throughout the night he made love to me with tenderness and care – long and slow and sensual, leaving my languid body liquid to his touch, and each touch a point of fire. By dawn I could no longer resist sleep and he sang softly as he held me, a sweet song of love and longing from his youth.

I woke when a sharp shaft of sunlight stung my eyelids. I mumbled recriminations and turned my head before I remembered where we were. Matthew lifted a hand to shade my face and I curled closer to him, his heart beating steadily beneath me.

"*Busie old foole, unruly Sunne,*
Why dost thou thus,
Through windowes, and through curtaines call on us?'"

He chided the sun and kissed my eyelids awake.

I smiled, sleepily content. "It's odd to think Donne did this all that time ago." I turned in his arms so that I could look at him.

"Surprisingly little has changed, or perhaps it's not so surprising – people are fundamentally the same, aren't they?"

"I suppose they are. On which note, don't you get bored waiting for me to wake up?"

"How could I after years of being alone? I like to watch you, and besides, I have plenty to think about."

I smoothed the fair hair on his arm and he tightened his hold on me. "Don't you miss being able to sleep?"

"Not now, no. I did at first, I have to admit; it's such a basic part of humanity, and not sleeping or talking in terms of sleep – 'I'm exhausted', 'time to hit the sack', 'I'm sick and tired', you know the sort of thing – was strange. I had to be careful to begin with, when it began to be noticed and commented on, but then I learned to imitate it, and now I can appear asleep, even if I'm not."

I thought of all the times we had spent in the same bed, together yet worlds apart. "I've never seen you do that."

"No, there's been no reason, but I can put myself into a sort of torpor which is quite convincing. I just have to remember to close my eyes or it gives the game away."

I imagined him asleep, waking with me, so normal as to be almost mundane, yet wholly beyond our reach. It didn't matter any more. What I had was more than I could have hoped for, and what we had was as near normality as we could get, and that was close enough for me.

"I always wanted to fall asleep with someone and to wake by them. There's that sense of security in it – permanency, almost."

A fleeting sadness escaped from him before he could disguise it. "I'm sorry; I could have pretended to be asleep for you, but now that you know…"

I put my finger against his lips. "I didn't mean you."

"Guy?"

I pulled a face. "Yes," I said shortly, but I didn't want him in bed with us, and even the mention of his name made me feel dirty. I unwrapped Matthew's arms from around me and sat up. "I'm going to have a bath."

The bath took an age to fill. I let it run as I did my teeth, and didn't hear him over the flowing water, until he gathered my hair and kissed my neck. "Would you mind if I join you?" I felt myself blush unnecessarily. His brow gathered into a frown. "If you would prefer to be alone…" He looked so serious over something so trivial that I had to laugh.

"No, of course not," I said and held out my hand to him.

At first I thought nothing of it, but as he dried me with intense focus, I saw he did so with more than a lover's consideration. "Matthew, you haven't hurt me."

Denim eyes met mine. "Are you sure?"

"Yes, positive. No bruises – nothing for which to reproach yourself."

He touched the tips of his fingers to the rise of my breast. "It's just that it can be difficult to judge, especially when it's been a long time…" He wasn't usually this tongue-tied, but as he stood there in front of me, he was young again, and unsure, and the years fell away from him like the mercurial drops of water from his skin. I wondered if he had been like this with Ellen on their wedding night and found myself swimming with a mixture of curiosity and jealousy.

"Did you ever hurt Ellen?"

At the mention of her name, he blinked once, as if retrieving a memory. "No, not that I'm aware of, never."

"Then why do you think you might have hurt me now?" I shivered as my skin cooled, and he whipped a soft, dry towel from where it hung warming and wound it around my shoulders. He hadn't answered me. "Well?"

He rubbed my arms briskly through the towel. "There, you're dry now, let's get you warm."

When he saw that I wanted an answer, he shook his head in resignation. "I was different with Ellen. I really don't want to talk about it; please, don't ask me."

That did it. Don't give a historian a tantalizing snippet of information and tell her to forget it. Like any unanswered question, I found the ambiguity both intriguing and disquieting. What did he mean he was different with her: different good, bad – what? I let my silence do the talking and walked through to the bedroom. He followed, uncertainty seeping in an amber vapour. "It's history now, Emma. All that matters is what we have – our present, our future."

From the chest of drawers in the bedroom, I rummaged for matching underwear. "You say you don't want to tell me, yet you keep letting little morsels slip, which is as good as a flashing neon sign saying, *'ask me'.*"

"I don't!" he objected. "Do I?"

"In so many words, or in what you don't say or in how you don't say it, yes, you do. I wouldn't mind so much but it's obviously something that's bothering you and it's niggling away like mad at me."

He ran his hand through his drying hair, giving it a tousled, just-out-of-bed look. "You must be hungry…"

"Not that hungry."

I struggled with unfamiliar hooks on my clothes and he came over to help me, letting his hands rest briefly on my shoulders. "Before we married, Ellen and I never discussed sex and had done nothing more than kiss and hold hands – all very tame by today's standards. It didn't surprise me; that level of restraint was more acceptable then. Now I think that it would appear unusual – odd even – not to show more interest. I accepted her moderation as modesty and, of course, I would never have expected her to sleep with me before we married. When we did marry, I thought that she just needed time to get used to the idea of lovemaking, and then, when I returned from the war, that she needed time to adjust to me being home and unchanged. But, as the years went on and our marriage survived, I began to wonder if it was me and I was the problem."

I twisted to look at him. "In what way?"

"I thought I might be too much for her; too – oh, I don't know, energetic I suppose you could say – although I did restrain myself as far as I could. Then I thought that perhaps it was because I was different, and that she saw something I didn't, something that frightened her."

I detected decades of anxiety in the note of self-doubt, the strain in his eyes, and the way he didn't meet mine, and I thought my heart would break for him because in that one relationship he had forged, a brittle fissure of doubt ran.

"My darling, it wasn't you; there is nothing wrong with *you*."

"There must have been…"

"No, I promise you, Ellen didn't see you as a monster. She didn't think you were wrong. She told me that she had never been that interested in sex and always thought that she must have been a disappointment. It seems that you both believed you had failed each other in that respect."

He laughed hoarsely. "A little honesty might have gone a long way to healing those wounds. I didn't want to put her in a difficult position by talking about it and…"

"… she wouldn't have known where to start," I finished.

He sucked in his cheeks. "Apparently not."

"Anyway, as you said, that's history and I think that you're neither a monster nor… how did you put it? Oh yes, nor are you too *energetic*, though I have to say that last night was a bit of an eye-opener."

His guarded look crept back again. "In what way?"

"I'm not sure if I can say…"

"Emma! Don't be coy now – what happened to honesty?"

"All right." I thought about how I was going to phrase the

next bit. "Let's just say that I have never experienced anything like it before."

"Oh, I see. I think." He looked away, chewing his lip, then back at me, with an anxious frown. "Is that a problem?"

"No, not at all; it was just a surprise. But a very pleasant one," I made certain to add.

He relaxed into a grin, his eyes warming. "I'm relieved to hear it." He cradled my face in his hands, searching. "I've waited a lifetime to find you."

I turned my head to kiss his palm, and held it with my own against my cheek. "And now you've found me."

"And now I've found you," he echoed, voice softening until it became no more than a whisper. "My beloved, my wife."

"That's better." Matthew stretched out in the sun, not bothering to shade his eyes against the glare. "We both needed some of this." We had found a warm spot sheltered from the mountain breezes. Colder by degrees than by the sea, the clear air tingled up here among the pines and hardier trees, and I relished each breath I drew.

"You needed to recharge your batteries," I agreed. "At least you don't get freckles." I held up my arms, ruefully noting that, despite the layers of sun cream he had helped me to apply, my freckles were beginning to join up as their fainter little cousins came to join the party.

"Your freckles are like constellations," he reflected, leaning on one elbow. "Here's Orion's Belt" – he tracked three prominent freckles with his finger – "and this is Cygnus – you can see the sweep of the wings – and all these lighter marks are the distant galaxies you can only see when the sky is really clear." He smiled. "I can navigate your skin; I can lose myself in its universe. I have found myself in you." He kissed the sensitive spot at the crease of my elbow and rested his head on the rise of my stomach. I wove my fingers through his hair, and together we listened to the tiny sounds of birds and insects, of stones cracking, green growing.

"You were going to tell me about my wedding ring," I reminded him. He found my hand and held it to the light, the plain gold band sitting snugly against my engagement ring.

"It was my mother's marriage ring. That doesn't worry you, does it?"

"Does it bother you that you're wearing Grandpa's ring?" I countered.

He raised his hand and placed it next to mine. The heavy gold band with its distinctive bar of platinum inlaid around its waist looked as if it had always been there. "No, I'm honoured to wear it."

"Well then, that makes us equal."

Until our wedding night, I hadn't had time to look closely at the ring he slipped on my finger at the altar. When, later that evening, he had shown me the words engraved on the inside of the band like a secret, I appreciated its antiquity at once.

"A poesy ring!" I exclaimed, as I read the inscription, "*'In God and thee all comfort be.'*"

"It seemed the most fitting way to express how I feel," he had said, and now – looking at it again – I understood just what he meant.

"So your mother wore this. Oh, that's odd, that's just... just downright... weird. But good weird," I hastened to say before he gained the wrong idea. With a whirr, a small wood-beetle landed on my arm and began investigating, its antennae testing the air. It tickled. Matthew placed a finger in front of it and it crawled on. He released it into the scant grass.

"My father gave it to her on their betrothal. It was the only ring she would ever wear as she said it was the only ring that mattered. She wore it until her joints became too swollen during pregnancy and my father offered to have it made bigger for her, but she wouldn't in case it damaged the inscription. I hoped it would fit you without the need for alteration." Matthew lifted his head at the sudden scurry and rattle of something small making a dash for cover beyond the outcrop behind which we sheltered. He settled back again and I continued stroking his hair. "She would be pleased to know you had it – not, perhaps, the peculiar circumstances in which we find ourselves – but pleased, nonetheless. When she died, my grandmother wore it on a ribbon around her neck until I was old enough to understand its significance and look after it. Now there was a tough character, but she also had her soft side and she was fiercely loyal. She stuck by my father, although she didn't get on well with my aunt. The two of them made a veritable fireball when they met."

"What about William?"

He sat up, seeking out among the frost-blown scree small stones he proceeded to lob at a stump some yards away. "William was a different matter; she adored him."

"Despite the trouble he caused?"

"Despite everything."

CHAPTER

20

Marking Time

Let us possess one world, each hath one, and is one.
John Donne (1572–1631)

We allowed ourselves a little over a week – just a week in which to be entirely ourselves and alone – but it was enough. In that time the mountain slopes shed the vestiges of winter, and sharp emerald replaced the snow.

We hiked from the cabin down the mountain early one morning to find Harry already waiting to meet us with the 4x4. Matthew swung the bags into the back. "Good morning, Harry. I thought Ellie was meeting us." Harry finished giving me a hug.

"She said something had come up and could I meet you instead." He opened the car door for me.

"Thanks. Is she OK?" I asked, hopping onto the high seat.

"Yeah, I think so, but you know it's kind of hard to tell with Ellie sometimes; she keeps things close. She said to say hi though. Oh, and Mom wants to know if you wish to be known as Dr D'Eresby or Mrs Lynes." He climbed into the car.

"I think I assumed I would be Mrs Lynes, Harry." It also gave a clear signal to the likes of Megan that Matthew was strictly off limits. Matthew smiled quietly to himself. "And why are you smiling, exactly?" I asked suspiciously.

Matthew held my hand to the light streaming through the window and rotated my rings until they sat true to my finger. "And isn't a man allowed to express a degree of happiness at the thought that his new bride carries his name?" His mouth twitched and I wanted desperately to kiss it, but Harry was driving and he didn't need any distractions from the back seat.

He left us at the front of our home. I craned to take in the full façade, remembering the first moment I had seen it before Christmas in times less certain than these, and when it was strange, and I the stranger. "Welcome home, my lady," Matthew said, scooping me up and carrying me across the threshold in time-honoured fashion. All the trappings of the wedding had gone, but the house smelled of fresh flowers and sunshine, as if new life had blown through on spring breezes. "Lunch, then presents," he said, putting me down and steering me towards the kitchen. "Pat said she would leave a meal for you. I think she believed food wouldn't be high on the agenda on our honeymoon, so she'll want to make up for it, no doubt."

After lunch, we sat around the old table in the dining room and opened the gifts that awaited our return, and, although we had asked for nothing, tradition dictated we received something. Given free rein, our guests had used their imaginations. I was still convulsed with laughter over Elena and Matias's present, when Matthew said in muted tones, "Emma, look at this." Amidst the tatty remains of sun-faded wrapping paper lay a large etching in an ornate gilded frame, white-flecked where it had been chipped on one edge. It appeared very old: small figures in front of the handsome moated building dated the image to the late seventeenth century. I didn't need to see the name at the bottom of the picture to know where it must be.

"Your home," I said softly, seeing at once the ground plan of the manor house we had traced through winter wheat together. Matthew said nothing. He studied it carefully and then I saw what he saw: blank-faced windows naked of glass, gap-toothed walls part-robbed of stone. Trees grew too close, and the moat was empty of water, but the eloquent heart of the building remained untouched.

"It's a beautiful house." It seemed such an inadequate thing to say, but he smiled in acknowledgment.

"Thank you; I thought so. I wish you could have seen it. Perhaps then we would be standing just here," and he pointed to the big oriel window suspended to one side, "talking about our future together." It seemed worlds away and yet close and real. And then came a thought so obvious I'd overlooked it.

"Matthew, who sent it? Who knows?"

"Don't worry, look," and he picked up a letter lying on the table. Cobweb writing skimmed the paper and here and there it faltered, but its voice was strong.

> *Old Manor Farm*
> *Martinsthorpe*
> *3rd April*

My dears,

I intended to give you this picture when you visited, so forgive an old woman's lassitude, but my years are long and time is short, and my memory is not what it used to be. I will give it to the young man who promised he would send it safely and, if you're reading this, he has done so. Roger doesn't know and I think he wouldn't care for it, but it belongs with the Lynes family and it is what my husband would have wanted.

I am feeling so much better now that spring is here. My doctor came to see me shortly after your visit and gave me some wonderful tablets. Such a revelation; I feel like a new woman.

Roger wants me to take a little flat in Peterborough. He says it will be much easier to keep warm and there will be somebody to keep an eye on me. I did take a look but it was rather poky and dark, and the noise of the trains quite shook me. Now that I feel much brighter, I think I will stay here until I am ready to leave. I have always rather liked the idea of a place in Oakham or Stamford near my friends, or at least near the ghosts of them and my youth.

I left the young man in the church while I finish this letter and I do not want to keep him waiting, so I will end by wishing you both much happiness and a long life.

Emma, please tell Matthew that I believe reincarnation is overrated.

Joan Seaton

"What does she mean by '*reincarnation is overrated*'?" I puzzled.

"I believe she refers to a conversation we had when you were making her lunch. She asked me if I believed in reincarnation. I said *no*, of course, and I thought she had forgotten about it." He turned the letter over and checked the date, and then back again to her last comment.

"Do you think she knows about you?"

"Knows? No, I don't think so, but suspects? Perhaps. I sometimes wonder whether as one nears death all things seem possible – or credible. Your Nanna certainly thought so."

"She didn't say."

"No, she wouldn't and who would believe the ramblings of an old woman anyway? Don't worry, I'm not concerned about what

Joan Seaton might say. I'm glad she's feeling much better, though; it'll help her stand up to her bully of a son. Now, where shall we hang this?" He picked up the picture and held it to the left of the fireplace for me to see. I gave him a thumbs up, and he placed it carefully to one side to put up later. He took a quick look out of the window and, seemingly satisfied, asked, "Are you ready for your present now?" I couldn't see what the weather had to do with anything, but I nodded again and together we went outside.

I couldn't see it from the drive and I hadn't looked from the kitchen windows, but there, where once the land rose and fell in curves towards the paddock, were now the heads of small trees. I shielded my eyes from the sun as we approached. "Trees? Apple trees? An orchard? You've planted an orchard!" I whooped and skipped to the first of the slim trunks. Each tree stood about seven feet high, the lower branches skimming my head. He had timed it perfectly and the blossom glowed in lustrous rose quartz petals in the rich light. I counted the trees in the newly turned earth. I swung around to face him, my eyes glistening. "My own orchard, Matthew. How did you know?"

"You told me. Once, some time ago, you said that it was where you would go to in your mind when you needed to escape."

I shook my head. "I don't remember telling you."

"No, well, I do. I remember everything you have ever said to me and it was something I have wanted to give you for a long time, but only now is right. I'm glad you like it. You have several types of apple, a crabapple, two pears, and a number of self-fertile plum trees to wander under to your heart's content, whenever you wish to escape."

Dancing up to him, I drew him close. "But not you; I'll never escape from you."

"And I'll never give you cause to. You didn't say why an orchard represents such a special place for you."

"Didn't I? It's something from when I was very little, or I might have dreamt it, I'm not sure. Grandpa and Nanna took Beth and me somewhere where there was an old orchard and stone walls. I don't remember much except Beth and I tried to catch petals as they fell, so it must have been spring, and we were happy – very happy. The day seemed immensely bright, an image I can play over and over again." I looked at the branches either side of us snagging Matthew's hair. "Grandpa sat in the sun and his hair was on fire with it and I thought I could never be that happy again." I smiled wistfully. "I wish he could have met you, but I'm glad Nanna did. There you are – that's why I like orchards. Now," I said, reluctant though I might be to leave the silk-scented bower, "it's my turn."

I had secreted the dull wooden box somewhere he wouldn't find it. I made him wait in his study while I brought it to him and carefully placed it on his desk. Picking up on my caution, he inched off the lid and removed the top half of the foam. Watching the muscles of his face, the hidden complexion of his response in the air around him, I held my breath and it was so long before he reacted that I drew another. An anxious minute passed in which his colours flowed dark to light and back again.

"A clock – a lantern clock," he stated. He lifted the brass clock from its womb of foam and set it on its ball feet. He rotated it slowly, examining the detail of the dolphin frets, the tulip engraving, the finials rising at the four corners around the bell dome, until finally turning it to face him. Still he said nothing and, worryingly, now I couldn't read his mood at all.

"It's second-quarter seventeenth century – pre-Commonwealth – by a London clockmaker," I ventured. "I know you don't have clocks in the house ..."

"No, I don't," he said quietly.

"... and I know Maggie said you don't want them because they remind you of the passing of time."

"Did she?" He quirked an eyebrow. "Well, I've never said so, but she is right enough." He paused for thought. "But that was before I met you, and now every moment is precious and should be marked and celebrated. Thank you, this is most fitting." He sounded so serious I wondered if I'd misheard him, until he smiled. "Maggie is very good at deciphering the present emotional state of a person based on their experiences, but she lacks the insight to see how they can move on from that point. She's too rigid in her thinking, too fixated on the past. You, however, are intuitive and perceptive. This isn't just what I wanted, but what I needed, and it's a very fine piece of craftsmanship. Talking of which, I have something else I want to show you."

"Ooo!" I pipped.

"Well, I couldn't have a new wife without getting a new bed. I wanted a full-tester, but couldn't find anything I liked enough at the time, so I chose this period colonial piece instead. I hope you like it. I was in two minds whether to wait until we could choose one together, but I rather wanted to surprise you."

I ran my hand from the delicate finial at head height, down over the smooth reeded column of the mahogany uprights to the carved footrest, finding his uncertainty rather endearing. I hopped on the bed and felt the mattress sink slightly as it resisted my weight.

He agitated his hair, leaving it awry. "I realize that all the furniture in this house – everything, in fact – is what I've chosen, so I thought that you might like to redecorate and make it your own."

I bounced once or twice, then rolled backwards, testing the springs, and lay there watching him watching me. He frowned, perplexed by my lack of response. "Emma, what do you think?"

Kicking my feet free of my sandals, I wriggled my bare toes against his stomach and felt the muscles contract delightfully beneath them. His expression changed, his eyes glittering. "You didn't give me an answer, my lady. I'm waiting for an answer." Bending slowly, he kissed one bare shoulder, and then the other.

"I think," I purred, wondering whether he could detect the thunderous reply in my blood, "that four-posters are overrated."

It had been a long day and the bed was very comfortable. "You still haven't answered my question," Matthew said sometime later.

I thought I had. Drowsily I found his arm and pulled it back over me. "They won't take back used items."

"I meant the redecorating bit. We could change the colour scheme, brighten things up, alter the kitchen, if you'd prefer."

Wriggling comfortably, I stretched out along his length. "No thanks, I like what's here."

He said something in an undertone as he slid out of bed and went to close the shutters.

"What was that?" I asked.

"I said, your father was right – you're an economy model. I'll bear it in mind when we get you a car."

"Very funny. There's something I've been meaning to ask. Why do you keep referring to me as *my lady*?"

He drew the heavy curtains across the shuttered windows, preventing the last of the evening light from creeping in around the edges. "Why? Does it bother you?"

"No, not really; well, yes, I suppose it does – it's irksome, like being called *professor* when I'm not."

"Is it indeed? Well, my lady, you'd better get used to it because that is what you are, and it's taken close to four hundred years for me to be able to say it."

There were few things in my life that had rendered me speechless and this was one of them. "Since… when?" I eventually stumbled.

"It's fairly complicated…"

"Of course it is! When isn't it with you?"

"All right, I'll tell you as we prepare dinner."

I washed my hands, fetched a knife and chopping board, waiting for his explanation while he located some things in the fridge and put them down on the table.

"The first part is straightforward. My father was made a baronet, which I inherited on his death, of course…"

"Of course."

"… and I was knighted as his eldest son when I gained my majority."

"I haven't seen any mention of it in anything Grandpa wrote."

He dried the long pepper, flinging the tea towel over his shoulder and setting a large frying pan over a low heat. "Didn't he? Perhaps he didn't know; it isn't obvious at first. If you take a close look at the Lynes window in St Martin's, you'll see a small red hand embroidered on the breast of my father's cape." I hadn't spent much time studying the detail of the window, and armorials had never been of great interest to me. "Baronets had the right to display the bloody hand of The Arms of Ulster – except my father wouldn't have it incorporated into our arms. I don't know why; he could be funny like that." He split the pepper and laid it in the hot pan. "I suspect he thought it might better my prospects of securing a good match and furthering the family name. He certainly didn't do it for himself."

I surveyed the lump of meat sitting on the chopping board and prodded it with the knife, thinking about his betrothal to the Harrington heiress, a good union for a gentleman's son.

His arms found their way around my waist and he kissed the back of my neck. "So you are Lady Lynes of New Hall."

"And you're Sir Matthew Lynes. Golly, Dad would be impressed."

"Much good it does us, I'm afraid. Not even Henry can know. My father would have liked to have been a grandfather, to know the Lynes carried on generation after generation and with it the title. It cost him a small fortune."

"Ah well, the title doesn't bother me; I only married you for your money after all…"

He tickled my waist for that, and I writhed to escape. "And my culinary skills. If you are to eat tonight, that steak has to be cooked." He let go of me and picked up a packet of green beans.

I suspended the steak between finger and thumb, inspecting it on both sides. "It's very fatty."

"That's marbling." He pointed to the fine creamy lines running through the meat. "It gives it flavour and makes it tender. This, on the other hand, is gristle, and needs cutting out, like this." He cut at an angle through the meat and handed me the knife.

"It's very tough," I complained, hacking at it crossly.

"Like this, Emma," he said patiently, and showed me again, his hand over mine. This time my knife severed tissue and soft flesh, and the smell of raw meat rose, sickly sweet. I took a shallow breath and turned my face away to find untainted air.

"Is this what a battlefield smelt like?"

He looked taken aback for an instant, then continued slicing beans before answering. "Not exactly, no – there were other smells too: sweat, horses, powder, mud – but most of all, fear." His voice dropped. "You never forget the smell of fear."

I concentrated on trimming the meat. "You said it was complicated, Matthew, but nothing you've said so far sounds out of the ordinary – if we put your circumstances aside for a moment, that is."

"It wasn't complicated until an incident with the Dutch in an occupation I pursued for a short period during the Dutch Wars. Then things became too warm for comfort and I disappeared again – over here for a bit, to be precise."

"Am I supposed to know what you are referring to or do I have to guess? And why do I have the feeling that I'm not going to like what I'm about to hear?"

"Well," he looked shifty, "you've heard of fireships, I expect..."

My temper flared and I slammed the knife into the steak. "What did you think you were doing in a fireship, of all things, Matthew Lynes? Life too dull for you or something?"

"It was a job that had to be done..."

"But not by you. What were you doing? Pushing your luck?"

"Along those lines, yes," he said. At his frank confession, I simmered down. He had alluded to such things before and perhaps I shouldn't have reacted as forcefully as I did. In some ways the thought that he had survived one of the most perilous occupations of the age brought an air of comfort with it. It hadn't killed him then – what could kill him now?

"You promised not to put your mortality to the test," I couldn't help but grumble, defying his attempts to win me over that were beginning to be quite effective.

"Sweetheart, that was before I met you. Be reasonable. It was well rewarded, exciting, and I was still a young man at heart. Besides, everyone else I had known was dead so I had nothing to lose."

"Except your life. You couldn't have known you were fairly indestructible." He let go of me and his hands flew as he finished preparing the meat. He tossed it into the waiting pan, watching it sear. "I still don't; that part of my life is as yet unknown."

I clamped my hands over my ears. "Don't you dare; your mortality is taboo in this house. I don't want to hear you mention it again. Understand?" He stared at the meat but didn't seem to notice it beginning to burn. The warm room chilled. "Understand?" I tried again, hesitantly.

He came to and saw the meat. "Taboo. Got it. Aye, aye, Captain." He flipped the steak. "We've forgotten to put the beans on, by the way."

Only once I had eaten did he venture, as if in passing, "So I take it you don't want to hear about my service in His Majesty's navy?"

My reply was unrepeatable.

Roadkill

I was late. Too absorbed in my own thoughts I missed the turning to Howard's Lake and ended up on a back road I didn't recognize, the trees bursting with leaves so I couldn't get my bearings through the shifting foliage. And the signage was lousy. Now I regretted not letting Matthew show me how to use the integrated Sat Nav system, so eager had I been to take my car, the colour of a blue jay, out for the first time.

Shiny – like a new toy.

The yellow line of the road curved out of sight, heading back towards the mountains. At some point it must cross the head of the lake on which the college sat. By continuing this way, surely the road would take me around the far end in a long loop.

Or I could go back.

I checked the clock: either way I wouldn't make it on time. I went on. Every now and again I caught a glimpse of the lake, sometimes closer, sometimes further away, and the odd summer lodge, hugging the shore, and then it disappeared altogether. I was about to give up and turn back, but the road suddenly straightened and dived across a narrow, wood-planked bridge barely wide enough for two cars to pass. Cautious, I slowed. The low ramparts hardly disguised the sudden drop twenty feet or so to the river below. Fast-flowing, it bulged around water-carved boulders and beaches of shingle, feeding the lake beyond. The bloodied body of a skunk lay thrown up against the farther end of the bridge where wheels had discarded it. I could smell it from here inside the car, and the stench stayed with me long after I had left its carcass and the bridge behind.

The campus seemed unnaturally quiet as students retreated to the darkest recesses on study leave. My four and I, however, had different plans.

"I'm sorry to have kept you waiting." I plonked the assortment of pastries on my desk. "I took the wrong turning. Where's Hannah?"

Josh raided the box for a doughnut and propped his feet on the spare chair. "She's gonna be a bit late – freaking out about the conference. Said she'll get here when she can. Hey, Dr D, we've all the time in the world, haven't we? No sweat."

I replied to his caustic grin by swiping his feet off the chair. "Glad you think so, Josh. I take it you're just about done?"

He nudged the folders next to him with his elbow. "Yeah. I added that reference you suggested. You sure Shotter's cool with this? I mean, has he had a personality transplant or have you got something on him?" Holly gave a nervous giggle, but Aydin, I noticed, waited for my reply.

I offered the others the sugary confections, licked my fingers, and fudged an answer. "I'll introduce the conference and set the theme on the Thursday morning. Then there'll be visiting speakers until noon. I'll give a short lecture after lunch, after which you four will be on. That's the plan, anyway. Josh, you'll lead, then Holly, then you Aydin, and lastly Hannah. There'll be the formal dinner on Friday evening, and I'll close the conference around midday on Saturday when we'll pack up all the delegates and send them on their merry way, replete with our combined wisdom." I smiled with a confidence that belied the truth and hoped they wouldn't notice the slight tremor of doubt. I needn't have worried because Hannah came in with a flurry of paper and a bad-tempered scowl. She sat down solidly.

"What on earth's the matter, Hannah?"

"I'm not doing it," she stated, her jaw jutting in imitation of a piranha. "I don't care; I'm not presenting that... that boring whale-crap at the conference." We stared at her.

"Hannah, you've left it too late to change now and you've no time to start a new project. If you don't finish what you've started, you'll fail your post-grad studies."

"I'll use my other work." She folded her arms across her chest and tried to stare me into submission, but since I had spent my youth practising that particular art form against my father, I wasn't going to let it worry me now.

"We discussed this, Hannah," I said evenly. "Your other research is seriously flawed. I won't let it pass in its present state. Let me have a look at what you've done so far on your current project and see if it can be revitalized."

"I don't need your help. I'll make it work by myself, or I'll start something new."

The others shifted uncomfortably and looked from her to me. Josh sat forward in his chair. "Aw, Hannah, c'mon. Dr D is just trying to help. It'd be stupid to chuck it in now. You just gotta do what it takes to pass, then you can do what you like. Isn't that right, Dr D?"

"Something like that, Josh. Don't let this stand in the way of your career, Hannah. Do what you need to pass, then your future is your own."

"You didn't though, did you?" she shot back. "You didn't do what you were supposed to and you've done all right." How in Heaven's name did she know that? She smiled in triumph as she read my expression. "I looked you up on the net – all your work's on there, including that research you submitted for your final examination. I know what you got away with and I saw what they said about you. If you managed it, then so can I. Or is it that you don't want the competition?"

Aydin jumped to his feet before I could respond, his normally placid features creased with anger. "This is rudeness. You do not speak to your professor like this; it is not respectful."

I put a steadying hand on his arm. "Aydin, it's all right – thank you, but please, sit down." I faced Hannah more regretfully than in irritation. "I'm sorry, Hannah. I cannot help you if that is your attitude. You're quite right, I did submit work that broke the rules, but my research was thorough and stood up to scrutiny, as you will have seen if you read all the documentation. I told you before – you cannot let your ambition lead your research. Submit your current thesis, or nothing."

She stood abruptly, stuffing the papers she had been holding into her stripy bag. "You're not the only professor who can help me," she almost spat, yanking the bag over her shoulder. She stalked out.

I rather thought I was. I had always known her to be strong-willed, but I didn't think she would be so stubborn as to ruin her chances of graduating successfully. She wasn't stupid – which made her outburst all the more puzzling.

"Well," I said in the ensuing silence, "and then there were three."

I didn't say anything to the others but I felt like an utter failure. I'd started the year with five students. Leo had fallen by the wayside because he was downright idle, but Hannah? She had vim and vision, but she also had an ego to match and she let it get in the way of her work. She needn't have done, and I couldn't help but think that, had I been able to keep a closer eye on her, we could have avoided this outcome. I still harboured the faint hope that she would calm down and think about it but, by the look she had thrown me as she left the room, the chances of that happening were as remote as my winning a lottery I didn't play.

We had a somewhat desultory tutorial where we went through the motions, but our hearts weren't in it and we decided to call it a day and meet up later in the week. Aydin stayed back after the others had gone.

"Thanks, Aydin."

He scratched his head through his dark, receding hair. "It is not your fault; you have tried to help her but she does not listen. It is her choice."

"Yes, I know it is, but still…"

"You think she is like you?" He laughed when I looked at him, surprised. "I, too, have read about your career, but I have a different – what do you say? – a different view, a different perspective. I think that we have to make choice of how we see things and then what we do about them. I think that Hannah is wrong about you – that is my view."

"Thanks," I said again.

He shrugged. "I would not be here if it was not for *your* perspective." No, he probably wouldn't be; he had nearly given up back in the autumn, and then there had been the incident with the police. "I have much to thank you for," he continued, then leant forward and shyly kissed me on both cheeks. "Thank you for believing me." He had almost left the room when he added with a grin, "You know, in my country, a husband would kill a man for kissing his wife. Do not tell Dr Lynes. I do not want to be shark-food."

* * *

It might indeed be Hannah's choice, but knowing it didn't make me feel any better. I mooched across the hall to Elena's tutor room and found her engrossed. She slung her bag over one shoulder and visibly brightened at the suggestion that we spend the afternoon together and catch up on life.

"*Da*! I have had enough of the Collectivization and the Great Famine. I need, how do you say… antidote? Yes, antidote. Wine for me, tea for you, and as much pizza as we can eat and the most ro-*mantic* film in the world…"

"Which is?" We linked arms and together made our way down the corridor.

"*Brief Encounter*, of course! I love it when Alec takes the speck out of Laura's eye. It is so romantic, so British."

"What, all grimy stations and postwar austerity? Or do you mean repressed emotions and unrequited love? Anyway, what's so romantic about a married woman having an affair with a married man?" I always pitied the poor passive husband rather than his wayward wife, although I had been young when I'd first seen it, and a harsh critic. Besides, it was a theme too close to home.

"Silly," Elena chided as we reached the stairs. "It is a wonderful film. Alec is a doctor like Matthew, and Laura is…"

I nudged her arm. "Is what?"

"Laura is very… nice."

"Nice! Are you saying I'm *nice*?"

"No, no – not nice; you are very correct, like Laura…"

"Oh, thanks a bunch."

"… and Matthew is very passionate."

I laughed. "True." She waited expectantly, but I wasn't in the habit of discussing the intimate details of my life, especially with someone prone to a glass or two in good company – or otherwise.

We opened the door to the quad and were met by a wall of sunshine. Cowed by the sudden light, I squinted as a sturdy form made his way towards us, raising his arm in greeting. I waved back. "There's Matias. Were you meeting him?" By her thwarted pout I rather thought not.

"Hey! Two gorgeous women, my luck's turned. Where are you off to?"

Elena returned his kiss halfheartedly. "We were going to watch *Brief Encounter* – alone."

"So that she can try to wheedle details of my sex life over a bottle of wine and a pizza. Unfortunately for her dastardly plan, tea doesn't make me particularly loquacious," I grinned.

Matias rumpled Elena's hair into a glossy bird's nest that settled back into place with a stroke of his hand. "But you can't blame her for trying, Emma. Matthew's not very forthcoming on that subject either. You shouldn't have bought her all those girly DVDs, and what was with the London policeman's helmet, may I ask? She's been making me wear it."

"Honestly, you two!" I exclaimed, laughing, but became distracted as Elena tugged my sleeve.

"Eckhart!" she said in a theatric undertone. "He's coming this way." Two figures made silhouettes by the sun – one short and oval, the other stiff and long – were making rapid ground towards us.

"Quick, hoof it." Matias made toreador movements with his arms, ushering us back towards the faculty door so we could make good our escape. Too late.

"Ah... ah, Professor!"

I groaned barely audibly and wondered if I could pretend I hadn't heard him.

"Professor!" Eckhart tried again. I halted, smiling apologetically at my friends. "Professor D'Eresby, just a moment if you w... will!" I turned, shielding my eyes against the glare. He could hardly contain his excitement. "I have su... such good news, s... someone I know you would like to meet."

The second figure moved out of the sun's path and became human, and my chest constricted sharply as the ground swayed and my lungs struggled to draw oxygen.

"Hello, Emma," the all-too familiar voice drawled. "Happy birthday."

Surprise

"Emma, you didn't say it was your birthday!" Elena gushed. She flung her arms around me. "Happy birthday!"

Remaining immobile, I was hardly aware of anything or anyone else, my eyes fixed and staring at the man in front of me. I forced my mouth to work. "Hello, Guy."

Elena took a step back, her smile fading as she recalled his name from my past. He had changed less than I would have expected – hair a little thinner, a tad more weight – but his eyes were exactly the same, and they scoured me as they had always done, seeking, delving, restless.

"I knew you would be p... pleased," Eckhart beamed, regardless of the sudden tension.

Guy almost smiled. "It's been a long time, Emma; you're looking very well, I must say." So was he. His shirt sat open at the neck and his olive skin had taken on a russet glow which suited him. He hadn't acquired a tan like *that* in the UK at this time of year. What did he think I'd say? How did he expect I would respond?

Eckhart ploughed on, oblivious. "Yes, yes, of c... course, Dr Hilliard is here for the conference. I wanted to introduce you last week but you were away on your... on your hon..."

"But the conference is three weeks away, Guy," I interrupted curtly, "and you weren't on the list."

Eckhart rubbed an inky hand over his nose. "Ah, no, there were some last minute changes, and when I heard Dr Hilliard was in the country publicizing his new book, I thought how fortuitous. You've seen Dr Hilliard's book, Professor, a brilliant work." *Shut up!* I yelled at him silently, my jaw aching with the effort to control my tongue. "You must remember, you had it a f... few weeks ago in your tutor room." He pushed his glasses up his nose. "On your desk."

Guy's interest quickened. "Did you now?"

I grew crimson. "One of my students read it," I said defensively, shoving my hands in my pockets to stop them from shaking. "What are you doing here, Guy?" I knew I sounded rude – I saw it mirrored in the baffled expressions of my friends – but they couldn't see what I saw, they couldn't feel what I felt.

If Guy took offence, he didn't show it. "I happened to be in the area and had the opportunity to take in the conference." Well, that wasn't true for a start; Guy never *happened* to be anywhere he hadn't planned on being with all the precision of a military operation. "I also wanted to do some research beforehand. I believe the library here has some interesting documents I might take a look at if I have the time. One or two of them are unique, I believe."

Avoiding his eyes in case he saw the panic swelling behind mine, I remembered to breathe, the frozen rivers of my veins becoming fissures of molten lead.

Eckhart's owl-like eyes swivelled in ecstasy. "Ah yes, the library – a magnificent collection. As you specialize in the s... same period, perhaps Professor D'Eresby could show you?"

Guy cracked a rare smile. "I don't wish to bother Emma. I'm sure she has better things to do than show me the library."

"I do," I said bluntly. "I'm far too busy."

Matias frowned. "Busy? But I thought you girls were going to spend an afternoon eating, drinking, and watching *Now, Voyager?*"

"*Brief Encounter*," Elena corrected him.

Guy's sharp mouth rose in a smile just short of derisory. "*Brief Encounter*? Not Emma's choice I think, so it must be yours, Professor…?" Guy turned to Elena. "Emma, you haven't introduced your friends."

Elena forgot to be cautious under his concentrated gaze. "Elena Smalova." She held out her hand, which he took and held a little over-long.

"*The* Elena Smalova of St Petersburg Institute of Historical Studies? I've read your insightful articles on post-Revolutionary popular culture with great interest. I believe you studied under Professor Sergei Bogdanovich? I had immense respect for the man. We must get together; I have a few questions you might be able to answer."

"*Da*, of course," she acquiesced too quickly, almost simpering at his flattery and ignoring my ferocious glare. Matias bristled next to her until she pulled him forward and introduced him. "This is my fiancé, Matias Lidström. He is a brilliant research scientist…"

She rattled on happily and Guy listened as if he cared. I'd had enough. I watched their faces; I sensed their gullibility. Even my friend who knew something of my history had seemingly forgotten, her initial watchfulness blown away by the strength of Guy's sincerity. And Matias, upon whom I could usually rely to exercise better judgment, seemed outwardly taken in. I couldn't really blame them – after all, what had Guy ever done to them to earn my disdain? But they were my friends and already he had insinuated himself into my relationships and cast shades of doubt in their minds, questioning my version of the truth.

"Excuse me." Detaching myself, I headed in the direction of the car park as fast as I could distance myself from them. I heard feet running on the soft earth behind me, but didn't turn around.

"Emma, wait," Elena called. "Please..." I slowed and she caught up with me. "Where are you going? What about the film and the pizza? What about your birthday?"

"Elena, how could you? How could you smile and talk with that man as if nothing happened? You know what he did, how I feel about him."

She shrugged, pulling her forehead into a dismissive frown. "Yes, you had an affair and he lied to you, but that was a long time ago, Emma. He seems to have forgotten it. Why can't you? You are married now and this man is nothing to you. Why can't you move on?"

Move on. Forget it. Forget what happened because it should be irrelevant now. Guy might be here for the conference, but he would leave, he would go, he would move on. She made sense, although not a fragment of me wanted to admit it. Perhaps she saw something I couldn't, something redeeming in him to which acrimony blinded me. She noted my hesitation and pushed her point.

"And Emma, you are wrong; he has changed now I think. I like him, he's really nice."

Nice. That's one thing Guy could never be accused of – being nice.

I hugged her longer than strictly necessary because I didn't want her to think I harboured any bad feeling between us, and because I couldn't find the words to tell her she was wrong without sour vitriol spilling from me like spikes. I let the car find the way back home, no pleasure left in driving Matthew's present to me, and let myself in by the back door.

* * *

Matthew found me in the kitchen some time later. "What are you doing?"

I didn't look around, my voice echoing in the metallic box. "Cleaning the oven."

"I can see that. Why?"

I rinsed the cloth in the bowl next to me, the water hardly brown. "I haven't cleaned it." I scrubbed at imaginary grease. I heard him move until he stood just behind me. I didn't turn around.

"We haven't used it since Christmas; what's going on?"

I dipped the cloth in the bowl again rather than answer, and my hands stung. He took the cloth from me, pulling me to my feet where I couldn't avoid him, and inspected my hands. "Sweetheart, your hands are raw. Tell me, what's wrong?"

I tried to pull my hands away, but he held on to them. I knew I would have to tell him and I had spent the afternoon on my knees doing pointless jobs because I didn't know how. Despite everything Elena said I couldn't believe that Guy had turned up on some random whim to kill time. And he wanted to see the library – he had specifically mentioned the library. Matthew waited.

I met his eyes. "He's here," I said flatly. I didn't need to say any more because across his face flashed instant understanding and something else soon concealed – anger? His fingers lingered for an instant over my wedding ring.

"I'll get something for your hands," he said.

Had it not registered? "Matthew, Guy's *here*; I met him. He's up to something. I don't trust him."

"He can't hurt you, Emma."

"He wants to see the library and you know what that means?" I tried to hide the rising note of fear. "What if he finds the journal, Matthew? What if he finds you?"

"Emma, he cannot hurt us." This time, he placed his palms either side of my face, willing me to believe him. "You are not alone any more and together we are stronger than anything he can throw at us. There's no reason to believe he will find the journal and anything in it that can lead him to me." He raised his head, listening. "Now, the family have planned a birthday party for you. Do you want them to know about Guy? We can tell them together if it's easier." I could hear voices now. I shook my head adamantly. This was my problem – our problem.

"OK," he breathed, "then now's the time to act surprised. Ready?"

Secret Smile

Quick-acting, like poison, he drew a mantle over my happiness so that every moment became tainted. I felt myself grey despite Matthew's attempts to maintain normality and, no matter how hard I tried, I couldn't persuade myself that Guy posed no threat.

In contrast, Ellie blossomed with the burgeoning summer, her honey hair brightening, and each step lighter than the last until she almost seemed to float with suppressed joy. She found me in the nascent orchard several days after my birthday, and she was hardly discernible from the sky because of the waves of pale blue that emanated from her.

"Hi. Matthew said I'd find you here." She threw herself into the lengthening grass and stretched in the dappled sun. "Mmm, I look forward all year to this weather – isn't it perfect?"

I put my book down and waited, in no hurry to disturb the peace I found there. She cast a look from beneath long lashes. "Emma, can I talk to you about something?"

"Of course you can."

"Sure, thanks, uh…" She smiled coyly.

"Who is he, Ellie?"

She laughed, high-pitched like a young girl, kicking her legs. "Is it that obvious? Mom hasn't noticed yet and I've been dropping hints like crazy." She rolled onto her stomach and plucked a strand of grass, sucking sweet liquid from its stem. "I've been seeing him for several weeks and we're sort of serious already."

"That's wonderful, but several *weeks*?"

"It's nearer a month. You know what it's like when you meet someone and it feels right? C'mon, I know you do. I remember how Matthew was when he met you; he couldn't hide it." Well now, she had a point. "Anyway, he'd hurt his back. It's lucky I was on call in the med centre at the time otherwise we'd never have met. He asked me on a date and I've seen him most days since then. He makes me feel special, Emma, as if I'm the only one that really matters. I know you'll like him. I kept it quiet until now but what I'd like – what I really want – is to bring him home to meet the family, except… I don't know how Matthew'll take it."

"He'll be as delighted as I am."

"You reckon? He's the one I'm most worried about. Do you really think he'll be OK about it?"

"Why shouldn't he be?"

She selected another stem, sucked it dry, and spat out the end. Turning over onto her back, she spread her fingers to the sky. "It was different with you; you were his choice. What happens if he doesn't like mine? It's not as if we're a normal family or anything, and I know I have to be careful. Mom said… Mom says that it was tough being accepted by the family at first. Matthew wasn't easy to persuade and I don't want him to make it hard for us."

"You know he doesn't take your welfare lightly, Ellie. He wants you to be happy and he won't make things difficult for you."

Her forehead crinkled. "Yeah, but you don't know that, Emma."

"But I know *him*. If things weren't easy for Jeannie it's likely there was a reason, even if it's not obvious. Do you want me to broach the subject with him?"

She suddenly smiled and sat up. "Would you?"

"Of course I will. I can't have my step-great-granddaughter pining now, can I?" I picked up my book and stood. "So, when do we get to meet him?"

She threw a handful of grass in my direction. "When you've kept your part of the bargain," she laughed.

I could hardly keep it to myself and her happiness was infectious. By the time I found Matthew in the study, I fairly burst with the news. He had replaced the handsome bronze stallion with the lantern clock and now stood back from the mantelpiece, assessing it. I wrapped my arms around his middle and he smiled down at me.

"Hello, what's brought out the sunshine?" He cocked his head, listening to the regular *tck, tck* of the clock.

"Why did you make it difficult for Dan and Jeannie when they met?"

He had been about to adjust the clock, but stopped, one hand still resting on the brass dome. "What makes you think I made it difficult for them?"

"Ellie said that's what Jeannie told her."

"Oh." He took the finest sliver of wood – a mere splinter – and eased it under one gold-balled foot and listened again. He seemed satisfied by the beat. "Jeannie," he stated. "Well, yes, I had reservations, it's true. I was concerned about her stability and therefore her reliability. We didn't need any more loose cannons after Monica. I didn't make it difficult for them, though, despite what she might choose to remember, but I wanted Dan to be sure before he committed himself to marriage. They were both young, and I asked him to consider waiting. Jeannie wasn't happy, but then she didn't know all the circumstances at the time. She tried to persuade him to leave the family and put him under pressure to accept the offer of a position in a firm in Washington he didn't want to take. Anyway, it was his decision to stay and I didn't try to sway him one way or the other, but she's never fully accepted that."

"But she thinks you persuaded him?"

"Coerced, more like. I didn't – the opposite in fact – but I was wrong about her in one respect."

"What's that?"

"Even though she's struggled with depression, she has never once placed the family in any danger. She adores Dan, and he loves her as much as he did when they first met. I find her inability to accept her children's differences difficult, and I can't say I've warmed to her, but she makes my grandson happy, and she's loyal, so I can tolerate her resentment towards me, such as it is." He slipped his arm around my shoulders. "You still haven't told me what's made you so happy. I doubt it's Jeannie somehow."

I picked up the single, silver-framed photograph of the two of us from our wedding that I had found waiting on my desk when we returned from our honeymoon. It was Henry's gift to us, and its presence spoke volumes. "No, it isn't Jeannie; it's Ellie. She's in love."

"Is she indeed! Who's this man who has managed to capture her heart?" Good point, we had been distracted before we reached that vital juncture.

"I don't know, but she wanted me to tell you because she wants you to meet him."

"Ah, it's serious then, and she thought I might make things awkward for her, so she sent you in to soften me up, is that it?"

"Something along those lines, I expect. I'm just so glad for her; she's moved on."

"From me as her stumbling block, do you mean?"

"It wasn't your fault, Matthew, but – yes."

He was thoughtful for a moment as the new sound of the clock filled the study with its comforting regularity. He looked at the photograph of the pair of us, a moment of intense happiness captured. "There's nothing I would like better than to see her settled," he said quietly. "There is nothing better than the love her parents, or we, or her grandparents share."

"You old softy," I teased.

"Less of the '*old*', if you will, madam," he grinned, ably demonstrating his youthful vitality until I gasped and begged him to stop. He put me back on my feet. "All right then, tell Ellie – in whatever way you see fit as her confidante – that her suitor may call and pay his respects. Only, do remind her that she doesn't need my approval, as I'm only her *uncle*."

I laughed, because he was trying to do an impersonation of a stuffy old man, and failing miserably. "If you go around like that he's sure to suss you're a fraud. Anyway, Ellie knows to be careful. Let's just hope she's equally sensible in all other respects." Matthew pulled a face of quaint disapproval. "What's that face for?"

"At the risk of sounding old-fashioned, I'd be happier if she waited until she married."

"Some women don't have that luxury, Matthew." I hadn't meant it to come out the way it did, but his regret was instantaneous.

"I'm so sorry; I didn't mean to imply anything. It's not as if you had any choice in the matter – Guy took that away from you."

"Yes, he did." I studied my toes. "Anyway, Ellie has parents to confide in, so unless she asks, I'm keeping my opinion to myself."

"And by that token, you think I should do the same?" he asked. I said nothing. "In which case, this young man of hers had better watch his step lest he incur the wrath of the Lynes family," he intoned theatrically, sweeping a length of my hair to form a copper mask in front of his face, over which his cobalt eyes gleamed.

"Daft ha'p'orth," I chided, laughing and repossessing my hair. "I'm going to let the poor girl know before she does herself a mischief."

Still feeling remarkably upbeat, later that day I received further good news. Hannah sounded contrite on the other end of the line. She had reconsidered her position and, although I could tell that she didn't find it easy, she accepted defeat.

"Great, Hannah, I'm really glad. Do you need any help getting it finished?"

"No," she said a little curtly, and broke off at a muffled sound in the background, like a voice on the radio, then corrected herself. "No, thanks, I'm good. I'll add those references you suggested before, then I'm done."

"Right," I said, both surprised and relieved. I didn't think she had been that close to completion. "I'll see you next week then."

"Sure," she said, almost dismissively, and rang off before I could say goodbye.

"That is what you wanted, isn't it?" Matthew asked when I told him later as I slipped into bed beside him.

"Yes, of course." How could I tell him that niggling away inside was an unsubstantiated suspicion that it felt like a victory too easily won. What, anyway, did it matter? Hannah had jumped back on board and only time would tell if it were a sinking ship she sailed and who, if any, were the rats.

It was as if Ellie's news helped dispel the grudging gloom meeting Guy invoked. I made up for my abrupt departure on my birthday by inviting Elena over for a film fest, and we settled in front of the big screen borrowed from Dan. Installed in the drawing room and with popcorn at the ready, we excluded the world. Matias and Matthew took one look at the pile of DVDs stacked and waiting, and departed for the study. An occasional burst of laughter confirmed Matias was enjoying the contents of the wine cellar that otherwise lay untouched.

I managed all of *Brief Encounter*, endured *Now, Voyager*, but drew a line at *Love Story*.

"I'll make some more popcorn," I offered, straightening stiffened limbs and standing up.

Elena surveyed her just-filled glass less than soberly. "If you do not want to watch it, say so. Choose another. Why don't you like romantic films? You are always making faces about them."

Was I? I hadn't thought I let it show. I slid back onto the sofa next to her. "It's not that I don't like them, but they hurt to watch. Too many broken hearts and damaged lives to make for comfortable viewing."

"Pah!" She rolled forward in an ungainly sprawl and snatched a DVD from the table. "Not like this! This is not com-for-table to watch!" She waved the box in front of me, nearly spilling her drink.

"Yes, but *Aliens* isn't real, Elena; there's the difference. I don't want to hurt. I had enough of all that to last me a lifetime."

She stopped waving the DVD, and her blood-tipped nails stilled, her brown-tilted eyes filling with curious concern. "This is to do with Guy, isn't it?"

"Yes, but don't spoil now with him. Let's watch something else." I picked a DVD at random, instantly regretting it: *Love Actually*. That had been a wasted evening; I didn't get past Emma Thompson finding the gift intended for someone else. The memory of her expression as her world collapsed lingered long after my abrupt exit from the cinema.

"Emma, perhaps if you talk with him, this demon you have made will go away."

I looked at her sharply. "What do you mean?"

"I think that you have spent so many years hating this man that you have made him into a monster from one of your books. He is not so bad."

"He's not what he seems."

"Maybe so, but who is? We all have parts of ourselves we do not want others to see, but it does not make us wicked people. Just because what he did ten years ago was wrong does not make him a bad man, Emma. He made a mistake; can't you forgive him?"

Forgive him? I knew I should. What he had done was trivial in the great scheme of things – merely an error of judgment, an omission. It was the last bastion I raised between me and my God, an open wound at which I picked and refused to let heal. To forgive Guy would be to lay myself open and relinquish the hate I clung to. It would free me, but I couldn't let go.

"I wish I could forgive him," I said, subdued, but in truth I didn't know how to begin, or whether I even wanted to.

"I know it is hard," Elena persisted. "It took me many years before I could forgive the man who attacked me as a girl. Sometimes, I do not think I have, but you should try, or your hate will eat you up." She made little snapping movements with her hand like a crocodile's jaw. "You should meet with him, and then you will see he is human after all."

If only it were so easy. For that to happen I had to look him in the eyes – remember what had passed between us – let it go. Part of me saw the truth of what my friend said, but how could I begin to find forgiveness for Guy when I had none for myself?

***

I skirted along the path between students pale and drawn from long nights spent in study, through the doors of the library and down to the silent vaults where the journal lay. There it was, undisturbed and at rest. From my pocket I drew a tiny scrap of paper, slipping it between the archive box and the shelf, where none but I would notice if it were dislodged.

I found now that I negotiated the campus with a degree of caution I had not used since the edgy days when Staahl was at liberty and a mere insinuation of a threat. I tried to justify my actions by telling myself that I didn't want to risk the distraction of meeting Guy when I had so much to prepare for the conference. The simple truth was that every time I thought I caught a glimpse of him, or imagined I heard his voice, my gut twisted and I grew cold despite the heat of the day.

I thought I hid it well enough until a door slammed down the corridor outside my tutor room one afternoon, and I started nervously. Matthew put the portion of my presentation he had been reading down on my desk. "Emma, this has to stop. You've been as jittery as a June bug since Guy Hilliard arrived." I twitched. "You see? I don't want you jumping at every mention of his name. This is where you work and you have every right to be here without this constant fear of meeting him. Do you want me to deal with him?"

"No!"

He smiled grimly. "It's only for a few more weeks and then he'll be gone. In the meantime have some fun; you're overworking again. Why don't you and Ellie take some time out together?"

"I would but she's a bit preoccupied at the moment," I reminded him. "*We* could go out though," I suggested hopefully.

"Yes, we could, but you might benefit from a little more balance in your life. I'm not sure if I have the right perspective on clothes shopping and cosmetics you seem to have."

That sounded like a cliché too far for my liking, and I was about to launch a pithy riposte when I saw his mouth tweak and concluded he was pulling my leg. He had made his point – I took life too seriously. With this in mind, when Elena suggested a day spent shopping in Portland, I accepted.

"On one condition," I demanded: "that we don't mention Guy."

"OK," she said pertly, as if nothing could be further from her mind. "On one condition…"

I looked at her guardedly. "What's that?"

"We go in your car. It is so pre-tty and fast. We can go in your car, can't we? Please, please, please!"

"You sound just like Flora," I laughed, feeling better already. "Only good girls get to go in my car. Are you a good girl, Elena?"

Her eyes widened innocently. "I'm always good," she said.

We passed Longfellow's venerable statue dominating its square, and headed for the attractive heart of the town where the oldest streets lay fronting the sea. A breeze lifted off the water, cooling the air. We spent our time mooching from one shop to another, laughing at the fiery red lobster toys and stuffed brown moose, admiring the Hopper prints and the quaintly kitsch white-painted lighthouses for the tourists. Elena kept checking her watch.

"Not keeping you, am I?" I asked after I caught her surreptitiously easing back her sleeve for the third time.

She jerked her sleeve back down. "*Nyet*, I am getting hungry, that is all. Are you not hungry, Emma?"

I consulted my stomach. "No, not particularly, but if you are, that's fine. There's a decent looking place we passed just up there." I nodded towards a side street. "Lunch is on me."

Instead of accepting, she moved in the opposite direction. "I think we do a little more shopping first – this way."

"I don't know this part of town very well," I said a few minutes later as the smaller boutiques gave way to larger institutional buildings and utilitarian stores. She darted into a shop specializing in camping equipment, flicked through racks of men's coats, checked her watch, and declared it to be lunchtime.

"OK," I said slowly, following her into a cramped, nondescript restaurant. She selected a table and sat down by the window. "Would you like to tell me what's going on?"

"I'm hungry." She thrust a menu in my hand.

"And I'm the Pope," I said drily. She didn't reply but ordered corn chowder and fries and waited while I cast my eyes down the menu.

"Just some fries, thanks," I said to the waitress, mildly astonished when Elena didn't comment on the paucity of my meal. "I like it when they leave the skins on." My random remark went unnoticed.

Elena grabbed her bag and stood up. "I've forgotten something," she rushed. "I'll be back in a few minutes; start without me."

I resigned myself to waiting, and rummaged in my bag for Longfellow's translation of Dante's *Inferno*. After ten minutes, I regretted sitting in the window, as the midday sun roasted my neck despite the air conditioning. People came and went. The waitress returned with my order. Still no Elena. I ate a few chips and considered moving further into the interior, but all the tables were occupied. I returned to Dante's "Second Circle" and his carnal malefactors. The table juddered as someone pushed past, making the cutlery rattle.

"Still on starvation rations, I see." Guy's dry inflection catapulted me into the present as he pulled out the chair and sat down. "And your choice of reading material is as erudite and sanctimonious as ever." He raised a hand and the waitress came over. "Americano," he ordered and looked expectantly at me. I shook my head, speechless with fury.

"Thanks," I said to the girl, as he hadn't. He moved the salt over in a clean sweep of his hand, resting his tanned arms on the barren table and looking particularly pleased with himself. I refused to give him the satisfaction of seeming surprised and I wouldn't leave; my pride made sure of that. The extra weight he carried suited him, made him less angular somehow, but it failed to disguise the vinegar in his blood. He had definitely aged, but he carried it well and the assertive aura he exuded was as beguiling as ever. The waitress certainly thought so as she placed the coffee in front of him. My heart stuttered for a few angry seconds as the sooty stench burned my throat. I leaned back as far as I could until my shoulders touched the glass and felt the vibration of the congested street outside.

"It's been a long time since we did this, Emma."

I stared stonily at him. "Why exactly are you here?"

"I have your friend to thank for this. It was her suggestion that we meet and heal some old wounds. Kind girl, attractive with it, but sentimental. Not like you, Emma; you were never one for slush. I must make sure I thank her, take her out perhaps."

"Leave Elena out of it. She's engaged and she's happy."

"I'm not interested in Elena." He didn't elucidate. "I see you're married now. That's a poesy ring, isn't it? Looks period. An interesting choice for a wedding ring in the twenty-first century, and that engagement ring…" I hid my hand and interest flashed in his eyes before the heavy lids masked it, an avaricious look I had seen before when he wanted something that wasn't his to possess: a book, information, me. A knot tightened around my gut.

"Congratulations," he continued. "I'm glad for you; it's what you always wanted." He didn't ask me *who* or *when* and I had the feeling he already knew. He smiled without warmth and always

– *always* – the suspicion that behind his words were layers of meaning, like strata. "We have some things to discuss, Emma, that's why I'm here."

"Do we?" I said, terse.

"We do, or at least I do. We have unfinished business. There are things I've had on my conscience for a long while."

"I'm not your confessor, Guy."

He eased forward in his chair, his tanned hands either side of his cup. "I know I've hurt you in the past..." I snorted with disbelief, "... but I want to say I'm sorry. I want your forgiveness, Emma. Can you forgive me?"

My mouth fell open. Guy wanted me to *forgive* him. Guy *asked* for my forgiveness. Guy never asked, he always took, regardless.

"Why?"

He shifted a fraction, the same sparse movements he always used. I tried to see beneath the exterior, tried to fathom his motives, but his words and colours matched – his contrition appeared real both inside and out.

"I've had a chance to re-evaluate my life over the last few years, take stock, put my house in order. Things weren't good after you left, I became quite low – you know that – and then I discovered Sarah had been having an affair."

I picked up a chip without looking and bit off its head. "I think it's called poetic justice."

He winced. "She took the children and left..."

"You divorced?"

"No, of course not." Someone dropped a stack of plates. In the brief hiatus as people craned their necks to look, we remained staring at each other. "I was in the V and A museum last spring shortly after the Edinburgh conference. You remember the conference, don't you? You should do – you were at pains to avoid me." He controlled a bitter smile. "There's an image in a little Book of Hours – a delightful thing, early sixteenth century – depicting King David praying for forgiveness for his adultery with Bathsheba, and it accompanies Psalm 6:

'O Lord, rebuke me not in thine anger, neither chasten me in thy hot displeasure.

Have mercy upon me, O Lord; for I am weak: O Lord, heal me; for my bones are vexed.

My soul is also sore vexed: but thou, O Lord, how long?'

You appreciate the irony, I'm sure, as much as you would value the object. I think you might say I had a cathartic experience, a revelation. I was being punished for my adultery and I had to ask forgiveness from those whom I had wronged."

"Really." I surveyed him across the table and tried to picture him conscience-stricken and repentant, but it just didn't work. "So you've seen Sarah since this lustral moment?"

"Not yet," he evaded. "I wanted to see you first."

So, she hadn't believed him either.

"You don't need my forgiveness to salve your conscience, Guy; if you really mean what you say you already have it from God. You could have repented and had done with it a long time ago. Why wait until now?"

He didn't like being thwarted, but then he never did. His expression soured. "I tried – remember? But you ignored my calls and you wouldn't see me. I even called you before Christmas when I heard you were home. You cut me dead, Emma. What more could I have done?" He picked up the cup, but didn't drink. "Look, I've moved on. I'm a different person from the one you used to know. After I left my post in Cambridge I took some time out…"

I couldn't resist the barbed, "You found yourself."

He drained the cup before answering. "You might put it like

that. I started writing again and my research has taken me in a new direction. The only thing that stands in my way is how we left it between us."

"You mean *I* stand in your way? It's my fault, is it?"

He all but threw the empty cup on the table. It slid towards me threateningly. I shoved it away again.

"I didn't say that. You always have to make everything so bloody complicated." The muted purples surrounding him flashed angry crimson.

"Is that all you wanted to say then, Guy? To say sorry and congratulate me on my marriage?"

He leant back and contemplated me. "You were never this hard."

I bit my tongue because he was a long way from the truth. "No, well, I had to learn rapidly." I caught the waitress's eye.

"What do you want me to do with your friend's order?" she asked as I paid and thanked her.

"She won't be back. This gentleman will have it." I stood and inched from behind the table.

"Emma..."

"I've already paid, Guy."

"I'm not talking about the damn food. Wait, for Pete's sake..." I threw his restraining hand from my arm and he followed me into the labouring street heaving with workers on their lunch-break and the first of the summer visitors, ambling.

"Emma, I need to know you forgive me."

I stopped abruptly and he almost bumped into me. "You haven't said why."

"Does it matter?"

It did. I couldn't say why, precisely, but his explanations were like an incomplete picture and I hated not knowing, because somehow – and for whatever unknown reason – it mattered.

"Because, Guy, you owe me that much." People edged around the obstruction we caused, shifting sultry air.

Eventually he shrugged. "It's part of my penance."

I almost laughed. Without warning, he bent down and forced his mouth hard against mine. I recoiled as soon as I could free myself.

"What do you think you're doing!" Furious, I wiped my arm across my mouth.

"To show you there's no hard feeling."

"Don't ever touch me again." Turning on my heel, I nearly collided with two nurses from the nearby medical centre. I apologized automatically and walked away, sensing his resentment boring through my back as I left him behind, leaving only the bitter aftertaste of the coffee and a discordant, ragged pulse in my veins.

The feeling of being watched remained with me all the way back to the car, and then I forgot about it because Elena waited for me there.

"Well?" she asked anxiously as the doors unlocked.

"Whose idea was it, Elena – his or yours?"

"I thought it would be a good idea…"

"His or yours?" I repeated.

"Guy said he wanted to see you and I thought it would be a good way of… of…"

I wrenched the door open without listening further to her explanation and climbed into the baking interior. The hot leather stung my legs. Grabbing a bottle of water I soaked a tissue, scrubbing at my lips until all trace of Guy and the coffee had gone.

She climbed in beside me, watching my rough movements with furrowed brow. "We were talking and I said you and I were going shopping and Guy mentioned he was in town. Did you not make up?"

"Oh sure, he kissed and made up all right." I could still feel the acid-etched pressure of his mouth on my skin. I felt dirty.

"Guy said he had things he needed to say to you, and Sam said…"

"Sam? What does Sam have to do with anything?"

"Nothing, but he was there with Guy in the staff dining hall, and they asked me to join them for coffee. It wasn't anything, Emma – just coffee."

But it was never *just* anything with Guy. And Sam? At what point had Guy met Sam, and why? I didn't believe in coincidence and, if there were such a thing, it was entirely of Guy's making. I wasn't cross with Elena – disappointed perhaps, but not cross. She had acted as she always did, with generous-hearted motives for the welfare of her friend. That this might be misplaced in Guy's case I thought clear; what worried me was that his motives were not.

As we approached the turning to the university drive, I broke the silence. "So you met Guy for coffee; that's nice. Had a good chat?"

Her smile brightened. "*Da*, he is very interesting. He told me about his travels and all his research. It sounds like your work."

"Oh? Did he say anything about my research?"

"No, he said nothing about you." She redirected the air vent onto her face. "But Sam did."

Blast. Sam knew little of what I did, but what he knew was too much in the hands of someone out to make mischief. I slowed for a red light, impatiently tapping the rim of the steering wheel. "What did he say?"

"Nothing much. I think he still does not like to talk about you. It hurts him – here." She placed her hand against her heart. We entered the long drive and she bent down, struggling with the strap of her fuchsia-coloured handbag that had wrapped itself around her feet.

"But he said something?" I pressed.

She yanked and the bag came free. "Oh, *da*, he talked about your research." Her hand hit the dashboard as I brought the car to a violent halt. "Emma, why did you stop?"

"What did he say?"

She looked over her shoulder. "We are blocking the drive."

"Elena, what-did-he-say?"

"Sam just said that you were researching an old book – a diary, he said. It was not important I think, is it?"

A car honked impatiently behind us. In the rearview mirror, Shotter's bulbous head glowered over the steering wheel. I took my foot off the break. "Did Guy say anything?"

"No," she dabbed at the perspiration on her forehead with a tissue. "He just smiled."

What do you do when your gut tells you something is wrong? Where do you turn when you have nothing more than instinct and insinuation to go on? I dropped Elena off in the staff car park and headed home the long way round to give myself time to think.

Less traffic crowded this route and I pulled over in a shallow lay-by near the bridge and climbed out. The bridge's planks had been worn smooth and silver by decades of wind and snow and rain. I leaned cautiously over the low metal parapet, corrugated where it had been struck by vehicles over the years. The river flowed tamer than it did only a few days before, and rocks that had lain submerged now held their bald heads above the water. Tail twitching furiously, a tiny startled squirrel rattled up the trunk of a nearby tree and sat swearing at me from a branch. I knew how it felt.

I didn't want to tell Matthew. I didn't want Guy to intrude any more on our marriage. I wanted to accept at face value the apology he offered, give him the absolution he sought for whatever reason he asked for it – and then be done with it, be finished with him once and forever.

The remains of the skunk had all but vanished, but its stink lingered in the grain of the wood. I held my breath and stepped past it. There might be nothing in what Sam had said about the journal that would whet Guy's appetite for fresh blood, not if what he said in the restaurant were true. I raised my head as the note of a car's engine rose above the gabble of the water – a harried noise, angry.

Too fast.

I made it to the other side as a small silver car sped around the angle of the bridge and tried to stop. Tyres skidded on the smooth planks, forcing the car into a spin and coming to a juddering halt against the low crash barrier that separated it from the drop to the river below. I sprinted to the driver's door as it flung open. "Are you all right?" A dazed boy of no more than eighteen fell out onto his knees. "Hang on, don't move." I leaned in and switched off the engine.

"My Mom's gonna kill me," he moaned, clutching his shoulder.

"Your mother will be thankful you're alive. You're OK, here..." I helped him sit with his back propped against the car, and put my jacket around him. "I'll call for help, then let me take a look at your shoulder."

The boy's face alternated between white and an odd shade of green. "I didn't know the bend was there; I couldn't see it. My Mom'll kill me," he said again. He seemed in one piece, just shaken, but the passenger door had caved in and the crash barrier had fared little better; it had been a close call.

* * *

"He was sure lucky," the stocky policeman said as the grey-faced mother collected her son. "Seen a number of fatalities here over the years. Something was supposed to be done about the bend. Spending cuts." He kicked at the loosened bulwark and it rattled unevenly. "I'll report it anyhow – lotta good it'll do." He eyed my sleek, powerful car. "You take care on the road now, ma'am. I don't want another callout tonight." He picked up a piece of discarded black trim and went back to his vehicle. I waited until he drove off and the recovery truck towed the lame car away, leaving the river to flow in peace once again with nothing more than the blackened marks of tyres and warped barrier as witnesses to what might have been.

Cat and Mouse

It was getting dark by the time I arrived back home. Tail lights bobbed and dipped like demon's eyes in my rearview mirror as I passed a car coming down our drive.

"Who was that?" I asked Matthew when I found him in the study deep in thought.

"Maggie," he replied shortly. "Had a good day?"

I dumped my bag on my chair. "It was interesting," I said noncommittally, but instead of asking me to clarify my remark, he just nodded without looking at me. "Is everything all right?"

He shoved his chair back from his desk, taking in my face, my mouth, my eyes. "I could ask you the same." He gave a tight smile. "I'm sure you're ready for something to eat; dinner's waiting."

He remained quiet all evening, and when I looked up unexpectedly, I found him watching me. Later, when I climbed into bed still damp from my shower, he wasn't there. When he didn't appear I went downstairs to find him. A single light lit his desk. He looked up when I came in. "I'll come to bed later," he said. "I have work to do."

Curling up alone, I pulled the covers over my ears, staring at my triptych in the faint light that crept from the landing under our bedroom door. Christ smiled down at me, and I yearned for the certainty that the dread I felt was unfounded, but my ears were filled with the sound of the river, and my dreams stained with blood.

Matthew lay beside me when I woke, as if nothing had happened. He reached out when he saw me stir and stroked my lips with his thumb as if cleansing them. "Bad dream?"

If I had I didn't remember, just the vague feeling that something wasn't right. I held his palm to my face and breathed him in. "I'm better now you're here." Already dressed, he withdrew his hand and slid out of bed. I followed his movements as he opened the shutters. "Matthew, is something bothering you?"

He opened the last shutter before answering. "Ellie's bringing her boyfriend to meet the family today. She has the afternoon off and they are seeing her parents for lunch, but she wants to introduce him to us after that – about tea-time. Do you think you'll be back by then?"

"I expect so. I don't see why not."

"So you won't be meeting up with Elena again?"

"Elena? No, we haven't arranged to." Did he know about Guy? Did he know and yet wouldn't ask me outright? I did my best to look nonchalant. "Nope, nor anyone else, but I can tell you one thing, I won't take the same road home I did yesterday."

"Oh?"

"It's pretty, but the bridge on that route is lethal – a boy crashed there yesterday. That's why I was back so late; I had to wait until his mum and the police arrived."

Matthew gave me a funny look – not so much one that questioned what I'd said, but rather why I'd said it. "You didn't say."

"No, I forgot." Still chilly in the mornings, I shivered and drew my dressing gown around my shoulders. "I'll be back by four."

* * *

Perhaps I should have told him about Guy. If he knew I had seen him would he not have mentioned it? Or did something else stalk him which he declined to share with me? I tussled with the wisdom of keeping it to myself as I made final checks to Aydin's work, and then again, as I made adjustments to my own. I was still pondering when I entered the library. The journal was where it had been and where it should be. Nothing had changed and I began to think that my growing anxiety amounted to nothing more than paranoia.

I made it home by two. By the time I opened the windows to let the grass-scented air run freely through the house, Matthew still hadn't returned, and I put on a load of washing and went to change into something lighter.

Pressing the damp, fresh linen to my hot skin, I began to hang it out. I had come to the conclusion that I would tell Matthew about the conversation with Guy, even if mentioning him made him more significant somehow, like an unwelcome weed. In the breeze, the sheet snapped damply against my legs and the peg securing one end sprang from the taut line, landing in the grass some feet away. Uttering mild oaths and stretching, I tussled with holding the sheet on the line as the freshening wind tried to tease it from my grip, and reached for the peg. Ghost-like, the sheet suddenly billowed into human form and a hand appeared beneath the veil of fabric and picked up the peg.

"Did you want this?" a disembodied voice asked. I stiffened.

"What are you doing here?"

Guy ducked under the line. "Your husband's tamed you, I see. What an image of domestic bliss; I never expected to see *you* hanging out laundry."

I ignored the peg in his outstretched hand. "How do you know where I live?"

"Does it matter?" he asked with a sardonic lift to his lip. "It would hardly be difficult to find out." The sheet flicked in my face and I pinned it to the line viciously without answering. "I like these." He bent down and lifted something from the washing basket. "I don't remember you wearing anything like this for me." I snatched my knickers from his hand and threw them back in the basket. I refused to be riled. So where was my resolve to forgive him? Vanished – the moment I heard his voice and realized nothing had changed.

"You didn't say why you're here, Guy. I thought we'd said everything there was to say yesterday."

"I didn't come here to see you, if that is what's bothering you. I told you; I've moved on. I'm here on other business."

What business could he have here if not with me? He wanted me to ask but I wouldn't give him the satisfaction.

A woman's voice called out from the direction of the house. "Guy!"

I felt the blood drain from my face and I looked at him with undisguised horror.

"Oh, there you are," Ellie laughed, lightly stepping between the sheets. "You've found Emma." She tucked her arm through Guy's. "I hope you've been helping with the laundry."

"No, Ellie," I whispered, my lips numb.

"Aw, Guy, that's too bad of you." She gazed up at him as he held my eyes. "Have you told Emma where you're from and what you do?"

"No, I haven't."

"Gee, what *have* you two been talking about?" She turned to me, her eyes shining. "I wanted to keep it a secret until today. Guy's from the UK, but you'd already worked that out, huh?" She laughed again. "But the best bit is he studies history like you.

Isn't that neat? I couldn't believe it when he told me. It's a real coincidence, isn't it?"

"But Ellie, she doesn't believe in coincidences – do you, Emma?"

Ellie's brow wrinkled into a puzzled smile. "How do you know that?"

"An educated guess. You wanted me to meet your uncle?"

"Oh, yeah, sure. Is Matthew back yet, Emma?"

"No. Not yet."

She appeared impervious to my stilted reply. "Can I show Guy the house?" She was already dragging him in the direction of the back door. "You'll love it; Matthew collects antiques. Come on." She didn't wait for my answer.

The distant sound of a car engine became audible as it climbed the rise towards the buildings. I raced around the front of the house waving frantically as the claret chassis came into view. Matthew leapt out of the car as I ran up to him. "What's the matter?"

"It's Ellie," I gasped, bending to recover my breath, but I didn't have a chance to explain.

"Matthew!" she called, waving from the front porch. She ran down the steps into the sun. "Matthew, come and meet Guy; he's dying to meet you."

Matthew's face clouded as he looked at me. I nodded, not daring to say anything in front of Ellie in case my voice gave me away.

"Hurry up," she said and danced up the steps and back into the house, disappearing from view.

"*Guy*? He's her boyfriend?"

"I didn't know, Matthew, I had no idea. What do we do?"

He swore quietly. "What does he want?"

"I don't know," I said again. "I don't trust him; this is too much of a coincidence to be one."

He looked towards the gaping mouth of the open front door. "Have you said anything to Ellie?"

"I haven't had a chance. He's in the house, in our home."

I must have looked upset because he said more evenly, "It might be more innocent than it appears. Let her introduce me – you never know, he could be genuine," he smiled, but without conviction. "Let's find out what he really wants. We'll play the long game. If he's after something, he'll reveal his hand sooner or later. Is he aware that I know who he is and about your relationship with him?"

"No, I haven't told him."

He gave a short nod and we started to walk towards the house. "Good, keep it that way for the time being."

"But we have to warn Ellie, Matthew, before it's too late."

"Yes," he said grimly, "we will, before it's too late."

A steady breeze from the open front door cooled the hall. Subdued voices came from the study. Matthew tensed and quickened his pace. They were standing by his desk surveying the bookcases, close together as they discussed the titles. As we walked in, Guy's eyes widened in surprise, then narrowed into calculating gashes. Matthew strode across the room, holding out his hand in an open show of conviviality.

"I'm Matthew Lynes. I apologize for not being here to welcome you, but I was held up at work. I believe you have already met my wife Emma?"

Guy shot me a look that I returned frostily. He reached out and shook Matthew's hand, weighing him up. "Yes," he replied slowly, "I have; the *pleasure* was all mine."

Nothing in his demeanour betrayed the deep rage that tore

through Matthew and only I could tell by the scalding vapour that suffused the air around him. He drew a smile out of nowhere. "You've met my brother Dan, and Jeannie, I believe."

Ellie beamed, taking Guy's hand in hers. "It went well, didn't it? Mom really likes you."

"Yes, your parents are charming. I can see the family resemblance in looks, if not in accommodation." His eyes travelled over the room and back to Matthew, resting on his hair before engaging his eyes again. "Your brother designed the conversion, I understand, Matthew, and your parents live in…?"

"The Barn," Ellie said.

"Yes, the Barn. And you have the main house," he stated as if the fact were significant. "An extended family – very traditional, very old-fashioned."

My heart thudded uncomfortably and Matthew put his arm around me. "Indeed, we are a close-knit family and protect our own." He smiled politely. "I see that Ellie has been showing you around."

"I took Guy to see the horses. Ollie's a bit jumpy today; he tried to bite Guy, but he just grazed his arm." She extended his forearm, revealing the reddened skin beneath the dark hairs.

"Shame," I muttered.

Ellie soothed Guy's arm. He twitched. "Ollie's not normally like that, is he, Matthew?"

"No. Not usually."

"I was telling Guy who you named the horses after," Ellie blithely continued. "He's a historian. He's written books; there's one in the library, he showed me."

"Really? What period do you study?"

"The same period as your wife." He smiled. "We share common interests – a common history, if you like."

I scowled at him, but Matthew succeeded in masking his

anger. "What a small world. What brings you to Maine?" He stepped aside and let Guy precede him to the hall.

"I came initially for the conference, but there's something of greater interest here I want to investigate." Ellie's face shone, but I had the impression it wasn't what he meant. For the second time that day, I shivered.

"Are you cold?" Ellie asked me.

Yes, from the inside out. I forced a smile. "No, I'm fine." I held on to her arm as she made to follow Guy and Matthew across the hall. "Ellie, wait a mo."

She examined my face. "You look awful, Emma. Sit down and let me take a look at you. Do you feel nauseous?"

She seemed so blissfully happy and I tried to find a way that wouldn't destroy her newfound joy. "No, but I need to speak to you. Ellie, what do you know of Guy?"

Her smile wavered. "Why? What's wrong?"

"What has he told you about himself?"

She giggled. "We haven't spent much time talking…"

"Have you slept with him?" I asked, aghast.

She dropped her gaze, running a hand through her hair and tucking the long strands behind her ear. Her mouth tightened. "Sure, I guess."

"For goodness sake, Ellie, you know nothing about him!"

I could have kicked myself as her eyes flashed defiance. "I know what I need to and that we're in love. He's older than me, sure, but I thought you of all people would understand. Mom really likes him."

"She doesn't know him."

"And you do, Emma?"

"Yes," I said. "Yes, I do." I took her hand. "Ellie, please listen to me. I know about Guy Hilliard…"

"I know he was married, if that's what you mean," she

interjected. "It's OK, he's told me. He had a really rough time – his wife had an affair. She even took their children. Can you believe it!"

"Ellie, she wasn't the only one. You can't trust him."

She snatched her hand from mine, her face hardening. "I don't know what's got into you; you've been acting odd since you met him. I just thought you'd be happy for me. Matthew's OK about it so why can't you be? Just forget it; I don't need your approval." She crashed out of the room and a few moments later I heard her elevated voice in the hall followed by a slammed door.

Matthew came in. "So you told her?"

"Not all of it. I tried to warn her but I made a mess of it. I believe she thinks I'm just interfering. He's told her he was married, but I don't think she knows he still is."

"Is he, Emma?" he said quietly.

How would I know that unless Guy had told me? "Matthew, there's something I want to tell you…"

The door flew open and Ellie stalked in, snatching her bag from the desk chair and giving me a filthy look before stomping out again.

"You were saying?" he asked as the clock counted the seconds into which the ensuing silence fell. I stared miserably out of the window – anything rather than read the colours that surrounded him in shifting tones of doubt.

"It doesn't really matter; I'll tell you later." I wondered if I imagined the slight exhalation that might have been a sigh. "What do you make of him?"

Subdued, all he said was, "It's too soon to say; he's convincing enough."

I whirled around. "You're kidding! Matthew, have you heard anything I've said?"

"I've heard everything, Emma. We'll see. In the meantime,

we'll take it one step at a time." Except for the darkness in his eyes, he had drawn a veil between us so that I could no longer read him. I wanted him to react, to rant, to yell – as I longed to do – but this calm acceptance was insufferable. "Have it your own way," I threw at him, and stormed from the room as the door crashed shut behind me, leaving him in no doubt how I felt, but without the words to say it.

I went to see Ellie later that evening at the Stables, but Jeannie curtly told me that she had a headache and all but closed the door in my face. I sent her a text instead, but none returned. I didn't press Matthew any further. I couldn't believe he would be taken in by Guy, not after everything I had been through, after everything I'd told him. When I said as much, he just looked at me calmly and said that people are not always as they seem. I slept alone again that night.

The following morning I couldn't wait to get out of the house despite the mist that crept up from the river during the night and masked the world in droplets. I made my way down to the little footbridge that spanned the water. The river was docile now, and my feet dangled above the surface as I leaned my head against the lichen-covered handrail. I never imagined I could forgive the river for nearly drowning Flora, nor the rocks for smashing Matthew's shoulder, but it had undergone a benign transformation, as Guy would have me believe he had done. But I didn't believe him, and what horrified me more than his unknown agenda was that others might.

"I thought I saw someone come this way," Henry greeted me from the riverbank. "I was out for a walk. Would you like some company, or would you rather be left alone to your thoughts?"

I smiled wanly. "I think that my thoughts and I need to part company for a bit."

He sat down next to me, resting his feet on the top of a specked boulder that poked its head like a grey seal out of the water. "Problem?" He waited as I watched the river, considering whether to tell my stepson what bothered me.

"Yes," I said eventually, "there's a problem."

I told him about Ellie. I told him about Guy. I told him more about my past than perhaps I would have done in any other circumstance but, like his father, Henry was a good listener, and my anxiety spilled out of me like water.

He ran a hand through his neat beard. "I see, and you've told Dad all this?"

"Yes, he knows, but yesterday it was as if he believed Guy despite everything I've said."

"And did he say that?"

"Well, no – not in so many words."

Henry smiled kindly. "Emma, at the risk of sounding patronizing, I've known my father for a very long time. He sees through people better than anyone. Whatever he might have you believe, he won't be taken in by this man, not after what you've told me."

"But Ellie wouldn't listen to me. Guy has her infatuated."

"And you don't believe he loves her?"

"No!"

"Then why do you think he's here?"

I couldn't answer that. I knew what I suspected – or at least, what I feared – although I had nothing but the grinding in the pit of my stomach and certainly no evidence to prove it. I picked at loose lichen on the splitting wood, buying time.

"Do you think he's here to make trouble for you?" Henry asked.

I flicked lichen into the water and watched it being carried away. "Possibly." I looked up at him. "I honestly don't know, but whatever I think, why ever he's here, he's trouble."

"And you just want somebody to believe you."

"Yes, because I don't know what else to do."

He placed his hand over mine as I picked at the rotting handrail. "I believe you, Emma, just as my father does. Ellie's blinded by love," he laughed gruffly, "and I know well enough what *that's* like; but sooner or later, she'll come to her senses. Let's hope for her sake that it's sooner rather than too late. In the meantime, you know where I am if you ever want to talk." He stood and offered to help me up. "Make sure you tell Dad everything; he'll know what to do with the information." He hauled me to my feet and I dusted myself down.

"Thanks, I'll remember."

I loitered a while, watching until he disappeared into the mist, all the time mindful that there was one piece of information I withheld and that, with each passing day, my reluctance to tell Matthew about the encounter brought me one step closer to complicity and guilt.

Matthew had gone out by the time I arrived back. A terse note lay on the table – "I'll be back by lunch" – but he hadn't said from where. The house felt empty and cold. I mooched about trying to occupy myself but I listened all the time for the sound of his car and couldn't settle to anything. Just before noon I heard an engine. By the time the door from the courtyard opened I appeared engrossed in a fifteenth-century transcript I had hurriedly opened.

"I was hoping my grandfather would be here." Maggie shut the door behind her. "But I see you are all alone." She hadn't bothered to knock. It was the first time I'd seen her since the wedding – and it was too soon.

"One of these days you'll forget and call him that in front of a stranger. He's out," I added, redundantly.

To my annoyance, she pulled out a chair and sat gracefully. "No matter, I'll wait." Neither of us pretended: I made no pretence of hospitality, and she expected none. It would be only a matter of time before the hostile truce collapsed. I turned back to the transcript, aware she studied me with transparent curiosity. She sat absolutely still except for the forefinger of one hand that tapped the time away. *Tac, tac, tac* – a neatly filed nail, plain and unadorned drummed. *Tac, tac.*

She broke the silence first. "Have you told him?"

It was no good trying to ignore her; I'd read the same sentence five times and still didn't know what it said. I didn't look up. "Told who what?"

"Have you told my grandfather – your husband – what you were doing the other day?"

For goodness sake. I put the book down with a thump. "Am I supposed to know what you're talking about, Maggie, or do I have to guess?"

"Did you think nobody would see you in that part of town and that you'd find anonymity among the masses? Or are you trying to flaunt it and don't care if he knows?"

Town? Had she seen me in town with Elena the other day? Idiot! No, not Elena – Guy. The hospital wasn't far from the restaurant and I hadn't imagined being watched at all. What did she think she saw?

"What of it, Maggie?"

"So you've told your husband you met a man?" She made it sound as if I had propositioned him.

I pushed back from the table and stood up. "That's none of your business."

"You made it my business when you married my grandfather. You made it my business when you kissed another man."

"I think you'll find that *he* kissed *me*. It was none of my doing."

"That's not what I saw," she said silkily. No, it wouldn't be, because it wasn't what she wanted to see. This fitted very nicely with her warped perception of me. A car door shut in the courtyard.

"Don't you ever get tired of all this?" I asked her. "Don't you have your own life to get on with without meddling in ours?"

"He is my life. I'll still be here when you're gone."

"Don't bet on it," I growled as Matthew walked in. He deposited two large bags on the table. He kissed me first, taking in my tight lips and taut atmosphere, before turning to his granddaughter.

"Maggie, we didn't expect you today."

"I came to see how you are."

"We are well; thank you for your concern."

She pulled a face. "No, I meant how are *you*?"

"*I* am fine; there is no reason why I shouldn't be. Are you staying?"

She looked uncertain for the first time. "I thought that after the other day…"

His eyes darkened and flared. "I said, we are fine. Now, if you are not staying, I have things to discuss with my wife."

We were both taken aback. I had never heard him speak to Maggie so brusquely; nor had she by the way she stared back at him. She left, and moments later the brief sound of a car engine bursting into life filled the courtyard.

"Matthew, she wanted to…"

"I know why she came," he interrupted. His face softened. "I'm sorry, I didn't mean to snap at you. I didn't anticipate her being here. Have you had lunch yet?" I shook my head. "I thought not; I've brought some back with me. You like chowder, don't you?"

It reminded me instantly of Elena's uneaten meal and what I wanted to tell him, what I needed to confess. "Yes, but…"

"Good, sit down. It should still be hot."

He wasn't in the mood to listen. He unpacked the bags with short, precise movements as I ate haddock chowder hot enough to scald my throat.

"What's all this for?" I indicated the pile of food in front of me. "We still have loads left from my birthday. I can't eat all this in a week."

He vanished into the pantry with an armful of goods and returned some minutes later carrying six bottles, which he lined up on the table.

"Wine, Matthew?"

He checked the bottles carefully, wiping dust off each shoulder. "It's for lunch tomorrow."

"Are we having guests?"

He avoided my eyes. "Yes – guests. We are having guests tomorrow." He leaned his knuckles on the table, bowing his head as if steeling himself for a fight. My fork hovered between my mouth and the bowl.

"Who, Matthew?"

"Ellie and Guy."

The fork chinked stridently against the porcelain as I threw it in the bowl and stood abruptly, my face burning. "Why? Why did you invite him here? To rub my face in it? Ellie's not talking to me and he's a… a *bastard*. You can entertain him if you want, but I won't be here to help you!" I swiped at the bowl and it flew off the end of the table, shattering against the floor, and ran from the kitchen and up the stairs before he could stop me.

He gave me a few moments before I heard the door to our bedroom open, and his soft tread across the floor. He crouched down beside me. "Emma." I turned my back on him and hunkered further into the armchair by the window, hiding my face. "Emma, please..." He put his arms around my hunched form. "My love, I know it doesn't make sense..."

"No, it doesn't," I spat.

"But please, trust me."

I nudged his arms from around me. "How can I? You didn't tell me, you didn't even ask. Did you assume I would be OK with this? Did you? I don't want him in my house – our *home*, Matthew. I don't want him poking around and I don't want him anywhere near me. Look what he's already done." I raised my hand and counted finger by finger. "He's persuaded my best friend I've broken his heart; he's quaffing coffee with Sam; he's somehow managed to convince Ellie he's in love with her... did you know she's sleeping with him? Ugh! She won't even talk to me now and Jeannie probably thinks he's ideal boyfriend material. He's wormed his way into our lives and no doubt I'll be cast in the role of village witch and nobody will believe anything I say about him." I broke off to take a breath before continuing despondently, "And he even has you thinking he's not so bad." I scrunched my fists because the pain of my knuckles cracking was preferable to the tears that wanted to flow. Matthew covered my hands with his and I felt his regret. I didn't dare look at him.

"No, Emma, he hasn't. I believe everything you've ever told me about him. I no more want him in our home than you do and I certainly don't want him near my wife, nor having sex with my great-granddaughter, but this is a case of 'know thy enemy'."

"I know him," I fumed. "I know him too well."

"Yes," he said patiently, "I know you do and that's why I believe you absolutely, but I want him to think he has the upper hand. If he's as arrogant as I think he is, he'll let slip sooner or later because, whatever else he is up to, he'll want me to acknowledge his superiority."

Angrily, I dragged my hand across my eyes. "Is that the real reason?"

"What else could it be?"

"I… I didn't tell you that I met Guy the other day – in town." Matthew remained expressionless. "I didn't go there to meet him," I clarified. "Guy got Elena to set it up. She thought she was helping me, but I didn't know that's what they'd arranged until it was too late and he turned up." When he still didn't respond, I added, "I didn't tell you because… well, because…" My excuses sounded feeble even before I'd voiced them. "Oh blast, I just didn't. I'm sorry." I checked to see how he was taking it, surprised to find him smiling.

"I know. Maggie told me that evening." The demon tail lights – that figured. "I would rather you had told me yourself…"

"I'm sorry."

"… because I think your account would be more accurate than Maggie's. She said she saw you in a compromising position outside a restaurant. 'A passionate embrace,' I think she said. She rather spoiled her quaint use of language by describing it as you gluing your face to his. Rather a gross depiction, I thought."

My face reddened. "*He* kissed *me*; I didn't want him to."

"I didn't think you did. I reckoned by her description that it must have been Guy."

"Why didn't you say anything?"

"Because you didn't. I trust you, Emma. Whatever your reason for not telling me at the time, I have no doubt your motives were blameless, although," he appended, "the coffee worried me – you still had tachycardia when you arrived home. You were lucky it was nothing more."

My hand went to my lips as they curled in revulsion. "I didn't drink any, but he had. I wondered if you knew about him; you've been acting oddly."

He frowned. "Have I? I suppose I have a lot on my mind, but it's nothing you've done. What did Guy want the other day?"

"My forgiveness."

Matthew's raised brows said it all. "And have you forgiven him?"

"I can't. I tried to, or at least I know I should, but how can I when I don't trust him? I can't put my finger on it. He says the right things, he sounds genuine, but his words don't add up."

"That's why we have to act as if they do."

I screwed my face. "It's deceitful – I hate lies."

"It's what we do, Emma; just remember why we need to do it."

"It's not something I'm likely to forget. I don't like the thought of him here, but I understand why you have invited him – keep your friends close and your enemies closer – but don't expect me to like it. I can't promise to be the perfect hostess."

"But you'll try," he encouraged, "for Ellie's sake as much as ours."

I shrugged my resignation. "Yes, I'll try. I'm sorry I let rip earlier; you caught me by surprise."

"You don't have to apologize. I should have broached it more tactfully. I'm out of practice." Truthfully, there would have been no safe way to tackle such an explosive issue. "And while we are on the subject of Guy," he slipped in, "I want you to tell me everything you know about him: his past, his marriage, his work, his interests. *Every* detail, no matter how insignificant it might appear."

"Know thy enemy?" I said.

"Know him, indeed," he replied.

Love Makes Fools

The following day grew stiflingly warm under the overcast sky. By the time Ellie and Guy arrived I had developed a headache that was more to do with the unrelenting tension than the oppressive heat. I greeted Ellie with a hug she barely returned. Guy, on the other hand, embraced me like an old friend as he handed me a large bouquet tied with an extravagant bow that matched the stunning pink of the gerberas it contained. Unnervingly, he wore a burgundy shirt, adding insult to injury, and I wondered whether he'd done so on purpose.

In the drawing room, Matthew threw the windows open and the sluggish air heaved. Guy wiped sweat from his neck. "It's hot as Hades; you could do with air conditioning in here. I don't know how you stand it."

Matthew interceded as I bristled at the implied criticism. "It's only for a few weeks of the year and if it becomes too hot we'll take a trip into the mountains until it cools down. Let me get you something to drink. Ellie, white wine as usual?"

"Sure, thanks. Guy'll have the same."

I didn't miss the slight rise to his lip. Guy loathed white wine and used to make a point of referring to it as a *feminine beverage* at college functions.

"Or perhaps you would prefer red?" Matthew offered.

Ellie nestled up to Guy on the sofa. "He bought me champagne the other week. I drank most of the bottle myself. I think he wanted to get me just a little tipsy." She giggled, and Guy gave a tight smile. I chewed an ice cube noisily and sipped iced tea.

Guy waited until Matthew had placed the drinks on the table and returned to the kitchen before raising his glass. "You're not drinking today, Emma?"

I fought the impulse to point out that what I held in my hand constituted a drink and instead resorted to a polite, "Alcohol doesn't suit me."

If he remembered the reference he didn't show it, but took a slug of wine as he wandered over to the cabinet of curios. I watched him catalogue every item, imagining him storing the information for retrieval and assessment later at his leisure. In an attempt at being companionable, I went to sit by Ellie. "I like your bracelet. Have I seen it before?"

She twisted the silver rope-work bangle on her wrist. "Guy gave it to me," she said shortly, putting her glass down and standing up. "Do you mind if I show him the cabinet?"

Yes, I did. "No, of course not."

She joined him, obviously glad not to have to talk to me, opening the door to the cabinet of treasures Matthew had gathered in his journeys around the world. I bridled as Guy picked out the nutmeg.

"Is there any particular relevance to this?" he asked me with a mordant twist, holding the precious nutmeg between thumb and forefinger as if it were dirt. I restrained the urge to leap up and snatch it from his hand, and was on the verge of answering when Matthew came back in.

"Ah," he said, putting a plate of my favourite olives on the table in front of me, and a calming hand on my shoulder. "I see you've found one of my most treasured possessions. It might look out of place, but it helps remind me to keep a perspective on what I value most." He took the nutmeg from Guy's hand and put it back where it belonged. "Has Ellie shown you this?" He lifted the dagger from its rosewood stand. "This is a particularly interesting piece. It was given to an Englishman after a dispute in which the Raja with whom he was staying betrayed the laws of hospitality and tried to kill his guest."

Ellie took it from Matthew, the rubies glowing blood red. "I didn't know there was a story behind this. Why did he try to kill him?"

"I believe the Raja thought the man a contender for the affections of a particularly attractive princess." He smiled. "But that was not the case at all." Ellie gave the dagger to Guy. He removed the blade, inspecting the intricate engraving and detailed gold work.

"This is a very fine piece – mid-eighteenth century?" He replaced the dagger and handed it back to Matthew.

"1733, or thereabouts. Are you interested in weapons?"

Guy cast briefly in my direction. "I am – seventeenth-century military pieces from the Civil War period in particular. I have a small collection, nothing spectacular, but all authentic. I find them a useful tool when illustrating certain topics with my students." Again, the merest glance towards me. I looked away.

"Really?" Matthew closed the cabinet door. "I have several pieces you might be interested in. Perhaps you can give me some advice?"

Guy visibly preened; there was nothing he liked better than to demonstrate his superior knowledge. I tried to gauge his emotions but found nothing to read. The colours that had been so clearly discernible the other day were indecipherable now. Coffee might have helped, but Matthew would have a fit if he caught me anywhere near the coffee jar.

"Lunch is just about ready," Matthew said. "Come on through. Emma will take you to the dining room."

Ellie had relaxed with the wine and the compliment paid to Guy. She led him, chattering animatedly, pointing out the antique furniture and the paintings, and all the while he was looking, looking. When he entered the dining room, he stopped. "Well, well."

"I thought you'd like it," she beamed. "It's all very old. Matthew's very particular about what he collects; it has to be exactly right."

"So I see," Guy said, *sotto voce*, taking in the early seventeenth-century furniture and ceramics, the paintings and the pewter. "A remarkable collection." His eyes came to rest on the old etched picture to the left of the fireplace, where they remained long enough to cause my heart to miss a beat. He didn't comment, but instead shifted his attention to the two swords hanging on the chimney breast. "And these must be the weapons Matthew mentioned: a knight's sword – late medieval – probably fifteenth-century German in origin, and this..." His hand hovered over the rapier's hilt, longing to touch it.

"Go ahead," Matthew said from where he stood in the doorway, "it lifts off the brackets." Guy eased the sword from its worn leather scabbard with due respect to its age.

He rotated the sword. "Pre-Commonwealth period rapier with a boat-form guard, very well made, well balanced – blade looks like Toledo steel. Belonged to a gentleman I should say; there's a remnant of gilding in the engraving. It's not ceremonial – it's too good for that – and it's been used in conflict, as the blade is notched." He studied the elegant quillons and then the detailed engraving. "This might be traceable through the coat of arms on the guard, and the lion's head pommel probably represents the family." He looked at Matthew keenly. "Where did you get it?"

Matthew removed the sword from Guy's hands and replaced the scabbard. "It was given to me," he said as he placed it on the sideboard between the pewter chargers, where it looked completely at home. "I'll bring in lunch."

I felt a swell of irritation as I noticed that Matthew had swapped the exuberant profusion of wild lupines and Maine roses he had picked for my birthday with the flowers Ellie and Guy bought. The bouquet shouted from the centre of the table.

"I haven't seen a collection so precisely dated as this for a long while, if ever," Guy deliberated as the door shut. He stroked the wood of the table but was taking in the paintings, the sideboard. "He seems to have a remarkable knowledge of a seventeenth-century interior for a... doctor. That is Matthew's profession, isn't it, Emma? A doctor?"

"Surgeon," I corrected tartly, "and there's nothing remarkable about it; it's just what he likes. Sit down, please. I'll help Matthew bring things in."

I welcomed the peace of the kitchen and leant against the table. Matthew laid a hand against my temple. "How's your head?"

"Bursting."

"I meant your headache."

"He's looking at everything, Matthew. I hate the way he's measuring it all up like a ruddy undertaker."

He gave me a large dish with something no doubt mouthwatering arranged over the salad I had prepared somewhat grudgingly that morning. "Let him look, it's not important."

Ellie momentarily forgot she wasn't speaking to me as she surveyed the dishes. "Wow, Emma! I thought you said you couldn't cook. This is amazing, isn't it, Guy?"

"Amazing," he echoed, and I didn't know whether he mocked

her or me. I served her, then spooned the spiced savoury sorbet into Guy's bowl and passed it to him, looking at him squarely.

"Matthew's the cook; I just do the donkey work. If it had been left to me you would've had gravel on toast." Matthew flashed me a warning and I shut up before I said something I wouldn't regret. He continued pouring wine. From what I could remember, Guy was always careful about what he drank, but not necessarily how much. He was on his third glass already and Matthew kept him topped up.

Guy admired the contents of his glass. "You keep a good cellar, Matthew" – *for a doctor*, he might have added. "Not joining us?"

"I ate something yesterday that didn't suit me. I'm on a self-imposed fast."

"No food or drink except water for twenty-four hours," Ellie added seamlessly, although she needn't have bothered as Guy had already turned his attention to me.

"Emma, I read your last paper on the schismatic persecution of belief. Interesting – that was a novel line you took." Roughly translated, that meant he thought it questionable. I counted silently to five before I answered.

"Hardly. There's a clear division between persecution on the grounds of schism, and that of heresy as defined by punishments recorded in religious court texts from the period I covered."

"More than three hundred Catholics would disagree with that assumption."

He trespassed on my territory trying to get a rise from me, but I stood my ground. "It's not an assumption, Guy; they were executed on political, not religious, grounds. They weren't tried for heresy, as you well know, but for treason. If it wasn't for the Papal Bull, *Regnans in Excelsis*, there probably wouldn't have been an escalation in executions at all." He was not my tutor any more, nor I his student. I had outgrown him and he knew it. We weighed each other up over the table.

"Do I detect bias along Protestant lines?" he goaded.

"No, you don't; you're just downright touchy when it comes to Catholic matters. I keep my personal beliefs out of it."

Ellie frowned. "You're Catholic, Guy? I didn't know that."

"Does it matter what I am?"

"Uh, no, sure it doesn't, but how come Emma knows and I didn't?"

I gathered the bowls. "Guy's religious roots are common knowledge among historians of our period, Ellie. He specializes in the Counter-Reformation."

Guy accepted another glass of wine. "So, what line of research are you following now?"

I outlined a plausible reply and he didn't offer a comment this time because I don't think he believed me. Frankly, I didn't care one way or another. I wanted to keep well away from the subject of the journal. Feeling stubborn and rattled in equal measure, I helped myself to some wine.

"Your recent work is interesting," I observed over the rim of the glass. "I note you've been collaborating with Antony Burridge on his book."

At my choice of semantics, his mouth warped. "He sought my advice and I was able to offer him some guidance. Originality was never his strong point."

"Not like you, Guy, is that it?" I didn't wait for a reply. "Where are you working now?"

"I'm not at the moment. I took a sabbatical to complete my latest book. I'm thinking of relocating to the States and making a fresh start." He took Ellie's hand in his, a calculated move. "There are more opportunities here, more avenues to explore."

Ellie's face glowed. "With his reputation he should be able to find a position at any university of his choice."

"Reputation *is* key, isn't it?" I said. "So hard won, so easily lost. Universities are pretty choosy who they take nowadays."

His lids lowered until they became mere slits. "From what I've heard, Emma, the question of reputation is something with which you've had a recent encounter. How secure is *your* position?"

I managed to nudge Matthew's leg before he detonated, and we were saved by Ellie's valiant attempt to intercede and diffuse the heady tension. "Hey you guys, come on, enough already. This is really good, Matthew. Gran would like the recipe."

I attempted a smile. "Yes, Ellie, of course; I'm sorry. It's just a little professional rivalry – it's endemic among historians." And the wine I consumed wasn't helping matters. My head thumped and my temper simmered. It wouldn't take much to bring me to boiling point. I pushed the glass aside and accepted iced water instead. I was making a real hash of this and I wasn't proud of myself, but I loathed the way Guy treated Ellie almost with disdain, and how she appeared blind to his neglect. Had he been like this with me and I, too, hadn't noticed? Until that moment, Matthew had remained quietly observant, although I watched his internal conversation through the fluctuating hues surrounding him. I had witnessed the same quietude before, when Sam misread him and ended up in the med centre. Would Guy do the same? I thought not. Guy's self-control was disciplined in a way Sam's could never be, and surely he wouldn't make the mistake of becoming a victim of his own conceit. Which is why I feared for Ellie because, from where I was sitting, she represented just another piece of a puzzle whose whole picture Guy kept to himself.

The conversation returned to less fraught ground as we served the main course and finished the third. Once or twice I thought

I saw Guy trying to focus on Matthew's hand, only for him to pretend otherwise, and look away. Eventually, we cleared the table and all that remained were glasses, which Matthew kept filled, and delicate chocolates he knew I liked. I passed them around. Guy declined the sweets but accepted a particularly good port. He had become flushed over the course of the meal, and his movements blurred.

"That's an interesting accent you have, Matthew. Ellie tells me you used to live in Idaho before you moved here, but that it's not where you come from. How long have you been in the States?"

I suppressed a sharp intake of breath. It might have been the wine talking but he wasn't the sort to make such a simple mistake. Matthew's hand hardly wavered as he poured water into my glass. Guy hadn't said, "Where did you stay in Britain?" or, "Have you lived on the east coast long?" No, he had made a distinction by implication that Matthew was somehow different from other members of his family. It bore all the signs of a hunt as Guy gazed steadily at Matthew.

Ellie laughed a little nervously. "Don't be silly, Guy. Matthew's always lived in the States; we all have."

I kept quiet, but my heart pounded in my throat and I clasped my hands beneath the table in case Guy saw them shaking.

"English furniture, paintings – accent. This room looks like a seventeenth-century recreation. You're a bit of an Anglophile perhaps?"

Caught between the two men, Ellie seemed unsure which way to turn. "Gramps is really keen to find out where the family originated, isn't he, Matthew? He's always said there's an English connection but he's never been able to trace it."

Guy pursed his lips in sardonic disbelief. "Really? I would have thought that given a distinctive name like Lynes and a few dates as a starting point, Emma could have rustled something up for you." It was fortunate he wasn't looking in my direction at the time as I felt my skin burn hot then cold. "I'm not a genealogist…" he went on, and Ellie gave a little gasp.

"That's just what Emma said!"

"… but Lynes is a name from rather close to home, isn't it, Emma?"

Silence.

Ellie looked first at me as I threw a furious glance at Guy, and then at him. "Have you two met before? You keep talking as if you know each other."

As if he had orchestrated this moment, Guy leaned forwards in his chair. "I have a confession to make. I have not been entirely honest with you, Ellie. Emma and I knew each other in Cambridge."

Ellie became very still. "Why didn't you tell me? What do you mean you knew each other? How? When?" Didn't he care what effect this might have on her? Altruism wasn't one of his virtues, nor honesty, but this plummeted to new depths even for him.

"Guy, this isn't the time…" I cautioned.

"Do you mean Emma hasn't said?" he questioned Matthew with one arched eyebrow.

"I'm sure she would have mentioned it, if it were important," Matthew replied evenly, refilling Ellie's glass with port.

Guy's mouth turned down. "Unless she had something to hide." He waited a few seconds for the implication to sink in before continuing. "I believe that complete honesty is the best foundation for any relationship."

"Huh, right," I said caustically.

Confusion spread across the girl's face. "You didn't tell me you'd already met him, Emma. Is that what you meant the other day? You could have told me outright."

With chilling deliberation and a smile short of a leer, Guy addressed her at last. "Emma was one of my students, Ellie; the best I ever had."

In her bewildered state, she missed the double entendre, but Matthew didn't. A carmine aura surrounded him instantly and glass disintegrated in his hand, port mingling with shards of crystal. He kicked back his chair, and I came between the two men as I saw Matthew's hand curl into a wine-soaked fist.

Guy flinched back, trapped by the table. "For Pete's sake, I only said…!"

"Shut up!" I flared, throwing my table napkin over Matthew's ruptured skin before Guy noticed it heal, and keeping a restraining hand on his chest until he reined in his temper. I rounded on Guy. "You've said enough. What do you hope to achieve with all this?"

He recovered his equilibrium more quickly than he should have done. "I'm sorry but there's no place for secrecy now. I can't have this on my conscience any longer. Ellie," he said, his voice almost breaking with remorse, "Emma and I had an affair. I came to the States to ask her to forgive me, but then I met you. I'm sorry I didn't tell you before. I'm not proud of what I did, but it's only right that you know." He turned to Matthew. "I didn't want to be the cause of any dissension between you and your wife; I thought Emma would have told you." In one fell swoop he hoped to discredit me in front of my husband and niece by making me out to be a liar or worse – a calculated risk, but it worked. I watched Ellie implode.

"You… you should have told me," she flung.

"I didn't know you were going out with Guy until the other day. I tried to warn you, Ellie."

She leapt to her feet. "But you didn't *say*." Her face crumpled, anger and disappointment flowing freely. "I trusted you – you were my friend – how could you do this? What about Matthew – did you tell him?"

"Ellie, it's not Emma's fault…" Matthew put his hand on her back and she threw her arms around him and sobbed into his neck. "Listen to me, there's more to all this than it looks. Let Emma tell you what happened."

Guy froze as he realized that Matthew already knew. He interrupted before Matthew could go any further, or I could explain. "It's true, Ellie, I'm as much to blame…" he began.

"Yes, you are," I hissed. "Don't try to take the moral high ground; it's a heck of a way to fall."

She gave a violent shake of her head. "At least he had the decency to tell me."

"He left it a bit late," I retorted.

Guy wiped his mouth and threw the folded napkin on the table. "I'm sorry, Ellie, you weren't supposed to find out this way. I seem to have rattled a few skeletons. Emma's never forgiven me for what I did and I can't say I blame her, although it was a long time ago. But then she always did harbour grudges – it runs in her family. I've let you down; I won't call again."

She raised her face from Matthew's shoulder, blotchy and wet with tears. "What do you mean? You can't go!"

Guy rose from the table. "I think it's best if I leave now."

"Yes, it is." Matthew barely contained his anger, but she pulled away from him. "Ellie, no, let him go." Too late, she already clung desperately to Guy.

"No, don't leave me! I don't care what you've done."

He stroked her hair as he looked at me over the top of her head. "But Ellie, how can you forgive me after all this?"

"Of course I do," she whimpered. "I forgive you everything."

* * *

"He's playing with us," I observed glumly, resting my chin in my cupped hands. The remains of the glass lay in a jagged mess on the table's glossy surface, my discarded napkin stained red. Matthew unsheathed the rapier and cast his eye down the length of its steel blade.

"He is."

I remembered the hope in the girl's face as she and Guy left the house together. "Ellie's going to get hurt." The rapier sliced through the air, catching the failing light.

"Probably."

"Guy's never forgiven me, has he?"

"No." The sword became an extension of his arm, a moving point I strained to follow.

"You heard what he said about your accent, Matthew." He didn't answer but did a practice lunge into the heart of the fireplace. "That's not all; did you notice the comment about your name? He specifically mentioned it came from our region. How does he know? It's hardly common knowledge and it wasn't a random error. He knows something, Matthew. I don't know how, but he does. I'd stake my life on it. Guy doesn't make mistakes like that."

As if by an invisible hand, a gerbera's head spilled into the air as the sword severed it cleanly from the stem. He caught it and laid it in front of me. "Neither," he said, "do I." And he sheathed the sword, in a single, precise movement, and suspended it on its brackets above the fireplace.

"What do you mean?" I asked.

He smiled darkly and said, "If nothing else, one thing is clear: Guy Hilliard came to Maine neither seeking your forgiveness, nor offering it."

Entrenched

If there was one mistake I thought Guy might make it would be that, in his arrogance, he would fail to recognize how seriously Matthew perceived the threat to his family to be and the lengths he would go to to protect them.

I didn't see Ellie again for days, but when I did, she made it clear it was under duress. Matthew wanted me to tell her exactly what happened in Cambridge. Dan asked if I would mind him being there too and, as I explained the full circumstances, he listened with increasing concern. Tight lipped and expressionless, Ellie sat on the sofa as I described the protracted corruption of my youth, the way Guy isolated me from my friends and played to my intellectual vanity. I made no bones about my part in it; I fully accepted my guilt in the seduction. Matthew said nothing until I skirted around the evening of my nineteenth birthday.

"He raped her," he said bluntly, and I shrank inside as I watched them recoil. Ellie didn't believe him.

"Guy wouldn't do that! He knows he shouldn't have had an affair with a student, but he was under a lot of pressure at the time and he admits he made a mistake."

I could imagine him saying it and convincing her lie by lie. "Guy doesn't make mistakes like that, Ellie. He knew precisely what he was doing then, and he knows what he is doing now."

"He's different with me. Whatever mistakes he made with you, he's changed." I wondered what other lies he had told her about me in the aftermath of his confession.

Dan rubbed his earlobe. "I have to admit I don't like what I've heard today, El. I think it would be as well to listen to Emma; she's known him for a lot longer than you have. Guy turned up out of the blue and this sudden affection he's declared for you seems rather..." he struggled for a word.

"Calculated," Matthew completed. "Whatever you decide to do, Ellie, you need to remember the unique situation you're in with regard to any relationship you choose to have. It could have consequences far beyond your own happiness. Guy mustn't be given any indication we are different from other families." Her eyes slid towards him and away. "Have you said something already?"

"No! Of course not, Matthew, but he has to know at some point." She wavered, and then in a single breath rushed, "He's asked me to marry him."

"Ellie, no, he's married!" I cried in dismay.

Was that triumph in her face? "He *was* married, Emma – he's getting a divorce."

I shook my head. "He won't; he's Catholic and he believes absolutely. Ellie, I know him..."

"But I know him better. I told you he's changed. He had to after what you did to him."

Matthew's eyes sparked and his voice took on a hard edge. "That's enough, Ellie. Emma's right. If Guy gives any credence to his faith he can neither divorce nor remarry. He remains married unless there are grounds for annulment – which seems unlikely – or he or his wife dies."

Crossing her arms, she became stubbornly mute. Dan put his arm around her shoulder and tried another tack. "Look, Ellie, this man is over twenty years older than you. He's married, he has children – three, didn't you say, Emma?" I nodded. "He's had a good portion of his life already. You have yours ahead."

"I didn't think an age difference mattered in this family," she whipped. "He's the same age as you and Mom and that's not old. It's not fair: there's one rule for Emma, but another for Guy. Matthew gave Emma a second chance." That was neither a wise thing to say nor true, and as soon as it left her mouth she regretted it. "Sorry, Emma," she mumbled under Matthew's scrutiny. It was no use; she had become so entrenched that her position was inviolable. I knew all the signs from my own battles with my father: the more he tried to undermine my foundations, the deeper I dug them. Nothing would change her mind now other than a fundamental shift in her thinking from within her emotional fortress, and what – heaven only knew – would initiate that?

Matthew appeared to have reached the same conclusion as he made a last attempt to breach her defences. "I understand that this must be your decision but, whatever you choose, protect your family at all costs. We are dependent on your discretion. Guy cannot know anything about us until he has earned our trust. Do you agree?"

She looked at him from beneath lowered lashes and saw that he was asking – not telling.

"OK," she said. "Just give him a chance."

We left it for the time being, but later, when Ellie had gone back to the Stables, Dan pulled up a chair in our kitchen and sat down wearily. He rubbed his knuckles over his eyes, looking more drained than I had seen him before, and nearer the mid-forties he was supposed to be than the thirty-something he usually looked. I placed a mug in front of him. "How is she, Dan?"

"I left her with her mother, sobbing her eyes out. I've been given the cold shoulder for siding with you. At least, that's how they see it." He raised the mug to his mouth and grimaced. "Thanks for this er... tea."

I smiled an apology. "Matthew's banned even the coffee jar from the house. He thinks I might be tempted to try something to get at Guy." I might well have done if I thought it could work.

Dan raised a tired smile. "I think we'll have to find another solution rather than put your life on the line. He's a slippery so..." He raised a hand in apology. "Sorry, but I don't like what I've seen or heard so far. The trouble is, Jeannie's as enamoured as El. I can't get through to her, and without her support it's like battling the three hundred."

"Guy has that effect on susceptible women," I said.

"It'll pass," Matthew commented quietly. "It always passes. Time will see to that." He left the table to close the shutters against the world outside. "In the meantime," he said, coming back to the table and sitting with us in the pool of light cast by the low lamp, "we need to take some sensible measures. Emma thinks there's more to him being here than her or Ellie, and whatever that might be, we can't take chances."

Dan nodded slowly. "OK. Do you want me to contact Joel?"

"I think it might be time."

"Joel?" I queried later once Dan reluctantly went home to what he ruefully referred to as his den of vipers, and we were making our way upstairs.

"He has access to information that would be difficult to get otherwise. It's just precautionary, my love, don't worry."

Which meant that I should.

Heart of Steel

It had been nettling me ever since he said it. I zipped my cross backwards and forwards on its sturdy chain and went through what Guy had said, for the umpteenth time. "*She always harboured grudges – it runs in her family.*"

Did I?

"Do I harbour grudges?" I asked Matthew as we pulled into the staff car park. The engine stilled.

"No, you don't. That was a comment intended to get under your skin. Don't give him the satisfaction of knowing it worked. Ignore it." Easier said than done. For more than a decade I'd struggled against the bitter tide that stemmed from years of conflict first with my father, and then with Guy. I had found some sense of peace through my faith – a spiritual release as potently physical as the pain of rejection and betrayal from which I fled – but recent events prodded old bruises, and they hurt. Matthew leaned over and kissed me. "I'll meet you for lunch. I've a departmental meeting at eleven and it should be finished by twelve-thirty, but if it isn't, I'll call you."

I stared blankly through the window at the heat haze developing in the distance. "OK."

"Emma?"

"Mmm?"

"Did you hear what I said? Lunch at twelve-thirty in the staff dining room." He frowned when he should have been smiling, his eyes starless. He had been keeping tabs on my food intake and making sure I didn't skip meals. Where hunger should have filled my stomach, Guy's presence had become a constant irritation that sapped my appetite and curdled my happiness. Within the awkward confines of the car, I pressed my cheek against his.

"I'm sorry; you didn't need all this..." I couldn't think of a better word, "... complication."

He smiled at the reference to our early days together, soothing the lines between my eyes. "This is nothing, my love. In a few weeks Guy Hilliard will be no more than a bad dream that will fade. Even the deepest wounds can heal with time." He pressed his lips against my wrist where the ribbon of silvered skin was all that remained of Staahl. I stretched my fingers to touch his hair, so unbelievably gold that even the strength of the early summer light could not fade its vitality, and then my eyes dropped to the slash across his collarbone, just visible in the open collar of his shirt.

"There are some hurts that will always leave a scar. I didn't know how much until I saw him again."

"I understand, but although they leave their mark, scars don't always need to hurt, do they? And they are a reminder that we can survive and, in doing so, we are stronger.

'In steel I fashion my heart,
Fire forged,
Broken, yet stronger still.'"

"Um," I said doubtfully, "I'm not sure if I like the thought of a heart of steel."

"No, well, I was going through a particularly challenging period at the time I wrote that. And that's the point, I – and my heart – survived to go on to better things." He kissed the tip of my nose and reached into the back of the car, pulling his jacket and tie from the back seat. "Now, onwards. We have work to do; I'll see you at lunch."

"Twelve-thirty," I confirmed, content to see his eyes were a more vibrant blue and to know he considered his heart healed.

I pushed all thought of Guy to one side for the rest of the morning, hammering him into oblivion with random tracks on my iPod so he couldn't creep in around the edges. I made a last-ditch effort to put my room in order before the conference, piling books and papers in stacks like brown pillars of salt, ready to be boxed and taken home for the summer. I then sought to bury myself in my work.

In a lull between tracks, I heard the door reverberating to impatient fists. Checking my watch, I groaned as I opened the door to Matias. He breathed heavily, and sweat gleamed on his brow and from beneath the collar of his shirt.

"Is that all the thanks I get for rescuing a man's wife from starvation? Your husband waited until past one but he had an emergency call and couldn't wait any longer. I said I was on my way to fetch Elena; otherwise he would have come himself and let the bloke die on the slab. Why didn't you answer your cell? And what's that awful racket?"

I turned the iPod off and switched on my mobile. It fired a rapid succession of beeps as the backlog of incoming texts registered my neglect. "Oops."

"That wasn't quite how Matthew put it. I've been charged with frog-marching you to the nearest purveyor of food and ensuring you consume a reasonably balanced diet of a suitably high calorific content."

"Golly, did he really say that?"

"No, that was the shorter, repeatable version." Negotiating his way through the piles of books, he scanned the quad through the window. "Have you seen Elena?"

"I didn't think she was in today. Have you tried David or Jess?" I selected some papers I needed to complete my presentation, saved my work to the memory stick, and closed the laptop.

"They haven't seen her and she isn't answering her cell, either. She said she wanted to get some work done." He nosed an errant book into line with the side of his shoe. He didn't look very happy.

"Perhaps she's gone to get something to eat, Matias."

He shrugged. "Yeah, maybe." He studied my series of posters. "These give me the creeps. I don't know how you live with them." He grimaced. "Are you ready?"

I heaved my bag onto my shoulder and tucked my laptop under my arm. "I honestly don't need a chaperone if you'd rather find Elena."

He smiled ruefully. "And how would I explain your emaciated form when I next see Matthew? Anyway, I owe him one."

"You do?"

"Here, let me take that bag." He took a step forward, but tripped, his arm colliding with the edge of the desk. He swore in Finnish; I didn't need a translation.

I dropped my bag and put out a hand to steady him. "Are you all right? I should have warned you."

"I'm fine," he said, his tanned face colouring maroon. "I'm used to being made to look like a blundering fool. What the heck was that, anyway?" He looked around accusingly and picked up the small, battered leather case that had drunkenly tumbled.

Taking it from him, I smoothed dust from its mottled surface. "It belonged to my grandfather; I meant to take it home. Sorry."

He grunted and rubbed his elbow. "Nothing a quick drink won't cure. Fancy one?"

"In this heat? I'll buy you one as recompense, but I'll stick to iced tea, thanks."

We crossed the quad to the cloister on thin-patched grass browned by the early summer heat. A groundsman wrestled with an automatic watering system. Matias glared up at the featureless blue of the sky. "Blasted heat; it shouldn't be this hot so soon. It can't last."

The cloisters provided welcome shelter from the sun. I waved to one of the porters sweltering in the stuffy atrium as we passed. "What did you mean earlier when you said you owe Matthew one?"

"Oh, that, well, er, he passed on some information – buddy to buddy – you know."

I didn't. He shifted my bag to his other hand as we neared the staff dining hall, and shouldered the door ajar. "He said to keep an eye on that bloke who's been hanging around lately, the one you saw on your birthday – Hilliard, wasn't it? Dating his niece, Matthew said. Got the feeling he wasn't too happy about it. Elena said you knew him once back in the UK?" The bag thumped against his hip as he attempted to fill a plate with something indescribable, and waited while I browsed the counter. The salad looked pretty good for once, but he twitched noticeably until I augmented the leaves with an overstuffed pepper, its bulging flanks shining with oil. "So you knew him?" Matias dug. "What's he like?"

I could supply the diplomatic, mature, professional answer, or the truth. "Why do you want to know?"

Instantly recognizable high-pitched laughter cut across the subdued hubbub in the dining hall. Matias followed the sound with a quizzical expression bordering on the comic. He stopped short. Sitting on the far side of the dining hall, her hands in animated conversation, Elena talked to someone obscured by another diner. The obstruction moved.

"That's why," Matias said. "She's been mentioning him a lot lately." Guy said something and Elena's hands flew to her mouth to stifle a squeal followed by a giggle.

"Yes, I'll tell you, Matias," I said quietly. "I'll tell you everything, but first you need to make your presence known."

He shifted uneasily. "Elena's a big girl; she can see who she likes. I don't want to come across as the overbearing male type."

"She's your fiancée, Matias. You might respect her independence, but he sure as anything won't respect you. There are times to back off, but this isn't one of them. Stake your claim – make it clear you won't stand any nonsense."

"I thought he was supposed to be dating your niece?"

"Oh, he is, but I don't expect for one moment that that will stop him. There are some boundaries he doesn't observe." A jaundiced nuance had slipped in where I hadn't meant it to be. Matias looked at me.

"Like that, was it?"

"Yes," I acknowledged, "it was like that."

I saw the expression on Guy's face and the glance he threw at me as Matias confronted him – a considered look, thoughtful, a game interrupted, but not thwarted. Guy gave a dismissive shrug, redolent of his Gallic heritage.

Matias returned with Elena. "That son-of-a…" he controlled himself, "… is making himself too damned comfortable around here if you ask me."

Elena managed to appear a little abashed, but not enough to mollify him. "We were only talking."

"No, Elena, that wasn't what he was doing," Matias growled. "If he comes near you again, I'll... I'll... Damn it – just keep away from him."

Guy held my gaze with a look I couldn't fathom. "I don't think you have to worry about Elena," I said slowly. "She's not what he's interested in."

"Then what the hell *does* he want?" Matias fumed, catching Elena's little pout, which did nothing to appease him.

"I don't know." Guy had been leaning on one elbow, stroking his top lip as he watched the effect he had on our tiny group.

Matias hunched his shoulders. "Well, I'm sure as heck not staying around here to find out. We'll go someplace else to eat."

I put my plate on the long table in front of me and slid onto the bench, dumping my bag and case next to me. "Thanks, but I think I'll stay here; I'm not going to be driven away by him. Mmm, this pepper looks rather good and I don't want to waste food." I picked up my fork.

Elena pulled a face. "But Em, it is disgusting and cold, and you always waste food."

I prodded the limp lettuce. "Well, perhaps it's time I turned over a new leaf. I'll see you later." They left and I surveyed the lifeless heart of the pepper, sinking the tines of the fork through the soft, red flesh. Oil seeped from the wounds, gathering on the lettuce in yellow pools. Oh, and a thought, so deliciously tempting that it stung, prickled my being. A shape passed between me and the light.

"That wasn't very sporting of you, Emma, but then you never played by the rules." His eyes flickered to my plate and back again. I looked down; I had stabbed the pepper unconsciously and the fork now lay buried deep within the body of the fruit.

"Only because you wrote them, Guy. My friends are off limits."

"You make me sound so scheming."

"Well, aren't you? Don't feel you have to keep me company."

He came around to my side of the table and I could feel the heat radiating from him. "Ellie sees you as being basically good-hearted, although she doesn't understand how you could have treated me so abominably. She'll forgive you – in time. Your sister-in-law, on the other hand, seems to think otherwise."

"My sister-in-law?"

He rested a palm lightly on the table. A few strands of brown hair protruded from his cuff. "Yes – Maggie – that was her name. Bit of a cold fish, I thought, and she doesn't like you, does she? I'm surprised; I thought you would have a lot in common. Still, I expect she has her reasons." His hand left the table and rested deliberately on the bare skin of my shoulder. "How is your husband, by the way?"

"Take your hand off me!" I fought the urge to turn my head and bite him, and instead shrugged violently to rid me of it. His fingers dug deeper and he bent close, his mouth grazing my ear.

"There was a time when my hand wasn't what you wanted."

I tried to prise him off. "I was a fool."

"It seems to run in the family. Does your husband know what you like? Should I tell him, or leave it to his imagination?" He squeezed the top of my shoulder, flesh on flesh, almost painful now. "Ellie's a lively girl; she reminds me of you. She's Matthew's niece, isn't she? She seems very fond of him…"

"What do you want from me, Guy?"

"I never used to have to spell it out." His fingers stretched over the curve of my shoulder and under the strap of my top. I grasped the fork, fashioning it into a weapon, but I looked up as somebody else joined us.

"Emma? You OK?"

"Sam!" Never had I been so glad to see him. His dark eyes took in Guy's hand and then my face.

"It seems I'm not the only one you made a fool of," Guy said in an audible undertone, straightening and leaving a hot, tacky patch where his hand had been. Sam's face turned sour. "I'm going to meet Ellie at the medical centre. Looking forward to the conference tomorrow. No doubt I'll see you around." He turned, his hand bumping against the case balanced next to me on the bench. He caught it without thinking as it slid precariously close to the edge. As he steadied it, his nostrils flared and he took one last, unreadable look at me before walking rapidly away, leaving me wondering what it was he had seen. Then I remembered Sam. He had recovered from the slight, and a little of the old gleam returned.

"Thanks," I said.

"Sure. I sort of know the signs. You didn't look as if you wanted him around." He allowed a hint of a smile to slip through the irony. "I haven't seen you lately, Em – heard you're married. I never got to say congratulations. Congratulations."

"Thanks," I said again.

"I guess you'll be staying in Maine now?"

"Reckon so," I drawled, not feeling particularly humorous.

"*Dirty Harry?*"

I shook my head. "*Josie Wales*. How are you, Sam?"

He grunted, nodding slowly. "Sure, yeah, OK – all things considered. You?"

I contemplated the door through which Guy had disappeared moments before. "I'm OK, thanks." I clutched the shabby leather handle of the case. "All things considered."

The tepid shower helped. I scrubbed my skin raw where Guy's hand had lain, smothering the lingering sensation in body lotion until I couldn't recall the feeling any more. Then, as Matthew still wasn't home yet, I went to sit in the light shade of the little orchard, taking Grandpa's heavy case and a bottle of water. The new trees were watered regularly, and here the grass – still long and lush under the protection of their branches – felt cool against my skin. In contrast, the hide of the case burned to touch. Something about this case caught Guy's eye. Nothing on the outside looked remarkable in the slightest and, except for Grandpa's initials in dulled chrome beneath the handle, it seemed nondescript.

The catches slid *t-chlik* stiffly aside under the persistent pressure of my thumbs. The distantly familiar scent of tobacco-impregnated paper and old-fashioned ink emanated from the worn pages, mingling with memories as sharp as yesterday. I ran my hand over the uppermost book, lifting it to my face, and inhaled.

Diaries.

Diaries covering the period from his early days at Cambridge through to the 1990s, with a gap in between for the war. Academic diaries in cloth-bound, foolscap books – later A4 – and each the thickness of thick-sliced bread. Day diaries recording the mundane. His journals. He often urged me to keep one, but they had seemed like a lifetime beholden to pointless pedantry when I saw so much more in history to explore. But then I had been young and eager to make my mark. I remembered him writing in one – this one. I lifted the red book with the sticky price still attached and a smear of ink across the cover. These were different to the little notebooks he used in his research into the journal, like the one that had led me to Matthew in what seemed a lifetime ago.

I leafed through the books, each with a gummed label declaring the first and last dates the diary covered, going back in time until I found the first. I opened the cover: a slip of paper stuck on a page, the glue yellowing the edges. The date, the time, the venue:

AUCTION

GOODS AND CHATTELS OF

EBENEZER HOWARD, ESQ

~

LATE OF

HOWARD'S LAKE, MAINE,

10AM, TUESDAY 18TH JULY

~

FINE ART & ANTIQUES

BOOKS~EPHEMERA ETC

OVER 1000 LOTS

Hanson & Sons, Market Street,
Portland, Maine

And the contact details of the auctioneer.

So, this is where it all started for my grandfather. Next to the flyer, he had written: "Visited auction at curious mansion somewhat west of Portland. Sale of effects, etc. Fine library. Bidding strong. Bought box of papers, etc." And that was it.

I shooed a small fly from my leg where it had settled in a spot of sun, more surprised than anything at the paucity of information. No fanfare of trumpets or triumphant declaration of an antiquity discovered, just "Bought box of papers, etc."

He had yet to sort through the box, to catalogue the contents in his meticulous hand. He did so some months after his return to his teaching position at Cambridge, and it seemed as if it injected life with a vibrancy that had been lacking, because – all at once – in page after page, he recorded hours spent transcribing the tatty wedge of papers he found at the bottom of the box tied with a faded red ribbon. Not the details themselves – that he did in a separate book – but his thoughts and impressions, his theories and conjecture, all of which infected me in the late days of his life, when I was just starting mine. Wind lifted a strand of my hair like fingers of copper across my face, calling my name in the purl of leaves, *Emmaa*, and in the heat, I shivered.

I traced my life through his in the history of those pages. Through his eyes I discovered the original journal, felt his keen disappointment when age and ill-health prevented his travel to seek out the rest of it for himself, but could not extinguish the ardour with which it consumed him. I began to read in him what my parents had feared to see in me – an obsession burning so hot that all else faded in comparison. Too hot, too bright.

Grandpa lived through Nathaniel Richardson's eyes, traced him back to the land from which he came. I read of his astonishment to discover how close to Cambridge he had lived, how over time he tracked him down to an obscure and lost manor in a peaceful corner of Rutland. Was it no coincidence, then, that he found himself recovering from his war injuries at the neighbouring manor where he met Nanna? Or by design?

I never thought of my grandfather as being calculating; he was always Grandpa. Yet, it became clear in page after page that he followed a route as precisely as if he had planned it.

"I wondered if I might find you out here." I smiled vaguely as Matthew dropped down in the long grass beside me, gifting a kiss on my upturned face. I had lost track of time. He raised the edge of the book with a finger and read the label. "Where have you been this afternoon?"

"Here."

"No, I mean where have you been transported to?"

"Oh – here." I held up the diary for him to see.

"Isn't this what your grandmother left you?" He picked up the next book in the series, flicked through the pages, and then, as he noted the content, lapsed into silence as we each became engrossed in the minutiae of academia half a century or more before.

Eventually, my eyes aching from straining to read Grandpa's tight script, I closed the diary, contemplating how easy I found it, surrounded by all the normality of life, to forget that the man I had married was the same whose name haunted these pages. Frowning now and again as he read the entries, Matthew appeared wholly absorbed, caressing my hair absentmindedly.

I watched the shadow-play of leaves against his face, the way his lips parted a little, then tightened again as he read. The heat of the day had yielded a comfortable warmth, and I settled further into the grass using his outstretched legs as a pillow. "Sorry about lunch earlier; did your patient make it?"

"He did." He turned a page, read on, then skipped a few. He seemed particularly intent on a section from the early 1970s. He didn't look up. "Did Matias find you?"

The sun cast a deep cleft at the hollow of his throat that I found mesmerizing. "He did." I twisted to get a closer look, the light fabric of my shirt riding up and exposing my skin to the touch of the warm air.

"If you keep staring at me like that, I'm going to have to do something about it," he declared, snapping the book shut. He ran his hands over my bared stomach, moulding them to my curves, and kissed the rise of my tummy. "So, you've had lunch?"

An image of thin, red flesh giving way to sharp steel supplanted the sensation of Guy's hand on my naked shoulder. I sat up, knocking the diaries to one side in my haste.

Matthew drew back in surprise. "What's the matter?"

Pulling my shirt down, I rolled onto my knees and started stacking the diaries. "Nothing. It's too exposed here." The placid, undulating grassland, devoid of all sign of humanity, sang with tiny birds darting from stalk to swaying stalk.

He watched my hassled movements for a moment. "OK, so I'm assuming this has nothing to do with sparing the blushes of the avian population?"

I stopped. "Did you know Guy's met Maggie?"

"Yes, Ellie told me she had taken him to meet her. What of it?"

"You don't think she might let something slip accidentally, or on purpose, do you? Only, Guy has a way of extracting information without someone noticing he's doing it."

"And you think that Maggie's too unstable or too vengeful to be trusted?" He secured the lid and then helped me to my feet. We walked slowly up the rise towards the house, our way heralded by the startled whirr of rising birds. "I think Maggie's recovered enough not to let slip anything accidentally, and I don't think she'll purposefully harm us – or you – for one simple reason." He swapped the case to his other hand, and took mine in his. "She thinks you won't be around long and it's just a matter of time before you leave. She won't say anything to Guy because she knows I will never forgive her if she does. She's willing to bide her time." He came to a standstill. "She's still delusional, Emma – stable, but delusional. Let her wait – she'll have to wait a very long time – and perhaps, by then, she'll have forgotten why she dislikes you so much."

We reached the courtyard and I was still thinking about my

reluctance to ask for help and pondering whether it represented stubborn pride or a lack of trust, when Matthew placed Grandpa's case on the kitchen table.

"Emma, if I've interpreted his diaries correctly, I'm surprised by the amount of forward planning your grandfather seems to have made. It wasn't the impression I gained from your description of him. He wasn't just scrupulous in his record-keeping, was he? He left nothing to chance."

"Yes," I agreed slowly, glad to shake ourselves free of the previous topic of Maggie like a dog shedding fleas. "I hadn't considered it until today. I always thought him a bit of a plodder, a duffer, in the nicest possible way, of course."

He smiled. "Of course."

"But he wasn't at all from what I can see. He seemed to have had an agenda, although he doesn't state it as such. It runs through everything he did, like a subplot almost." So Grandpa proved to be more systematic than I remembered, and that would have been fine, but for one thing: reading his diaries reminded me of reading notes from a more recent past; it was like reading Guy.

Between the Lines

It bugged me.

I tussled fitfully between broken sleep – words, phrases, half-remembered, warped by time, running like a seam of quartz through the dull obscurity of the everyday.

"She always harboured grudges – it runs in her family."

Runs in her family. Family.

The reference to my family had struck me as odd at the time, dropped in as a seemingly careless remark, which meant it couldn't be; but I had given it no other thought beyond the hurt Guy intended. I had assumed he referred to my parents – to my father – whose fist ensured Guy had taken a week off work with "flu". At the time I wondered how he explained his bloodied nose to his wife, and what lies he told to appease her curiosity. Yet, despite his sudden rage, Dad pursued the matter no further, so it wasn't a reference to my father, I felt sure of that.

Faint sounds of running water from the direction of the bathroom beckoned dawn. Matthew was halfway through shaving and I folded my arms around his stomach and laid my face against his back. His muscles undulated beneath my cheek. "Did I wake you?"

"No, I couldn't sleep." Resting my chin on his shoulder, I watched the razor make a clean path through the snowy foam until the foundations of his face were revealed. He washed his face, and rubbed it dry. In the silvered reflection of the mirror, he met my eyes. "Are you worried about the conference?"

"Not the conference, no, although I should be. I bet my students didn't get much sleep last night."

"About Guy, then?"

"Guy? Yes – always."

I wasn't prepared for the sheer number of delegates, already stewing in their suits in the morning heat, crowding the glass-roofed concourse outside the main lecture theatre. Neither, by the look of it, was Eckhart. I saw his balding head with its fringe of tonsured hair bobbing up and down like a cork among the tide of faces. His eyes went round behind his thick-rimmed specs as he spotted me, and his arm went up like a drowning man. "Ah, Pro… Professor!" He pushed through the bodies, clipboard clenched beneath his arm. "Professor – you're here!" I was only a few minutes later than planned and still in plenty of time – a miracle given the amount of traffic this morning. Clutching the clipboard like a lifebuoy, he launched before I could return his greeting. "Almost everyone is here. The delegates have signed in but Professor Maas is recovering from s… sickness and he won't be here until later this afternoon." His hands shook. "As agreed, you will open the conference and your keynote lecture has been rescheduled for after lunch as you requested… and then if you would introduce the second speaker, Professor…" he checked the board, "Professor Geo… Geog…" Poor man; Eckhart looked as if he would combust as he struggled with the unfamiliar Irish name.

"Professor Geoghegan," I offered. "Yes, of course I will; I've met him before." An uncomfortable burning sensation set up between my shoulder blades, becoming more intense as seconds passed. I looked behind me and Guy raised his cup in mock salute. I returned it with a scowl and turned my back on him.

Eckhart peered at me. "Are yo... you quite all right, Professor?"

Unsettled, I smiled weakly. "It's the heat," I explained. "I couldn't sleep."

He blinked. "The heat. Yes." Although the temperature already neared eighty degrees, and delegates undid buttons and loosened ties, Eckhart perspired profusely into his velvet jacket. His jitters were catching and I found myself itching to escape. "I must let you get on," I said as firmly and kindly as I could. "Let me know if I can help. Good luck, Professor."

The overhead lights scorched, reducing the faces of the delegates, ranked row upon row to the back of the lecture theatre, to mere smudges. I should have been more nervous, but by the time I mounted the podium my mind was elsewhere. I introduced the conference, outlined the next few days' proceedings, and gave my own thoughts on the subject matter. I barely heard the applause as I finished speaking, nor again as I introduced the next speaker with the impossible name. I left the platform aware that Guy's slow ovation made a mockery of my attempt, and made straight for the door where Matthew waited. We slipped outside. He exuded an irresistible calm.

"You didn't have to come, but I'm glad you're here."

"I couldn't miss the opportunity of seeing my wife in her element; you've worked so hard for this. Well done; that will keep them thinking for some time yet. Do you have any evidence to support your supposition?"

I broke away from him, ready to be cross, but saw he joked. "The only evidence is from a primary source, Matthew, and I'm not ready to reveal him – yet."

"Touché. Is Colin Eckhart aware of what you've done to his schedule of speakers? You seem edgy – are you all right?"

"As I'll ever be. No, Colin doesn't know and I daren't tell him – he's such a bundle of nerves, poor man. I wish I hadn't agreed to do this. Guy's making it very clear he's not impressed."

"You don't have to prove anything to him. It's your career; it's important to you. Don't give him the satisfaction of thinking he's spooked you." Easier said than done because no matter how hard I tried, Guy still made me feel like an inadequate undergraduate on the edge of her seat, even if I *had* earned my place here today. I drew a hand across my neck; it came away wet with perspiration.

"Try to look hot, Matthew, for goodness sake. It's baking in here and you're the only one who looks as if he can stand it."

"This heat won't last." He loosened his collar and tie nonetheless before reaching into his pocket. "Here," he said, taking my hand and pressing something into it. "Keep me close to you."

I looked down: the brown nutmeg sat snugly in my palm and I couldn't help but smile. "Thank you."

His eyes met those of someone behind me. "Merhaba Aydın; o seni görmek güzel. Nasılsın?"

I looked around; Aydın had approached and stood quietly waiting for a break in our conversation. He gave a little bow of his head.

"Günaydın, Doktor efendim. Thank you; I am well. Good morning, Professor." He smiled shyly. "Your introduction went well, I think. There was much… alkış." He looked to Matthew for help.

"Applause."

Aydın inclined his head in agreement.

"Thanks, so will yours. Are the others here? We'd better

organize a time to meet to go through things one last time while we have the chance. Matthew…"

"I know, I'm in the way. I'll meet you at home." He briefly touched the cross hanging at my throat. "God bless; keep me close."

I pressed the nutmeg against my heart. "I will."

During the break for lunch, I herded my group into an empty room where at least the air conditioning seemed to be working. Instantly recognizable by his stack of gelled, bleached hair, Josh's only concession to conformity was the suit he had recently purchased for the event. He took a slug of cola, trying to look nonchalant.

"You'll be fine, Josh, but take off the paperclip chain; it'll rattle if you get nervous." I searched their faces for any glimmer of confidence. "Look, you'll all be fine. You too, Hannah."

"I'm not nervous," she said, and went back to surveying the library from the window. It was the only thing she had said since entering the room, holding herself separate from the others – aloof, almost.

"Well, I am." Holly had the paper between her hands screwed into a tube, dark hair sticking damply to her neck.

"Yeah, we all are. It's a rite of passage, isn't it, Dr D? We'll get through it." Josh fingered his dark, three-day stubble and gave Holly a comforting hug. I closed my eyes and counted silently before opening them again to find my students watching me.

"Yes, we'll all get through it." I smiled as confidently as I could. "Let's go."

The air conditioning had been turned up as the temperature soared. I blanched in distaste when pungent glacial air struck us, as delegates, full coffee cups still in their hands, filtered into the conference room. I made my way to my reserved aisle seat in the front row. No sooner had I sat down than the Dean appeared at my elbow. Glistening jowls hung over his buttoned collar and, despite the refrigerated interior, plumes of sweat stained his shirt beneath his open blazer as he bent towards me. "A landmark event in your career, my dear Professor. I'm sure your paper will prove memorable." I detected no warmth in his voice, nor did he wish me well. I watched him walk to his own seat directly in front of the podium, and wondered what it was that had made his seemingly benign remark sound like a threat. I heard my name announced. I didn't dare look at the little group of students, whose page-pale faces were expressionless with nerves.

Touching my cross to my lips, and clasping the nutmeg in my hand, I rose to deliver what should have been the lecture of my life. Standing there under the spotlights, fingers of one hand grasping the edge of the lectern, the nutmeg in the palm of the other, if I had harboured any doubts about what I decided to do, I didn't now. I hoped Grandpa would have understood I had no option – that the journal must remain concealed for as long as Matthew lived, and that for as long as I lived, I would ensure its anonymity.

So, instead of presenting the journal to the world and ensuring my place in it, the lecture I gave was short and to the point, the research sound, the concept interesting. It was not what I had spent my life pursuing, nor what Grandpa meant me to do. It would neither break new ground nor set the world alight, but it was safe and, from the platform of its mundane solidity, I could launch my students' careers at the sacrifice of my own.

As I spoke, I became aware of the hues of my audience reacting like a shoal of fish to my pursuing words: changing direction, now silvered light, now wraithlike dark, with individuals breaking free in purples of disagreement, or bright blues as my thoughts chimed with their own. No longer victim to their emotions as I had been at the trial, I found myself able to read and respond to them, liberating me. Only one I couldn't map: Guy sat next to Shotter, opaque and unresponsive and far from impressed.

My abrupt conclusion left the lecture hall stunned. Without delay, I introduced Josh, and watched as Shotter suffused with anger. I left the platform and took my seat, avoiding his eyes, with Eckhart stuttering incomprehensibly to one side. First Josh, then Holly, followed by Aydin – winning over the battle-hardened historians in front of them, who saw their young selves in the stumbled sentences and missed words, until the clarity of my students' arguments won their respect.

I welcomed each back with a hug and saw in their faces, and heard in the applause, the only justification I needed. Then it was Hannah's turn. I hadn't seen her paper for a while now, and as the last speaker of the day, she would push the boundaries of tolerance. Her short skirt wrinkling as she mounted the stage, polite boredom brewed along with hunger among the academics. Behind me, two middle-aged men maintained a running commentary in subdued tones. I threw a cautioning look in their direction and they shut up. I nodded to Hannah to begin.

The moment she looked at Guy for approval I guessed what he had done. From the second she opened her mouth I understood what had happened. And I could do nothing. Her argument was riveting; her argument was flawless; her argument was *mine*.

What bait had he laid, what enticements, what flattery? And what promises of fame and recognition did he make off *my* back, off *my* work? It had taken me months of painstaking research to complete the project in my second year at university, only for him to hand it to her on a plate.

The intense heat of the afternoon couldn't compete with the rage on which I had to keep a lid for the rest of her lecture. *My* lecture. I didn't wait for the announcements at the end of the day. No sooner had Hannah finished to wide acclaim than I made for the door, only to find the Dean waiting for me outside. His fingers pinched my arm, his eyes wintry.

"I'll not have my college made a laughing stock by parading complete unknowns. Don't think I'll forget this. You're not irreplaceable." With the sound of people pushing their way through the door, he let go of me, pulling his blazer taut, buttoning it as he walked away, smiling as if nothing untoward had happened. I launched daggers at his retreating back, wondering what he planned.

"You've got balls pulling that stunt."

I forgot the Dean in an instant. I whirled around. "What the heck were you doing giving Hannah my work?"

Guy tucked a leather portfolio under his arm, looking unruffled. "And I thought that you would be pleased that one of your students had a break."

"Not off *my* research. You had no right, Guy, and you haven't done her any favours. You know I can't pass her MA now."

His calm infuriated me. I wanted to thump him. He inspected his nails. "No, *you* can't."

"What is that supposed to mean?"

Shading his eyes, he squinted at someone on the other side of the concourse. "All's fair in love and war, Emma; you should know that by now. In love. And war." He slung his jacket over his other arm. "Now, if you don't mind, I have people to see."

Impotence fuelling my temper, I raged across campus to my car, reversed at speed and sped down the drive and onto the back roads home. I took the road across the bridge, slowing enough to cross it safely before giving the car its head, feeling it surge with all the unrestrained power beneath its bonnet.

Matthew appeared at the door as I drew up. "How did it go?"

"Malodorous skunk," I threw over my shoulder as I tore off my shirt. He looked taken aback. "Not you – Guy. I'll explain later." I ran up the stairs, undoing my skirt as I went, slipping off my shoes and diving into the shower as he appeared behind me with my discarded shirt in his hand.

"What happened?"

I let the water quell my temper before I could tell him without using expletives as conjunctions. I then repeated Shotter's threat, word by word. Matthew handed me a dry towel as I stepped from the shower.

"Did he indeed. That was most brazen of him. He might just regret saying that."

I stopped towelling my hair. "Well, if you do decide to do anything, just let me take a pot-shot first. Hannah aside, the others were brilliant. I doubt I could have done what they did at this stage of their careers. It's downright intimidating facing an audience of crabby historians at the best of times. Shotter should be celebrating their success, not trying to bury them." I hunted for my hairbrush. "I'll bury him; just give me a pickaxe and shovel..." I ceased ranting. He hadn't said anything and seemed distracted. "What are you thinking?"

His eyes – azure in the strong afternoon light – refocused. "Mmm? Nothing. Your hair's wet. And you'll need to dress if you're going to poleaxe anybody with any dignity."

I went into our bedroom. "Pickaxe," I said, pulling on clothes and looking around for my ring. "Not poleaxe. Does much the same job, I suppose."

"Indeed," he murmured, "it does." He didn't elaborate, but from his distant expression, I guessed he drew on personal experience.

***

The study felt cooler on this side of the house where the sun only penetrated first thing in the morning, but it was still hot. No birds sang. Distant voices crossed the courtyard to the Stable and a door slammed. The loudest sounds were insects in their lazy dance on the torpid evening air. Behind the house, suspended above remote mountains, the sun exhausted the last of the day, and the land, saturated by heat, waited.

We waited, and it seemed to me that it must be all part of the game Guy played: he made all the moves while we waited. Always one step ahead of us and we waited; he knew where he wanted to go while we waited to find out.

Impatient, I huffed, "What are we waiting *for*?"

At his desk, Matthew powered down the laptop. "Would you like to go for a walk?"

"It's too hot." I batted an inquisitive mosquito out of the window. "And I don't want to get bitten to death." The sash slid shut with an indelicate thump. I wanted to shout, rant, explode.

He closed the notebook in which he had been writing and put down his pen. "One of the worst parts of battle used to be the anticipation of it."

I folded my arms. "I suppose that does put things into perspective."

He came and stood behind me by the window, curving his arms around my middle. "On the eve of battle, while we waited to engage the enemy, a peculiar stillness would overcome the camp. Some men sang, others prayed – many would have gone to the local ale house or played dice if they could have got away with it. One man I knew carved a new animal for his children before each battle. They were barely bigger than my thumb, detailed, and each with a character of its own. He whittled away until we were called to arms. He kept them in a little leather bag

with a letter, and concealed it in his buff coat against his heart."
I pressed against his chest, my back resonating with his voice
when he spoke. "I think he poured himself into the toy so that
it bore his hope and love for his family in case he didn't return."

"Did he live to give them to his children?"

He dropped his arms and I felt their absence. "No."

It wasn't what I'd hoped to hear, but then happy endings were
the preserve of stories, not real life.

"What did you do?"

"I wrote poetry."

I conjured an incongruous image of men on the eve of battle
quietly engaged in pastimes more readily associated with peace.
"I still hate waiting," I moaned, and then capitulated and took
the hint. "Oh, all right then, I'll find something to do."

The diaries spanned the floor in chronological order, recording
a lifetime of discovery. Like Nathaniel, Grandpa used a series of
abbreviations throughout his work. He loved riddles and puzzles
and could complete the *Times* crossword faster than anybody
I had ever known. *A mind like a pin*, Nanna would say; *sharp
and bright*. Some were self-evident: initials for people he knew
– students, other academics – and acronyms for institutions
or organizations. I tussled with PK, until the penny finally
dropped and I found myself laughing as I remembered his own
pet name for me – Pipkin – because I was little and his beloved
granddaughter. Many were familiar, some I had to work out,
but several abbreviated references remained ambiguous and I
struggled to place them within a context in which they would
make any sense. By the 80s, he noted one student in particular
– Vir – who cropped up increasingly. *A potentially brilliant mind*,
he wrote, *but currently flawed by ego*.

By the middle of the decade, Vir had fulfilled all early

expectation, and worked towards a doctorate. Grandpa returned to the Old Manor to continue his research, taking the young man with him and delegating assignments, much as Guy had done with me. Curiosity tingled. I recalled Mrs Seaton mentioning a student accompanying him, although she hadn't remembered his name.

The lantern clock struck the hour with a clear note. I stood up and let the blood flow back into my legs before flopping back to the floor.

My name cropped up time and again. I checked the date – late 80s – I would have been nearly ten. I mentally toured my childhood, pinning dates, events, names to each reference he made to me. "Took PK to Ely", to Peterborough, to Tickencote. I remembered every trip we made. "PK fascinated by..." this or that. "PK transcribed..." such and such. Had I? I didn't recall. "PK finished reading Woolrych's 'Commonwealth to Protectorate'." I remembered *that*. "Shows insight..." "Intuitive understanding..." Reference after reference – sometimes as a single word, sometimes noted in a margin as if late at night and, more often as not, as comments strung between tutorial notes or criticism of another academic. A pattern developed as I read through the months until, with a jolt, I worked out what I read: a syllabus. Step by step, my grandfather had been training me – grooming me – for my future career. I sat back on my heels, not sure how I felt about that. Was that all I had been to him – a project, just another student to be initiated into the rites and rituals of a historian? Not special at all?

"Was that it, Grandpa?" I asked the ether.

I was alone and my question remained unanswered. I licked gluey chocolate thoughtfully, not tasting it, and the heat did it no favours. I went to the kitchen and returned with toast. The room had become insufferably stuffy and riding the tall sashes into their frames barely moved the air at all. Haze-hung, the distant trees glowed with the dying sun, and Siren-like, the diaries beckoned. I read on.

Vir and I continued to figure large until one day, apparently, we met.

I was no more than eleven. Grandpa would have retired by then but he still played an active role in college life.

13th October. "Took PK to lunch with A.S. et al. Held her own on Putney debates – drew quite a crowd. Put Vir's nose out of joint." Grandpa obviously found this amusing, but I thought it sounded precocious. I racked my memory but found no recollection on which to draw. I had been taken to so many lunches, with so many historians, that they tended to blur. They all seemed like old men – even the women – and this twenty-something-year-old student apparently made little impression. Shortly afterwards, however, Grandpa recorded a day I could never forget: "Introduced PK to the journal."

He was sitting in his usual place at his desk by the window of his bedroom, and it was snowing. Early snow, it had taken us all by surprise. I remembered the smell of it in the air mingling with the aromatic tobacco he savoured but rarely smoked.

"Emma," he said so quietly that I turned from where I pressed my nose against the cold glass, thinking I had imagined his voice. "Come here. I have something I want to show you." And he tapped a ragged stack of paper secured with a frayed red ribbon on his desk in front of him. I climbed onto my chair with its cushion so I could reach the desk.

"*Verba volant, scripta manent.*" He smiled tolerantly as I fought to translate his wisdom, and failed. "'Words fly away, writings remain,' Pipkin. These words are very old. This is part of a transcript of a diary written by a man called Nathaniel Richardson, and he lived not far from here a long time ago. I want to tell you his story, or what I know of it, and the rest will be for you to discover when I am no longer here." And from that moment on, as he wove the magic of the journal into my eager heart, I became enslaved as surely as he had been.

"Emma," he said at last, long after dusk crowded the room and hunger had been forgotten. "I have very little to give you when I die, but I will leave you this." He laid a wasted hand upon the inked page. "Perhaps you will do what I have failed to do: find the journal, make it your own. The journal holds the key." He closed his eyes and let out a long, slow exhalation as if he had waited forever to say those words.

"The key to what, Grandpa?" I asked, visualizing a seventeenth-century man holding out a golden key.

"The key," he said again. "Nathaniel holds the key. *Mundus vult decipi* – the world wants to be deceived, my Pipkin, but not you. *Veritas lux mea* – the truth is my light. Find what it is he hides, Emma – read between the *lines*." He laughed quietly at some private joke, but I was hopelessly lost, and his talk of mortality drove all thought of keys and journals from my mind, until the battered tailor's box had been placed in my hands on the day we buried him.

"What key, Grandpa?" I whimpered into the night, cast adrift without him to guide me, hugging the box close until I had cried enough to sleep.

For years after, I clung to those words. Grandpa wanted me to find the key, and I had kept my promise – I had married him.

Had he known? Did he suspect?

Shortly before he died, when I read to him from the journal as his mind wandered between the living and the dead, he looked at me regretfully with faded blue eyes. "What have I done?" he whispered. "Pipkin, forgive me."

I held his frail hand between mine and stroked freckled skin as translucent as parchment.

"Don't be silly, Grandpa," I chided gently in all my teenage wisdom, "there's nothing to forgive."

He turned his head away, and in the failing light from the window, a slow tear had gleamed in his hollow cheek. "Forgive me."

Sitting on the floor of the study, surrounded by his diaries, I recalled his last words. "Grandpa, what have you done?" I picked up the diary with the smudge of ink across its cover. Reading carefully and with a more open mind, I continued.

Dining at Kings. A lecture at Oxford. Martinsthorpe. The Old Manor. "JS" for Joan Seaton. Rolling my shoulders to ease them, I focused on references to Martinsthorpe, ignoring all else.

4th May. "Set Vir on cataloguing all source material at OM" (Old Manor?).

A few weeks later: 22nd May. "OM. Seaton papers ref: 1643/ WL. Vir impatient to trace records of trial at Oak'm." Then, a week later: "Vir following up WL lead."

WL. William Lynes? Did this Vir know the story of William's betrayal of his brother that Joan Seaton had been so eager to tell me? I read on.

1st June. "The Glorious First! (That's what Grandpa used to call my birthday.) Vir traced WL grave. Reburied at some expense within church post-Restoration, poss. 1669 by unknown benefactor." Now that was interesting on several counts. A frisson of curiosity ran through me.

5th June. "Went to WL memorial. Curious inscription. S. A. (l. 1,170) Error in dating? Played down relevance, but Vir persistent."

On a plain sheet of paper, folded and stuck between the diary's pages, Grandpa had sketched, with infinitesimal detail, the handsome, unadorned memorial. In fine white marble with black marble columns, it had been embedded in the wall of a church in what once would have been the Lady Chapel, the inscription still clear. After William's name and his age at death, there appeared to be a quote:

"These evils I deserve, and more... Justly, yet despair not of his final pardon,
Whose ear is ever open, and his eye Gracious to re-admit the suppliant."

And beneath, the Lynes coat of arms and the date – 1669. No mention of his execution, or what had led to it, nor evidence who commissioned the monument, or why. Fleetingly, I became lost in the tragedy of it all, then gathered myself. Why was there an error in dating and what did it matter anyway? Grandpa had thought it sufficiently odd to hinder Vir's curiosity and that was enough to kindle mine. I hopped to my feet and went out to the kitchen to make a cup of tea and clear my head.

Matthew found me there when he emerged through the pantry door from the Stable, making me jump. "Where's my pipe and slippers then?" he grinned, swinging me around and putting me back on my feet. "I fail to amuse, it seems."

Shaking my head, I grabbed his hand, dragging him towards the study. "I can't make head or tail of these diaries. I need your help."

"Ah," he said, stepping over the piles of paper spread across the floor. "You've been busy. Looking for something?"

I started examining the books on the study shelves for anything that might help. "Your timing's perfect. I'm looking for a quote. I don't recognize it and I wondered whether you mi..." I heard an exclamation behind me.

"So, he found it!"

I turned around. Matthew hunkered down and was examining the sketch of the memorial with a curious expression of nostalgia mixed with regret. I should have known. "You had William reburied, didn't you? So you know what the quote is?" Weaving between the diaries, I knelt next to him.

Tracing the outline of the stone, he summoned memory from the page. "It's taken from Milton's *Samson Agonistes*. I thought it fitting. I couldn't leave him where he was, unremembered and as if he'd never existed. It didn't seem right, despite what he did."

"Why did Grandpa think there was an error in the date, and so what if there was?"

Matthew looked puzzled. "Did he?" Then his face cleared. "Ah, well, that might be because I had William reinterred in 1669."

"So?"

"And *Samson Agonistes* wasn't published until a few years later – 1671, I believe. Your grandfather did well to spot the discrepancy; it's not exactly common knowledge. I didn't think anyone would notice at the time and I certainly didn't think I'd still be around to worry about it being discovered now."

I chewed my cross, deep in thought. "But he wasn't the only one. His research student – Vir – noticed, but Grandpa wouldn't tell him anything more. He seemed to be suspicious of him. I wonder why. What are you looking at me like that for?"

"You like a conundrum, don't you?"

I wrinkled my nose. "I took you on, didn't I?"

He laughed. "You did."

"How come you came into possession of a quote that hadn't yet been published?"

For a second I thought he might tell me, but he shook his head, gave a half smile and just said, "It's a very long story," before quickly moving on. "So, your grandfather's student found William and they noted the mismatch between dates, but what did they make of it?"

We searched the next few pages together, silently reading, heads almost touching: a colleague's birthday bash, dining in Hall, a lecture published in a periodical and so on, until I found what I wanted. "Vir curious about window. Wants to access primary material. Told him records didn't survive." Then later still, "OM a mistake – Vir pushing for information. Visited OM without telling me. Not what he seemed." Finally, a curt: "Spoke to Davies. Offer terminated."

I puffed out my cheeks. Offer. What offer? "Who on earth *is* Vir?"

"Vir," Matthew snorted a laugh until he saw my expression.

"What's so funny?" I demanded.

"My apologies; I'd forgotten Latin is not your strong point. Vir can be translated as 'man' or 'hero'; does that help?"

I was already leafing through the diary. "Vir was helping Grandpa with his research. He took him to the Old Manor, but Vir became overly curious and something happened. Grandpa took a dislike to him, but he doesn't say why. Vir. Man. Hero. I can't see why. An anagram, perhaps? No – that doesn't work. A play on words? Grandpa was always mucking about with words."

Matthew reeled off a list of synonyms. "Man: Gentleman. Fellow. Chap. Bloke. Lad…"

We looked at each other. "Guy?"

I forced myself to breathe, but each word hurt. "Tell me it wasn't Guy. Tell me his being here has nothing to do with you."

Matthew's face said it all. "It could just be chance," he hedged.

"But I don't believe in coincidence."

"No." We observed each other bleakly for what seemed like an age.

"It would make sense," I said eventually. "It would fit, but Guy never said he knew Grandpa. He never said he had met me.

In all the time I knew him, why didn't he tell me, Matthew?" I slumped to the floor, shaken, bewildered.

"I don't know, but this puts a different light on things." He glanced at his watch. "Let's talk to the family before it gets any later. They need to know – especially Ellie, before she says something to him." He sprang to his feet, but I stayed put, my mind already racing down dark avenues, looking for a glimmer of light.

"You go; I want to think this through." He was in the hall when something occurred to me. "Matthew!" I called. He reappeared. "Henry doesn't know who you really are and if Guy has any knowledge about the Lynes or where you come from, he'll use it to sow dissension."

He didn't waiver. "Then I'll just have to make sure that he doesn't." And he left before I could ask him what he meant.

I waited for him in the study. I hadn't the heart to shut out the dark, and against the unshuttered windows, moth wings beat in a futile attempt to reach the light. Whatever the family decided, I had come to a decision of my own.

He returned in the early hours. "Well?" I asked, no sooner than he stepped through the door.

Leaning against the desk, he picked up the ivory letter opener, running a finger down its edge. "As Ellie's parents, Dan and Jeannie will ask Guy to a family meeting this weekend under the guise of discussing his intentions. Dan managed to persuade Jeannie, although she's not wild about it. She likes Guy well enough, and believes he loves her daughter. Ellie's certainly infatuated with him."

I couldn't see this working. "She's an adult, Matthew. Even if he does agree – which I bet he won't – Ellie can do what she likes. She doesn't need her parents' permission. You might be from another era, but she isn't. There's nothing stopping her from raising two fingers and refusing to cooperate. You said yourself she's infatuated."

"She'll cooperate, Emma, and Guy will agree to a meeting because, if you're right about him, he'll want as much contact with the family as he can get. The closer he is, the more information he can gather."

It felt as if we were being backed into an impossible situation where there could be only one outcome. I folded my arms against my chest, squeezing the fear and frustration from between my ribs. "And we're going to give it to him on a plate, is that it? And then what?"

He raised an eyebrow at the note of irritation. "And then we'll see," he said calmly. The clock chimed sweetly, unable to sugar the pill he expected me to swallow. I fumed at the piles of paper still strewn like the aftermath of a bomb across the floor. "Now, it's late, and you have a conference in the morning; you need your sleep."

Conference? I'd forgotten the blasted conference. Who cared anyway?

"Emma, until we know what Guy is up to, until we know what he wants, life goes on as usual. It's part of our masquerade. To all intents we are a normal family. Let's not give him – or anyone else for that matter – any reason to think otherwise. What could he have possibly discovered that would reveal my identity? If he does have any evidence, from your knowledge of him, is he likely to have told anyone else?"

I shook my head. "Guy would want to keep that sort of information to himself until he could use it to further his career. I didn't get primary recognition for the work I did for him; he always ensured his name appeared first. It was how things worked."

"Good," he said grimly, "then let's keep it that way."

Mad Dog

The haze which had developed overnight did nothing to alleviate the seething heat of the morning.

Guy was talking with a group of French academics when I spotted him at the far side of the concourse, holding court.

"Emma, join us for a coffee. We were just discussing *Le Roi et la Croix*. I know you'll have something to say on D'Aubigne's ridiculous assertion…"

I wasn't fooled by his false affability, even if they were. "Why didn't you tell me you knew him?"

There was a momentary hesitation before a condescending smile replaced the surprise. "You know Françoise, of course, but have you met Professors Bayard and Leveque?"

I realized I must seem outrageously rude. I bit my lip and greeted each stiffly before facing him again and he could see I wouldn't let it drop. He shrugged apologetically.

"*Pardon, ces affaires de coeur. Tout est juste dans l'amour et la guerre, n'est-ce pas?*" I knew enough French to get the gist. The exchange of sympathetic looks fuelled my anger and I really didn't care whether they knew I thought him a conniving bastard or not.

"Don't flatter yourself, Guy; love never had anything to do with it. Why did you lie to me? Why didn't you tell me you knew my grandfather?"

The French professors drifted away. Guy dropped all pretence. "You pick your times, Emma. Couldn't it wait?"

"For what?" I shot back. "Another ten years? It isn't just something you forgot to mention, is it?" My voice echoed across the crowded concourse.

He lowered his voice. "Not here; you don't want the whole world to know."

"Why not? I've nothing to hide."

"Haven't you?" He needed to add nothing to the shrewd, sharp look he gave me in the eloquent seconds that passed. It told me what I wanted to know and was enough to send a shockwave rattling through me.

"What do you want, Guy?"

"Meet me at my hotel..."

I shook my head emphatically. "No, not there. You can come to the house after the dinner."

That sardonic lift to his mouth again. "Don't you trust me?"

I raised my eyes and stared directly into his. "When have you *ever* given me reason to trust you?"

Purgatory – the only word I could think of to describe the torment I endured throughout the rest of the day. I sat through the series of presentations with what I hoped appeared to be attentive interest but, in reality, mentally scoured every source I knew to see what Guy could have discovered that justified the expression of smug satisfaction he openly wore.

During the brief interval for lunch, I snatched a few moments to phone Matthew.

"What time did you arrange to meet?" he asked.

"After the conference dinner tonight – probably nearly eleven by the time I get home."

"Do you want me there?"

I wanted to shout: "Yes! Don't leave me alone with him," but I couldn't. "No, I have to do this by myself."

I visualized him closing his eyes on the other end of the phone before answering. "All right, but I won't be far if you need me. Don't let him... keep safe... *please*."

I imagined how hard it was for him to let me go and silently prayed that I had enough strength for the both of us.

The interminable afternoon drew to a close too soon. I wasn't ready. Now without my own flat on campus, I went back to Elena's apartment to change for the conference dinner. The heat of the day lay trapped in the confined space and she had not yet returned. I opened the windows to capture the mountain air, but they remained steadfastly distant, and our brief days of happiness among the slopes seemed so long ago that I struggled to recall them. Something tickled my face. I touched my cheek and to my surprise found it wet. I tried to quench fire in my throat, but bottled-up tears continued to seep for all the wasted years spent in the shadow of this man, for all the joy I had found with Matthew, for his family, and the threat hanging over us.

When Elena returned in the early evening she found me sitting in the darkening room, alone and brooding. "Are you not going to the dinner?" she asked, switching on the overhead light. I squinted in the glare. "Are you OK?" She came closer. "Have you been crying?"

Rising to my feet, I tucked the sodden hankies out of sight. "I'm all right. I'll get changed."

"Emma, wait, what is the matter? You look so sad."

"Do you believe we get what we deserve?"

"I do not understand what you are saying."

"Do you think we're punished for our sins, Elena? Is that

why Guy is here – as a reminder of what I did to his wife, as retribution for my crime against an innocent woman?"

Her brown eyes widened. "What are you talking about? This is crazy nonsense. You did not know he was married…"

"I didn't ask."

"No! He did not say, and you assumed…"

I laughed – a hollow, raw sound that grated my throat still sore from grief. She grabbed my elbows, almost angry. "You take this on yourself, but you always say to me that God forgives. If it is so, then He forgives you."

"For me to be forgiven I have to ask for forgiveness – and give it in return."

"Have you not done so for this woman?"

"Constantly."

"Then, it is so," she declared, but she didn't know what I hid so deep inside me that I had forgotten until recently to look.

"But not for him, not for Guy. I thought I had, but… but now, after all this…"

"Are you angry because he wants to marry Matthew's niece; are you jealous?"

"No, Elena! You don't understand." I hid my face in my hands. "I can't tell you. I don't know what to do."

She swept her arm around my shoulder. "In Russia, we have a saying: 'if you rely on God, you won't fail.'" And it was something I believed, or thought I did; but how could I look God in the face and ask for help when I so stubbornly refused to do this one thing required of me? "But," she went on, "we also say: 'we should hope for God, but lock your house just in case.'" I managed to raise a smile at the simple pragmatism. Elena clapped her hands. "Ah, so you have not altogether lost your humour – this is good. Now you get changed and we do not talk any more of this man. Matias will not let me mention his name. 'Elena,' he said to me,

'I should be enough man for you; this Guy is trouble.' And I let him show me how much man he is. It was so romantic. I think I shall have to make Matias jealous again."

I thought that it wouldn't be so very hard, but he had little to be jealous about – Elena wasn't going anywhere. A natural flirt she might be, but she adored him as much as he loved her, and adultery would not blight their lives in years to come.

I blew my nose. "I must look a fright – and I've used half a box of your tissues. Sorry."

"Hah! There! See? You are good at asking for forgiveness. Why don't you stay here with me and we can have a girls' night in?"

"I can't; I promised Eckhart I'd be there. I think he's relying on me to do some of the socializing for him – he's dreading it."

She shrugged and went to answer a solid knock at the door. I felt flat, drained, all the highs and lows of the past weeks rendered featureless and out of reach. *Me ask forgiveness?* I said to myself as I sought the seclusion of her bathroom to wash and change. *Not when it really matters, clearly. Not so that it counts.*

Occupied with my own thoughts, by the time I emerged I'd forgotten there might be someone else with her. Sam stood up when he saw me.

"Emma – hi."

"Sam," I acknowledged. He looked more together than I'd seen him for ages – happy, almost. From the sound of it, Elena was in the kitchen putting something in the oven. I waited until she slammed the door shut and joined us again.

"I'm off. Thanks for letting me blub. Don't take any notice, it's probably PMT." She gave me one of her *don't be daft* looks. "Anyway. Thanks."

Dawdling awkwardly by the apartment door, Sam picked up my jacket and held it out to me. I took it from him.

"See you, Sam."

"Elena says you're going to the conference dinner," he said. "I'll walk you there."

"No, thanks, I can manage." I remembered all too clearly the last time he insisted on walking me home and so, it seemed, did he. He fingered his chin.

"Sure, I know you can, but I wanted to say something. Give me a break, Em – please?" His mahogany eyes smiled at his own joke. "Yeah, I know, I deserved to get the crap knocked out of me. My jaw's healed fine. No hard feelings, OK?"

We ended up walking slowly down the hall to the stairs to the lower floor with Sam struggling to begin a conversation. "Elena said you were upset because Guy's been bothering you. She said…"

"Elena's said too much already…" I stopped myself. "Sorry, go on."

"I thought he was OK when I met him – thought he could be a buddy, you know?" He gave me a quick glance. "Look, if I've said anything that's made things difficult for you, then I'm sorry, OK? I'm really, really sorry."

"Why – what have you said?" We came to a standstill halfway across the iron-hard square of ground that made up the quad, still dead brown, not green, despite the watering. He took his time answering, so I risked looking at him. "What have you said, Sam?"

He scuffed at a patch of dry turf with his heel, avoiding me. "Stuff I shouldn't – about you. Yeah, you probably gathered that." That came as a relief; it must have shown because he went on, "And about Ly… Matthew. Sure, I know I shouldn't have, but you know I was jealous, right? OK?" He crammed his hands in his pockets in his familiar defensive gesture. "It's no excuse, but I was off my head, annihilated, butt-toast…"

"You thought Guy was a friend. He got you drunk. You talked. It's what he does, Sam, forget it."

We started walking again. Most of the delegates had gathered in the main reception room for drinks before dinner. Guy would be there, waiting, watching. Sam came to a sudden halt, curiosity replacing his painful remorse. "Em, you remember that picnic we went on? Yeah, sure you do. You mentioned something about a "sleeping dog". You said you'd been bitten – once bitten, twice shy, you said – and when I asked you what happened, you said, 'What happens to all dogs that bite – he was muzzled.'" Laughter flew from the windows, not a pleasant sound, but one fuelled by alcohol and ego and heat. "The dog – that was Guy you were referring to, wasn't it?"

I raised my face to the sky, seeking some sign of a breeze to cool my flaming skin, but found none. "Yes," I said eventually, "that was Guy."

"And now he's back to bite you?"

I checked to see if he mocked me – enjoying my torment, revelling in revenge – but he wasn't. If anything he looked genuinely concerned.

"Yes, Sam; he's back to bite me." Across the quad, a viperous *hisss* announced the evening watering. Welcome cool drops sprayed my bare arms and raised musty humours from the ground, but we stepped out of range and back into the fetid air. The dinner gong sounded. "I've got to go. Thanks for... well, you know, just thanks."

For the first time since that day of the picnic on the shores of the lake, he smiled with uncompromising warmth. "Sure, Em – you too." I watched him as he started to walk the way we had come, the irrepressible Sam I remembered from our first meeting evident in his buoyant step. As I made my way towards the open door, I heard him call, "Hey, Em, you know what we do with mad dogs in the States?" I turned, and he raised two fingers in imitation of a gun. "We shoot 'em." He fired off a couple of shots through the open window into the body of the crowded room. "Yes'm, dead dogs don't bite."

I waited in a corner of the outer hall until I could be certain to avoid Shotter and Guy, and then slipped in among a group of Swedish delegates as they made their way to the great hall. Just like at the All Saints' dinner, the Dean displayed the college's sumptuous wealth on each of the three long tables, and the room droned with the visitors' approbation. Even though I knew Staahl couldn't hurt me any more, sweat chilled on my skin at the memory of that night, but Eckhart saw me and ushered me towards a place at the table from where I played host to the people around me. Guy sat next to Shotter at the far end where Matthew had once been, and now and again they exchanged comments and Guy's eyes would challenge mine.

It helped playing a lie and I found myself grateful for it. The great hall lacked air conditioning and my skin crawled with heat, my tights constricting stickily, perspiration gathering beneath my collar and at the base of my spine. By the end of the meal I had eaten next to nothing, leaving my temper raw and exposed. My clothes hung limply, but inside a slow fire smouldered, ready to erupt. Like the clashing colours of canvas chairs on a beach, the voices of the people around me were strident and abusive, vying to be noticed in the choking smog that permeated the soul of the room.

By ten to ten we rose from the table and I could escape the cloying tincture of coffee grounds lingering in empty demitasses, but there was nothing I could do to avoid the brooding dread of the impending confrontation that had dogged me all day.

"Professor, before you go..." Eckhart scurried up. I was

surprised he was still speaking to me, but he had been impressed by my students and had been overheard saying as much to Shotter. What the Dean said in reply I hadn't been told. Beyond Eckhart, I caught sight of Guy, no doubt charming the pants off the small group of women gathered around him, not because he wanted to, but because he could. He raised his eyes to me. I looked away.

Eckhart swayed a little, his tie stained and his glasses awry, but the moderate consumption of alcohol had rendered his speech fluent and his gaze direct.

"Professor, there has been a slight change to tomorrow's scheduled guest speaker. Professor Pornelli has withdrawn his paper at the last minute, very inconvenient – he didn't say why – but it seems we have an admirable substitute. Indeed we are honoured to…"

"Let me guess," I interrupted. "Dr Hilliard has stepped into the breach. How fortuitous."

Colin Eckhart pushed his glasses onto the bridge of his nose, looking like Mole. "H… how did you know?"

"Because she's a little witch," Guy broke in, raising the glass he still carried in silent salutation, which I answered with a hostile glare.

Eckhart beamed. "Excellent, excellent. How appropriate for the conference. Witch – very good, most humorous. And we know what happens to witches, don't we?" he guffawed in his good-natured way, his glasses slipping down his sweaty nose again.

Guy's eyes flickered over my face, his mouth barely moving as he breathed out, "They burn."

Eckhart chortled. "Quite so, quite so. We have much to celebrate. Yes, yes – such a success. Care to join me for a drink, Dr Hilliard? You too, Professor?"

I was too angry to answer. Guy ran a finger around his collar, finding the knot of his tie and loosening it. Releasing the top button, he revealed a dark, mouth-shaped smudge against his olive skin, which he stroked with a finger – a deliberate movement even Colin couldn't fail to see.

"Dr D'Eresby – or is it Mrs Lynes now? – and I are otherwise engaged this evening, Eckhart. Give me a lift back to your place, Emma?"

Colin had not drunk so much that he missed the innuendo, or perhaps because of the wine the full implication of what Guy said revealed itself in all its tainted glory. He stammered out his confusion, but I was beyond caring because, as far as I was concerned, it was just Guy and me now. Him and me.

"Get yourself a bloody taxi," I flung at him, and left him to do just that.

It was past eleven when I finally arrived home. The house sat in darkness bar the single light in the hall. Guy's taxi drew up at the front minutes later. He told it to wait and, slinging the strap of his case over one arm, followed me through the hall to the study.

"No husband waiting for you? I'm surprised he's left you all alone in a big house like this. One could never tell what he might come home to."

I declined to answer. Soft yellow light washed the room as I switched on the desk lamps, comforting and so at odds with how I felt. I had spent all day working out what I would say to him – all day – but it came down to this: "Why didn't you tell me you knew Grandpa?"

Guy looked around for somewhere to sit, pushing several things to one side on Matthew's desk and, in perching, took possession of it. I chewed my cheek.

"Doug? Still harping on about him after all these years? I

often used to wonder what lay behind your infatuation with him; it was quite infantile. You know, his obsession with you was unhealthy..."

I restrained my temper – just. "Answer the question."

After a brief pause during which, stony-faced, I returned his gaze, he shifted off the desk, casting a hand in the direction of the books. "He would have liked all this. He liked poking around minutiae, meddling in the infinitesimal. Meddling – it's what he did best," his lip curled, "old *Doug*. How did you find out?"

"His diaries."

"Of course, his bloody diaries – always going on about the importance of keeping notes like a damn antiquarian. 'My journals' he used to call them. Journals." He paused as if expecting me to react, but went on when I didn't. "I thought they'd been destroyed a long time ago. I was surprised you never mentioned them when we met at Cambridge, and then I realized you didn't know." He threw his head back and laughed. "That was a gift."

I still grappled with the fundamental question he seemed reluctant to answer. "Why didn't you tell me you knew him, Guy – that we had already met?"

He whipped round and I stumbled back, caught off-guard by his sudden irritation. "Because I didn't want you to *know*!" With a spiteful finger, he tapped his head. "Haven't you worked it out yet? Didn't your grandfather spell it out in his journals for you? Do you really believe that it was all a coincidence? Why do you think you were accepted into one of the best colleges in Cambridge? Why do you think you got onto my course when there were dozens of spotty little undergrads fighting for a place? You didn't even have all the basic entrance requirements – you're functionally innumerate, for Pete's sake. They wouldn't have given you a second glance if it weren't for me."

I must have looked like a drowning fish as he tugged his tie from around his neck while he waited for his words to sink in. "Yo… you gave me preferential treatment?"

He folded his tie into fifths, dragging out the moment. "What do you think?"

Blood rushed back to my face. "I earned my place. I worked my guts out to get there…"

His lip curled in a derisory leer. "You thought it would be handed to you on a plate."

He had hooked me, and now he played me out on the line. I fought back, but the rising note in my voice was the sound of desperation and he knew it; he relished it.

"I didn't! You know I didn't. I didn't expect anything other than what I'd earned. If you really thought that, you wouldn't have accepted me on your course, Guy – not you – you despise nepotism as much as I do. You didn't make it easy for me – I earned it."

He leaned forwards over the back of the chair. "I made sure there were no obstacles. Straight firsts – no seconds for you."

"I earned it!"

"On your back."

"What?"

He tucked the tie into his top pocket, the gold silk protruding like a head above a parapet. "You heard me. You were a willing little lay out to buy herself a degree. You earned it all right." My head spun. This was all wrong. I concentrated on controlling my breathing and let my head clear. Something wasn't right about the air around him; his words and emotions didn't rhyme. I had paid too much credence to the words and not enough to what lay behind them.

"And you were willing to be bought by sex, Guy? I don't think so." There, I saw it again, that distinct flash of colour, but too quick for me to determine its complexion. "Why did you want me on your course if I didn't deserve to be there?"

A salacious rise to his mouth, but he avoided answering the question. Instead, he pulled a volume from the bookshelves, opened it to the frontispiece, checked the date, and put it back. Hands on hips, he scanned the spines of the adjacent books as if looking for something. "You know, Doug cried the day you won the scholarship at school. He was so proud of you it was pathetic."

Disregarding the jibe, it nonetheless struck me as odd that he thought it significant enough a memory to be commented on. "You remember that?"

"Why shouldn't I?" More to the point, why should he? I detected more to his sniping than his desire to get a rise from me; more, even, than a long-harboured resentment of my rejection. Unravelling Guy was worse than the Gordian knot. I tried pulling another loose end.

"Grandpa called you 'Vir' in his diaries."

"Vir," he spat. "His hero, he called me. I was come to save the day. I would take up his banner and seek the Holy Grail of Knowledge. I was his heir presumptive until..." The air became suffused in green rancour, a bitter bile he could neither control nor hide.

"You were *jealous* of me? But I was only a child, his granddaughter, Guy. What did you expect? Of course he loved me."

"It was more than filial affection; he doted on you – he invested in you – he gave you the key..."

His eyes narrowed to slits as my head snapped up. "You know what I'm talking about, don't you? You heard him mention it." He took a step towards me. "Did he tell you what it was?" His eyes became greedy, a look I had seen so many times when knowledge was tantalizingly within reach. But he didn't *know*. Guy didn't know what – or who – the key was. A slight speckled moth with wings of ermine danced desperately against the lampshade, going nowhere. I undid the window and lifted the sash.

"If he'd wanted you to know, he'd have told you," I prevaricated, cupping the moth in my hands. "He didn't trust you, Guy. It wasn't just me; you did something and he saw you for what you really are. What did you do?"

He barked a laugh. "He wrote about it, did he? Stupid old fool."

"He said that the offer was withdrawn. What offer? Why?" Moth wings beat against the cage of my hands. I offered it the freedom of the open window, but it flew back in, drawn irresistibly to the light.

"Your grandfather promised me his position when he retired; it was mine by rights. I'd worked damn hard to get where I was. I worked all the vacations, weekends. He used me like a dog on his pedantic project, throwing me the bones to chew, but never the whole bloody joint. He never trusted me enough to tell me what he was looking for; he never *trusted* me."

"You haven't answered the question."

"No, I haven't." He wiped sweat from his top lip. "It makes no difference now, so you might as well know – he made sure I wasn't given his post when he retired, vindictive bugger. It went to Stevenson, much good it did him." Stevenson: a vague memory of a floridly jovial man in a loud checked tweed jacket and long side whiskers the colour of dying grass. A relic of an older age when eccentricity in an academic was tolerated.

"I remember him; he was always kind to me. He died not long after Grandpa." I shook my head. "My grandfather wasn't vindictive; he must have had his reasons. You gave him a reason not to trust you, Guy."

He took off his jacket and threw it over Matthew's desk, knocking several items like bowling pins. "The old sod found out I'd been having it off with Emerson's wife. Didn't think it was the done thing, thought that sort of behaviour was not the conduct of a gentleman." His mouth twisted. "What century did he think we were living in? What did he think the gentry had been doing for the last effing knows how long?" He stabbed a finger in my direction. "What right did he have to say I wasn't a gentleman? My family owned half of the Loire valley…"

"He wasn't referring to your class, Guy, only to your behaviour." So, this is what it was all about: thwarted ambition and being jealous of a child. How pitiable. I could think of nothing to be afraid of here, nothing at all. I laughed and then found I couldn't stop. I covered my face with my hands, and sobbed out long peals of relief until my chest hurt.

"What do you think you're laughing at, you little…" He grabbed the tops of my arms, but I didn't care. He shook me roughly, his fingers bruising, and I saw spite in the way he lowered his head until his mouth came close to mine. I flinched back but he held me rigid.

"I screwed you like a whore because you were his little Pipkin. I screwed you like he screwed me for his quaint ideas of chivalry and honour. You were on my course so that I could screw you. My only regret is that he's not here to know what it is I've done to you, and what I'm about to do." My eyes widened in fright. "No," he said slowly, "that wasn't what I had in mind. Ellie's a lively little thing, thighs like a vice, stronger than she looks, but if you're offering…"

I finally managed to wrench myself free. "What do you want?"

He scratched at premature stubble with his thumbnail, eyeing me. "You ruined my marriage. You ruined my career. What do you think you can do to make up for that? No, nothing? Can't think of anything? Well, I'll tell you, shall I? I'll have your job, for a start..."

"You can't!"

A thin smile slid over his face. "Can't I? I already have. The good Dean offered me the contract today. Seems he wasn't happy to discover that your qualifications are not quite what you led him to believe. Falsification of official documents is considered a very serious offence in the States – as it is in Britain. I think you'll find the authorities in Cambridge are looking into several claims that you obtained your degree in less than... savoury circumstances..."

"You... you bas...!"

He didn't let me finish. "I wonder what your friends and family – especially your father – will think of that?"

"They won't believe you. They know I wouldn't do anything like that, and I have all the documentation to verify my degrees."

He shrugged in the knowledge he had me over a barrel. "But you will be suspended until a full investigation is carried out and, whatever the outcome, mud sticks, as you well know. Remember the trial? A little poison in a receptive ear... oh, come on, Emma; did you really think I would forgive and forget?"

"How do you know about the trial?"

"I was always good at getting information. I have contacts." Fleetingly, the moth distracted him, dancing unsteadily in the whorl of air his hand created as he flapped it away. "Now, where were we? Ah yes, your career. You don't seem as upset as you should be; perhaps you don't need job security as much as you once did? You're well set up here..."

"You want *money*?"

"I'm marrying money. The little cash cow will provide me with everything I need. Keep up, Emma."

"You're already married!"

"And?"

"And you used to believe it was wrong to divorce. What happened to 'I can't get a divorce; it's a sin, Emma'?"

"*You* happened." With a swipe he caught the moth and crushed it in his hand. "Or perhaps I never believed it in the first place. Whatever." Dispassionately, he inspected the remains and brushed the frail carcass to the floor. "Anyway, Ellie's young, rich, and a good lay. She'll see me through to my old age. Which is more than I could say of your marriage. Now, you have a couple of choices: either you can '*fess up*, I think the Yanks say, spill the beans, come clean – you get the drift – and resign your position here and in Cambridge without a fuss, and I'll marry Ellie and we'll all live as one big, happy family, or..." He paused, raised his head, and looked me dead in the eye.

"Or what?"

His voice ached with threat. "... or I'll expose your husband for the fraud he is."

He must have seen the fissure rip through the surface of my control. I turned my back and stared sightlessly through the window into the solid night. Like an apparition in the gloss-black reflection of the glass, he hovered close behind me.

"Aren't you going to ask me how I know?"

Dead, devoid of emotion, I asked, "How do you know, Guy?"

"It was something your grandfather said a long time ago when researching the Lynes family in Martinsthorpe. Never told me why, but he had a real bee in his bonnet about it – was on to something – he must have told you?" He was fishing again. This time I wouldn't take the bait. "No? Well, he was a secretive old bugger. Anyway, he'd had one too many..."

"Grandpa didn't drink," I said flatly.

"He did that night. With encouragement. 'Vir, my boy' – how I hated his sentimental tags – 'Vir, my boy, the Lynes are not all that they seem.' I asked him what he meant, but he wouldn't tell me, and he never mentioned it again. I think he forgot he'd told me, but I don't forget – I *never* forget. I found the monument to William Lynes – did he mention that in his diaries? I found it and he dismissed it as nothing, of 'no importance', he said. But the way he said it I knew there must be something significant about it." His breathing quickened, his eyes reflecting sharp interest, a rare excitement. "I did my own research but came up blank. I lost interest for a while, but never forgot. And then I heard about your little escapade in the States – caused quite a stir for all of a minute in the department at home apparently – we don't get many academics being attacked as colourfully as you were. I had to find out of course and tried to get in contact, but your father wouldn't let me speak to you. Getting on a bit, isn't he? And then there was the trial, and the publicity, and the name – *Lynes*." He dragged out the final "s" in a sibilance. "That kept eating away at me so I did a bit of digging of my own." He moved closer, raising the hairs on the back of my neck. "There was a time when the thought of a riddle would have turned you on. Do you know what the answer is yet? Am I boring you? Shall I stop or carry on?"

My answer came automatically. "Don't stop."

"No, well I wasn't going to. This is making me horny – fancy a quickie?"

I closed my eyes in disgust, clamping my mouth shut against the flow of vitriol that wanted to burst out and consume him like a mouth, like flame – a cleansing fire. Steel through flesh.

My eyes snapped open and I saw my reflection, grimly determined.

He hadn't noticed. "Never mind. Ellie's a game girl; I'll give her one later on. What's the matter? Too vulgar for your refined sensibilities? What does your poor sap of a husband have to do to get his?"

"Get to the point, Guy – if you have one."

Customary irritation broached the surface. "You always were so bloody impatient." He turned away and picked up something from my desk. When he spoke again, he had regained control. "The Lynes of Rutland were supposed to have died out with the heir – Matthew – although I could find no record of his death. Matthew Lynes – now that is quite a coincidence, isn't it? 'But surely,' I hear you say, 'there are lots of Lynes,' and of course you would be right. It's a relatively common name – not as rare as D'Eresby, for example – but enough to make it traceable. I must admit that my original plan was to put a spanner in your works – vengeance is sweet, they say, and I'm certainly enjoying mine." He moved slightly, and I stiffened as the glint of metal confirmed he held the photograph of our wedding. He flicked the silver frame with his nail. "The Lynes connection might have been nothing more than a passing interest until, that is, I went to visit the old lady. Deplorable state she was in. She'd been quite a lively old bird when I last saw her with your grandfather. Doug was always very protective of her. She was full of stories, but he wouldn't let her share them with me." His shoulders hunched and a sour note crept into his voice. "Now that was a mistake." He replaced the photograph. "She was as sweet as pie when I went to see her this time. Lonely old girl, doesn't get many visitors, likes a good chat."

I circled around in dismay. "What did you do to her?"

He snorted. "What do you think I would do to a decrepit old woman? I'm not a monster; I wouldn't leave my mother to rot like her son does. I'd at least put her in a home, for Pete's sake. I let her talk – that's all I did – talk. And she did. She told me all about your visit – you and your fiancé – and she told me that he's a descendent of the Lynes of Martinsthorpe – the most handsome man she'd ever laid eyes on, as if he'd stepped out of history – 'out of the window,' she said. When I told her that the family had died out, she said, 'I don't believe in reincarnation.' I thought she had lost it then, but it was worth looking into, given your grandfather's obsession."

He waited for my response. He wanted me to ask him what he knew – his game, his rules – but I wasn't ready to give in, not yet, not on his terms.

"So what if Matthew's descended from an English family? You're wasting my time with trivia."

The clear bell of the clock made his answer all the more sinister.

"But Ellie doesn't know, does she? More to the point, Matthew's father doesn't know. I find that very strange and I've been racking my brains over why a son wouldn't want his father to know something as basic as where he comes from. Don't you find that odd? Doesn't that set up an itch that's desperate to be scratched? Come on, Emma, don't tell me you haven't asked yourself the same question, or has marriage to a dull doctor tamed your intellect?"

The airless room had become rank. I lifted the window higher, breathing the saturated night air until I couldn't tell whether my skin was wet with moisture or fear-induced sweat. "Matthew doesn't know…"

I balked as he ejected contempt like vomit. "Who the hell do you think you're talking to? I'm not some amateur here. Of course he knows; there's a picture of New Hall above the mantelpiece – the one the old girl had me bring here like an errand boy. He has an exact recreation of a seventeenth-century dining hall, a sword that belonged to the Lynes family, and he wears a ring with the Lynes coat of arms on it. Or hadn't you noticed?" Interrogating my reflection, he demanded, "What's the story, Emma – you know, don't you?"

"You said you would reveal him as a fraud, Guy. There's nothing in what you've said that could be deemed fraudulent."

"So it won't matter when I tell Henry his son's been keeping family secrets then? You obviously have no respect for your father-in-law, so I will see it as my duty to inform him…"

"Go ahead."

"You're a cool little vixen. Perhaps the family won't mind that Matthew's not what he seems, but I think the authorities might… Ah, I thought that would get your attention. Having your welfare in mind, I decided to look into your husband's credentials, and then I found that he didn't have any – or that he does – a list as long as your arm, but they don't add up. Quite literally. Like his esteemed relative's grave, the dates don't match. What's more, he seems to have appeared from nowhere: no date of birth, no state records. Ellie couldn't tell me where he was born – although she can give me precise dates, times, and locations for the rest of her family. Then she clammed up. That means only one thing…" He hung back to let the gravity of the situation sink in, but he didn't need to; I was already there, wallowing in the mire at the bottom of a deep, dark lake, drowning. "… your husband's a fake, he's phony, he's a sham. So, who is he?"

My nail snapped as I gripped the windowsill, ripples of fear flowing up my arms and choking the hope out of me. I could see no possible solution but an inevitable death. Without answering, I wheeled around and pushed past him as I left the room.

The dining room was unlit. I didn't switch on the sidelights but used the glow from the hall to find my way to the fireplace. I didn't think. I didn't need to think. I acted as anyone would to protect what was most dear to them.

The scabbard slipped seamlessly from the iced blade, the sword perfectly balanced. I turned swiftly and found my way blocked. I opened my mouth to scream but a hand clamped over it, stifling all sound.

"Shh, quiet, it's me." Matthew removed his hand and put a finger to his lips, his eyes gleaming fire on blue. Moving silently, he closed the door to the hall before returning to me. "I'll take that." He prised my fingers from the grip and laid the rapier on the table. It rocked once, then lay still.

"He knows too much! I'm going to kill him." I reached again for the sword, but he blocked me.

"No – you're not."

"You don't understand," I said, my voice hoarse with suppressed rage and desperation. "He knows too much. He's not leaving; he wants to expose you as a fraud. He won't give up until he's done whatever he can to hurt you – to hurt me. He's never forgiven me; he's never forgiven Grandpa. He'll do anything he can – anything… he's got to die. I want to *kill him*."

"I know. I heard what he said. He has no proof. He has enough to make things very difficult for us, but no proof – not yet. You're not going to kill him, Emma."

I couldn't understand how he could be so calm when his existence lay within a breath of exposure, when the solution appeared so clear, when the answer to this knot was… Alexandrian.

"Matthew, I have no choice…"

"Yes, we do." That quietude, when he said everything in nothing. An anguished gasp escaped my lips as the veil of anger that blinded me slipped. I grabbed his arm as he moved to take the sword. "No, not you, I won't let you kill him. He's my responsibility, I brought him here."

He picked up the sword and in that moment I saw midnight resignation where before there had been light. "Emma, my love…"

"No! Matthew, no!" I tried to drag his hand from the sword. "I won't let you do this to yourself!"

In the thin light from beneath the door, the fine blade shone, newly honed, as he rotated it slowly, his intention clear as he followed the line of the rapier to its point. "Have you ever seen a sword cut flesh? Seen muscle pared from bone? Bone splintered by blade? Have you spent each night with the faces of the men you've killed pressed against your own, and carried their image through your waking day? Have you heard, in the depths of the night, their dark despair and added to their cries your own? I have, Emma; I do. My soul is heavy with their blood, and their fear. Once you have taken that step you can never go back; their death is your responsibility forever." He drew a hand slowly over his face and then pierced me with a blazing look from which I shrank. "You will not give up your innocence to save me. I lost mine a long time ago." He shook me free and, aligning the sword, took a step towards the door.

Channelling panic and without thinking, I balled my fist and hit him in the small of his back as hard as I could. He grunted as I suppressed a yelp of pain.

"What in Heaven's name did you do that for?" He dropped the sword and reached out to me. "Your hand, Emma, let me see it."

Clasping my jarred limb against my chest, I hissed through my clenched teeth, "Get off! I don't want you near me. I don't want a *killer* touching me." It hurt like blazes, but it had worked – he felt my pain.

Exasperated, he shook his head as cold intent left him. "All right, you've made your point, you win. He lives – for now. Let me see your hand." He felt the fine bones, and along each finger. "It's not broken, just bruised. I'd have thought you'd have learned not to hit me by now." He covered it with his own, drawing out the discomfort.

I didn't give a jot about my hand; the immediate problem had yet to be resolved. "What do we do, Matthew? We can't wait."

"No, we can't, but we need to buy some time. Can you stall him, do you think?"

"He's supposed to be giving a presentation tomorrow at the conference. He won't give up a chance to be centre stage, not if he thinks he has me cornered. He'll be in no rush to play his hand, but we have until tomorrow noon. That's all."

"Tomorrow." He went quiet for some seconds as he thought. "Then tomorrow will have to do. Buy me some time, Emma."

"You won't kill him?"

I'd grown accustomed to the dim light in the room enough for me to make out the unyielding set of his mouth. "It'll be dawn in a few hours; just buy me some time."

The front door swung ajar. Tail lights and the acrid smell of fumes were the only evidence that remained of the retreating taxi. I ran to the study; it was empty.

"He's gone!" I cried, nearly colliding with Matthew as he saw for himself. He swore under his breath.

"Wait here!"

"Where are you going?"

"Wait until I get back; don't move." He left before I could insist on an answer. Moments later, the sound of his car speeding down the drive filled the room. Then silence, and nothing more than the ticking of the clock, the passing of time.

CHAPTER

30

A Matter of Time

It must have been later than I thought. Dawn crept through sheets of cloud pressing in on all sides as it smothered life from the dry land. It would be hotter than the day before.

The clock claimed five. Six. I showered and changed, but Matthew still hadn't returned. The initial shock abated, leaving me as arid as the earth. I had eaten and drunk little since the day before and, after a night without sleep when my whole world seemed on the brink of collapse, I began to tremble, and then to shake.

Low blood sugar. I reached into my desk drawer for chocolate and only then noticed something missing: the forbidden photograph of our wedding.

I checked the drawers, the floor, and then Matthew's desk, and saw the empty space where something once stood. It was gone. The tiny photograph in a new silver frame of him with Ellen on their wedding day – the one he had always kept in his wallet, the one I insisted he keep now because it represented part of his life and an element of him he shouldn't forget – was gone. He'd put it away? I wrenched open the drawers one by one. I slid the chair away from the desk. I checked under the cushion. Nothing.

Primary evidence.

I didn't hesitate. I grabbed the keys from the hall table and ran to my car.

The day choked. The yellow haze from the previous evening had thickened into a suffocating membrane between earth and sky through which I drove, tearing the heart from the engine. The campus was stirring, but not yet awake.

"Ma'am!" I almost ran into the security guard as he blocked my path. "Professor D'Eresby, ma'am!"

I had seen him around; I didn't know his name but he seemed to know mine. "What is it? I'm in a hurry."

"I'm sorry, ma'am, I can't let you on campus – the Dean's orders."

"What do you mean? I work here."

"Yes, ma'am, but the Dean has told me to accompany you from the premises. I'm sorry."

So soon.

I dodged past him. "I'll be back in a minute." The path rang hard under my feet, the air heavy in my lungs. His shouts faded as the distance grew and the library came into view, rising like thunder.

Sanctuary.

A pause to catch my breath, then I ran to the lifts and sank down through the heart of the building to the secure door. The numbers. The code. The key. "Come on, come on!" and the swift sweet air escaping as the door released. I halted in front of the racks and my heart stopped with me. The box hadn't moved, but the paper had gone. On the floor by the toe of my shoe lay a tiny white scrap, invalidated by its position. Checking the box became mere formality: where the journal had once lain was now a brazen void.

"*No!*" The empty room echoed. Why did I leave it to chance? Whatever I had done, Matthew didn't deserve this. Shoving myself from the racks, I forced leaden legs to move towards the door.

The guard waited by the main entrance to the library looking sweaty. "Professor…"

"It's OK, I'm leaving. You can tell the Dean I won't bother him any more."

Guy had the journal.

I was fairly sure that last night he had had nothing more than fragments of evidence against Matthew, too disparate to draw any real conclusion, but today he possessed the journal and it would be only a matter of time before he read it. And he had the photographs.

Time. A matter of time. My watch said seven-twenty. Guy would be in his hotel in town. I could make it there before he left. I could get there and confront him and retrieve the journal and the photographs before… before what? Who was I kidding? Could I really stroll in there and ask him for them? *Hey, Guy, you seem to have some items that don't belong to you. Please may I have them back?* He would smell a rat even if he hadn't done so last night. And where there were rats, there would be sewage, and Guy had always been good at sniffing it out.

What then? I couldn't kill him; the moment of blind fury had passed and that only left desperation. But desperation wasn't enough to fuel murder – because that is what it would be. Matthew knew what it would do to me, how it would corrupt and eat away at me until I could no longer look at myself and I would turn away from all that I loved, and be lost. That he had been willing to do so haunted every minute that had since passed. What was more, I had no idea where he was now.

I used the back roads to avoid the worst of the morning traffic over the main bridge into town. Even at this early hour, heat rose in torrid waves from the mirrored surface until mirage merged with memory and I drove on silvered glass. I'd driven through this part of town only a couple of times before, but faintly recalled where I could find Guy's hotel.

Except for the odd suited executive, the modern foyer was all but empty.

"Dr Hilliard," I said to the reception clerk in a voice that meant business.

"Is he expecting you, ma'am?"

I considered lying, then found a better way. "Please tell him Dr Lynes is here."

Guy opened the door, his expression changing from languid anticipation to curious satisfaction when he saw me. The room behind him seemed vacant. No Matthew. "*Dr Lynes*, is it, today? I would say this is a pleasant surprise but I'm short of time. What do you want, Emma?"

"You have something that belongs to me."

"Can't it wait un…"

"No," I blocked.

He shrugged. "In that case, you'd better come in." Leaving the door open for me to follow, he went over to a glass-topped table sitting in front of the window letting in feeble day, and held up a coffee jug. "Want one?" I didn't answer and he poured himself a cup. Next to the tray with the partial remains of breakfast and a knife smeared in butter, lay a pad of paper and a pen, and beside that, the journal. It was open, and he'd used a napkin to mark the page. How far had he read?

"I would offer you breakfast but that might give the staff the wrong idea, and I wouldn't want Ellie thinking I've screwed her aunt – again."

I kept my eyes from drifting towards the journal and

marking my desire, and fixed them on his face. "I want the photographs."

He viewed me speculatively. "I expect you do. Did your husband send you? Didn't have the balls to get them himself, or doesn't he know they're gone?" The insulated coffee jug chinged noisily as he set it down. He picked up the two photographs from where they lay side-by-side as if he had been comparing them. He'd taken them from their frames. I held out my hand.

"You know, I find it curious that you haven't asked me why I took them." He flipped one against his thumb and then squinted at it. "These two men are extraordinarily alike. Ellie said Matthew takes after his grandfather, but they could be the same man. It even looks as if it's the same signet ring. Impossible to tell, I expect, as this picture is so small, and perhaps he inherited it – you never know." He smiled briefly at my frozen expression. "You look shocked, Emma, but you must have seen the similarity yourself. When I first met Matthew, do you know who he reminded me of? Of course you do – your grandfather – it's that signature hair. I'd know it anywhere. It always struck me how similar it was to the young man in the Lynes memorial window at the Old Manor – you know which one I mean, don't you? The one old Joan Seaton said you fainted beneath when you saw it for the first time. That puzzled me. You – *faint*? Reminded you of your grandpa, did it? Or of Matthew?"

He wandered over to the window and seemed to be deliberating. I took the opportunity to inch closer to the table. His edgy scrawl covered the lined pad; he'd been making notes. Dates and names jumped out, sending spirals of jangled alarm. I could take the journal and run. I was smaller than him, but faster, and I had fear at my tail. I could be out of the hotel in less than the time it would take for him to call security. But he stood too close. I opted to bluff it out until I found a clearer way.

"This is all very interesting, Guy, but I never took you for a fantasist, although Grandpa did write something about you…"

He swung round; I'd touched a raw nerve. "What did he say?"

I decided against finishing the sentence. "It doesn't matter; it's all in the past. I'm going to be late. I want my photographs, and I want them *now*."

For a long moment I thought it had worked, but I was a fool to think he'd give up that easily.

"I think I'll hang on to these for a bit – as a memento. Then, perhaps when Ellie and I are settled…" He smiled. "Or perhaps not." He picked up the leather portfolio lying on a nearby chair, slipping them in.

It was now or never. The instant his back was turned I snatched the journal from the table. Too late. His hand slammed down on mine, pinning it against the journal until I let go or risk him breaking my fingers. Picking it up, he held the volume in front of my face like an allegation as I nursed my already bruised hand. "This is what you came for, isn't it? *This* is what it's all about. The damn journal you harked on about as an undergrad." I tried to grab it from him but he lifted it higher. "Your grandfather wouldn't tell me his source material, tight sod, but it was this, wasn't it? He said he'd only a portion of it, that the rest was elsewhere, but he wouldn't tell me – he'd only ever entrust it to his beloved little *Pipkin*." His face contorted, grinding out my pet name like an insult. "Do you know how I knew I would find it here? Because it was the only reason I could see why you'd come to this forsaken pit of a college – for this tedious…" he slapped the fragile book against his hand, "… crap."

"Give it to me, Guy! You'll damage it!"

"You want this? Then you're going to have to do something for me in return."

I let my arm drop, taking a step away from him. "What?"

"What do you think? I said we have unfinished business, Emma."

I always knew him to be self-centred – it gave him the edge in his ruthless pursuit of knowledge – but I had also imagined that somewhere, somehow, there might be a decent core to the man that conscience would one day prick and reveal.

"What about Ellie?"

But I was wrong. He seemed surprised at the mention of her name, as if he had forgotten she existed.

"What about her?"

What remorseless conceit. I could see nothing of the man I had been attracted to as a girl. What I admired turned out to be no more than his single-minded narcissism.

"Not even after what you did to your wife and children did I imagine you could be so callous. I was a fool to think there is any semblance of decency in you. All that talk of forgiveness, Guy, was a smokescreen. I don't understand how I could have been taken in by you so easily. I should have trusted my instincts."

He moved closer until I could smell the soap on his skin and the taint of coffee on his breath. Close, too close, and too physical a presence to ignore.

"Because you saw what you wanted to see. Because you are as ambitious as I am. You're greedy for the truth, Emma; it's what drives you – your lust, your insatiable desire for knowledge – at any cost. We are kindred spirits..."

I turned my face away in disgust. "We are not! *I* am not."

"Then why are you here?"

Why indeed? What did I think I could achieve? He held the journal just out of reach, holding my life in his hand as surely as he held the secret to Matthew's past. He had only to open the diary and read on and the final disparate pieces would be drawn together. In that book lay all the evidence he needed for the fissure to become a fault through which our lives would fall.

"Just give me the journal, Guy – *please*. It's my research; it's what I came for."

"Is it? Are you sure about that?" I recognized the look in his eyes. His voice thickened. "What's it worth, Emma? What are you willing to give in exchange?"

Lumpen distaste lodged in my throat. I shuddered. "I have nothing to give."

His eyes slid over my body. "Oh, I wouldn't say that."

"I'm married and you're engaged to my niece."

He brought the journal within tantalizing reach, and with each breath, I inhaled its age like incense, its secrets bittersweet and lethal, leather-coated suicide.

"I won't tell if you don't."

I hung my head, frantically trying to find a way out but discovering every path barred. He took it as rejection. He didn't appear surprised and only mildly disappointed.

"In that case, if you're not interested you leave me no option." Discarding the napkin, he opened the journal. "Now, where was I? It takes a bit of getting used to even for me. Richardson's style hardly makes for scintillating reading. Ah, yes, late June 1643 and it seems things between the Lynes brothers have become a bit tense, but – what's this? The young master is at hand. I wonder what happens next...?"

"All right," I snapped. "You win."

Game, set, and match. He closed the journal and placed it on the table where my eyes followed it. "With a little more grace, if you would, Emma; you don't sound as if your heart is in it."

I glared at him. "I said, I will sleep with you if you give me the journal. What more do you want?"

"Sleep? I didn't say anything about sleep." A taunt in every movement, he started to unbutton his shirt. My mind racing, I couldn't think straight. His shirt fell open; I looked away. He reached for me. "Well?"

"Later, Guy. After the conference."

He moved closer, close enough to feel the heat of his body. A crack of thunder tore the brooding sky. "No, Emma – *now*."

Eking out time, I slowly started to undo the buttons on my blouse. His eyes pursued the stumbling movements of my fingers and his breathing shortened. He used to relish this moment, when fabric fell from my body revealing golden skin, but each time had been a new violation, hoping that one day it would feel like love.

Guy moistened his lips. "You never know, you might even enjoy it like old times, perhaps."

Like old times? Sex with Guy had been like cardboard – flat, grey, and dry. It was all I had known until I encountered Matthew's passionate tenderness and understood what had been missing. Had Guy's ego been so inflated he never realized? His shirt came off and he started to unbuckle his belt. Nausea rose in my gullet.

"I have to go to the bathroom."

"Don't be long," he called after me. "We have to go soon. I don't want to miss my lecture."

A single window let thuggish light into the small bathroom. Outside it began to rain – thick and engorged with heat. There was no wind, and humidity bloated the space between each drop. I was buying time, but for what? Postponing the inevitable? Did he honestly believe that I could want sex with him? After all that had passed between us, could he be so delusional? He had said last night that he seduced me in vengeance, but I felt certain it wasn't the whole truth. I closed my eyes and forced myself back in time, remembering his face and the wretched despair in his eyes as he lay in the hospital bed following his suicide attempt. He had said many things last night, and I believed he thought they were true, but time and bitterness had warped his perspective and I remembered otherwise. That might be so, but of what use was it to me now?

The extractor fan whirred overhead and I ran a basin of cold water as I tried to get things straight in my mind, but water could not alleviate lack of sleep. He couldn't possibly find me desirable in this state, but what had desire to do with power and control? Sex with him would be a betrayal of my marriage and all that had come between us in the first place, and I had no intention of giving him what he wanted. He would make it public knowledge because he could, and I doubted he would relinquish the journal, for the simple reason that I wanted it so much. There had to be another way.

Buy me time, Matthew had said. I found my mobile in my handbag and, smothering its telltale voice, switched it on. The text took only moments to send.

"You took your time."

I made myself look at him lying still partially clothed on the bed, and dawdled, putting my bag on the glass table, bumping against the breakfast plate and making the knife sing. I reached out to still it, my fingers lingering on its cold blade. Even through the expanse of the window, dull daylight struggled into the room.

"I've been thinking." I sat on the bed closer than he expected, tracking the quilted lines on the bedspread within inches of his thigh. "After the conference we could leave, go away – together."

He hadn't expected that. "What about your husband?" he asked guardedly. Moving closer, I pulled a pillow towards me.

It felt cool against my hot skin. I leant on one elbow, letting my hair unfurl and lie in copper scrolls against the rich green fabric of the quilt. He reached out and touched it. I had his full attention.

"I've got what I want out of him. If I divorce him, I'll have all the money we need. He's loaded."

Threading his hand through my hair, his frown gave way to a mystified smile. "You little witch – you do intrigue me. I didn't think you had it in you. What's changed your mind?"

I ran my tongue over dry lips. "You reminded me of what it used to be like between us."

Tugging my head back, he exposed my throat to his mouth, slipping his other hand down my blouse. "You'd better show me."

Pulling away, I gritted my teeth and formed a smile. "Later. We don't have time now."

He pushed me back onto the bed. "I'll take something on account as a token of your... intent. It won't take long."

I fought the urge to leap up and run as his mouth crushed against my neck, his free hand yanking my clothing from my hips, roughly nudging my legs apart with his knee to leave marks on the soft skin of my thighs, like accusations. I thrust a hand beneath the pillow and felt the slippery steel of the butter knife hidden there. Blunt, it would still do the job driven beneath the armour of his ribcage and into his heart.

Self-defence.

Curling my fingers securely around the handle, I began to draw it out, but the shrill summons of the mobile sliced the air. I released the knife. He grunted.

"It's my mobile," I said, needlessly.

"Shut the effing thing up; I can't concentrate."

He rolled off me and I went to retrieve it from my bag. "Hello?"

"Don't answer the bloody thing!"

I partially covered the phone. "Shh, it's Elena. Hi... what's up?" Guy made to get off the bed and take the mobile from me, but I waved him back with a frown. "No, I'm at the hotel with Guy. Yes, that's the one – in the centre of town. Elena, I can't explain, but I'm leaving with him. Yes, you heard me – I'm leaving now. He's got what it takes to make me happy, and I can't go on living a lie." I listened for a moment, biting the nail of my thumb. "What do you mean? He's coming here? Blast... no, I'll go to college first, he won't expect that – pick up some things and get out of here. I'll leave my phone on; call me if you hear anything." Grabbing my blouse from the bed, I hurriedly began dressing.

Guy sat up. "What are you doing?"

"It's Matthew – he's guessed where I am and he's on his way here now."

"You can tell him you're leaving him for me..."

"No!" I shouted in his face so that he flinched back. "You don't understand. He gets really jealous and he'll kill you if he thinks I'm leaving with you. He's a crack shot with a gun and he's always suspected I never got over you. Hurry up and get dressed. He can't touch us at college; he wouldn't dare with everyone else there." Stuffing my feet in my shoes, I crammed the journal into its bag. "Come on, Guy! We've got to get out of here!" Using my movements to cover the sound, I ripped the used pages out of the notepad when his back was turned. I shoved the blank pad into the portfolio and then thrust it into his hands.

I didn't have a plan as such; I was just buying time.

Purple tumescent clouds disgorged a steady rain, becoming torrents as we left town in my car, windscreen wipers in a futile battle against the storm. Guy vetted every passing vehicle through distorted glass. "Is that his car? What does he drive? You can't possibly see in this."

"I can see enough." Headlights barely visible through the rain, I nonetheless kept up a steady pace, water parting in sheets on the deserted highway. Occasional lights reflected in my rearview mirror, and once I thought I saw a low red car close behind, only to look hard and find it gone.

White-knuckled, Guy clung to the portfolio on his knees, body braced against sudden turns in direction. "You're driving too fast, slow down – I want to get there in one piece." Blue flashing lights pierced the gloom in front of us. "For Pete's sake, slow down!" He lurched forwards as I brought the car to a sudden stop, the highway blocked by a single police car. Already drenched despite waterproofs, the patrolman leaned forward to shout through my window over the hissing rain. Water cascaded off every angle of him and he used a hand to shield his eyes.

"Road's closed, ma'am. There's no way through here; the bridge is close to going under. Turn back."

"I need to get to Howard's Lake, we're late."

"Road's all closed between here and out of town. Worst storm in a century. It'll not last long, so you'd better go back and wait it out. Be safe now." He tapped the roof in salutation, returning to the shelter of his vehicle.

The car purred expectantly as I worked out what to do next. I couldn't go on; I wouldn't go back. I would have to find another route.

Guy seemed relieved as I circled the car in the middle of the road under the watchful eye of the patrolman, and set off the way we had come. "We can go to another hotel. Your husband won't be able to find us and we should still make it in time for my presentation. We can entertain ourselves until then."

"No, we flippin' well won't," I muttered, taking a sharp right turn. He slipped his hand under my skirt. "Take your hand off me!"

To my surprise, he laughed. "I wondered how long you'd keep up the act. I didn't think you'd be prepared to give up all this..." he indicated the luxurious interior of the car, the rings on my finger, "... for an impoverished academic. But it was worth a punt – I nearly got to screw you."

I seethed at his assumption that I had married Matthew for money. "None of this has anything to do with money."

"No? What is it for then? Love? You would have screwed me for *love*? What has love to do with anything? Love is a delusion. You deluded yourself that your grandfather loved you, that you loved me, but it was all about ambition, wasn't it? His, yours, and this..." He yanked the journal in its bag. "This is what drove him – and you – and this is what will ensure I am remembered as the historian who rewrote history."

He knew.

Rain battered the windscreen, nail-driven drops through my flesh. I forced out words. "How long have you known?"

"For certain? Not until this morning. I had my suspicions of course, but then Richardson filled in the gaps and you – you confirmed them."

The engine screamed as the car skidded on a sheet of water, neatly aquaplaning for a dozen yards before the tyres found the surface again, and I regained control.

"How?"

Beads of sweat gathered on his forehead as he clung to the armrest. "Slow down...!" His words were lost as I cut him dead.

"How did I confirm your suspicions?"

"You turned up."

My heart attempted to keep up with the frenetic beat of the blades. Breathing too fast, too shallow, my head dazzled, and all I could see in my memory was the mutilated wreck of a car and the eyes of a dead woman staring back at me, ermine-faced, crushed, beyond life.

"Emma!"

I came to, yanking the wheel over as a car, blaring its horn in an extended bleat of complaint, narrowly missed us.

"For Pete's sake, are you completely insane? Stop, will you!"

I didn't stop – I had come too far to stop now. Too much had been said, a line crossed. There could be only one way to go, and that was forward, to the end.

We left the main highway and joined a side road. Storm drains had reached their capacity some time ago and water flooded all but the centre of the road. I used the yellow stripe to mark my passage without slowing. In my bid to buy time Guy had revealed his hand as Matthew said he would. Now I needed to find out what he knew and how far he had uncovered the truth before I took it from him and buried it. Devoid of emotion, I said, "Tell me what you know."

He must have been waiting for me to ask. Despite the circumstances, he couldn't resist rubbing my face in it, revelling in his discovery. "Matthew Lynes, born 1609, died – well, he hasn't, has he? A miracle, a phenomenon, a mutant – whatever you want to call your freak, I don't give a toss. You must have thought you had it made when you discovered him. How did you do it – or did your grandfather give you a helping hand? That's why you came out here in the first place. When were you going to reveal it?" I swerved to avoid a rock washed onto the road, and my mobile slid across the dashboard. *It*, not *him* – like an object, like an animal. He reduced Matthew to a convenient meal ticket. Guy enjoyed the moment too much to notice the speedometer creeping up as I steadily increased the pressure on the accelerator.

He continued. "That first day at the conference I thought you'd beaten me to it. Or had you something better planned? Tell me, Emma, does he know why he didn't die, or does he put it down to divine intervention? Do you? Don't tell me you buy all that miracle rubbish now you've found Jesus."

If he stopped, if he just shut up or gave some sign that there might be another way, I could perhaps find an alternative to what he was driving me to do.

"You'll be the laughing stock of every history department, Guy, in every university – globally. Do you really think anybody in their right mind will believe you?"

"Why not? You did. Besides," he stroked the journal, "this makes compelling reading, and the photographs are the icing on the cake, so to speak."

"They prove nothing."

"Keep up, Emma – where have you been? Technology is an amazing thing. You can take two photographs and, using forensic digital analysis, compare facial features that are unique and specific to the individual. They don't even change over time. A hundred per cent accuracy – guaranteed. One photograph taken in... when was Ellie's great-grandmother married – 1936? and the other taken only last month. With digital analysis it will take seconds to confirm they are one and the same man. I've a contact who owes me a favour in the Forensic Investigation Unit who can confirm it..." He broke off at my sudden choked exclamation and gave a self-satisfied smile. "But we both know the outcome, Emma, don't we?"

Yes, I knew the outcome; I knew how one thing would lead to another, how our fragile existence, so solid and everyday, would be blown apart like ash in the wind. "What did you say to them?"

"Now that would be telling." He peered through the rain. "Where are we going? I don't know this route."

"To college via a back road. Nervous?"

He looked at me sharply. "No."

He should be.

Rain-slick clapperboard houses and small commercial units with empty forecourts gave way to trees hugging verges. The road twisted in long curves and blind bends that on any other day I would have approached with caution. But this was no ordinary day, and caution was something I used to observe when I had something to live for. Unnaturally calm as I suppressed the storm raging inside me, my voice was oiled water, waiting for a match. "What do you intend to do with the information?"

He looked at his watch. "In exactly forty-three minutes I will announce to the gathered brotherhood of our discipline something that will blow... their... minds."

No, you won't. Don't make me do this.

"It will destroy Matthew and his family, and I can't let you do that."

"That's their hard bloody lookout; what do you think you can do to stop me?" I didn't respond. He stared at me incredulously. "You don't think you're going to *kill* me? You are out of your mind! You won't kill me – you're too soft. I could stick a gun to your head and you'd help me pull the trigger."

Behind us, a car's headlights momentarily distracted me. And again. I sped up. "I don't think you're capable of understanding me and you never have been because you can't see beyond your own self-interest. You're right – I wouldn't kill you for myself, Guy – but I might do it to protect those I love. I'd do it for Matthew."

The road took on a familiar bend. He rammed his foot against an imaginary brake, swearing viciously. "Slow down!" The silvered planks of the bridge were oil-black with rain, the churning river unrecognizable in its fury. Lights flashed ahead and Guy suddenly shrieked, "Watch out...!"

The ABS system prevented the car from skidding out of control as I packed the brakes, engine roaring. Braking too hard, too late, the driver of the oncoming truck saw us, spinning into our path, spewing the load of metal rods like spillikins across the bridge. Appalled, I watched powerless as the driver battled with his wheel, eyes rolling in terror as the truck slid across the worn planks, ploughing its flank into the low metalwork which split and peeled apart as we slewed to a halt in front of it. There was nowhere we could go. For a fleeting second all was still, and then the air shook as the full impact of the truck hit us, the windscreen collapsing into an opaque mosaic, the airbag exploding in my face, smothering sight and sound for an instant. And then a shudder and the slow scream of metal tearing as the car tilted forward, hanging suspended long enough for me to register what was happening, and then falling, falling into the river below.

My ears were full of rushing, and something crushed my legs to my seat. I took a gulp of air, and then another, blinking water out of my eyes, spitting gritty water from my mouth. Through the gap where the windscreen had been, I could just make out the banks of the river through the rain.

"Guy?" I called, but the sound of the water drowned me out. I couldn't see him; something blocked my line of sight. Water coursed through the car and it rocked and lifted slightly. The current found its weakness, and slowly, the car began to tilt.

"Guy," I yelled, "we've got to get out – it's not stable!" He said something I couldn't make out. "For goodness sake, come on!"

We were wedged against the remains of a tree trunk slung at an angle across a narrow channel, itself lodged against an outcrop of rock in the shadow of the bridge. A heavy branch, thrust through the space where the windscreen had been, held the car temporarily in place and kept us from sinking any further. The river was rising fast, threatening to wash us clear over the barrier. We had minutes before the car lifted free and fell victim to the torrent.

The flaccid remains of the airbag sucked at my hands, and I managed to reach the seatbelt beyond the imprisoning spur, but couldn't undo it. "Guy, you've got to get out; we haven't much time." I tried to slide up but it was no use. "I'm trapped. Get out."

The car jarred violently, pivoting on its spur, and weight lifted from my legs. Now able to shift, I wasn't strong enough to pull myself over the bough. I tried to open my door, but the force of water held it shut. Blurred movement to one side caught my eye, then a voice called out over the violent surge.

"Don't move." Balancing on the only rock still above water, Matthew assessed the car before slipping into the current. He grasped the edge of the chassis with one hand, trying to wrench my door open with the other.

"Matthew! I'm trapped."

"I know, hang on. Turn your head away and cover your eyes." I heard glass shatter and opened them again in time to see the skin of his knuckles heal. Without hesitation he leaned through the driver's window and punched the airbag out of the way. The window gone, water piled through the car, pulling it further down. He put his arm around my waist, supporting me above the water as he fought to free me from the seatbelt tangled around the stump.

"I think Guy's hurt. It happened so quickly. I... I couldn't stop it," I stuttered.

The car lifted and, for a split second, threatened to roll. Matthew braced himself. "Let's get you out of here."

"Help him, please, Matthew..."

He glanced over at the passenger seat, grimaced, and hooked his arm securely around me. "You first; I'll deal with him later. Push with your legs as I lift..." He suddenly gasped, partially loosening his hold as pain flashed across his face.

"What is it? Matthew, tell me!"

Compressing his lips he bore my weight again. "It's nothing. Push." My legs slipping, on the second attempt I wriggled myself free. The car shifted again and Matthew moaned and creased in agony. I cried out, but he straightened. "Hang on to the car; I'm going to lift you onto those rocks." He nodded to a scattering of foam-crested boulders, not yet submerged. "The water's rising fast – I want you out of here."

"What about Guy?"

Now free, I tried to twist around and look at him, but Matthew began to pull me away. "There's nothing I can do for him."

From the other side of the spur, Guy's voice – weak at first, but gathering strength as he spoke – loomed eerily calm, words slurring a little. "It's alll-right Em-ma. You've nothing t'be worri'd about. No witnesses." And he laughed, but it sounded like bubbles. I wrestled free of Matthew and around the spur of wood, fighting the water. Speared like a fish, Guy sat upright. A long rod of steel pierced his chest and pinned him to his seat. Around him the water flowed, a steady stream of his blood staining it red as it ripped away his life.

"Guy!"

Glassy eyed, his forehead creased in a familiar frown. "Don't cry; you... won." He licked at the blood oozing from his mouth. "Last... man... standing." He closed his eyes and I started forward, but he drew breath and coughed, blood coating his mouth and chin. Matthew reached around my waist; I could hear the pain he tried to suppress in the urgency of his voice.

"Emma, come away; the car's not secure."

"I can't leave him."

"I'll stay, just let me get you to safety first."

The sky had rained itself dry, and a first weak gleam of sun broke through.

Guy opened his eyes and my heart wrenched as I recognized the look I had last seen after he tried to kill himself – the look of a man with nothing to lose – honest, unveiled. "Em'a..." The car lurched deeper and Matthew hauled me back as water rose to Guy's shoulders. His eyes lost focus, glazed, and found me again, haunted, pleading.

"I forgive you," I whispered, before Matthew succeeded in dragging me from the car. The last thing I saw of Guy Hilliard – the last thing I remember and which will haunt me for the rest of my life – was the sunlight fading from his face, leaving nothing but the trace of a smile.

Paramedics and police wove down the sharp slope, slippery with mud, towards us. Matthew lifted me from the current as it tried to take my legs from under me.

"Matthew..." I began.

"I'll go back to him. I won't let him die alone."

The first of the paramedics reached the banks. Matthew called out to him, "She's all right – no sign of internal trauma, just shaken and with superficial contusions. I'll be back to look after her."

He started into the water. A policewoman, still encumbered by heavy waterproofs, raised her voice at his retreating back. "Sir, don't go in there; the water's still rising." He raised his hand in acknowledgment, but didn't turn around.

Once we reached the bridge, I made straight for the remaining parapet, stepping between the long bars of steel, until I found somewhere from which I could see the car. I was dismayed to see how little remained above water. Another paramedic wrapped a shiny blanket around my shoulders. "Ma'am, we need to get you to the hospital."

From where I stood, I couldn't see Matthew, but several policemen crowded the bank and one waded into the water towards the car as far as he could go. They were calling out.

The paramedic became insistent. "Ma'am, we need a doctor to take a look at you."

"I'm not hurt, I'm OK, my husband's a doctor."

He must have thought I had concussion because he looked sympathetic and concerned. "Yes, ma'am, but you need to see a doctor."

I couldn't take my eyes from the car. "He's down there – in the car. They're both down there."

The paramedic took in the scene as the patch of blue that was all that remained of my car grew smaller while we watched, the policemen withdrawing steadily up the banks as the river rose. They ceased calling and stood in a huddle, throwing quick, hopeless glances as the car finally gave up and, floating like a bloated cadaver over the branch, was cast downstream.

There was no sign of Matthew.

"Ma'am, I'm sorry…" the paramedic began. I looked at him; he had a kind face.

"He's not dead. He can't die."

Heavy tyres ground to a halt beyond the overturned truck. A door slammed. The paramedic attempted to lead me towards the ambulance, but I resisted all efforts and he waved to his colleague for help. My voice rose shrill over the sound of rapid footsteps across the wooden planks. "He's not dead!" As the steps neared, I broke free, foundering over my own feet towards the wheat-haired young man. "Joel! Joel, he's not dead."

Joel quickly read the river, the expression on the face of the paramedic, and caught me as exhaustion finally took my legs from beneath me.

Policemen fanned out along the bank, beneath the bridge, and downstream where rock projections obscured a bend in the river. In full spate, water the colour of clay shredded the banks in a relentless attack on the saplings growing too close. A policeman, ahead of the others by a hundred yards, began gesticulating towards the river, his shouted words drowned by its roar.

"They've found the car." Joel canted his head towards the river. "There's a body in it." He grabbed me as I pitched forward. "Only one body, Emma; it's not Matthew."

I slumped onto the deck of the bridge from which I had refused to move ever since the search for the car began. The wooden planks steamed in the strong sun, and above the trees a golden mist rose. Such agonizing beauty. Joel had stayed with me, although I begged him to join the search. It was just as well. In my stupefied state I kept repeating, "I killed him, I killed him," in response to police questions, and he had produced an ID card, and they left me alone.

Dazed, I let him fill in missing pieces of information, barely registering when he gave them Guy's name and his next of kin. He didn't reveal Guy's relationship with his sister, nor did he mention the dead man's connection to me. He explained what Guy had been doing at the conference, and where we were going in my car. I wasn't asked where we had come from, so didn't have to lie about the hotel, but when they tried to push for the details of the crash, all I could give them was, "I killed him", and Joel soon put a stop to that.

He tried to forestall the approach of a young officer, but I struggled to my feet, grabbing the damp object from his hand. "Where did you find it?" I asked, my voice gravelly from shouting over the snarl of the river. He indicated several police officers analysing skid marks on the bridge planks, the truck driver waving his arms as he described the crash.

"Is it yours, ma'am?"

The brown leather hung limp, but, inside the bag, the journal remained unscathed. I closed my eyes. "Yes," I said, "it's mine."

"And this?" He held out a small, shiny object. I took my mobile from his hand.

"Yes," I nodded. "Thanks."

He became distracted by movement along the river. An officer managed to reach the car. He raised an arm and beckoned. For a split second I thought Guy might still be alive, but then I caught sight of the empty zipped bag being passed along the line. I don't think the enormity of it had fully registered until that point.

One man used powered metal cutters to remove the roof; two held on to him against the current. I stood transfixed by the scene. "I killed him, Joel. I killed Guy."

The roof peeled back like a tin can. "Don't look," Joel advised, but I continued to gaze with undisguised horror until he moved, obscuring the scene from view.

I don't know what made me look around – perhaps it was the rattle and tang of the steel reinforcing bars being gathered to one side; perhaps the shouts as they finally pulled Guy's body from the wreckage. Yet neither of these seemed as significant as the sound of quiet steps across the bridge, nor the wash of hope like mountain air that inextricably flowed through me. Joel spoke first. "Hey, old man; thought the river'd got the better of you this time."

Matthew raised a tired smile. "Not this time, Joel; not yet."

Wordlessly I went to him. Neither of us spoke until, eyes closed, he leaned his forehead against mine. "When I saw your car go over the side, I thought I'd lost you."

I ran my hand over his chest, his shoulders, my fingers over the frame of his face. The fire had gone from his eyes, and he looked grey in the bright noon light, but he was whole.

"You promised you wouldn't put your mortality to the test."

The weighty body bag being carried carefully along the rock-strewn bank compounded his hesitancy. "It pleased God to bring me back to you."

"Matthew..."

"It took me some time to get out of the car, that's all. I had to swim downstream until I could find somewhere to climb out. The current was very strong." I wasn't meant to see the exchange of looks between the two men.

"Yes, but so are you."

"I'm not invincible." He lifted his face and it looked as if he had aged over the last hours as he drank in the sun. He breathed the warm air, his colour returning. "Let's get you home."

"Sir, wait up there!" The sturdy policewoman making her way towards us halted when she took in the state of his clothes. Matthew pre-empted her next question.

"The river carried me downstream and it's taken me this time to get back here. I'm fine," he added as she began to hail the paramedics making ready to leave.

"Sir, I understand you're a doctor." She pronounced it "docta", the Mainer way, comforting and familiar. "You were in the car with the deceased. Was he already dead when you reached him?"

Matthew increased the pressure of his arm around me until my involuntary shudder passed. "He died shortly afterwards."

She had been looking at her notebook when he said it, so she wouldn't have seen the telltale tight line that formed around his mouth, but I did. She asked him a few more questions, thanked him, and, with a curious look in his direction, went back to her colleagues.

After a brief conversation, Joel left. As Matthew led me past the emergency vehicles, he said, "Joel's going to the hotel to tidy up any loose ends, just in case."

Once in the safety of Matthew's car, I spoke. "What happened to Guy?"

Matthew gripped the steering wheel in both hands, eyes fixed on the gap in the bridge where he had last seen my car whole. "I didn't let him drown."

"You... *killed* him?"

"I could do nothing to save him; it was only a matter of time." I remembered the steel-pierced flesh, and the blood. I remembered Matthew's face when he saw him, and the agony as he endured the dying man's pain.

Lips compressed, he faced me. "I couldn't let him drown, Emma; it was the only thing I could do for him. He didn't suffer."

He had put him down as you would a dog.

He reversed neatly, negotiating the parked vehicles. Guy's body lay loaded in a strapped gurney. Then the door of the ambulance closed, shutting him from view.

So he had killed him after all. Like an animal in distress, he chose to end his life rather than let him drown. Compassion had killed Guy – not hate, or fear, or vengeance. Matthew had acted out of compassion, but nothing could change what brought Guy to the brink of death. Where had my compassion been then? Where my faith?

"Emma, there will be more questions from the police. They will want to know the details of the accident, of course, but they will also ask why you were at the hotel at that time of the morning." The journal lay mutely on my knees, shouting, "*murderer*" where once it had screamed, "*thief*". I picked it up. "He had the journal?"

"Yes."

"And you went to get it?"

I nodded.

"But he didn't give it to you?"

I clasped the journal to my chest in an attempt to still its accusing voice.

"Emma?" He watched me carefully. I shook my head.

"Th... there's a knife under one of the pillows. On the bed."

Tyres protested as he drove the car off the road and brought it to a standstill in a wooded track. Wild-eyed, his pupils burned. "Tell me..." he bit hard on his lip, his voice straining. "Tell me he didn't touch you – he didn't hurt you."

The book dug into my skin. "No, it wasn't like that."

"Like what? Like what, Emma?" His face twisted in revulsion. "No – no you didn't. You couldn't..." The car shook as his door slammed back. In misery, I saw his heart break in waves of magenta as he crashed through the undergrowth. I couldn't bear to watch. Still clutching the journal, I clambered from the car and, stumbling blindly, ran.

Guy had won after all. He had pitched himself against my better judgment and, against my conscience, won. Not for us his certain, quick death but a lingering dusk at the dawn of our marriage. Matthew would never trust me again. I wish I had died; I wish the life had been crushed from me along with my years of guilt.

Scrubby bushes tore skin from my legs as I rushed headlong for the open road. My foot touched tarmac and I felt myself dragged backwards as the bass roar of an engine blasted past in the form of a slab-sided lorry. I landed on my back, staring into Matthew's terrified face.

I swallowed. "I... I didn't see it."

"Why were you running?"

The sodden ground rapidly saturated my just-dry clothes.

I tussled to free myself from the prickly shrubs, but he lifted me bodily and put me back on my feet. I avoided his eyes, but couldn't evade his question. "You looked so upset…"

In exasperation, he threw his hands in the air. "Of course I'm upset. What else would I be if my wife placed herself in such a situation as… as…"

"I didn't let him – I wouldn't let him, but I had to get the journal, Matthew; he had all the evidence he needed. I had to buy some time and I didn't know any other way, and… and he said he would let me have it if I slept with him."

"And you believed him?"

"No."

"Is that when you texted me?"

"I needed a get out."

"And the knife?"

"In case you didn't get the text."

He bowed his head, pressing his knuckles against his brow. "So you decided to drive off the bridge."

"No! I didn't; it was an accident. I didn't mean to… well, I did at first when he said he knew who you were, but I couldn't when it came to it. Matthew, you have to believe me. I didn't mean to kill him." My voice climbed higher and higher until it broke. The anguish in his face made it worse. He held me against him as the woods steamed around us. I clung to him as the occasional car sped past. We held each other even when one slowed and came to a halt close by.

"You folks OK there?" I heard the gentle burr of the policewoman.

Matthew lifted his chin from the top of my head. "Thanks – we'll be fine."

"Just be sure you are now," she replied.

The sound of her car driving away left us in peace. Matthew

placed both hands around my face and raised it to look at me. "And we will," he said. "We'll be just fine."

31

Epitaph

"So, where did you go?" I asked him once he had run me a bath and I had soaked the gritty mud from my hair and from every crease of my skin. The patch of late afternoon sun shone hot, and this time I welcomed its heat, letting it drive away the memory of the cold river. Matthew continued squeezing water from my hair. He had checked the various bumps and abrasions accumulated from the crash, but I hid the marks on the inside of my thighs, glad to see they had already faded as if lessened by the flood.

"I went first to the library but the journal had been taken, then to Maggie's. Ellie stays with her sometimes. Neither was answering her cell so I went over there to check it out, but they hadn't seen Guy. I wanted you to stay at home, Emma; I wanted you to be safe."

I had apologized tenfold when I appreciated how my sudden disappearance caused aeons of panic until Matthew received my text. His phone call in response had saved me from killing Guy... I choked – no, that was something his call had postponed; my subsequent actions ensured Guy's death as surely as a knife driven into his heart.

"Matthew, I had to find him. When I guessed he had the photos, I knew he must also have the journal." I slithered around to face him. "Guy hadn't slept in his bed and I don't think he'd been back long. Where had he been if not with Ellie?"

"Taking the journal, I presume."

"No, he must have had it for a few days because he'd transcribed enough to work out who you were. He only needed physical evidence to prove it and he took that last night when he stole the photographs. He must have seen them that time Ellie showed him around. Matthew, I was so stupid. I shouldn't have kept that photograph…"

He shook his head. "Hindsight is a very valuable commodity that wasn't on the market last time I looked."

"Huh! He must have known I wouldn't go back to the hotel with him after the dinner. He must have been laughing all the way back from here." I sat upright. "He said he had a contact in a forensic laboratory. He said he was sending the photographs to have them analysed. Sending or sent? I don't know – I can't remember."

He stopped rubbing the wet tails of my hair. "When did he contact them?"

"He didn't say, but it must have been after he left with the photographs. Could he have scanned them, sent them digitally?"

Matthew jumped to his feet, reaching for his mobile. "Any idea which lab he would send them to?"

Wrapping the towel around my hair, I slid off our bed and started to hunt for clothes. "I think he said something like the Forensic Research Unit. I'm not sure; I wasn't thinking straight."

He gave short, succinct instructions. He listened intently, spoke again, and then snapped the mobile shut. "Joel's on to it. He did a sweep of the hotel room before the police arrived and retrieved the knife and various other items. He'll go down to the morgue and see what was on Guy's body. I'm guessing that anything Guy did he will have saved onto a flash drive."

The initial elation of being home and safe quickly wore off as the implications of what Guy had said – what I had done – loomed ever larger in my mind until they blotted out the sun, and this one loose end created shivers of apprehension.

"Emma, it will be all right."

I gave a wobbly smile, but everything felt flat. "I don't see what Joel can do; no one will take any notice of a soldier."

"No, they probably wouldn't. I'm sorry – I thought you knew. Didn't you ask Joel about his new job?" Puzzled, I shook my head. "He was headhunted by a national intelligence agency. His test scores were in the upper limits – one of the best candidates they'd seen. It gives him access to restricted information." It explained the police officers' sudden change of attitude on the bridge, and why – even in my fuddled state – I thought Joel had grown into himself. Matthew raised a smile. "It's only a pity he can't let his mother know."

"Why not?"

"It helps if he keeps a low profile, even at home. People are less wary if they think he's… ordinary."

"Like you, you mean?"

"I try my best. So you see, everything is under control."

"For now."

"And now is good enough."

Or it would be had I not remembered that in all this, there was one person who would not greet Guy's death with guilty relief.

Matthew took it upon himself to tell Ellie.

When, a few days later, she at last let me see her, she opened the door to her bedroom, her face drained of colour and avoiding my eyes while her own were pink-rimmed. Wordlessly, she went and curled up on her scrumpled bed. All around her lay evidence of bereavement in the untouched mugs, the scattered clothes, her dishevelled hair.

"Ellie, there's nothing I can say to make this any better for you, but I am sorry."

She hugged her pillow closer, bedraggled hair sticking to the wet patches on her cheeks. This was not the girl I had met all those months ago in the med centre, whose self-assurance bordered on arrogance and with a promising medical career ahead of her. Here was another of Guy's castoffs, except this time I felt complicit.

I sat cross-legged on the floor next to her bed, plucking at a random piece of fluff on my trousers. I had been thinking this through ever since Matthew returned from seeing her on the evening of the crash. I had begged him not to tell her everything and reluctantly he agreed, although against his better judgment. "She needs to know the truth," he said, but I persuaded him otherwise and he kept to the story we devised of a tragic accident that cut short the promise of their life together.

Days on, as I surveyed her colourless face, I admitted I had been wrong. "Ellie, I am sorry about what happened to Guy, but I think you ought to know the truth."

Her eyes focused on my face. "Matthew said it was an accident," she whispered.

"Yes, it was, but I didn't want him to tell you everything, so please don't blame him."

I told her about my grandfather, about Guy's relentless pursuit of his grudge because I supplanted him, of his own wilful conceit that had led him here. I even told her that his desire for revenge was such that he had taken my job and destroyed my career, and would – if he could – have destroyed my marriage. I told her he knew that Matthew was long-lived and how close he came to exploiting it for his own profit. But I didn't tell her about the journal, nor how her great-grandfather's fate was bound between its pages. I didn't tell her how close I came to killing Guy and how – had it not been for the accident – I might still have done so.

I spent restless nights with the thought gnawing at me. What madness had I been driven to, what senseless disregard for life? How could I have suspended my conscience long enough to contemplate murder, and knowing that I did so, find peace? Finding me awake, Matthew had pressed me until I spilled my guilt before him.

"I've tried to pray, but…" I lifted my shoulders, avoiding the gentle prompting of my triptych. Matthew sat next to me on our bed.

"Would you like me to pray with you?"

I picked at my torn nail. "I… don't think I can." I felt his disappointment. "What did you do when you'd killed someone? How did you cope?"

He took moments to answer. "I didn't very well, not at first. I had nightmares, felt beleaguered by it and, like you, couldn't find the words to express my regret, and part of me didn't want to."

"Why?"

"I suppose because it would have meant facing what I'd done, accepting my culpability – and letting go." He looked at me. "That's the hardest part, isn't it? Letting go."

I nodded, words stuck behind the walls holding me together.

"There is nothing that is not seen, nothing that unconditional love cannot heal. No more is asked of you than you can give. Let yourself be healed. Let go."

Heat scalded my eyes. "I don't know how."

"Then begin by doing what you can for others and let God work through you."

"As you do? I haven't anything like that to offer."

"You have yourself. God is in the little things, Emma, the small acts of kindness, the everyday."

I had nothing left to resist, nor the strength to do so. I nodded. Yes, I could manage the small things; I could do that. Even I, in this shrunken form, could do that.

Ellie listened, dark-eyed, without interruption. When I finished, she said nothing but rolled onto her other side with her back to me. I put my hand on her shoulder; it shook slightly.

"I'm sorry, Ellie," I said for the umpteenth time, "but you had to know. I couldn't let you live a lie; it would have eaten you from inside – believe me, I know."

She looked over her shoulder and I was shaken to see the vehemence in her eyes. "I could have lived with the lie, Emma, but now that I know the truth, what do I tell my baby?"

The fact that Guy had come so close to revealing Matthew's identity sent a surge of disquiet around the family, but this latest news shook them to the core, like having a cuckoo in the nest.

Joel was livid. "How could you have been so stupid, sis? You're a doctor – you know what can happen if you have unprotected sex. Geesh, you've really screwed up big time."

Folding his arms, Henry settled on the arm of the sofa. "This is not helping, Joel; you're supposed to be supporting your sister, not telling her what she already knows."

"But it had to be with that son-of-a-..." Joel swung on his heel and continued pacing the room in short, angry steps. "Have you any idea how close he came to destroying everything we have? Have you?" He stuck his face up close to his sister. "If it weren't for Emma we would have had to take extreme measures to deal with him."

"If it weren't for me, you wouldn't have needed to," I pointed out.

Ellie darted me a look of seething resentment. She held me fully responsible for Guy's death because, whether about to expose the family or not, he was no longer around to defend himself. She turned her face from me and glared at her brother. Dan stepped rapidly between them.

"Back off, son – what's done is done."

"Yeah, and we're left to pick up the pieces."

Hands linked behind his back, Matthew now turned from the window where he had followed the course of the sun as he listened to the arguments being played out behind him. "That's what families do, Joel – they stick together no matter what. Guy Hilliard caused enough dissension when he was alive, and we'll not let him continue his game now he's dead. Ellie, what do you want to do?"

Shoulders slumped, Ellie twisted the remains of her hankie into a knot resembling her strained mouth. Jeannie stroked the hair out of her eyes.

"Ellie, think about your career. You can have other children later when you're ready. Put yourself first. We can arrange a termination and you'll be back to normal in no time, as if nothing's happened."

Harry rolled his eyes and threw his hands in the air. "Mom!"

"I'm with Mom on this one." Joel folded his arms, looking just like his grandfather.

Harry raised a caustic eyebrow. "That's a first. I'm not in favour of abortions – you know that. I'll look after you, El, but I won't condone a termination."

I secretly suspected Pat looked forward to being a great-grandmother and her next comment confirmed it. "We'll all look after you and the baby, sweetie. It'll be lovely to have a baby in the house again."

Voices rose in a chorus of dissent. With his head bowed and his arms crossed on his chest with just his thumbs sticking out, Matthew's stillness set him apart. His voice rolled quietly over the others. "It's Ellie's decision; let her make it." He looked at his great-granddaughter. "Whatever you decide, we will abide by it."

"But her career..." Jeannie began, but faltered under his direct gaze.

"*Whatever* you decide," he reiterated.

"What do you think I should do, Matthew?"

He crouched in front of her, taking her two small hands in his and looking earnestly into her drawn face. "I think you should do whatever your heart tells you, and that will be the right thing." He smiled, and in that instant her face cleared.

"Then I know what I want," she declared, eyes shining. "I want to keep my baby."

Matthew squeezed her hands. "Then so be it," he said. "So be it."

"This will make me a great-*great*-grandfather," he mused, with his hands behind his neck as he stared up at the ceiling where several moths cavorted. "It makes me sound old, but I don't feel it."

He didn't appear too put out by the prospect. I finished my last mouthful of omelette without enthusiasm, took the plate to the sink, and slowly washed it, watching the suds foam and gather around the plug before disappearing into the vortex. Matthew took a clean tea towel from the drawer, and waited for me to finish. "Emma, it's not the baby's fault who fathered him."

I handed him the plate. "I know." I took my time washing the fork. Matthew waited, sensing my internal struggle. "I don't know how I feel about having his child in the house. I mean..." What did I mean? I took a deep breath. "I mean I don't know what I'll say to it – how I'll be – knowing I killed its father, knowing who its father was."

Putting the tea towel down and taking the fork from my hands, he turned me to face him. "This baby – not *it*, Emma, but *he* or *she* – will not be Guy Hilliard. This baby will be accepted and loved, and in doing so, will accept and love us back. The sins of the father died with him; don't let them taint how you feel about the child. You've so much love in you, Emma Lynes; let the baby have some, and, in years to come – and it will be years from now – we will decide how to tell him about his father. We don't have to decide that now, do we. Do we?"

"I suppose not," I acknowledged, "but it's going to take me time to get used to the idea. In the meantime, what do we do about the journal?"

"Well now, I've been thinking. We have several choices. We can return it to the libr... no, no – all right. I didn't think that would be a prime option." I settled down again. "We can destroy it..." He waited for me to react, but continued when I didn't, "Or, we can keep it."

I weighed up the choices. "If we kept it, where would it be safe?"

In answer, he took my hand and led me through to the study. The journal had been given a temporary hiding place behind some books where it could dry out without being seen. It had survived remarkably undamaged, as it had done through the long centuries of its existence. He pressed a section of bookshelf, revealing the hiding place. Taking out the obvious papers, he released the catches on the deeper safe and removed the battered metal box. The mechanism whirred and clicked and finally the lid stood open.

"We will keep it in here," he said, and stood back to let me reverently lay the book and its bag in its resting place.

"It's where it belongs," I reflected as he closed the lid upon it, and the locks engaged.

"Yes," he said, resting his hand on the lid as if sealing a promise, "and here it will remain."

Coming September 2016

Fearful Symmetry

In the final book in *The Secret of the Journal* series, how can Emma and Matthew escape when the past is only one step behind them, and the enemy unknown?

When history catches up and past and present collide, where is there left to go but the future?